Please let me take away his pain . . .

She heard his breath beside her. The hasty intake of air gentled by degrees until he began to breathe deeply, slowly. . . . As he leaned toward her, she caught his scent. Warm. Musky. Mingling with the salty tang of the sea.

And then she felt his mouth on her forehead, imparting a gentle kiss. His lips soft, his kiss as delicate as the brush of a butterfly's wing. They lingered only fleetingly, but in that time she felt her love for him shudder through her, filling her, consuming her. Swamped by emotion, she felt the rise of tears at the back of her throat.

Give it all to me, she beseeched him silently. Surrender . . . the word sprang to her mind like a mantra. *Surrender* . . .

Also by Katherine O'Neal

Silent Surrender

Katherine O'Neal

Bantam Books

SILENT SURRENDER
A Bantam Book / June 2003

Published by Bantam Dell
A Division of Random House, Inc.
New York, New York

ISBN 0-553-58124-4

Manufactured in the United States of America
Published simultaneously in Canada

OPM 10 9 8 7 6 5 4 3 2 1

For my husband Bill—
without whose help,
support, love, and
understanding these books
never would have been written—
with all my love.
This is really your book.

Silent Surrender

Prologue

Paris
June 6, 1916

Where was he?

Liana stared at the clock on the wall of the empty salon in the vast Musée du Louvre. It was almost five in the afternoon, nearly an hour past their regular meeting time. He was a punctual man. Had he been detained? Or was it because of last night?

Last night . . .

What have I done?

Restlessly, she paced up and down the long corridor filled with vibrant, colorful canvases of the South Seas: the paintings the man she was waiting for loved so much that he came here every day of his leave, as if unable to get enough of their primitive glory. Meeting her here was like a sacred ritual.

She'd known him for only ten days. Such a short time. And yet, in that brief span, her life had changed forever. In those ten days she'd finally found the happiness she'd sought for so long.

And then . . . last night. Disaster! In their first real moment of physical intimacy she'd apparently done or said something to offend him. Sending him bolting out of her room, leaving her to wonder what had gone wrong.

Now, she had to talk to him, to understand what had happened and make up for it.

She heard footsteps on the tile floor. Turning, her heart leaping in anticipation, she saw not the man she hoped for, but the museum attendant coming her way. With the instinctive interest of a Frenchman, his admiring gaze took in the sight of the young woman: dusky black hair tucked up beneath a chic Parisian hat, dazzling green eyes that through their worried glare were feverishly bright, lithe yet curvaceous body clothed in a flattering blue dress that showed a tantalizing glimpse of slender ankle. A beautiful woman whose delicate face exuded the kind of vulnerability that brought his masculine instincts to the fore.

"Pardon, mademoiselle." In French, he told her the museum was closing at once.

"But you can't close," she responded in the flawless French her mother had taught her as a child. "I'm waiting for someone."

"But mademoiselle, it cannot be helped. The Germans have taken Belleville, and Verdun is threatened. If it falls, Paris herself will be defenseless. The government has declared a state of emergency. You would do well, mademoiselle, to rush to the safety of your home."

A dramatic new attack. Of course! That's why he hadn't shown up. It probably had nothing to do with last night. No doubt all furloughs were being canceled, every man ordered to return to his unit.

If he *was* leaving, she had to see him one more time. Somehow, she must get to him.

But how? She knew so little about him, really. Not his squadron . . . where he was assigned . . . where he was billeted in Paris . . . not even his name. This, the mystery of it all, was part of what made their romance so thrilling. She knew him only as Ace, a dashing American captain in the Lafayette Escadrille flying corps who'd done what she'd thought no man could: brought her back to life.

When she left the museum she came out onto the Rue de Rivoli to find chaos all around her. People were rushing home from work. Soldiers lined up in front of the Métro station, many kissing sweethearts for perhaps the last time. A snarl of taxicabs, government limousines, and horse-drawn carriages clogged the thoroughfare. The forced merriment, the devil-may-care facade of home-front Paris in the depths of war, had vanished instantly in a seizure of panic that mirrored her own.

As she pushed her way through the heart of Paris, people packed the sidewalks of the wide boulevards, bent on evacuating the endangered city. Some dragged with them mattresses for the old and infirm who followed, or were carried, weakly in their wake. Others jealously guarded their precious stores of hoarded silk stockings, sugar, and other black-market delicacies, even as they left their jewelry and silver behind.

Liana moved among them, going from one municipal agency to another, vainly trying to find out where her young officer might be staying while on leave, always receiving the same exasperated response: *"The world is ending, mademoiselle, and you want me to find for you a soldier with no name!"*

Desperately, she searched the features of the passing soldiers—French, British, and Russian alike—and saw the fear bright in their faces: the realization that their fleeting respite in the carnival atmosphere of Paris was over, and the reality of their young lives was war. But none of the faces was the one she sought.

Then she was struck by an idea. Perhaps in the midst of this bedlam *he* was searching for *her*. With renewed hope, she crossed the Pont Neuf to her modest hotel in St.-Germain-des-Prés, where the traveling entertainers of the Frank Callow Troupe were quartered. Breathlessly, at the front desk, she asked the harried concierge, "Is there a message for me?"

"No, Mademoiselle Wycliffe." He turned to answer the ringing telephone.

"Are you sure? There wasn't an American flier here looking for me?"

Cupping his hand over the mouthpiece, he repeated, annoyed, "There was no one, mademoiselle."

So he hadn't come to find her after all. As the man turned his back to her, Liana stood numbly, uncertain what to do next.

Just then, a hand touched her shoulder. She wheeled around. But it was only Maggie, one of the English actresses in the troupe.

"Have you heard the news? We're off in the morning."

"Off?" Liana asked. "For where?"

"Back to London. Frank fancies himself a brave bugger, but he doesn't fancy entertaining the Huns."

She chattered on, but Liana heard none of it. They were leaving France. With the war deteriorating, it was unlikely they'd return.

So this was the end. She'd never find him now.

This once-in-a-lifetime love would become, as it had for so many others, just another passing of strangers in the tumult of the Great War.

* * *

In a life abounding with disappointment, this was the most devastating. Most of her twenty-one years had been a struggle to hope, to believe in herself, to convince herself that happiness was possible, despite the wretched twists of fate. Because she'd lost hope so many times. But Ace had made her want to believe, despite the evidence of her past that this kind of happiness wasn't destined to be hers.

Born in the last years of the old century in the windswept, isolated seaport of Mendocino, California, she'd started life happily, the only child of doting parents. But at age thirteen, it was all snatched from her. Her parents died tragically, leaving behind financial ruin. To pay off creditors, all the family's assets were seized by the court. And then, in a final humiliating defeat, her mother's precious black pearl necklace—her most valuable possession and Liana's cherished birthright—was confiscated by the sheriff and sold at auction.

With no means of support and no family or friends, she was placed in a San Francisco institution so brutal and horrific that it was like being hurled into some Dickensian nightmare. After only a few months, she no longer recognized the cherished child she'd been. Taunted, bullied, half-starved, her hair tangled and unkempt, she was forced to fight even to keep the sole blanket that was given her to withstand the fierce winter of 1908. And fight she did.

It proved an increasingly hopeless existence. All she saw around her was sickness, greed, filth. Her surroundings lent her a scrappy sense of survival, but gnawed at her normally optimistic soul. So she kept to herself, insufferably lonely, retreating into the refuge of her own mind.

Those daydreams always centered around acting. Her mother had been the daughter of actors and had seen and encouraged Liana's talent at an early age. During her rough days in the orphanage, Liana relived those happier times, when she'd performed bits of plays to the delighted applause of her parents. She'd surface from these daydreams feeling as she had then, loved and appreciated, only to find herself once again surrounded by despair.

She knew she couldn't bear it. If she stayed, she'd become like all the rest—hollowed out and destitute of spirit. She'd lost everything except her dreams of the stage. Her only chance of survival—of salvation—was to leave that hellhole and pursue those dreams. And so she let the vicious taunts of the other girls make her strong. She'd show them, she vowed. She'd become a great actress.

One night, as the orphanage slept, she climbed out a rear window, crept her way by moonlight along the building's third story ledge overlooking the Central Pacific tracks, and, taking a breath for courage, leapt onto the first passing freight train, nearly falling to her death in the process. She clung to the rail all through the night, staying awake with an iron will. The next day, exhausted but triumphant, she arrived in Denver. There she landed a job as the ingenue of a local stock company by lying about her age, telling them she was sixteen. The ruse worked. Already a striking beauty, the unusual mixture of her mother's fresh-faced English wholesomeness and her father's black Irish sensuality lent her a sophistication beyond her years. Her instant success filled her with a heady confidence. Why shouldn't she succeed? She was, after all, the granddaughter of two of Victorian London's most celebrated thespians. Her talent was natural, and her deceptive air of vulnerability invariably attracted strong men to her aid. For the next two years, she toured the West—from Salt Lake City to San Diego to Vancouver—living out of a trunk but learning her craft, playing everything from Shakespeare to Sheridan to Gilbert and Sullivan.

Finally, feeling her apprenticeship served, she packed up her belongings and went to New York with a letter of introduction to David Belasco. For over an hour she stood on the stage of the Victory Theater on Forty-second Street doing Portia from *The Merchant of Venice* and bits of other roles she felt showed off her gifts. Through it all, the renowned impresario sat patiently, not moving so much as an eyebrow. But when Liana finished, he took her aside and held her hand as he delivered his difficult verdict.

"My child, you are one of the loveliest human beings I have ever beheld. You are possessed of a charm that makes men want to carry you away to their caves. I can see you playing spunky daughters and perhaps even best friends. But you don't have the spark of a great actress, a star. You will never be a Bernhardt or a Lillian Russell or a Mrs. Leslie Carter. You have neither the stature nor the voice that projects to the rafters. You have the gift of intimacy, the stock-in-trade of the artists' model. But you do not have the grandeur that fills an auditorium with your presence."

It wasn't, of course, what she'd hoped to hear. But once again she swallowed her disappointment, dusted herself off, and decided to head for London, where American actresses were in particular demand that season. She'd actually wanted to go to England for some time, to visit her parents' homeland and seek out whatever relatives might still be living there. So she sailed for Southampton in the summer of 1914, only to discover on her arrival that her relatives had long since passed away and the England of her parents' memories was nowhere to be found. What she found instead was a world exploding into war.

Suddenly, everything was changing. London, in a patriotic fever, had little interest in frivolous entertainment. Half the West End theaters were dark and chances for employment were slim. But she realized that the troops now flooding across the Channel would soon be in dire need of diversion. Haunting the theatrical offices along the Strand, she finally found her opportunity, an open audition for a daring new venture: to form the first company to entertain the soldiers in France. The repertoire included plays by Oscar Wilde. Liana knew Wilde by heart. He'd even been a confidant of her mother's. And the prospect of being part of this mounting conflagration appealed to her sense of adventure.

For the next two years, the Frank Callow Troupe toured the trenches, brightened the hospitals, and played theaters in Paris, Orléans, and Cherbourg. The quality of the production was inferior even by Denver standards. Producer Callow was a drunk and a lecher who cast most of the lesser roles to fill his bed. Often they were in physical danger, within sight of the Kaiser's troops, sometimes having to dodge a wayward bomb blast. But despite these hazards, Liana found the work fulfilling. It warmed her to see those war-ravaged faces brighten at a barb of Wildean wit. Their laughter was like sweet music. For the first time in her life, she knew she was doing something good, bringing a little joy into a haunted world that desperately needed it.

And eventually, it brought her to the man of her dreams: to Ace.

It began at a matinee of D.W. Griffith's motion picture sensation *The Birth of a Nation*. She'd gone to the Gaumont Palace in Montmartre out of curiosity, to see what all the fuss was about. Until now, moving pictures had been a mute shadow of live theater, an arcade novelty, a toy. But this! It was, indeed, as President Wilson had declared, like seeing history "in flashes of lightning." The lack of audible speech, rather than detracting from the drama, heightened it, creating an enchanting, dreamlike ambiance. She became a participant in the process, providing the voices, in her own imagination, as she read the title cards. The musical score, played crashingly by a full orchestra, carried her away until she was soaring with emotion. This was spectacle but in its most personal form, a revolutionary style of acting where emotion was expressed not through the voice, but by pantomime and facial expression. As Liana watched, transfixed, she understood the true power of the cinema—that, while she'd been providing respite to small numbers of war-shattered soldiers, this astounding new art form could raise the hopes and spirits of people the world over. Stunned by the emotional impact, she sat arrested in her seat, even as the lights came on.

The effect of the film was so startling, in fact, that she hardly noticed the departure of the audience. Only when she heard an American voice did she return with a start to the reality of her surroundings.

"Come on, Ace, we don't have all night."

The theater was all but empty now, but a few rows ahead of her, two soldiers stood in the aisle, prompting a third who sat staring at the blank screen as if he, too, had just had a religious experience.

"Paris awaits," coaxed the other, a French major, "and there is much to see, *mon ami*."

They wore the khaki uniform of the Escadrille flying corps—the jodhpur pants, tightly fitted jackets, gleaming knee-high boots. As their companion reluctantly rose and turned, she noticed the captain's bars and a row of brightly colored ribbons across his chest that spoke of numerous triumphs in the air. A handsome man with a tumble of sun-streaked hair and, with his gaze lowered, a slightly boyish cast to his face. Straight nose; firm, sensuous mouth with a full lower lip. There was an indentation between his nose and mouth, as if a gentle finger had touched the place and left its imprint behind, and the hint of a cleft in his prominent chin. These seemed to frame his mouth, drawing attention to it. But when he lifted his lashes, startling blue eyes, as cold as ice, dominated the face, transforming it from boyish charm to rugged masculinity. As the others accused him good-naturedly of having been bewitched, he gave them a hard glare with just a hint of cynical amusement. But when he passed, his gaze met Liana's, and she realized he'd been just as dumbstruck by the film as she. For just an instant, those piercing, glacial eyes locked with hers. And she knew that she'd been struck by the thunderbolt twice in the same afternoon.

The next day she returned to the theater, surprised to find that he, too, had come again. But this time he was without his boisterous compatriots. This time, when the picture ended and they were alone in the huge auditorium, she sat with held breath, knowing he'd approach her, waiting for him to come. He did—slowly, warily. When she beamed at him and said, "It's the most magnificent thing I've ever seen," he swept her with a scrutiny that made her loins tingle. They spoke briefly of their admiration for the motion picture. But even as they chatted, it seemed that something unspoken lingered between them. In the midst of their talk, he stopped and peered at her intently, then asked in a whiskey-tinged voice, "You wouldn't want to have coffee with me, would you?"

The tentative invitation was a stark contrast to his flinty, haunted glare. She sensed in him a mystery that intrigued her beyond initial attraction, as if he, like her, had known pain and was determined to disguise it. But while she concealed hers with a bright charm, he presented an impenetrable facade. He smiled with closed lips, as if what little humor he found in life wasn't worth the effort of a real smile, and as he did, a hint of secret sadness dimmed his eyes. It presented a challenge—to see if she could penetrate his reserve and make him laugh out loud.

As they discussed the film, she found her heart beating fast, riveted by his intellect, his obvious recognition of what this seminal motion picture represented to the future of dramatic art. By the romantic figure he cut as a member of the Escadrille flying corps—this band of expatriate American adventurers, too impatient to wait for America's entry into the World War, who'd come to fly for France but who, fiercely independent, were the sole romantic renegades of a grim conflict.

The mystery of the man was irresistible. He seemed reluctant to talk about himself, even declining to give his last name. "I want to remember you always as the beautiful princess I found in Paris," he told her with that tantalizing sadness in his voice.

She'd known her share of men in her twenty-one years, but never anyone like him. She discovered beneath the hard facade a man with a surprising artistic sensibility. He listened intently to all she had to say in a way other men, craving her beauty alone, didn't. A visionary glint softened his features when they discussed the power and influence the fledgling art of the cinema could wield on a war-scorched and disillusioned world.

All of it captivated her, but what won her heart irrevocably was his innate sense of daring. He approached life with fearless determination. Like the father she'd adored, he possessed, without seeming to be aware of it, such an unaffected flair for leadership and action that it took her breath away. Once, in a large, crowded Pigalle dance hall, a fight broke out between rival factions of "Apache" gangsters. Knives flashed, bottles sailed through the air, chairs splintered over unsuspecting heads, until the floor was a sea of clashing bodies. As gendarmes streamed in, blowing whistles and endeavoring to break up the fight, Ace gallantly hoisted her up onto his shoulder and maneuvered his way through the ferocious melee with the skill and dexterity of a prize fullback on his way to the goalpost.

This vision of him as dashing hero wasn't just the gauze of romantic infatuation; she saw the same image reflected in the opinions of his two best friends: Tommy, the American, and Philippe, the Frenchman, who'd given him the nickname "Ace." It was obvious from the start that they regarded him as their natural leader, even though Philippe outranked him and was a decade older than his twenty-six years. They deferred to him, bought him drinks, and bragged about his astonishing twenty confirmed German kills. Tommy, a Kansas farm boy with brown eyes behind round, wire-rimmed glasses, worshipped him as if he were a god sent from Mount Olympus. "I'm telling you," he gushed to her one night, "when Ace is back on the front, the Red Baron can't sleep at night." Philippe, a charming, towheaded former pilot who was now the French liaison officer of their unit, was more cautious with his praise, but it was obvious that he, too, was in awe of the captain. "In the air, ice water runs in his veins," he confided to Liana over a cognac in the Café de la Paix. "I've never seen such courage. Or determination. He is, to be sure, the Tom Mix of the skies."

One night Ace came to see her in *Lady Windermere's Fan.* His analysis of the play and her performance was astute and unpatronizing. He told her matter-of-factly that she was in the wrong medium. "Your style of acting is too natural for the theater. Your emotions aren't expressed with your body, but with your face. You're dwarfed by the scope and scale of the theater, which makes you seem small. You don't belong in a proscenium. You were made for the new showcase of naturalistic acting. You were made for the cinema."

To prove his point, he grabbed Tommy, who, it turned out, was an aerial photographer. Inspired by *Birth of a Nation,* they'd bought a Bell and Howell motion picture camera and had been teaching themselves to use it. Tommy brought along his French girlfriend, Marie, and the four of them spent the day touring Paris, using the city as a backdrop to film Liana in different locales. She felt ridiculously self-conscious at first, and pulled Marie into the frame with her. Soon they were giggling and cavorting like schoolgirls bent on mischief. Marie was a cute, petite Métro worker from Bordeaux who clearly adored Tommy and so distracted him with playfully blown kisses that Ace soon removed her from the scene. Alone before the camera's attentive eye, Liana began to love it in no time. Soon Marie was forgotten and the three of them were behaving like old pros, Liana joyously posing for the camera Tommy cranked, with Ace murmuring astute suggestions.

She had no expectations of the outcome. But the following afternoon, Ace took her to a deserted coffee house, where a rented projector had been set up. The waiters turned down the lights and Ace began to crank the handle. And all at once, her image filled the stucco wall in a shaft of silvery light.

The spectacle of her magnified self was astonishing.

It was Liana, but a Liana she'd never seen before. A shimmering stranger whose image was pure sorcery. Captivating. Playfully seductive yet implying, in her delight with life, an unaffected innocence. Not the wounded inner self she hid from the world. Someone she'd like to be.

In that magical, projected self, with Ace at her side, she saw at last the means of attaining the elusive happiness she'd desired: a glorious future that combined stardom in this new medium with a storybook love.

Wanting to repay him in some small way for the gift he'd given her, she used her savings and bought him a solid gold pocket lighter. A thing of beauty with clean, masculine lines and a name plate on which she'd had engraved: ACE. When she presented it to him, he seemed baffled. But she laughed and prompted him to use it. He took a cigarette and lit it and, as he exhaled, held the lighter in the palm of his hand, just staring at it. His eyes gleamed with a mixture of emotions: wondering why she'd done it, and touched that she had. He seemed, endearingly, at a loss as to what to do.

She laughed again. "Hasn't a woman ever given you a present before?"

"No." He glanced at her, then back to her present and said simply, "Thank you." But he said it the way someone else might say, "I'll keep it forever."

And yet, he remained a mystery. Over the next few days, they spent their time together strolling through the Luxembourg Gardens, flying kites in the Bois de Boulogne, haunting the cinemas of the Champs Élysées, and returning to the Gaumont Palace to see Mr. Griffith's masterpiece three more times, dissecting every sequence, scene and frame. He held her hand. He kissed her cheek. And sometimes, in the process, his mouth would linger, as if wanting to turn and capture her lips in a more possessive kiss. But something always stopped him. Sometimes it seemed to her, as they spoke of Paris, the war, and the cinema, that he was on the verge of revealing some private part of himself. But again, some inner obstacle held him back.

Until one day, in the middle of a sentence, he stopped abruptly and told her he wanted to show her something that meant a great deal to him. Grabbing her hand, he pulled her across town to the Louvre to see its new acquisition: artist Paul Gauguin's provocative, resplendently primitive paintings of life in the South Seas. Standing before them, he began to speak in a mesmerized tone.

"When I saw these for the first time, they had a shattering effect on me. I couldn't believe how perfectly this man has captured the unspoiled innocence of the Pacific I knew as a boy in Hawaii. An innocence that's dying out fast." He turned to her and said, "You remind me so much of someone I used to know. Someone who was more important to me than anyone else in my life."

"A girl you loved?" she asked, her heart skipping a beat.

"Not the way you mean. But someone I cared for nonetheless."

It was the first time he'd ever revealed anything about his past. A boyhood in Hawaii. A lost innocence. Someone dearly important to him. Intuition told her he'd never shared this with any other woman. She glowed with the unexpected privilege. And knew he was the one she'd been waiting for: the one man she could love for the rest of her life.

She'd never felt so close to anyone. Growing up, she'd led an isolated existence, devoid of friends. She'd never shared her feelings, or her secrets, with anyone but her parents. Yet now, astonishingly, she wanted to tell him everything. All the things she'd buried deep inside. Knowing she trusted him enough to tell him everything, all the things others had never understood. But he didn't refer to his past again and she didn't ask him. There would be time for that later, a lifetime of shared experiences after the war ended and they had the leisure to explore each others' souls. She tried not to dwell on the fact that pilots were being killed by the dozens every day. Ace would survive, she told herself. He had to.

In the days that followed, as if to reaffirm their new closeness, they met by the Gauguin paintings every afternoon, readmiring them before heading out into the city, to walk its streets and have a quiet dinner at a sidewalk café before her seven o'clock performance, meeting immediately afterward and escaping into the night, to surround themselves with couples in similar circumstances. The very air of Paris was one of desperate romance, of stolen kisses and rash promises. Every instant was precious, heightened by the terror of war, the urgency of snatched pleasures before furloughs were over and a new batch of soldiers came to take the places of men on their way to die.

A passionate young woman by nature, Liana felt this urgency keenly. Every beat of her heart seemed to echo the ticking of the clock. Ace's leave would end in a few days. Falling more desperately in love with him with each passing hour, she felt her hunger for him build until her impatience began to push aside all other needs.

Increasingly, as he spoke, she'd find her gaze lingering on the sensual mouth with its guarded smile—a mouth that had so far only kissed her good night on the cheek. She'd watch the way his hands moved, masculine but graceful, as they fingered the stem of a wineglass over dinner—hands that had never once touched the aching swell of her breasts. The buttons of his jacket strained against the flexing of the muscles in his chest and made her wonder what he looked like beneath the dashing uniform. Her body starved for him. But still he made no move. Their pleasures were innocent: the touch of his leg against hers in the movies, the sharing of some lovely sight during which he'd whisper intimately in her ear, the protective guidance of his hand on her arm as they crossed the crowded Place de la Concorde. He treated her with a romantic solicitude she'd never experienced before, as if she were made of crystal, and might break at his manly touch.

It began to drive her mad.

Until last night when she'd known she could bear it no longer. Her body on fire, her heart racing in anticipation, she'd lured him to her hotel room on the pretext of seeing its view of the Seine and Notre Dame. As he'd stood at the window, taking in the sight, she'd come up behind him and wrapped her arms about him, stroking his chest and raining his shoulder with kisses of invitation.

He'd recoiled as if genuinely shocked. But she'd turned him around gently, murmuring, "It's all right, you know." She grasped his head in her hands and drew it down, her lips seeking his.

He seemed reluctant at first, as if fearful of offending her. But she persisted, enticing his lips with gentle kisses until at last he responded. Until his arms tightened about her back and his mouth caressed hers in a sweetly tender kiss.

She felt a surge of triumph as he swelled against her thigh, proof of his mounting excitement. She wanted him so badly now that she pressed into him, moaning defenselessly, deepening the kiss. Transmitting to him through her body the craving for him that had gone unheeded for far too long. Her hand left his chest to wander until at last it closed upon the rampant erection in his aviator breeches.

Abruptly he jerked back, as if the touch of her fingers had burned him. He took her shoulders in both hands, examining her as if seeing her for the first time. She couldn't read his expression. It seemed to her that his arousal was at war with his gentlemanly instincts.

To relieve any doubts he might have, she murmured, "I want to feel you inside me so much I can't stand it."

She stood on tiptoe, stretching to meet his lips again. But he held her back. Shaking his head as if to clear it, he said, crisply, "It's late. I'd better go."

And before she could protest, he'd bolted out of the room. Leaving her to ask herself what had happened. Sensing that she'd spoiled things, but at a loss to understand how.

Now it was too late. He'd return to the front without answering her nagging questions. And she would leave Paris without the promise of a future together. With no way of finding him. With no hope that she'd ever see him again.

She spent the evening in a numb haze, packing, avoiding the other girls, going to bed early. Endeavoring to ignore the periodic booms of distant cannon fire and the fear of what it might bring should the Germans break the lines. But she couldn't sleep. Again and again she reran the scene in her mind. The way he'd jerked back, after proving his desire. Was it possible, she wondered now, that he'd received some wound that affected his ability to make love? But no. There was no mistaking the swell of him in her hand.

Just then, she heard a commotion coming from the lobby below. Raised voices. Then booted footsteps on the stairs. The concierge crying, "But you can't go in there, monsieur."

Her heart pounding, Liana sat up in bed. With a mighty crash, her door flew open. Light flooded the room. In the doorway, Ace stood like a colossus, weaving ever so slightly from the impact of his foot against the door. The concierge struggled with him, trying to hold him back, but Ace shook him off. "I told you," he snarled. "I'm an *invited* guest."

Reaching into his breast pocket, he withdrew a hundred-franc note and tossed it at the man. "That should take care of the door. Now get the hell out of here."

Just then, the air raid siren began to blare. Newly panicked, the concierge turned and made a dash for the stairs. Ace stepped into the room and closed the mangled door. Then, ignoring the alarm completely, he stood and waited for her in the moonlight.

A part of her brain told her that she should head for the cellar and safety. Yet all that mattered was that he'd returned to her.

With a cry of delight, she sprang from the bed and ran across the room to fling herself into his embrace. He clutched her like a vise, lifting her off her feet, dragging her close for a fierce kiss. She tasted the whiskey on his breath. But it didn't matter. He'd come to claim her after all.

"I tried to stay away," he muttered against her lips, his voice slightly slurred. "But I couldn't."

"Don't say anything. Just make love to me."

Her words were cut off as his mouth came crashing down on hers. This wasn't the genteel kiss of the night before. Instead his hand twisted itself in her hair as he crushed her lips. A blinding kiss that in itself was utter satiation. Her body coiled with desire so intense that she felt herself shiver beneath his hands.

A yearning moan escaped her throat and was muffled by his mouth. Still kissing her, he picked her up in powerful arms and carried her to the bed. There he lowered her into the feather mattress, lips still clinging to hers, his tongue probing her open mouth with a desperation that matched her own.

The nightgown she wore fell away beneath the forceful exploration of his hands. His palm found her breast as he deepened his kiss, igniting her body with raw licks of arousal. Her moans were coming nonstop now, punctuating the wail of the siren. But the outside pandemonium was little more than counterpoint to her elation. She was drifting in time, drowning in his lips. Her body enflamed, highly sensitive to his touch, completely swept away by his bold invasion, already on the verge of heart-blasting explosion.

Never had she felt so vital, so bursting with life. Her soft body molded itself to him like liquid silver, honed to his every touch. Sharing his breath, she knew without conscious thought that she could go on kissing him until the end of time. Wanting nothing more than this.

His hand wandered feverishly as their tongues entwined. Cupping her breast. Trailing her rib cage, her belly, with a rough mastery that caused her to arch up against him. Expertly kneading the flesh of her sensitive inner thigh. The surprise of it, after last night's hesitation, electrified her.

His roaming hand found the slick aperture of her thighs. She spread her legs with a joyous gasp as his fingers slipped inside. And as they did, her body soared, erupting as she cried out her release into his mouth.

He continued kissing her as she clung to him, quivering beneath him with a rapture that seemed too extraordinary to bear. Helpless to the power of his touch and the consummation of his long-awaited kiss.

She had no way of knowing how long she shuddered beneath him. It seemed that she could go on and on, pulsing to his heartbeat, surrendering completely, her breath one with his. But finally the shivers quieted and she felt awash in startling bliss.

She felt his hands tug at his uniform, felt him shrug free, never once taking his mouth from hers. And then she felt him push open her thighs, felt the heat and steel of him against her juicy core. As he entered her with a forceful thrust, she cried out once again into his mouth.

Supreme, commanding, clutching her head and thrusting into her with frenzied power, he seized control. He grabbed her slender calves and shoved them back, clenching them with an iron grip, opening her wide, slamming into her so deeply, with such devastating might, that she came again as his mouth muffled her cries.

At last he fell back, steaming, into the rumpled sheets. She lay beside him, her heart refusing to slow. She felt jarred even as her body sang in luscious satisfaction. What had just happened? It was like nothing she'd ever known before. As if their two bodies had been fashioned for one another, and had just realized where they belonged.

He lay beside her, just as quiet, as if he, too, needed time to sort it out. Sometime since, the alarm outside had ceased without their realizing it. The room was redolent with a silence that seemed eerie. Only their breathing, slowing now by varying degrees, broke the unspoken communication that seemed to throb between them. She went into his arms, never loving him more than she did now, after her body had told him so eloquently of the love she hadn't dared express in words. But her contentment was bittersweet. "We leave in the morning," she whispered.

"So do I."

"What will we do?"

He rolled over, covering her again with his body, slickly naked now. Once again, he was hard.

"Morning won't be here for hours," he told her.

And kissed her again.

They made love through the night, not speaking by consent. Again and again he turned to her, rousing her anew with demanding kisses, then drowning in her body like a man whose passions, once unleashed, knew no bounds. As if he couldn't get enough. As if the gentlest touch of her hand on his damp flesh was all that was needed to bring him back for more.

Finally Liana slept, nestled in his arms. Luxuriantly serene. Happy as she'd never been. Knowing this was what she'd wanted when she'd bolted from the orphanage to find her way in the world: this sense of belonging.

She awoke the next morning to the realization that he was gone. Outside, she could hear the rumble of heavy vehicles. Rushing to the window, she saw a convoy of military trucks filled with soldiers returning to the front. She turned back to the empty bed. Obviously, he'd found it too difficult to say good-bye. . . .

She threw on some clothes and hurriedly ran down the stairs. Could she catch up with him before he left? How long had he been gone?

In the lobby, the sight of a soldier at the front desk stopped her. Not Ace, but his shadow, Tommy, handing a note to the concierge.

When he saw her, the color drained from his face.

"Is that for me?" she asked.

She took the note and held it lovingly. Tender words of parting. The only letter Ace had ever written her. Surely, after last night, a promise for the future. Perhaps he'd asked her to stay in Paris and wait for him. . . .

Watching her, Tommy flushed a deep, embarrassed red. "I'm sorry, Li."

She came out of her daydream and saw the consternation on his face. Flustered, she asked, "Sorry? For what?"

"I—"

Something was wrong. "Tommy, what is it?"

"This is really hard for me. I told him I didn't want to be part of this, but . . ."

"What are you talking about?"

He couldn't bring himself to look at her. "You'll know when you read the letter," he murmured.

The note seemed to burn her hand. A plain white envelope that no longer seemed welcome and loving, but ominous instead.

"He's the greatest guy in the world," he continued in a rush. "But when it comes to women . . . it's not that he's cruel, exactly, he's just . . . and look, I'm not justifying it . . . it's just that I thought with *you* it would be different . . ." He trailed off, clearly helpless.

"Where is he?" she asked in a small voice.

He shifted uncomfortably. "He doesn't want to see you."

"But I *have* to see him. I have to talk to him. It *was* different with us. He's just scared, perhaps, or—"

"Li, for God's sake! Don't make this any harder on yourself than it already is."

She clenched the letter. "What did he say about me?"

"I don't—"

"I know he told you something. I think I have a right to know."

She stood there before him, head held high, a heart-breaking attempt at dignity keeping her back ramrod straight.

"He *did* think you were special . . ."

"But . . . ?"

"Don't make me say it."

"Say what, Tommy? *What?*"

Thinking it kinder to tell her the truth, he took a breath and blurted it out. "He said, 'I thought she was the embodiment of purity. But she turned out to be just another . . .' "

He didn't finish. But the word he couldn't use hung between them, more cruel than if he'd spoken it aloud.

1

September 19, 1920

Four years later

She heard their voices first—harsh, male, threatening. The raucous laughter of drunken men bent on forcing their attentions on a woman they knew to be alone. The pail dropped from her hands, into the stream where she'd been gathering water. She turned and ran for the safety of the cabin. But even as she bolted the door, she heard them coming closer: along the pathway, stumbling up the wooden planks of the stairs.

She thought of screaming, but who would hear her in this isolated cabin in the remotest part of the Sierra Nevada mining country? Her husband was miles away, buying supplies. And these men—the loathsome Bromfield brothers—knew it. Crude, illiterate, starved for the feel of a woman, they'd spied on her from a distance, awaiting their chance.

Please, she prayed, *go away.*

But she felt herself being watched. Hesitantly, she

turned her gaze toward the left window and gasped at the horrid sight. Horace Bromfield, the youngest of the brood, was leering at her, his rotten teeth bared as tobacco streamed from the corner of his mouth. She reeled toward the second window where his brother Joshua stroked his matted beard as his lips formed a filthy kiss, his rancid breath fogging the window.

Just as suddenly, the faces disappeared. Silence. Her heart pounding, she prayed, *Please, God, let this be enough!*

Her prayer was answered by a tremendous thud against the door. Then another and another until it splintered. Feeling faint, she backed away, falling down on the threadbare bed. *If they touch me, I'll kill myself!*

Another thud broke the door completely. As it crashed open, the three dreaded brothers stood like lumbering bears, their huffing forms framed by the mountains in the distance, their features obscured and made more menacing by the rays of the setting sun.

Terror gripped her as they stood taking stock of their prey. *I'm going to faint. . . .*

An inner voice told her: *Now . . . faint. . . .*

But instinct took over. As Horace stepped forth to be the first to violate her, she found her right leg rising to kick the man squarely in the groin, sending him sprawling to the floor to roll up in a ball of pain.

"Stop film!"

The voice, boomed through a megaphone, brought things to a halt. The two standing Bromfield brothers turned in the direction from which the voice had come. A man who'd been hand-cranking a motion picture camera a few feet away stopped with a disgusted expletive. The mood music, coming from an accordion player, died on a sour note.

A short man wearing puttees and riding boots

stormed onto the set. "*Miss* Dare," he shouted through the megaphone he still held, "what the devil do you think you're doing?"

Rising from the bed, Liana, acting under her most recent stage name of Veronica Dare, said, "I'm sorry, Mr. King. I just couldn't do it." Her voice was husky and low. She went to help the wounded actor rise from the floor. "I didn't hurt you too much, did I, Sam?"

"Like hell you didn't," he grumbled, wrenching his arm away.

"You were supposed to *faint,*" the director continued his attack. "These brutes are going to ravish you. The only thing that can save you is your husband getting back before they *do*. How many times do I have to tell you?"

"I know what you told me. But that's not what a real woman would do."

"You're not a real woman, for crying out loud. You're an actress in a photoplay. And only the third-billed one at that!"

"But the whole thing is absurd," Liana argued, forgetting her resolve to obey without question. "Are you telling me this woman's husband would go off and leave her alone, knowing these marauders live close by, without even a rifle for protection? And even if he did, what sort of woman would faint and risk rape waiting for her husband to come rescue her? These Bromfield brothers are imbeciles! Even if I couldn't overpower them, I could outsmart them without lifting a finger."

"Miss Dare, this is beside the—"

"This is 1920, Mr. King. Queen Victoria's been dead for two decades. Look around you. The shop girls you hope will line up to see this picture are no shrinking violets. They're getting laid in the backs of Model T Fords. Not because they're being ravished, as you call it.

Because they *want* to. Do you think any of them would lie down and take this? They'd fight like wildcats!"

As she'd spoken, the director's face had progressively hardened to stone. "That's it!" he exploded through his megaphone. "You're fired!"

In the aftermath of his eruption, Liana stood staring at him. Reality began to set in. She had a dollar and thirty-six cents in her purse. Not enough to pay her rent. Barely enough to eat. She couldn't afford to be fired.

Swallowing her pride, she said, "Very well, Mr. King, we'll do it your way."

"That's just the thing, Miss Dare," he raged. "You *can't* do it my way. We've been through this too many times. You just can't take direction."

She raised her chin in a rebellious gesture. "I can if the direction makes sense."

The director, accustomed to reading emotion, saw past the rebellion to the flash of vulnerability. It was that "I can do it myself" defiance that had made him want to help her in the first place. Despite the sensual beauty and provocative allure that had made him want her at first sight, she'd aroused his masculine instincts with her childlike naïveté that she could make her way without any assistance. It had made him want to protect her from herself.

Now, boiling with frustration the equal of her own, he lowered his voice so only she could hear. "Veronica, I gave you this part against my better judgment. I knew your reputation for trouble. But you convinced me you could do what I said. You're talented. You're beautiful. The camera loves you. But you're your own worst enemy. Where do you think this kind of behavior is going to get you?"

"Don't you see, Mr. King?" Her voice lost its defiance

and took on the urgency of persuasion. "You're asking me to play a complete ninny. A fool! What kind of woman would see herself as that character? And why is Gloria Swanson the biggest star in the world? Because she's sexy *and* clever. Let me play someone like that. Why can't this woman react like a human being instead of a helpless bump on a log?"

Her passion didn't move him. "That's fine if you're Swanson, but you're not. And wanting to be won't get it for you." He slumped when he saw her face. "I'm sorry, Veronica, I tried. But no movie company can function with players who don't do as they're told. You're fired and that's final. Turn in your costume, go to payroll, and get your two dollars for the day."

She was seized by a sudden impulse to beg. To do anything she had to in order to keep this, the only job she'd had in months. But in the quiet all around her, she could feel them watching her. Even the carpenters had ceased their building and were staring at her, hammers and saws in hand. Standing there, the focus of attention, she knew she couldn't give them the satisfaction.

Gathering together what was left of her dignity, she squared her shoulders and, head held high, walked off the set. But she couldn't resist pausing at the door and calling back so all could hear, "Tell me, Mr. King. Would things have been different if I'd said yes when you tried to get me into bed?"

When she entered the makeup department, a long bungalow on the southeast corner of the Universal lot, she found two young bit players putting the finishing touches on their makeup. Dressed for the French Revolution, they were an incongruous, if familiar, sight, sharing a cigarette and gossiping in Brooklyn accents.

Their elaborate powdered wigs lay on the table before them. Their hair—red and blond respectively—was flattened against their heads beneath skull caps.

"They're shooting the whole thing in Tahiti," said the redhead, smacking her gum.

"Where's Tahiti?"

The redhead shrugged. "I dunno. Somewhere in the South Seas."

"The South Seas . . . say! Ain't that the place where naked women throw themselves at sailors? And where they spoon all day under palm trees?"

"Ain't it just!"

Liana passed them and went to the last of a long row of makeup chairs. Automatically, she reached for the cold cream, but found she couldn't summon the energy. Defeated, she sank back in the chair. What was she going to do? When word of this got around, no one would hire her. Already she was thought to be on her last legs. A playgirl who danced till dawn in local speakeasies, then showed up late to cause trouble on the set. She'd been offered fewer and smaller roles since her brief flush of success two years before. She was nearly twenty-five years old . . . well along for a woman in this still-new business of moving pictures, where ingenues of fifteen and sixteen weren't uncommon.

King hadn't said so, but she could see the writing on the wall. She was finished.

But she couldn't be finished. She'd allowed for nothing else in her life. She'd come to Hollywood four years ago filled with determination, burning with ambition to make it in pictures and create a new kind of woman star. Not the weak sisters of Victorian melodrama, but the newly emancipated woman she saw all around her: the kind of woman her mother had taught her to be. Independent. Resourceful. Daring. Unafraid to take pleasure in her own sexuality.

But what had gone wrong? Her affairs with men had been brief—she'd put an end to them before they had the chance to call it quits. Once or twice it had seemed to her that one of her lovers wanted more, that there was the possibility of some genuine emotion and deeper ties. But even as she entertained the possibility, she was jolted back to that fateful moment in Paris, when her heart had been ripped in two. And she'd sworn to never let that happen again.

As for her career, it *was* true that she'd been inconstant and self-destructive. When she thought back on the person she'd been during the war . . . how she'd been slapped to the ground, and how it had tarnished the legacy her mother had given her . . . even the thought of it made her burn with anger and shame. It hurt to think about it, and so she didn't.

Instead she sought escape in the frivolous pleasures that were rising up in postwar America to define the raucous new decade of the twenties. Four years of becoming increasingly notorious as a high-living party girl, no gathering complete without her, kicking up her heels with many of the town's biggest names, but never taken seriously. Laughed at behind her back. Acknowledged to have an exotic screen presence but not at all like sweet Mary Pickford. And everybody wanted Pickford. At first rejecting anything that smacked of the "damsel in distress," but finally giving in and playing them indifferently. Discovering that the offers dwindled and came from less distinguished studios. Until she'd finally been reduced to the ultimate humiliation: playing a Pickfordesque bit part in a ridiculous melodrama for a third-rate director at Universal. When everyone knew Universal was the lowest rung on the

Hollywood ladder. Universal was where movie people went to die.

Reaching into her purse, she withdrew a flask and tossed back a swallow of bootleg gin, feeling the fire slide down her throat and the warmth begin to spread. Soon forgetfulness would follow, if only for a time. She tipped her head back and took another gulp. But as she did, she opened her eyes and saw herself in the mirror. The foolish makeup they'd made her wear gave her the appearance of a down-and-out clown.

And as she stared at herself, her mother's words from long ago came back to her. "Women like us don't just lie down and die. When confronted with a challenge we don't wallow in self-pity. We get what we want by making it happen."

But what could she do?

"That's why everyone's talking about it. The way I heard it, they're spending a million dollars on just this one picture. Can you beat that?"

The chatter of the young actresses penetrated Liana's thoughts.

"But what's it *about*?"

"Some Polynesian babe. They're calling it *Tehani of the South Seas*. They say it's gonna be the raciest picture ever made. Nude scenes and everything. *That's* why the director's filming it so far away, and *that's* why he won't say nothing about it! He don't want no studio censors within a thousand miles."

All at once, Liana's mind was sharp and clear.

Beside her she spied a stack of magazines. She brushed through them quickly until she located that day's edition of *Variety*. Its front page headline pronounced:

MILLION-DOLLAR PRODUCTION TO TAHITI

Hastily, she glanced through the story. Spencer Sloane, famed director of *Devils In The Air,* was embarking on Hollywood's most ambitious production to date. Lavish expedition to the South Seas. Antimissionary. Sex in the Sand. A bold departure from the kind of saccharine pictures Hollywood had been turning out by the hundreds. A vanguard film for the new decade. A heroine with so much courage that she'd stand up to the most sacrosanct of all villains: the church. Hobart Farnsworth, last year's top box office star, to play the male lead. Massive talent search for an actress to play the Polynesian beauty.

The blonde was saying, "I'm gonna go for it."

"You!"

"And why not? I just happen to have an in with the casting director at Paramount."

"Yeah, that's why you're here. Listen, honey, the biggest stars in town are lining up to try out, including Pickford herself."

"Pickford," the blonde scoffed. "Imagine the prissy dame rising naked from the sea. And Polynesian, at that." She let loose a squeal of laughter.

"You can laugh and I can laugh. All I know is this Sloane fella's already turned his nose up at the biggest actresses in town. *Including* Pickford. *And* Mae Marsh. *And* Bessie Love . . ."

"Great cats! What's he looking for?"

"All I hear is something . . . different, he says."

Liana dropped the trade paper and peered into the mirror once again. But this time she ignored the ridiculous makeup to study herself with fresh perspective. The luxuriant black hair, unfashionably straight, so different from little-girl Pickford's blond ringlets. The hooded green eyes that lent her an air of exotic mystery. The lush mouth that seemed—so she'd been told—perpetually swollen from kisses. A face that was a unique blend of wholesome innocence and raw sexuality. A face that no director could figure out what to do with. But with the proper makeup . . . a face just made for rising naked from a Polynesian sea!

"Different, how?" the blonde persisted.

"Beats me. Something he ain't seen before, that's all I know."

We get what we want by making it happen. . . .

Suddenly Liana knew exactly what the illustrious Spencer Sloane wanted. He was looking for *her!*

He just didn't know it yet.

2

By 1920, the Hollywood movie industry had exploded into America's third largest industry. In the Los Angeles area, forty-nine studios, employing some twenty thousand workers, cranked out seven-hundred and ninety-seven features—with an average budget of sixty-five thousand dollars each—for which over thirty-five million people queued up every week. Over eight thousand unsolicited screen scenarios were received by Hollywood studios on a weekly basis, and two thousand new aspiring actresses flooded into the Los Angeles basin every month.

It was the greatest entertainment gold rush of all time: the Hollywood of Charlie Chaplin, Fatty Arbuckle, and the Keystone Kops; of William S. Hart, Erich von Stroheim, and Rin Tin Tin. In March, king of the swashbucklers Douglas Fairbanks married America's Sweetheart Mary Pickford and they moved into their twenty-two-room Beverly Hills mansion complete with its own canal, which the press dubbed "Pickfair." In June, *Motion Picture Classic* published the first fan magazine article about a young Italian actor, formerly a gigolo, named Ruldolph Valentino, who'd been picked from out of nowhere to star in Metro's *The Four Horsemen of the Apocalypse.* Just this month, Lillian Gish had scored a huge success in D.W. Griffith's melodrama *Way Down East,* playing the ultimate Victorian damsel-in-distress as she collapsed on an ice floe about to go over the falls and Richard Barthelmess saved her in the nick of time. And yet change was in the air—this same month Gloria Swanson had almost as big a hit playing a very different, more modern, and subtly sexual heroine in Cecil B. DeMille's *The Affairs of Anatole.*

Universal City was located in the San Fernando Valley, some distance from Hollywood proper. Liana caught a streetcar just outside the main gate on Lankersham Boulevard and settled back for the hour-long journey over the Cahuenga Pass. The streetcar line ran parallel to the sparsely paved dirt road that had developed out of the original pioneer trail. The view was mostly of isolated farmhouses and fruit orchards with their neat rows of lemon, orange, and pecan trees. Elsewhere in the country, crisp fall days presaged the winter chill, but here, a pleasant warmth had replaced the heat of summer, infusing the countryside with a mellow golden light and giving the air a crystal clarity.

As the rattle of the streetcar signified their descent into the valley of Hollywood, she could see increased signs of urbanization. Four years ago, this was an idyllic little farming community. When she'd first come in on the train from New York, she'd been greeted by luxuriant fields of flowers on either side of the tracks. Legend had it that people in the early days used to toss wildflower seeds from the train and they'd taken root in the fertile southern California soil. Now, those same fields had been taken over by the motion picture studios and their backlots, or the homes of those who'd come here to profit by the boom of the movies. Mary Pickford was famous for saying, "When I came here, Hollywood was a paradise. Now it's ruined."

Contemplating the panorama spread out in the distance before her—the glass-enclosed stages of the Fox lot, standing sets of Paramount, and the hodgepodge of "poverty row" studios along Gower Street—intensified her dilemma. In the same four years of the rapid growth around her, Liana had achieved practically nothing. Now, at last, opportunity was knocking on her door.

But what to do? Every actress in Hollywood would be after this part. Obviously, this Spencer Sloane couldn't see them all, and would have to rely on the expertise of the top casting agents. No doubt they would send what they deemed the best of the screen tests to Sloane's office at Paramount. He'd consider those and make his choice. Her task, then, was to make a test, somehow add it to that collection, and trust that he'd be able to see the qualities that made her perfect for the part.

A brave plan, but how to go about it? She'd burned her bridges with most of the top casting agents. She had no contacts among the Paramount executives. She'd once briefly been under contract there, but her last assignment had ended so disastrously that she'd been dropped and barred from the studio by no less than B.P. Greenburg himself. Clearly, she couldn't go through normal channels.

She disembarked at Hollywood Boulevard, deciding to walk the half mile to the Hillview Apartments where she had a one-room flat. She had to think in more unconventional terms. *What would Mother do?*

All at once, a plan began to take shape in her mind.

* * *

"My dear girl, this has *got* to be the craziest stunt you've *ever* pulled. And that's saying a lot."

The slight man stood behind her, examining her image in the mirror with a professional air, one of his long, delicate hands stroking his chin, the other holding a makeup sponge.

"You call it crazy. I call it resourceful."

"Your brand of resourcefulness has a nasty way of landing you in trouble."

"Ah, but *this* time I'll have my fairy godmother to help me out."

He put a hand on his hip and glared at her with mock fury. "Just who are you calling a fairy, toots?"

She turned to face him. "Nelson . . . *darling* . . . you know I didn't mean it that way. I meant it in the Cinderella sense. I've got the services of the greatest unsung makeup man in Hollywood fixing me up for the ball."

He went back to studying the contours of her face. "Flatterer. You know just how to twist me around your little finger, don't you, you hussy?"

She laughed at his customary hissing. Nelson Reilly was Liana's pal and frequent escort through the mad swirl of Hollywood nightlife. He was one of the few men who wasn't interested in her romantically, and therefore made no demands on her. They were comfortable together. They shared an interest in art and drama. And he had a genuine appreciation for her unique beauty, seeing it as a canvas for his makeup artistry. The first thing he'd ever said to her was, "I'd kill for cheekbones like yours."

An hour earlier Liana had appeared on the doorstep of his bungalow at the Garden of Allah, the fashionable new palm-enclosed cluster of cottages just off Sunset on what had been the estate of the Russian actress Alla Nazimova. Still half asleep, he'd opened the door to find her loaded down with an armful of books and beaming a determined smile. "You're going to transform me into a perfect Polynesian beauty," she'd announced.

She proceeded to spread the books out on his coffee table, opening them to pages she'd earlier flagged, talking all the while. "I've just been to the library and grabbed everything they had on the South Seas. These pictures will give you an idea of what I'm after."

"Tell me you're not going after that Sloane picture, too. Get in line, honey."

"Not *only* am I going after it, I'm going to get it."

"Oh, please. Not again. I can't take it one more time. You beat your head against the wall, get your heart broken, and I'm the one who has to pick up the pieces."

"This time it's different. This role has my name written all over it."

"You must be kidding. This is the plum role of the year."

"Yes, but what *kind* of role? Not the same old blushing ninny. A Polynesian woman, Nelson. You know what that means?"

"I haven't a clue, dear. Do tell."

"Read these books. To the women of Tahiti, sex was a free and natural part of life. They didn't know shame or guilt or hypocrisy in matters of love. They were women who were actually empowered by their sexuality. That is, until the missionaries got their hands on them. The same missionaries who are the villains of this picture. Which means this is a movie that's going to celebrate the raw sexual power of an exotic woman. Now who's going to play that? Bessie Love? Blanche Sweet? Or Veronica Dare?"

He said nothing, just observed her excitement.

"I can do this, Nelson. With your help. All I need is a test that'll show this guy Sloane what *we* already know. I talked to Todd at Vitagraph, who's agreed to meet us here and shoot the footage."

"That alley cat? All he wants is to get into your knickers and you know it."

"Let him think what he wants. He's got a good eye and ambitions to be a director. He'll do a good job. All *you* have to do is transform me into a Polynesian goddess rising from the sea."

As she spoke, he took on the gleam she recognized as the artist perusing his subject. Thoughtfully, he sauntered over to the coffee table and flipped through the pictures she'd laid out for him, then back at her. "The trick here will be to get the skin tone just right," he mused. "If it's the breath of a shade too light or dark, the camera will make it look ludicrous. It has to be just the perfect color to photograph like natural Polynesian skin."

"And you're just the genius to do it."

He took his time, experimenting with various creams he himself had developed over years of trial and error. When he was finally satisfied, he began to apply it to her skin. "Yes, that's it," he cried, as enthusiastic now as she. "This will wash off easily, but if you get the role, we may want to replace it with a stain that will make the color last for a week or so at a time."

He shaped and combed her sleek dark hair, but had to do little else as its one drawback—the lack of natural curl—was unexpectedly an asset. She'd brought with her a length of bright blue cloth that she'd picked up in a bargain fabric shop along the way. Together, studying the pictures closely, they wrapped, tucked, and tied it about her body, exposing her slender arms and long, shapely legs. The task of applying foundation to all of her exposed skin was time-consuming and arduous. Once finished, he concentrated on her lips and eyes.

As he worked, he chatted away. "You know, of course, that everyone is talking about this Midas whose every picture turns to gold."

"What have you heard? I need all the ammunition I can get."

"Oh, well, most of it's the usual new-guy-on-the-block gossip. Ladies' man . . . wouldn't you know it? Just ask him. War hero . . . but who wasn't?"

"I looked him up in the library, but there's not much about him. Paramount seems to be selling him as a man of mystery. He shot his first two pictures in Europe, so no one here has ever worked with him before."

"Tilt your head higher." He began to line her lid. "You remember when we saw *Devils of the Air*? I was so excited, I practically wet myself. And you know I *detest* war pictures."

"I loved it. But I liked his second one better."

Actually, she'd been devastated by *The Wounded Heart*. Sloane had followed the daring feats of *Devils in the Air* with the last thing she'd expected—a tragic love story that was so real, she was too moved to speak for hours after seeing it. He'd set up what appeared to be a simple and innocent love story and had skillfully, surprisingly, turned it into a tragedy worthy of the Greeks. He'd displayed on screen something that Liana had carried in her heart since that last night in Paris, but hadn't articulated until she'd seen the picture: the conviction that this sort of ideal love wasn't possible. That it was a lie. She'd come away choking back her tears, thinking, "Now *that's* a man who knows what it is to have a broken heart."

"That's just it," Nelson was saying. "His first picture came from nowhere and went through the roof. Everyone wrote him off as a fluke. But then he came back with *The Wounded Heart,* and showed he had a deft hand with emotion, not just men in battle, and it did even better. So now he can write his own ticket."

"I know all that," she said. "I want details. What's he like personally? What does he do in his off time? Where does he go? What's his favorite color?"

"Well, how am I supposed to know? You'll have to find that out for yourself. Hold still, for God's sake. Do you want your eyes down about your chin?" He dabbed at the outer corner of her eyelid with his pinkie, then stepped back to admire his handiwork. "I've done it. Gracious, but you're a wonder. If I could work on faces like yours all the time, I'd be as exalted as I deserve to be."

He took her hand and helped her to her feet, then stepped aside so she could view herself in the full-length mirror. He never let her see herself until he was finished, so she was stunned by the image she saw reflected back at her. His carefully customized makeup gave her skin a natural sun-kissed glow. The sarong hugged every curve of her body, giving the impression that she was clothed in nothing save the blue wash of the sea. Her breasts appeared lush and generous, threatening to spill from over the top of the knot that held the fabric in place. Her arms, legs, and feet were bare. Her black hair streamed over her shoulders, shining like onyx. The very embodiment of a Polynesian Eve. The skillful makeup had brought to life the wholesome innocence of her features, yet had managed to impart the natural, subtle, and exquisite sensuality the part required.

"You really *are* a genius," she told him sincerely.

"Well, I've done *my* bit."

"Oh, no. I still need you."

"I want no part of this foolishness."

She gave him a smile that was half entreaty and half pure mischief. But all she said was, "The foolishness, as you call it, has just begun."

"There it is!"

Two days later, from their vantage point behind a cluster of hillside weeping willows, Liana and Nelson watched the polished black Duesenberg turn the corner and begin its descent from the enclave of luxurious homes known as Whitley Heights.

"This is insane," Nelson wailed. "Let's turn back. It's not too late."

"No. Benny's getting into position now."

"See how fast the car's traveling? He could be killed."

"I told you, he'll be fine. Benny's the best stunt man in the business."

He ducked his head. "I can't look."

"Don't be such a sissy. He does this every day. Watch."

She nudged his arm. Unlike her reluctant partner, Liana was bubbling with exhilaration.

Several hundred feet up the hill from them, a man in overalls and cap stood partway in the street as if waiting for the limousine to pass before crossing. But as it reached him, he took a sudden step into its path, colliding with it and taking a backward fall. The driver slammed on his brakes and the big car ground to a halt. As the victim lay writhing on the dirt road, the driver leapt out to bend over him. At nearly the same instant, the back door swung open and two horrified figures emerged: Gloria Swanson and her director, Cecil B. DeMille.

As a small crowd began to gather, a policeman appeared and pandemonium erupted. Gloria Swanson rushed to the injured man. The traumatized driver frantically pleaded his innocence to the stern policeman—never dreaming he was, in reality, an actor acquaintance of Liana's. DeMille raised his arms to push back the gathering bystanders as if directing a crowd scene from one of his epics. And all the while, Benny the stuntman lay moaning pitifully for effect.

"All right," Liana said. "Let's go."

But Nelson begged, "Let's forget this. It's never going to work."

"It *will* work. 'Officer' Jimmy should be able to hold them there for at least half an hour, and that's all the time we'll need."

"What if a real policeman comes by?"

"What would a police car be doing on *this* stretch of road?"

She opened the door of an identical Duesenberg she'd wangled from a pal who worked in the prop department at Metro. Pulling the protesting Nelson into the backseat with her, she signaled the chauffeur, Bobby, who, like the policeman and injured pedestrian, was a fellow actor doing her a favor. He started the motor and they sped off toward Hollywood Boulevard.

Nelson fell back into the rich leather seat and whined, "I'm so scared, I swear this bridge is going to melt right off my nose."

Liana rolled down the window to give him some air. "But Nelson, didn't you see? You're the spitting image of the man. And *me* . . . even her own mother would be fooled. How can you *possibly* doubt that it will work?"

He thawed a little. "Well, I have to admit, this is my pièce de résistance. A pity no one can ever know."

"When I get the part, we'll tell everyone. We'll put it on your resume!"

Early that morning, Nelson had toiled for hours to

transform them into perfect replicas of Swanson and DeMille. He'd even shaved his head of the luxuriant auburn hair he was so proud of. Puttees, a white coat and Panama hat completed the masquerade, while Liana was dressed in the height of understated chic as befitted the modish actress's style. Her features were similar to Swanson's to begin with, but with the makeup and veil the metamorphosis was uncanny.

Her confidence was further buoyed when they stopped at a red light and a young woman peered curiously into the car, then cried out, "It's Gloria Swanson!" Soon there was a crowd of people staring in. "Miss Swanson," the first woman cried, "I loved you in *Male and Female*. Could I have your autograph? *Please?*"

Nelson nearly choked, but Liana graciously extended her hand. "But of course, darling," she cooed.

The woman fished in her purse for an envelope and handed it forth with a pencil.

"The light is *green,* Gloria," Nelson muttered between clenched teeth.

But she waved him away. "We have time. I *always* have time for my public."

She signed Swanson's name with a flourish and grandly handed the paper back just as Bobby put his foot to the accelerator.

Nelson grumbled, "There's something about you, Liana, that I never noticed before."

"And what's that?"

"You're certifiably insane."

She laughed. "No, I'm just having fun. I feel alive for the first time in years."

He turned and stared at her. "You're having the time of your life. You actually *like* the danger!"

"Like it? I *adore* it! Come, Nelson, when have you ever enjoyed yourself this much?"

"My God, you really *are* a crook at heart."

For a moment, she was tempted to say: *Yes, I am. An outlaw woman, as Mother used to say. The daughter of a highwayman* . . . But the old instinct against trusting men—even Nelson—too intimately came to the fore, and she kept it to herself.

They pulled up to the Paramount gate on Marathon Avenue. Nelson surveyed the narrow opening to the fortresslike studio and the armed uniformed guard coming their way and visibly shrank in his seat. But he straightened abruptly as Liana leaned toward the open window. "For mercy's sake," he hissed, "don't offer to give him your autograph!"

"I have to say hello. Swanson is always chummy with the little people. *Noblesse oblige,* you know. Don't worry. I was at a party where she was holding court. I've got her voice. Watch." Turning to the guard she managed to give him a kind yet at the same time condescending smile.

"Morning, Miss Swanson. Lovely day."

"Good morning Eddie," she greeted in an impressive mimic of the star's voice. "I'm doing a test this morning. Do you know where it's supposed to be?"

"Imagine," he grumbled sympathetically, "our Glorious Gloria having to test for a role. Whatever is this world coming to?"

"We all have our crosses to bear. Even *I*, on occasion, have to prove myself to the Philistines."

Nelson groaned but Eddie nodded sagely. "You're a saint, Miss Swanson. It's Studio Three today. Mr. Greenburg's there with some of the New York brass, waiting to greet you."

"Thank you, Eddie. I can always count on you."

As the car began to pull slowly away, Eddie peeped

inside and hastily added, "And a good day to you, too, Mr. DeMille."

Liana elbowed Nelson' ribs. "What am I supposed to do?" he asked without moving his lips.

"Just give him a jaunty salute."

He did so, but as they drove into the lot, Nelson turned on her. "Greenburg! The New York brass! Jesus, Liana, you're taking us right into the lion's den. They're going to want to *watch* you film Swanson's test which, may I remind you, you can't do."

"Just keep your head and follow my lead. But most of all, remember: you're Cecil B. DeMille. These men are nothing to you. You eat flunkies like them for breakfast."

"That's all well and good. But have you forgotten Greenburg knows you? That he personally told you never to set foot on the lot again?"

"Forgotten it? I'm going to make him *eat* those words!"

Several hundred yards down the main driveway, they could see a gathering of executives waiting before the entrance of Studio Three. It appeared as if a party was in progress. Two boys wearing luau shirts were strumming ukuleles while the executives ogled a trio of Hawaiian hula dancers. A crescent of hibiscus had been placed around the studio doorway and a sign read "Good luck, Gloria."

Inside the car, Liana and Nelson exchanged cryptic glances. "Can you *believe* this?" she whispered, trying her best not to laugh.

"I think I'm going to be sick."

"Nonsense."

He turned to her warily. "Liana, for pity's sake . . . *please* . . . don't make a spectacle of yourself. Just do your business and let's get out of here as fast as we can."

She patted him on his newly bald head. "Don't you worry, C.B. Just leave it all to me."

Bobby, in his borrowed uniform, grandly opened the door and she stepped imperiously out. When they spotted her, the executives burst into a spontaneous round of applause. Liana stood there in all her Swansonesque glory, head held high, carriage erect, nose firmly planted in the air. As the ovation died down, she took a long, dramatic pause, making them wait. And then, in a haughty tone, she cried, "How *dare* you!"

Greenburg's fleshy cheeks dropped. His eyelid twitched in panic. "But Miss Swanson . . . Gloria—we only wanted to—"

"Humiliate me with this tawdry display?"

Greenburg glanced nervously at the New York brass and managed a hollow smile. "But we thought this would please you."

"*Please* me! After the audacity of asking me to test in the first place, you add insult to injury by creating this . . . spectacle! Hula dancers! Ukuleles! You're not even in the right part of the world!"

The executive was turning beet red. "I'm sorry, Miss Swanson. We thought—"

"Shame on you!" she denounced him in ringing tones. "You insensitive boor! I am here to recreate the soul of a Polynesian maiden. I am here to create *art*! And you dare to greet me with this carnival sideshow?"

Distraught now, Greenburg snapped at his ever-present assistant, "Hula dancers! Who told you to hire hula dancers? Get them out of here. Now!"

"*All* of you get out," Liana commanded. "Crawl back under your rocks. Clear the set. If I must go through this humiliating ordeal in the first place, I want no one here but my director and the camera. Mr. DeMille has generously agreed to act as cameraman as well as director. So all of you, out of my way, out of my sight!"

Eager to be away from this harangue, they scurried off. Red-faced, Greenburg continued to berate his underling for misjudging Miss Swanson's wishes.

When they were out of sight, Nelson clasped his hands to his chest. "I think I'm having a heart attack," he moaned.

"What are you complaining about? I got rid of them, didn't I? If I hadn't done that, they'd be fawning over us still and we'd be forced to go through with that damn test."

"Okay," he whispered. "Let's just get on with it and get out of here fast."

At Liana's signal, Bobby turned the Duesenberg around and drove off. The plan was for Liana and Nelson to deposit her test in the select group her wardrobe-girl spy had told her was kept in a nitrate storage vault at the back of this shooting stage. After that, they'd discard their disguises, don the street clothes Liana had secreted in a tapestry bag, and nonchalantly exit through the gate. Entering a studio was difficult, but leaving was no problem as personnel and visitors were only checked going in. Then they'd walk three blocks west on Melrose, where the car would be waiting to whisk them away.

Inside the glass-enclosed stage, they found a cameraman and assistants waiting. Liana dispatched them with some more of the same star temperament, but they were slow in leaving and the clock was ticking. By the time they were finally out the door, Nelson had turned a vivid puce. But Liana lost no time. With a determined stride, she quickly found the vault, opened the heavy metal door, and rapidly scanned the ten shelves stocked with reels of film of varying sizes. Nitrate film, being chemically unstable and highly flammable, had to be stored in safety vaults. She found the row labeled "Tehani Tests" and was just taking her own reel from Nelson's pocket when a tyrannical male voice froze her in her tracks.

"What in the name of Moses is going on here?"

They turned to find two people staring at them—two people with equally startled expressions. Because the two intruders were the *real* Gloria Swanson and Cecil B. DeMille.

3

On their heels came a vigilante group composed of Greenburg, his contingent of yes-men, a detachment of uniformed security guards, and Eddie, the gate man who'd obviously sounded the alarm when the second Swanson and DeMille had made their appearance. They were all talking at once, vying to be heard above the commotion. DeMille waved his riding crop at the production chief, yelling, "Greenburg, you son of a bitch, what's the meaning of this?" Swanson just continued to peer at Liana as if fascinated by the impersonation.

Liana felt Nelson grip her arm. " 'Don't worry,' " he mimicked in a sarcastic tone. " 'Just leave everything to me.' "

Greenburg was sputtering with fury. His whole body trembled with indignation for the impostors who'd made a fool of him twice in one morning—first in front of the brass and now before his biggest star. Clenching his cigar between his teeth, he charged forth and demanded, "Just who in the hell are you?"

Liana moved the hand holding the footage behind her back to keep him from seeing it. Stealthily, she nudged it toward Nelson, urging him to hide it. But Nelson, too alarmed by this unforeseen disaster, didn't notice.

Greenburg noticed. He reached behind her and yanked her hand around. When he saw the small reel of film, he asked, dumbfounded, "You did all this to steal a piece of film?"

Liana's eyes flicked her contempt. Swanson, watching her closely, saw it and said, "Far from it, my good man. This remarkable young woman came here today not to take anything from you, but to give you the gift of her talent. She obviously brought you a screen test."

Greenburg's gaze darted to Swanson, then hardened on Liana. "So that's your game." He studied her more closely. "Do I know you?"

"Not to speak of," Liana answered vaguely.

He reached forth and ripped the hat and wig from her head, releasing the tumult of long, dark hair.

"Come, dear," said Swanson, not unkindly. "You've proved your tenacity by going to all this trouble. You might as well tell us your name."

"My name is Liana Wycliffe," she admitted, knowing it wouldn't register, since she'd worked at Paramount under her stage name Veronica Dare.

Greenburg was staring at her closely, trying to discern the true features beneath the expert makeup. Suddenly he straightened with a jerk. "You! You're that—that Dare woman! I ordered you off the lot!"

"Why do you think I had to go to such lengths to get back on it?"

"After that stunt you pulled last time, you're not *wel-*

come on this lot. Of all the unmitigated gall . . . this tops everything! You must be some kind of loony. Did you really think you could waltz in here and go to the head of the line?" He yanked his cigar from his mouth and began to jab it at her to emphasize his point. "You, young lady, would be the last actress on the planet Earth that I'd give this role to. You hear me? Not if a flood drowned every other actress in southern California . . . not if an earthquake swallowed them all . . . not if—"

Coolly, Liana cut him off. "If you don't get that cigar away from this reel of film, it's going to blow up in *both* our faces. And then you'll never know how right I am for Tehani."

"*Tehani* . . . You're gonna be cooling your heels in the L.A. county jail for the next six months! Criminal trespass is a serious offense, little lady." But, enraged as he was, he heeded her warning and shoved his cigar at his underling, snarling, "Get rid of this, you idiot!"

Far from being upset, as expected, Swanson seemed amused by the whole affair. "Really, don't you think jail is a bit extreme? She is, after all, just a struggling actress trying to get ahead. One who mistakenly feels she's right for a role that was obviously meant for me."

"Just look at the test," Liana urged Greenburg. "For a minute, put your wrath aside and be a wise executive. Show the world why Paramount is the most successful studio. Show my test to Spencer Sloane, and you won't regret it. I promise you."

As she'd spoken, Swanson's famous brow had risen in a feline arch. "On second thought," she pronounced, "jail may be just the place for her, after all."

Liana impatiently tugged at her handcuff, which only served to hurt her wrist in the process. She'd been placed in the front room of a bungalow in the southeast corner of the lot that served as the headquarters of the studio police, her wrist held taut by a single steel cuff bolted to the wall. She'd expected to be whisked away by the city authorities within minutes of her incarceration, but three hours had passed and she was still here. Even the guards who'd watched over her all this time seemed mystified by the delay.

She didn't even have the comfort of Nelson's company. Hours ago, he'd been escorted to the front gate and given the bum's rush. By now her nerves were raw. What could they possibly be doing? If they were going to throw her in jail, why didn't they just get on with it?

Just then the phone rang, making them all jump. One of the guards answered it. As he listened to the voice at the other end, he turned and gave Liana a bewildered frown. "Very well, sir. Yes, sir. Of course, sir."

Slowly, he hung up the phone before turning back to her. In a puzzled but solicitous tone, he said, "Mr. Greenburg is on his way to see you. While we wait may I offer you a cup of coffee? A cigarette?"

It was the first time in all the hours they'd been together that he'd offered her anything. "A last cigarette before the firing squad arrives?"

"Don't know. Mr. Greenburg just said to make you as comfortable as possible."

"*Greenburg* said that?"

"Yes, ma'am."

With an apologetic air, he unlocked the cuff and set her free. Rubbing her chafed wrist, she dropped into the closest seat, truly baffled by this odd turn of events.

Within a few minutes, the door opened and Greenburg entered the bungalow. His face was ashen, as if he'd just received a devastating blow.

Liana shot to her feet. "This has gone on long enough. I want a lawyer."

His gaze was unfocused, as if still trying to come to terms with whatever news he'd brought. "A lawyer you don't need."

Liana peered at him. "Since when?"

He shrugged. "Things change. The past is the past. It's the future that counts."

"You're planning to visit me in jail, I suppose?"

He sighed. "As much as you deserve jail, it seems it's not to be."

By now, Liana felt as if she was in a whirlpool, being sucked down the drain. "What's going on here?"

"What you need to know, you'll be told in time. Just come with me."

"You think I'd go anywhere with you after the way you've treated me?"

He took a breath as if to control his temper. "I was told to bring you, so bringing you I am."

All at once it hit her. "It's Sloane. He wants me! That's it, isn't it?"

Reluctantly, Greenburg nodded.

It was too staggering a thought for her to grasp. "Did he see my test?"

"He saw it."

"I knew it! I knew if he saw me he'd want me." She spread her arms and twirled around, crying, "Spencer Sloane, I love you!" *Nelson will die,* she thought. Turning back to Greenburg she added giddily, "Where is this man of such impeccable taste? I want to meet him."

"You'll meet him, you'll meet him. He wants us to come to Screening Room B right away."

"A screening room? Why?"

"He wants to introduce you to a few people. But

first he wants to show them . . . why you're right for the role."

They walked across the lot in the golden afternoon sun, past a succession of grips, carpenters, and extras costumed as Roman gladiators, Barbary pirates, and Babylonian slaves. All of them turned to stare at her. By the mysterious osmosis of the studio grapevine, they already knew! They looked at her as if she'd been magically transformed into a star. And as they passed, whispers followed in their wake.

"When we get there," Greenburg warned, "don't mention our earlier misunderstandings. And try not to say anything . . . controversial. The New York brass will be there. If they find out you were once barred from the lot—and why—we could all end up looking like jackasses. Just remember, from now on we're one happy family."

"Don't worry, B.P., I've been waiting for this all my life. I'm not about to sabotage it."

A small crowd of curious studio employees was clustered at the entrance of the screening room. Publicity people, wardrobe girls, and a few actors who remembered her from her brief stint here last year. "Nice going, Veronica," a voice called out.

Greenburg stiffened at the sound of her former, troublesome name. "This is Liana Wycliffe, *not* Veronica Dare," he announced sternly.

Liana winked at the well-wisher.

The crowd parted as they stepped into the foyer of the theater. Greenburg opened the door and ushered her to a seat in the front row. She caught a brief glimpse of twenty or thirty people seated and waiting for the show to begin. As they took their seats, Greenburg nodded toward the projection booth. Momentarily the lights dimmed and a square of white light filled the screen.

In this moment of supreme glory, a thousand thoughts flashed through Liana's mind. She was glad she'd taken such pains with the makeup in the test. Glad she hadn't given up at what had seemed a brick wall of resistance. Glad she'd had the audacity to go to absurd lengths to showcase her talent.

Women like us make things happen. She could feel her mother's presence strongly, bestowing approval. If only she could be here to see it for herself. . . .

The white light was replaced by the flickering backward numbers of film leader followed by a succession of shots: city streets . . . crowds of people . . . young men in uniform . . .

This wasn't her test. What picture was this? It wasn't familiar. Had they loaded the wrong film? Or was this some early two-reeler she'd forgotten?

The scene changed abruptly. The camera panned up to show the Eiffel Tower dominating the city skyline. And then, in closeup, a young woman standing before it. Shimmering with a smile of exquisite innocence and beauty. Radiant with happiness, glowing with the certainty of endless possibilities ahead of her. A face whose power and charisma generated a collective gasp.

As she cavorted in front of the famous monument, dancing lithely before it, removing a hairpin to let her hair tumble down, toasting the cameraman with a glass of champagne, she seemed the embodiment of natural womanhood. The kind of woman every shop girl, every seamstress, every dreamy schoolgirl would like to be. A woman whose zest for life bubbled forth in a spirit that lifted the soul.

And in a blast of recognition, she realized this

enchanting creature was herself. A self long buried and forgotten. A self still open to the possibility of joy.

She shot to her feet, blocking the flow of images so they flickered, malformed, across her rigid back. Wheeling around, she searched the semidarkness for the face she knew must be there. Struggling to perceive the features of blurred faces and indistinct forms. Her breath heaving in her chest.

The lights snapped on and she stood like a statue in the midst of an audience who gaped at her as if they'd just seen Botticelli's Venus. The silence in the room was deafening. The kind of silence that comes when people are so moved they don't, at first, know how to react. The silence of awe.

And then, as she scanned the rows of faces, they broke into a burst of spontaneous applause. And as they enveloped her with their admiration, giving her the kind of approval and sense of belonging she'd longed for, she found him. Sitting in the back row. Watching her with eyes that blazed like blue ice. Waiting . . . just waiting . . . to see what she'd do.

Ace . . .

Spencer Sloane!

The man who'd taken that girl on the screen and stolen her ability to trust. To love.

She had to tear her gaze away. Beside him sat his shadow from the old days, Tommy. She recalled now the credit on Sloane's two pictures: Camera work, T. Crenshaw. She hadn't put it together. Fool! she scolded herself. *Again* a fool!

Tommy smiled and waved. As if nothing had happened. As if he hadn't witnessed the most humiliating episode of her life.

The applause died down. One of the executives said, "You're right, Sloane, she's perfect."

Another addressed her directly, standing and extending his hand to her. "Congratulations, Miss Wycliffe. You're a lucky young lady. You've just landed the role of a lifetime."

Liana ignored the offered hand. Glaring at Sloane's impassive face, she said, "You're wrong. I wouldn't take this role if my life depended on it."

With that, she turned and fled the room.

4

Churning with a mixture of turbulent emotions, Liana stormed toward the front gate. Beyond it was freedom. Freedom from the pain, the humiliation, the outrage of a past that was reaching out to repossess her, a past she only wanted to forget.

She almost made it. But just as she was passing through, she heard the voice of the guard Eddie calling, "Wait a minute, you."

Instinct told her to run. But before she could, two hands grabbed each of her arms and lifted her from the ground—the same security men who'd detained her earlier. "Mr. Sloane says he's not through with you yet," one of them announced.

"Well, I'm through with him," she declared. Twisting, she kicked the man who'd spoken in the shin. He howled, but didn't loosen his grip. She tried to break away but fingers dug forcefully into her flesh.

"Take her back to the security office," Eddie told them. "Mr. Sloane will meet you there."

Spencer Sloane charged back and forth across the tiny bungalow like a lion pacing the confines of a cage, wanting—uncharacteristically—to be anywhere but here. Feeling the need to vent himself in something physical: to run until he dropped winded to his knees, to beat a punching bag until he was exhausted and drained. Or better yet, to feel the roar of an engine beneath him as his plane soared high above, carrying him away.

It had staggered him to see her again. What had he expected? That he'd deal with her as an actress, calmly, dispassionately, the past forgotten in the necessity of his mission. Instead, when she'd stood and met his gaze, it had seemed to him that his whole world came crashing in on him. Again.

Because the truth was—whether he wanted to admit it or not—she'd broken his heart. He'd done something on that fateful leave in Paris, in the midst of the desolation of war, that he'd thought impossible: He'd fallen in love. Despite a past that had taught him not to trust and a present that showed him the folly of hope, he'd opened himself up to her, believing in the illusion and the promise she'd presented like some kind of lovesick dope on his first trip from home. Thinking her special—that one girl in a million. Wanting to *marry* her. Even—he balled his fists at the memory—envisioning her as the mother of his children. But she'd turned out to be just one more good-time girl using the excuse of the war to fling her morals to the wind. She'd taken him in with the skill and cunning of a supreme seductress. It had nearly finished him. More so because he'd been fool enough to believe in the possibility of a happy ending when life had taught him such things didn't exist. She'd given him hope, then had shown it up for the lie it was.

And so he'd walked out, leaving nothing but a polite note behind, too raw to look his defeat in the face. In a desperate attempt at self-preservation, he'd run and never looked back. Even though, at that point, there was little of himself to save.

But that was four years ago. When he'd realized that Liana was the only actress who could do his Tehani justice, he'd set out in search of her. Fully confident that he could approach her as a professional and treat their past as nothing more than an unfortunate memory. He'd even watched her screen test with a director's eye, approving her transformation to Polynesian maiden, admiring her beauty and her astonishing star quality only from the standpoint that it justified his insistence on finding her.

But then she'd stood and glared at him with such suffering burning in her eyes that he saw standing before him the illusion of the woman he'd once thought she was—the woman he'd had the misfortune to love, the one who'd proved, with her ability to play a role convincingly, to be nothing more than a mirage—and he'd felt flayed anew. Once again he relived that moment in Paris when he'd penned the good-bye note, wishing even then that things could have been different, slamming the door to his heart and shutting out any further potential for love.

And yet . . . how was it possible that, after all this time, the sight of her could cause his dead heart to ache? It was more than disconcerting. It was horrifying.

But what a Tehani she'd make! What an actress . . . what a presence on film. He'd never forgotten that. It's why he'd sought her out for this role—because he knew no one else could embody the Tehani he envisioned. That, too, was why he'd shown the Paris film first, planning to move on to her screen test, because her charisma was already so obvious. He'd fallen in love with that image and found it wasn't real. She wasn't the vision of pristine innocence she appeared to be. She was, in fact, little more than a tramp. But he'd never lost respect for her ability to convey that illusion.

Over the years he'd thought he was able to separate the two in his mind. But when he'd seen her again in person, he realized he hadn't at all. He was just as susceptible to the deception of her magic as he'd ever been.

He had to get hold of himself. His reaction to her proved she was still a danger. But how? To him personally? Absurd! Once he'd discovered what she was really like, he'd turned his back on any tender feelings for her.

To his mission, then. It was the picture that mattered now. It had only been through his art—purging himself of his demons by making them into films—that he'd finally risen from the ashes of Liana in the first place. But in order to purge *this* demon, he needed her. His task, then, was to change her mind. He couldn't afford to let anything get in the way, least of all himself. Because this was his salvation. Because perhaps, by making this picture, he could put his other past to rest—the past before Liana—the pain of which still throbbed like an open wound.

Liana fought the security men every step of the way. But she was no match for their burly strength. They all but carried her up the steps and into the bungalow. And there, waiting inside, was the last man she'd ever wanted to see again.

He'd collected himself by the time they arrived. He

sat propped against the edge of the desk with a negligent air, deceptively casual, as if his pulse weren't thundering within his chest.

Liana watched him warily. He was just as she remembered him, but somehow more vivid. The hair more sun-streaked, the gaze more intensely focused. Weather lines crinkled the corners of his eyes in a way that aged him magnificently, as if the promise of youth had sprung into full-blown masculine splendor. Harder. Confident. More commanding. He filled the room like a threat of danger to come. She could almost smell his allure.

She shattered beneath his effortless assault. Like a trapped animal, all she wanted was escape. But she heard the door close firmly behind her. And suddenly they were alone.

Neither spoke. Sloane measuring her with a closed, introspective gleam, as if gazing inward to thoughts she couldn't discern. Liana fought with everything she had to keep from trembling visibly, resolving not to let him see his effect on her.

Finally, he offered a smile. The same smile she remembered—*why* did she have to remember?—all too well: the lips closed, the corners of his mouth imperceptibly upturned. "I came bearing gifts. It never occurred to me that they might be thrown back in my face."

Unconsciously, she stiffened her back. "I've learned a thing or two about Greeks bearing gifts since we last met."

"Meaning?"

"Meaning I wouldn't touch your precious picture if you offered me the entire million-dollar budget."

"That's not in my power, I'm afraid. But it *is* in my power to make you a star."

"Just like that. As if Paris hadn't happened?"

His jaw tightened. He didn't want to be reminded of

Paris any more than she did. He watched her a moment, deciding it was safer to ignore Paris completely. "I knew from the inception of this picture that you were the only one who could play it. I've been trying to track you down for months. But I was searching for Liana Wycliffe, not Veronica Dare."

"That's another thing I learned from you: that the use of real names just leads to—how would you put it? Messy entanglements?"

He let out a slow, cautioning breath. "I can see you're resistant. Things ended badly between us. And I'm sure this whole thing is a great shock. But I'm asking you to put the past behind us for the sake of something that could come to mean a great deal to both of us. This picture is going to be the biggest thing to hit the screen since *Birth of a Nation.* But I can't do it without you."

"Why?" she asked, feeling lulled by the conviction of his words, by his director's charm.

"I showed you earlier why. That face you saw on screen today possesses exactly what this character *must* embody."

"What?" she breathed.

"Innocence."

She blinked in disbelief, the spell shattered. "Innocence!"

"The quintessence of innocence and heartbreaking purity," he continued, leaning forward as he warmed to his subject. "The purity of a paradise being ravaged by the evil emissaries of the white man's world. The human face of the rape of Polynesia."

"A victim."

"Very much a victim."

"I thought this was supposed to be a bold and controversial picture."

"It will be. We're not just ruffling feathers here,

we're going for the throat of some of the most powerful and protected villains in all the world: the bogus men of the cloth. The missionaries who, in their zeal to bring their own narrow vision of God to the so-called heathens, have devastated their culture and robbed them of the dignity that was their birthright. We're going to expose these evils as no one has dared before."

"What happened to 'Sex in the Sand'? Tehani rising naked from the Polynesian sea?"

He dismissed this with a wave of his hand. "That's nothing more than cheap gossip-column speculation. Our story's so powerful it doesn't need a lot of tawdry sex to embellish it."

"Tawdry sex . . ." she repeated thoughtfully. "Yes, sex *is* tawdry to you, isn't it?"

She recalled the way he'd walked out of her life with nothing but an insultingly dismissive note, all because she'd been brazen enough to want to sleep with him as an expression of her love. Recalled, too, when she'd seen his second film, *The Wounded Heart,* the tragic love story that had proclaimed his belief that there was no more innocent love to be found, that had shown the world just what he'd thought of her. Incredibly, it all fell together. Through his art, he'd revealed himself to his faceless audience in a way he never had to her. As—of all things—the injured party in their doomed romance!

Flushing with humiliation but keeping to the subject, she said, "Your Tehani, then, is another imperiled virgin."

"Not *just* another imperiled virgin. A profound metaphor."

"Why don't you just get a Polynesian woman?"

"If I could find one who had the same quality I see in you, I'd cast her in a minute. But I'm convinced you're the only one who can make the character live."

"And you thought I'd jump at the chance to play her."

"Once I explain more about the role, I hope you'll—"

She held up a hand. "You don't have to explain anything. I understand perfectly. This is just the sort of role I've been resisting for the past four years. It's everything I hate about Hollywood. I'm not even *remotely* like your Tehani. That innocence you say I embody never existed."

"I know that now. But you fooled me. You can fool anyone."

In the silence that followed, a surge of rage erupted through her. Of all the insufferable arrogance! To make assumptions about her nature that were never true, then blame *her* for his misconception . . . to reject what she was in the cruelest possible way . . . and then, when she'd finally succeeded in putting it all behind her, to sweep back into her life like some mogul prince bestowing favors . . . to grandly imply that he would overlook her shortcomings so that he could *use* her for his own egotistical purposes . . .

"You must be out of your mind!" she gasped. "Make your little masterpiece without me."

He lunged to his feet. Damn her! She was thwarting him out of spite, when he'd done his best to rise above it, tried everything possible to be reasonable, even accommodating. He felt his patience stretched to the breaking point. His eyes creased and a flinty gaze hardened on her face. "I didn't spend eight months searching for you so I could make this picture without you."

"I'd say that's *your* misfortune. Because I'm not doing it."

"I intend to change your mind."

"You won't."

"No? I could fix it so you never work in this town again."

She stared at him, trying to determine if he could possibly be serious. "You're bluffing."

In a hard tone, he said, "I never bluff. Ask anyone."

It was too ridiculous even to consider. "There's nothing you could say or do that would change my feelings for you."

He scanned her with a look that penetrated her very soul. "Nothing?"

Slowly he stepped closer, towering over her in a way that made her feel small, hunted by a beast much larger than she. She caught a whiff of the clean, manly scent of him. A scent she remembered. A scent that made her knees feel weak. Bringing with it images of his hard body pressed against her . . . his hot mouth clamped on her nipple . . . the commanding way he'd parted her thighs and . . .

A chill shuddered up her spine. Unconsciously, she took a step back. Then another. And another. Until the wall at her back stopped her.

He followed, leaning over her, bracing his arms against the wall on either side. Forming a prison with his masculine frame. As he brushed against her, she felt the swell of his erection. She jumped back, as if burned, but the wall behind left her nowhere to go. She felt his presence closing in on her, overwhelming . . . suffocating . . .

His manner was tenderly seductive, but there was ice in his stare. As if saying to himself: *If this is what it takes . . .*

"I'm thinking back four years ago to a beautiful leave in Paris," he murmured in his whiskey-tinged voice. "The bombs rumbling in the distance . . . the air charged with danger and excitement . . . two people finding each other in the heat of the night . . ."

He moved in closer. His lips found her neck, nuzzling persuasively. Her body, pressed against his now, leapt to life, her breasts throbbing, her loins aching from the torture of having him so unexpectedly near. Hating herself because her body craved him every bit as much as it ever had, responding on a primitive level, even as her mind screamed outrage that he would use the memory of the most painful night of her life as a cheap tool of seduction.

He thinks I'll give in. He thinks I'm a whore who loves sex so much, she can't resist.

She tried to jerk free. And as she did, heard a metallic jangle. A sound that gave her an idea.

Pulling herself together with an effort, she reached up, stroking his arm. "So you thought about me all these years," she purred.

He paused, his lips halted on her neck. "Well," he said, more grudging now, "we did manage to make some sparks."

"We were good together, weren't we?"

A moment of indecision. Then, "Yes," he growled, as if she'd ripped it out of him.

"And when you saw me again . . . you couldn't help but think back on that night we spent together. Did you want me right away?"

His lips returned to her neck. "Right away," he admitted, his voice muffled by her flesh.

"You couldn't help yourself, could you?"

His hands came up to clasp her face in preparation for a kiss. "No."

He dipped his head, seeking her lips.

"Good!" she said. The sound of a metallic click broke his spell. The dangling handcuff that had bound her earlier now fastened his wrist to the wall.

When he realized what had happened, he gave a

mighty jerk, attempting to pull himself free. Then he turned and glared at her.

"Unlock this thing *now*."

She didn't bother to answer. Sliding past him, she moved the phone out of his reach, then left the bungalow, closing the door behind her. Just up the way, she saw the two security guards. By now it was late afternoon and most of the studio employees were leaving for the day. With a smile she told them, "Our business is concluded in there. Mr. Sloane says he won't be needing you boys anymore."

"No hard feelings, miss?"

She winked at them, thinking of Sloane spending the night under lock and key. "Not in the least."

That night, Liana sat with Nelson at a table at Earl's. Located in an alley off McCadden Place, it was the favorite speakeasy of the aspiring Hollywood crowd—bit players and extras who came to share their frustrations or forget them in the profusion of bootleg gin. While the rest of the country was suffering under the restrictions of Prohibition, Hollywood was wide open. Speakeasies had sprung up in every part of town, while stars used their money and influence to stock their parties with every kind of liquor imaginable. Rather than deter them, the new law made drinking more fashionable than ever before. It was forbidden, and therefore all the more appealing to a society which, on its own in a town that flaunted convention, was hell-bent on having a good time, whatever the cost.

Raucous laughter filled the smoky air. A young musician banged out the latest tunes on a tinny piano as couples danced like wild things, kicking up their heels with the abandon that was even now beginning to define the new decade of the twenties. The regular patrons were a young crowd, fast and loose and flamboyantly modern. Before the night was over, a brawl or two could be expected. But it was early yet.

Liana had asked Nelson to meet her here, delaying his frantic questions. She wanted noise, confusion, even chaos around her. She was still too wounded to tell it in the hushed loneliness of her shabby apartment. She'd gone over things so often in her mind that she felt numb and battered, and so she sought the escape of a crowd. It would do her good to get out, to dance. To drink. To occupy her mind with something besides the shock of seeing Ace again.

Sloane, she reminded herself.

And so she'd spent the evening dancing feverishly, obliging the steady stream of men who cut in, accepting the drinks they offered, laughing with brittle gaiety as the liquor took hold. Nelson sat watching her, nursing a drink. When she finally fell back into her chair he moaned, "I can't believe you *handcuffed* him to the wall. The hottest director in town! We'd better call someone—"

"And spoil my revenge? Don't you dare!"

"So, fine. You've had your revenge. Now what? I thought you wanted this role. Isn't that why we carried out that crazy plan of yours in the first place?"

"It's not the role I thought it was. It's another woman-as-helpless-victim, but on a grander scale. It's *Tehani of Sunnybrook Farm.*"

"You're an actress, Liana. You're supposed to play a lot of *different* roles. Let them make you a star, then you can call your own shots. All you have to do is play the game. Give them what they want."

She squirmed in her seat. "It's not just that."

"Then what is it?"

"It's him. Sloane. I can't have anything to do with him."

He sat up straight as the magnitude of the revelation hit him. "You *know* him!"

She lowered her lashes to hide the vulnerability in her eyes, wishing that she'd kept her mouth shut. But Nelson had caught the scent and was closing in for the kill.

"You actually *know* this Mr. Wonderful, and you never breathed a word!"

Grudgingly, she admitted, "I didn't know him under his real name. Anyway, it was long ago."

"This is a story I *have* to hear!"

She peered at him speculatively through the smoky haze. As a rule, she'd never had any close friends, and her experience with Sloane in Paris had effectively killed her trust in men. She had a passing camaraderie with a number of out-of-work actors around town, but her breezy cheer was little more than a mask that hid her isolation. Nelson was the closest thing she had to a true friend, but even with him she felt the need to hide.

She did so now, succinctly. "Forget it, Nelson. Spencer Sloane is a closed subject. I came here to have fun and that's exactly what I'm going to do."

He watched her drain the glass and signal for another. "You must have loved him something fierce."

She stopped in the act of replacing the glass on the table. For just an instant, her fragility showed. But she raised her chin a notch and answered in an insouciant tone, "I love no one. You know me, the original party girl. Love 'em and leave 'em." The waiter brought her drink and she held it high in a derisive toast. "If I'd known you were going to play sourpuss, I wouldn't have asked you to come. Run along home, dear. I don't need a watchdog." Raising her voice, she called out to no one in particular, "My toes are twitching, boys. Who wants to dance?"

A dozen youths scurried to the call. She laughed and exclaimed, "What riches! You choose for me, Nelson." When he shrugged, still pouting, she added, "I'll just have to dance with all of you. Come along, lads. The lady's hungry for fun."

They descended onto the wood floor and Liana, with drink in hand, danced with renewed abandon within a circle of her admirers, pulling one then another into the spotlight with her, laughingly exchanging partners with the speed of lightning. Once or twice fights threatened to break out as her enflamed partners battled for their turn. She shrugged off their antics—this was par for the course.

But as she drained her glass and turned to ask for another, she spotted a lone figure standing at the outskirts of the crowd. Dressed like a gentleman in black evening clothes and stark white shirt, impeccably tailored. Reeking of money and prestige. Making her surroundings seem shabby in contrast.

Spencer Sloane.

Somehow he'd escaped and was standing across the room with a thunderous scowl on his face, the very essence of retribution in human form.

When he saw that she'd spotted him, he began to walk toward her with a purposeful stride. She couldn't have felt more panicked if Mephistopheles himself was marching toward her. Hazily, she cast about for some refuge. But before she could think, he'd maneuvered his way through the crowd and was standing before her. With a calculated gleam in his eye, he raised his hand. Dangling from his index finger was the handcuff and chain he'd torn from the wall and removed from his wrist. "I thought you might like a souvenir."

"Why don't *you* keep it. It'll give you something to remember me by."

He pocketed it with the air of one who'd forgotten it already. "I'd like to have a word with you."

The youths surrounding her glowered at him. Seizing the opportunity, Liana said to the crowd at large, "Tell the big man to go away."

One of her admirers obliged. "Be gone, old man. She's spoken for."

With a disdain like the lash of a bullwhip, Sloane sneered, "By everyone in the room, it seems."

The swain who'd spoken made a move as if to shove Sloane aside, but was rewarded with such a glacial glare that he thought better of it and stepped back.

Sloane moved toward Liana as if intending to drag her away. Like a cat, she sidestepped him, scrambling onto the nearest chair and atop the table. There she stood, mindless of the glasses and ashtrays that littered the surface. "Help me, boys," she appealed with a deceptively teasing smile. "The big bully's trying to get li'l ole me."

Only Sloane noted the sarcasm in her tone, contemptuously invoking their male desire to safeguard a helpless female. Thinking it a game, the others flanked her table in a protective line. But Sloane ignored them, stepping through as if they didn't exist.

He was approaching her when Liana spotted a familiar face across the swirl of dancers, recognizing him as a bit actor from Universal. He held his arms out to her and called, "Come to Papa, baby." As Sloane stepped to the table, Liana leapt into the air, sailing past her line of defenders, and into the outstretched arms. But the actor had imbibed as much as she. He swayed under the impact, and together they went tumbling to the floor.

Liana felt the gin she'd drunk engulf her in a swirl of

dizziness. She was giggling when she felt Sloane's presence above her. She noted the disgust on his face and her laughter died in her throat. "No wonder no one will hire you, if this is how you behave."

Her eyes spit fire at him. *I behave this way because of you,* she thought bitterly. But she'd die before she said it aloud.

He reached down and took her arm in his hand. She jerked away, but his grip tightened and he hauled her to her feet. The stunned crowd parted as he dragged her across the room toward the exit. She struggled with him, but his hold was too strong to break. The gin had left her feeling disoriented. She couldn't seem to think clearly. She only knew that she couldn't—wouldn't—let him see the effect he was having on her. She must continue to play her role. Disgust him enough that he'd leave her alone for good.

Along the way, she passed a waiter with drinks on a tray. Grabbing one, she gulped at its contents as Sloane opened the door and shoved her outside.

The night air was cool after the hot flush within. She leaned back against the brick wall, taking a breath, then, when she saw his furious face, lifting the glass once again to her lips. But before she could drink, he put his hand on hers, halting the motion. The shock of his touch sobered her at once.

"I'll take that," he said, relieving her of the glass.

She glared defiance at him. "And what will you replace it with?" she taunted.

His cold blue eyes—damn those eyes!—swept her with a slow, measuring assessment. Finally he said softly, "With the self-respect of doing good work."

She stared at him, astonished. "*You* are going to give *me* self-respect?"

"If I can."

It was too much. She snatched the drink from him and tossed the contents into his face.

He didn't flinch, didn't move. He just stood there, letting the alcohol drip from his face with the dignity of a stone statue.

It shamed her. Flinging the glass so it shattered against the wall, she reeled past him to lose herself in the night.

The next morning, Liana stood in line with perhaps eighty other young women outside the gate of Monarch Studios. An open casting call at a third-rate studio—a step down even from Universal. She'd awoken early, head splitting, but determined to put the horror of the day before out of her mind and get on with the necessity of paying the rent.

At first, the ordeal of waiting in line fed her determination, made her feel she was doing something positive. But gradually, as the minutes ticked by and her body began to ache along with her head, a sense of discouragement began to seep into her. Here she was, back where she'd started. Just a faceless part of the constant influx of people drawn by the lure of stardom on the silver screen.

Some of those hopefuls surrounded her today: young girls who'd come on buses and trains, using the last of their meager savings for a chance at Hollywood glory. Pretty girls who'd come with high hopes but who'd quickly found that pretty girls were a dime a dozen, and the talent that had wowed the folks back home was dismissed as ordinary by a town already overrun with talent and ambition. Some of them were buoyed by naïveté, certain that stardom was just around the corner. Others were near despondency, their faith dulled, only a step away from begging or selling themselves on the streets to survive. For these girls, this was their last chance, and they knew it. The air of desperation was oppressive.

An unfamiliar male voice calling her name distracted her. She turned to see a man approaching. A short man with a wide mouth and the instantly endearing manner of a country boy. Tommy.

The sight of him brought it all rushing back again. The degradation of their last encounter. A hotel lobby with the faint whiff of croissants in the air. The presence of this man, sidekick to Sloane, bearer of a brush-off worthy of a Pigalle whore.

He was grinning at her. Through his glasses, his calf-like brown eyes brimmed with admiration. "Boy howdy, are you something!"

"Am I?" she asked coolly. The impulse to flee was strong upon her. But she'd been standing in this line for two hours and didn't want to lose her place.

"You've just got some of the most powerful people in this town cringing at your feet, lady."

"I don't see anyone cringing."

He glanced down the line. A pathetic spectacle. "Well, you've got them over a barrel, anyhow. The Ace has got to leave for Tahiti in two weeks." She flinched at the old nickname. "Everything's set. Ship chartered, equipment rented, crew on payroll. And Paramount's gettin' nervous. *Variety*'s crack about 'controversy' caught 'em off guard. They haven't seen a scenario yet. Between you and me, I think if they have any more time to think about it, they'll get wet feet and pull out. So the Ace has to sign a star and hightail it out of here as fast as he can."

"Let him get Swanson, then."

"He wants you."

By now, some of the girls closest to them were turning their heads, listening while pretending not to. She lowered her voice.

"I *told* him I'm not going to do it. If he thinks I'll change my mind, he's crazy."

"Who's more crazy? Him for wanting you, or you for turning down the chance of a lifetime?"

She rubbed her aching forehead. "Aside from everything else, the part sounds dreadful. I wouldn't want it no matter *who* was directing it."

"But if it makes you a star, you can play any role you want from then on."

It was the same argument Nelson had used. It made sense to everyone but her.

"There's no use talking about it. I can't work for that man and live with myself."

"You could live pretty high on a thousand dollars a week."

"A thousand—" The color drained from Liana's face.

The girl behind them piped up, "*I'll* take it!"

Ignoring her, Liana asked, "Don't you remember what he did to me?"

He shifted. "I remember." She caught the sympathy behind his spectacles. He moved closer and lowered his voice. "Li, let me tell you something about Spencer Sloane. In the war, I saw him—*routinely*—perform acts of courage and heroism I used to think only existed in books. I was just a hick farm boy from Kansas when I went to France. I went with dreams of glory, but the truth is I never even got to flight school. Bum eyes." He tapped his glasses. "Without the Ace's kicking my tail, I never would have become a photographer, much less T. Crenshaw, hotshot cameraman. He pushed me every step of the way. Now, I'm pretty good with a camera. But I don't have Ace's flashes of genius or narrative skills. There were times during the making of *Devils and Heart* when I felt like I was the fellow holding the brushes for Mike Angelo or Leo-Bob da Vinci."

Liana felt herself warming to him. She sighed. "Tommy, you're sweet, but I've heard all this before. What a great man he is. Big war hero. But let me tell *you* something. He . . ." She broke off, choking on a rush of remembered pain.

As she struggled to regain her composure, he said, "You really loved him." As if he hadn't realized it until now.

She turned her head away.

"If I'd known that . . ." His face hardened briefly before giving way to sympathy. "Honey, if it makes you feel any better, I think you *were* special to him. In all the years we've been buddies, I've never known him to have more than a one-night stand with anyone else. He doesn't have much regard for most women. He pursues them, beds them, then once he does . . ." He shrugged. "Do you remember Marie?"

She cast about in her memory. "Your girlfriend in Paris."

"That's right. I got it into my head that I wanted to marry her. But the Ace talked some sense into me. He said 'Sleep with her, but don't marry her. You don't want some tramp you met in a Pigalle bar to be the mother of your children.' "

"Pompous bastard!"

"Maybe. But if I *had* married her, I probably wouldn't be here now. Anyway, the point is, he sees women either as saints or . . ."

"I know what he thinks."

"But that doesn't change the fact that he's a visionary. An artist. And if you ask me, I think he's using this film to work out his problems with women. Not that he'd admit it, or even knows it. But isn't that what artists do? Turn their demons into art?"

She thought of his using their tragedy as fodder for his second film and burned anew. "Get this straight, Tommy. I have absolutely no interest in helping him work out his problems with women."

"Fair enough. Forget that. What he's trying to say about the missionaries in the South Seas is important. And you're a big part of it. So I'm begging you . . . for him, for you, and hell, for me . . . swallow your pride and at least go talk to him about it."

At that moment the gate opened and a coarse voice called out, "All right, let's have the next ten."

"That's me," Liana said as the line in front of her began to move. "I'm sorry, Tommy. I just can't."

"If you change your mind," he called after her, "or if you need any help, I'm in suite one-oh-one at the Hollywood Hotel."

"I won't change my mind," she assured him. "But thanks just the same."

5

Dusk was rapidly descending on Sloane as he sat in an overstuffed leather chair in his bungalow office on the Paramount lot. Around him were mementos of his meteoric career: framed posters from his two earlier films, the *Photoplay* and *Motion Picture Classic* awards these films had won him, an inscribed megaphone given him by the admiring cast and crew of *Wounded Heart*. Mixed in with this were souvenirs of the war years: a model of his Neuport 16 biplane, a German air corps emblem ripped from the fuselage of one of his downed adversaries, his aviator jacket and goggles hanging from hooks on the wall, and his Croix de Guerre, personally bestowed on him by the President of France.

But, despite these trappings of victory, the office today was hardly a scene of triumph. His large desk was covered with unanswered phone messages regarding the *Tehani* project. The steamship was fully chartered—the first payment made that morning—and a departure date set for two weeks from today. The crew and male lead had all been hired. A mountain of supplies and equipment was in the process of being packed and transported to the dock in San Pedro. Paramount was having last-minute jitters and demanding to see a script that existed only in his head. The New York brass were hounding him day and night to hire a box office star: Gloria Swanson, Lillian Gish, Mary Miles Minter, Mary Pickford.

He took a sip of bootleg bourbon, always plentifully available at the studio, and sank lower into the Moroccan leather, head back, long legs stretched out before him. He was tired. His left wrist was badly chafed from the night before. When no studio policeman had come to his aid, it had taken him a quarter hour to rip the bolted handcuff from the wall, taking a portion of it with him before he could retrieve the key from the desk and free himself completely. A minor annoyance, but symbolic of a larger problem.

After years of painstakingly overcoming every obstacle, he finally had everything in place toward achieving the goal of his life. Everything except the most important detail: The only woman who could play Tehani refused to have anything to do with him. Not only did she resent him for ending their hopeless affair, but in a colossal gesture of self-destruction she was willing to sacrifice any chance she might have at a career for the sake of never seeing him again.

He reached into his coat pocket, withdrew his wallet, and took out a worn photograph, brown with age. Gazing again at the lovely Polynesian woman whose large, dark eyes radiated a kind of childlike serenity and playful purity restored his strength and determination. Tehani. *I'm almost there,* he told her. *After all these years*

I'm going to get my revenge for what happened to you. I've been ruthless. I've pushed everything else out of my life. I've stayed awake each night feeling the pain you endured. You're my reason for doing this. And I promise you, I won't let anything get in my way.

As he stared at her picture, it struck him again how uncanny was the resemblance between the two women. Not that they looked exactly alike. They had in common a quality he couldn't quite define, but which was as tangible, unmistakable, and unique as the scent of night-blooming jasmine. No. No other actress could do this. Not Swanson or Gish or *anyone.* Without Liana, there would be no *Tehani of the South Seas.*

So how to get her? Not with the promise of fame or money—no matter how much he offered. If that was what she was after, she would have found a way to rationalize her acceptance immediately, no matter how she felt about him. What, then, did she want?

He laid his head back against the padded seat and closed his eyes. Unbidden he recalled the feel of her skin. Soft as silk, luminous as pearls beneath the rough texture of his hands. Skin that made a man want to taste it on his tongue, the way a cat lapped up cream . . .

He shook himself and took another drink. Be careful, he warned himself. But his mind wandered back to that last night in Paris. The depth of her passion, the explosion of her climax, the way she'd come when he'd done nothing more than kiss her. The utter abandonment of that kiss. *That* was what she wanted.

There was an undeniable physical attraction between them. And, despite the way she'd led him on the day before, then so ridiculously rebuffed him, he couldn't help noting his effect on her. The unconscious parting of her lips. The subtle deepening of her breath. He found himself growing hard just thinking about it. She wouldn't respond to reason. She wouldn't respond to bribery. But she *would* respond to seduction. He was certain of that.

He'd do it, he vowed. Not because the memory of her was driving him mad. Not because he really wanted her. He wanted the illusion, that was all. He'd do it not because he needed to, but for the sake of the picture. Because it was the only way.

Having justified himself, he put the photograph away, rose, and went to his desk. Pushing the intercom button, he said, "Mabel, have my car brought around."

Liana sprang from the streetcar on Hollywood Boulevard in an elated mood. After a discouraging day of open casting calls, she'd had an amazing piece of luck. She was summoned from among the crowd by producer Barry Levine at Fox. Thinking she was being interviewed for a minor role in a forgettable comedy, she was astounded when he offered her the female lead in the period drama *When Knighthood Was In Flower*. Considerably more than she'd bargained for. When she asked why, he showed her the morning's *Herald*. There, on the gossip page, was a picture of Liana with the story of how she'd declined the role all the big stars were scrambling for.

"You're the talk of the town," he'd told her.

She'd floated back in a triumphant daze. She'd beaten Sloane, and on her own terms!

She checked her mail, then bounded up the stairs of the Hillview Apartments, to the room she'd rented for the last year and a half, since her fortunes had taken a nose-dive. Built around a Mediterranean-style courtyard, it was inexpensive, a favored spot of New York actors who'd come to Hollywood. Anticipating the luxury of a hot bath and a celebratory drink, she opened the door.

And stopped dead in her tracks. For there, in her shabby sitting room, sprawled in a threadbare overstuffed chair, was Spencer Sloane.

He was dressed in casual but obviously expensive clothes which only served to amplify the decayed surroundings. She stood, frozen, staring at him, the shock of his presence in her sanctuary making her feel violated and vulnerable.

"Well, well, well. Captain Sloane." She went through the motions of taking off her hat and laying down her purse as if she was in no way agitated by his unexpected visit.

"My name is Spencer," he told her.

Ignoring this, she asked instead, "Don't you ever give up?"

"Not when something's important to me."

His reply unsettled her further. "How did you get in here?"

"I promised your landlady a screen test."

"Good. Then let *her* play Tehani."

"Is this any way to treat someone who's trying to do you a favor?"

"*Me* a favor? You're trying to do yourself a favor. As always."

He heard the rancor in her tone and backed off, changing tactics. "I'm sorry we got off on the wrong foot by talking business. I didn't come for that."

"What *did* you come for?"

"I thought we might become reacquainted."

"I know you as well as I care to, thanks."

He stood up, suddenly seeming to fill the room. "But that's not true, is it? When you get right down to it, neither of us knows much about the other. I was hoping we could remedy that situation."

"*You* remedy it."

He moved closer. "I can't do it alone." He reached up and stroked her lower lip with his thumb. "What you said yesterday . . ."

He broke off, as if loath to finish. Despite her resistance, Liana couldn't help but ask, "What?"

"About how I've thought of you . . . being close to you again brought it all back . . . and you were right, you know. I *did* want you right away."

Involuntarily, she shivered and took a step back. But he followed her, stalking her like a panther on the prowl, reaching forth with both hands to cup her face and bring her close. As he lowered his mouth until it barely brushed her lips, a jolt of treacherous longing shot through her.

"If you don't get out," she breathed, "I'm going to call the police."

"Is your kiss as sweet as I remember?"

He pulled her closer, so her breasts were flattened against the granite of his chest, and captured her lips in a kiss that made her feel drugged. Panic bubbled within her and she shoved him away. She made a dash for the door, but he grabbed her arm and wheeled her around, pulling her up against him so her breath left her body as his lips found hers.

She fought him. But he held her with a relentless grip, deepening his kiss against her impregnable mouth until slowly she relaxed, her struggles melting in remembered bliss. Against all the forces of her will, her lips parted, letting him in, feeling his arms strong about her back, drowning in a temptation so sweet, so profoundly remembered, that it nearly broke her heart in two. The pain of it reminded her again of the danger, bringing to the fore an instinct for survival that had been honed to a razor-sharp edge.

Coming to her senses, she pushed herself away and,

wrenching up a hand, slapped his face. It felt so good that she did it again and again, until her palm stung. He didn't resist. He just stood there, taking her assault stoically, waiting for her wrath to subside. And when it had, when she'd exhausted herself in pummeling him, he firmly picked her up and carried her to the bed, to lay her down and sit beside her, leaning over for another kiss.

But just as his mouth was about to touch hers, she challenged in a lifeless voice, "What are you going to do? Rape me?"

He stilled. Slowly, he rose to a sitting position with a horrified yet strangely hollow gaze, as if she'd just held up a mirror and he'd caught a glimpse of himself that had stopped him cold. It seemed for a while that he would never speak. But finally he said, beaten, "No, Liana. I'm not going to rape you."

She sat up, brushing her tangled hair from her face. "I don't need you, and I don't need your part," she told him, struggling to bring her breathing under control. "In fact, I've just been offered a great role over at Fox. And I'm going to take it. So I'm telling you once and for all, get out of my apartment, and out of my life."

He deliberated for a second more. Then, without another word, he rose, picked up his hat, and left.

Minutes later, when the telephone rang, she still hadn't moved. In a daze, she picked up the candlestick phone and held the receiver to her ear. The voice on the other end belonged to Barry Levine at Fox. He was sorry, he told her. He had to rescind his offer.

"But . . . why?" she asked, still trying to digest it.

"The word is out, sweetie. Anyone who hires you has just made some powerful enemies. You're a hot potato. No one will touch you."

"Sloane called you, didn't he?"

"It's just that—"

"I know he did."

"As much as I'd love to hire you, honey, I can't afford to alienate—"

"Coward!" She slammed down the receiver.

I never bluff. Ask anyone.

Furious, she went to her dresser, opened the top drawer, and took out the bottle of gin. Her hands were trembling so badly that as she poured, it spilled down the sides of the glass. Taking it in both hands, she raised it to her lips. Just a sip to calm her ragged nerves.

But as the alcohol singed her tongue, she recalled the contempt and distaste on Sloane's face at Earl's the night before. And felt again a flush of shame. Staring at the glass, she saw before her all the wasted years of the path she'd tread. She saw herself as he must have seen her, a pathetic, squandered shadow of her former self.

And as she did, she realized that her hands had stopped their shaking. Staring at them, she put the glass aside. That was over. She had a purpose now. To put this colossally arrogant man in his place.

And she knew just how to do it.

First she telephoned the Hollywood Hotel and found out Sloane's room number. Then, opening the bottom drawer of her dresser, she fished around until she found what she was hunting for. With a sense of sublime satisfaction, she put it in her purse, and prepared herself for battle.

The Hollywood Hotel was a sprawling wooden edifice built at the juncture of Hollywood Boulevard and Highland in 1903 in a rather gaudy mission-Moorish style. It was originally the mecca of tourists who flocked to see the area's natural wonders and the famed gardens of painter Paul de Longpre. When the fledgling motion picture business came to town in 1911, it soon became the unofficial headquarters of Cecil B. DeMille, Al Christie, Mack Sennett and the like—New York motion picture makers who'd come to Hollywood for the sunshine, the varied natural settings, and often, to escape the law.

It was after two in the morning when Liana arrived. She'd waited until she was fairly certain Sloane would be asleep, then had walked the short distance from the Hillview, reinforcing her determination with every step. The large lobby was deserted at this hour, the lone attendant snoring into his hand. She crossed on soundless feet and went up the wide main stairway to the second floor. Suite 108 was the last room at the end of the hall occupying the entire corner of the hotel.

Liana's anger bubbled beneath the surface. *I'll be strong,* she vowed. *I won't let him get to me.*

She rapped on the door, but had to knock again before a sleep-thickened voice asked from inside, "Who is it?"

"Open the door and see," she replied.

A brief pause, then he cracked it open, widening it when he saw her standing in the hall. He was wearing a royal blue silk robe that had been hastily knotted about his lean waist. She caught a glimpse of bare legs and naked chest. His hair was slightly tousled, lending him a casually dashing air. He raked a hand through it. "Come in," he invited, clearly caught off guard.

Just as I want him, Liana thought with a secret smirk.

She stepped past him into a luxurious sitting room. The curtains were drawn, the only light coming from a small lamp. She noted Victorian furnishings: plush, overstuffed chairs, a huge tufted, round ottoman, a circular claw-footed table in the center of the room with a massive bouquet of brilliant birds of paradise.

She removed her coat and draped it over the nearest chair. Underneath, she wore a dress of black chiffon sporadically sprinkled with silver sequins, stars in an inky night. Cut on the bias so a cowl dipped tantalizingly about her breasts, it showed a great deal of calf, clinging subtly to every curve. A dress elegant enough to wear to any fashionable function, but sexy enough to hint at delights to be discovered underneath. A holdover from the wardrobe she'd bought during her brief flirtation with success.

"I didn't expect you."

"Good." Once again she felt a surge of anger, but repressed it with an actress's skill. She sauntered to the center of the room with feline grace, surveying her surroundings as if they consumed her completely. All the while preening for him, letting him watch. Feeling him study every inch of her through the gauzy gown.

"You intended it to be a surprise, then. May I ask why?"

She glanced over her shoulder at him. "Why don't you have a drink? You seem a little tense."

As he went to pour bourbon into a glass, she reached into her sequined bag and took out a cigarette, positioning it in a stylized black-and-silver holder. "Want to give me a light?"

He reached automatically into the pocket of his robe. But, thinking better of it, he instead removed his hand and walked over to an end table. Picking up the heavy lighter, he flicked the flame, lit her cigarette, then stepped back. She took a puff, blowing a thin stream of smoke into the air.

"I didn't know you smoked," he said, before taking a sip of his drink.

"I only smoke when I'm having sex. Or . . . when I'm about to."

He choked on the bourbon. When he'd cleared his throat enough that he could talk, he asked, "Why are you here?"

"I couldn't sleep." She went to the window and parted the drape just a bit, pretending to scrutinize the lighted gardens below. "I know I accused you of wanting to rape me, but . . . the truth is . . ."

"What?"

"I couldn't help wondering what it might be like to be spanked by you."

A long silence followed her words. The impulse to look at him was overwhelming. But she had to stick to her script. *He thinks I'm a tramp. Fine. I'll just give him what he wants.*

"What kind of game are you playing?" he asked.

"I thought we might call a halt to games. At least, for the time being."

"If that's your intended effect, you're failing miserably."

"Oh? What effect am I having on you?"

She took another puff of her cigarette then exhaled it slowly through pursed red lips, turning ever so slightly to allow him a glimpse of her profile as she did.

"You kick me out of your room with the threat of calling the police. But then you show up at my door in the middle of the night, dressed like a Park Avenue temptress, smelling of . . ." He moved closer to sniff the back of her neck. ". . . wicked perfume. Inviting me with every move you make. Until all I can think of is how your body felt beneath mine. You hold it from me, but all the while your eyes beg to be touched."

His hands reached around to cup her breasts. A moan of ferocious desire mewled low in her throat. She could feel his erection against the crack of her buttocks. *Careful,* she warned herself. But she couldn't help quivering beneath his hands.

"They have a name for women like you," he growled in her ear.

He took the neckline of her dress and yanked it down. It slid to her feet in a fluffy heap of sequins and chiffon. She stood with her naked back to him, dressed in nothing but black stockings and garters, shivering now with uncontrollable arousal.

One hand found her breast again as the other smoothed itself over the rounded cheek of her ass. "You *should* be spanked," he said. Then he took his hand away and gave her a resounding smack. She gasped at the sting. But her body surged in euphoric abdication. *Yes,* she thought, giving herself up to it. *Let it be like this. No tender caresses. No heartfelt sighs. Just sex. Wild. Feral. Free from expectations.*

Because she had no strength to deny him now. She'd placed him in her mind as something forbidden and, because of it, had ended up wanting him all the more. She'd make him suffer . . . but she'd have him once more before she did.

His hand left her breast to roam her trembling body. Strong. Powerful. Supremely confident of its journey. Past rib cage and flat belly, to bury itself between her thighs. To find her already wet with need. To play with her with such skill that she had to bite her lower lip to keep from whimpering aloud. Pinning her to him, he smacked her rear again and yet again, not hurting her, but striking from her the last vestiges of her will to resist.

"Is that how you prefer the game?" he demanded, nibbling on her ear.

All her denied longing boiled to the surface like lava, hot and uncontained. "Exactly," she told him, truthful now.

"You didn't really think I'd rape you."

"No."

"But you like it when men are rough."

"Yes." His fingers played with her unmercifully, demanding obedience to his will.

"You want me to take you like a pirate seizing his prize."

She leaned back into him, so weak with wanting him, so thrilled by the lash of his words, that all she could do was sigh.

He put his hands on her shoulders and turned her to face him, assessing her with a scalding glare. "Then that's what you'll have," he told her in an oddly controlled tone.

He took the cigarette from her and tossed it into the ashtray on the table. With a motion so swift that it took her breath away, he locked both wrists in the prison of his hands and thrust them behind her back. Then he shoved her back onto the ottoman and lowered himself onto her, still pinning her arms behind.

The impact of his body jolted her with desire. He caught both wrists in one mighty hand then crashed his mouth down on hers. With his free hand he kneaded her breast just before his mouth left hers and clamped itself upon her nipple. She gasped aloud in hot, wet, wanton need as he sucked and licked and nipped, driven by the grinding of her body into his, by the helpless moans as he feasted on her flesh. His mouth blazed like an inferno, kissing, devouring, branding her as it moved lower, his hand trailing a path for it to follow.

Her head began to spin. With her hands imprisoned behind her, she felt like a conquered slave being ravished by a Viking lord. Her efforts to free herself only added to the delicious sense of seizure. As in Paris, she'd once again unleashed in him a sexual fury that was absolutely thrilling. She shimmered in carnal heat, her body soaring, spiraling beneath the onslaught of his mouth.

His free hand shoved her legs apart. Pinned beneath him, she felt completely exposed. His tongue found the sensitive flesh of her inner thigh, causing jolts of heat to spark her loins like lightning. She cried out, her body writhing uncontrollably, trying to bring him closer to the apex of her desire. But she couldn't control him. His mouth moved with an infuriating will all its own, feasting voraciously on the silky skin of her thigh, her belly, everywhere but where she wanted him most.

Panting her need, her body strummed tight in agonized anticipation, she taunted him with a voice raw with passion. "You'll have to do more than that to satisfy a woman like me."

His mouth stilled. Then, with a snarl like a starving beast, he clamped it on the pouting lips between her legs. His tongue moved swiftly and with rapacious skill, parting the lips, digging inside, finding the swollen, ravenous bud. She jerked with a cry but he held her down, impaling her to the ottoman as he assaulted her with such blinding mastery that she began to whimper deep in her throat. He tongued her relentlessly, urging her higher and higher until she was arching against his mouth.

The pleasure was exquisite. Waves of heat and raw, unbridled lust shot through her, filling her with mounting exultation. He worked feverishly now, pushing her past the precipice until she was flying free, soaring like an eagle on the propulsion of his breath, spilling her juices into his mouth with a cry of helpless surrender.

"Let me go," she cried. "I want to taste you."

He let go of her wrists. Ripped off his robe and tossed it aside. But even as she brought her arms up to reach for him, he shifted, straddling her chest so his knees pinned her arms to the ottoman on either side of her head.

"You're not in control," he told her through heaving breath. "You use men. Make toys of them. It's fun for you, is it? Well, not *this* time."

His erection jutted up against her mouth. She wanted to take him in her hands, to feel the velvety steel, to marvel at his rugged beauty. But he wouldn't let her. He thrust forward against her mouth. She took one slow swipe up the shaft with her tongue. The taste of him aroused her anew. When she reached the head, her lips parted and she took him in. Her mouth closed over him and he exhaled a ragged breath. She took him deep inside, the whole bulging length of him, into her throat then slowly, ever so slowly back again, feeling with her tongue every cord and vein along the burgeoning shaft. Luxuriating in the feel of him in her mouth, pulsing, throbbing, filling her throat.

With a savage groan he grabbed her head and began to pump into her mouth. She took him willingly, moaning her delight. He thrust harder and harder still, until she could feel him swell with the need for release.

But he wasn't finished. He withdrew and shifted his weight, freeing her for a brief span. She lunged up and grabbed his head, kissing him with all the desperation that had intensified with the passing of every minute of every fever-soaked night without him. Electrified by the searing sovereignty of his kiss. Beyond thought or the chaos of emotion, needing now nothing more than for him to come inside and make her whole.

"Fuck me," she begged against his lips.

He reared back at her use of the word. But when he saw the excitement it had engendered, he brought his mouth to her ear. "I'm *going* to fuck you," he rumbled. "I'm going to fuck you like you've never been fucked before."

He spread her wide and plunged inside like a madman seeking release from demons in hot pursuit. Grabbing her wrists again in a punishing grip, thrusting them high over her head, binding them to the ottoman as he drove into her with such force that she opened her mouth to scream. His own mouth cut short her cry, silencing her with a pressure so fierce, so feral, so demanding that he stole her very breath. Restraining his need for release with superhuman control, thrusting hard, again and again, until she was swept away by one voluptuous explosion after the other as he pinned her down and pounded into her like a man who could never get enough.

Only when she felt she could go on no longer did he allow himself the luxury of release, kissing her all the while. Letting go of her wrists so that her arms came up to hold him close. Growling his deliverance into her mouth.

He collapsed on top of her, both of them reeling as their breaths slowed, their bodies steaming. Finally he lifted his head.

"Is that what you needed?"

She felt dizzy, the intensity of their union shocking her now, even as it had four years before. "Yes," she whispered.

"Good. Then we understand the rules of the game."

Yes. She understood. Despite her earlier determination, she'd been swept away by him once again, her defenses shattered, her will overtaken by his. And she'd loved it so much that she felt immobilized. She could barely remember why she'd come here.

"Meet me at the studio in the morning," he told her, "and we'll sign the contract."

She picked up her tattered dress, put on her coat, and left him without another word.

She departed the suite in a fog. The doors along the hallway seemed to drift by her as she passed, as if in a dream, the numbers blurred, until one of them penetrated her jumbled mind. Suite 101. Tommy's room.

And then she remembered why she'd come. He answered her series of knocks dressed in a robe, but unlike Sloane he wore pajamas buttoned to the neck underneath.

"Li . . ." he said uncertainly, squinting at her as he put on his glasses. "What are you doing here? What time is it?"

"Would you do me a favor, Tommy?"

"Well, sure . . . anything."

"In the morning, tell Spencer Sloane he can find someone else for his precious movie. And give him this."

She handed him an envelope. "Read it, if you like."

He withdrew the single page, wrinkled and worn. The same kiss-off letter Ace had asked him to deliver to her in Paris. The letter she'd kept all these years to remind herself of her folly.

On the bottom she'd scrawled, "Paid in full."

6

For the first time in ages, Liana felt good. Her show of integrity had been cleansing, leaving behind the feel of having freed herself from a power that was seeking to destroy her. For two days, she carried herself erect, with a sense of pride.

But on the third morning, a banging on her door awoke her from a sound sleep. When she dragged herself from bed and answered it, Nelson shoved a rumpled copy of *Variety* into her face.

"Have you seen this?"

She shoved back her hair and shook her head to try to clear it. Taking the paper, she squinted at the headline that was splashed across the front page:

Boy Wonder Pulls Plug on Pacific Pix

She was still too sleep-drugged for the words to penetrate. "What does it mean?"

"It means your old friend Sloane has called off the whole thing."

"The whole thing?" she repeated numbly.

"He's pulled out of the picture completely. It's finished. Canceled. They're writing off everything that's been spent so far as a loss."

She was suddenly wide awake. "I don't believe it."

"It's true. Read it. It's all there. He says he can't cast the picture to his satisfaction, and without the perfect Tehani he won't do it at all."

She scanned the story as he talked. "That's absurd. It's some kind of trick."

"If it is, it's one that could ruin his career. Paramount's furious. This was their biggest picture ever, don't forget. To pull out at the last minute after this kind of ballyhoo—well, it's unheard of. With a million dollars riding on it, a lot of which has already been spent . . . Paramount was taking a chance on him as it was, but now . . . *well* . . . no one will trust him after this. He may never work again."

The news was finally penetrating her early morning fog. "My God, he's really done it! But why?"

"Use your head, goose. I'd say if he can't have you, he doesn't want anyone. Which leads me to wonder exactly what went on between the two of you, anyway."

She held up a hand to silence his chatter so she could think. Was it possible that Sloane had really meant it when he'd said no one else could play Tehani? Enough that he'd jeopardize everything—his career, his future, his life? If so, she saw herself facing such a monumental sense of integrity that it made her small show seem trivial in comparison.

But more than that . . . she felt strangely moved. Did he really trust her that much? Did he have such faith in her that he really *believed* no one could play the part but her?

Or was he bluffing? Was this nothing more than a calculated attempt to change her mind? Knowing she'd realize she had him over a barrel and could demand anything she wanted? Was it nothing more than a colossal attempt at bribery?

I never bluff.

Could she trust him? Of course not. But maybe it wasn't a question of trust. Maybe the real issue at stake here was power. She'd been prancing around for two days feeling powerful because she'd told him to go to hell, and yet it wasn't real. She'd gained nothing. But to have a million-dollar production canceled because of her—*that* was power she could use to her advantage.

But how?

Her father's words of long ago came back to her. *Let them think you're giving them what they want, then turn it on them.*

"Nelson, you were right all along."

"*Was* I? About what?"

"Running away gets you nowhere. The only way to win is to somehow find a way to take Tehani away from Sloane and make her my own."

He was peering at her suspiciously. "I don't know that I like that gleam in your eyes."

"Nelson . . ." She turned to him. "*You* call his office. Tell them I'll take the part on one condition: that you come along to do my makeup."

Nelson flushed suddenly and fixed his gaze on the floor. "I—uh—can't do that."

"Why not?"

"Well . . ." He continued to stare at the ground. "It seems the diva Swanson was so impressed by the way I made you up to look like her that she's offered me a job. As her personal makeup artist, no less."

She stared at him incredulously. "You'd rather make her up than *me*?"

He put a hand on a hip and snapped, "Well, how was I supposed to know you'd change your mind? The last I heard it was 'over my dead body.' The least you can do is be happy for me."

She relented, kissing him on the cheek. "I *am* happy for you. Although you realize you're missing a trip to Tahiti."

"I'll live. I get seasick on the Catalina ferry."

"You *can* take the time to call Sloane's office before you desert me?"

"Of course I can. I'm not a *complete* louse."

"Good. Then tell them I want . . . star billing equal with Farnsworth and two thousand dollars a week."

"*Only* two thousand?" he quipped. "Gloria gets twenty-five hundred."

She grinned at him, heady now with the enormity of her plan. "Well, let's not get greedy."

"Heaven forbid. What did they pay you at Universal? Two dollars a day? I'll say one thing for you, doll. You get a little taste of power and you don't just run with it, you go for the Olympics."

"I have to have *something* to compensate for losing you to Swanson, don't I? Besides, let Sloane think I'm being a typical petty actress, worrying about money and billing. I want him off guard. I've learned something today, Nelson. I'm going to play Tehani, but *my* Tehani, not his."

"How are you going to do *that*?"

She wound a tendril of hair around her finger. "It won't be easy. He's cool and stubborn and likes to be in control. But I have one weapon that I can use against him. He has one weakness, and I know just how to use it to get what I want."

Nelson raised a brow. "And just *what's* this chink in the great man's armor?"

She turned and fixed him with a steady gaze. "Me."

Two weeks later, the main conference room of the U.S. Port Authority at the San Pedro dock was packed with reporters covering the official departure of the *Tehani of the South Seas* company. It was one of the largest press gatherings Hollywood had ever seen: not just the usual industry newshounds and photographers from *Photoplay, Motion Picture Classic,* and *Bioscope,* but reporters from all the Los Angeles dailies and the West Coast correspondents for most of the big New York papers. Up the dock, the chartered ship that would take the film expedition to Tahiti was in the final stages of loading equipment and supplies.

Sloane had hoped to sneak away quietly but Greenburg, as head of West Coast production, had insisted on this public spectacle as a way of deflecting attention from the near-calamity of Sloane's shutting down the picture. It had become apparent in recent days that Greenburg was an enemy not just of Liana, but of the film itself—considered it a folly and had gone along with it only because he didn't want to buck Adolph Zukor, Paramount's boss in New York and a huge fan of *Devils of the Air*.

All this was explained to Liana by Tod Perkins, Paramount's publicity chief, who drove her to San Pedro, thirty miles from Hollywood, in a studio-owned Bugatti roadster. "Greenburg will be there, but don't let him intimidate you," he advised. "He's bound to be a little hostile, but Zukor has the last say. And Zukor thinks Sloane used his threat to slam the brakes on the picture to convince you to come aboard. Which, from his point of view, is only good business. You and I know different, but if Zukor's happy we all rest easier."

Liana felt her heart flutter at the thought of presenting herself to open questions from reporters dying for a juicy story to pass on to their readers. "This is my first press conference," she told him. "What do I do?"

"Nothing to it. We'll meet in a back office, then go out to the press room as a panel: you, Sloane, Greenburg, Hobart Farnsworth, and myself."

Hobart Farnsworth was one of the top male stars in the Paramount stable and had been since coming to Hollywood from the Shakespearean stage in 1915. She'd admired his air of quiet strength spiced with just the right touch of dash and flair in films by major directors like DeMille, D.W. Griffith, and Marshall Neilan. Now she was going to be starring with him.

"We'll answer a few questions about the film," he continued, "introduce you and Farnsworth, then depart for the ship in a stream of confetti and well wishes. Fifteen or twenty minutes at the most. If a question throws you, I'll answer for you. All you have to do is sit there and look pretty."

When they arrived, Perkins took Liana down the hall into a back office where Greenburg was briefing Sloane. Hobart Farnsworth lounged back in a chair, idly smoking a pipe and ignoring everyone around him. He was in his early forties, still striking with a square jaw, dark hair, and large, expressive eyes that the camera loved. Now those famous eyes flicked over her with aimless boredom. "So this is our Cinderella," he drawled with a theatrical sneer.

In an attempt to be accommodating, she said, "I'm

glad to meet you, Mr. Farnsworth. I've been a fan of yours for years."

Lifting his shoulder in a conceited shrug, he drawled, "Well, naturally, my dear."

With that, any of Liana's lingering movie star fascination vanished. He was just another aging ham, like a hundred others she'd met in the course of her career. Her first impulse was to deflate him with a retort about how she'd been a mere tot when she'd first seen him on the screen. But caution stayed her tongue. In her battle of wits with Sloane, Hobart might prove a useful ally. She knew how to handle men like him. Giving him her best ingenue smile, she told him, "I'm not as experienced or gifted as you are, Mr. Farnsworth. You may have to help me, I'm afraid."

He puffed up in surprise. "Well, my dear, naturally I'll do all I can to help. I always feel it's the duty of an established player to lend newcomers the benefit of his vast experience."

He was so serious, she felt an impulse to laugh. Instead she gave him a gracious smile.

Off to the side, the austerity in Greenburg's tone as he spoke to Sloane captured her attention. "This project was approved over my head by Mr. Zukor. I still don't have any clue what it's about. That's what he wants, fine by me, it's his problem. But when rumors start flying about antimissionary themes, I gotta worry about that. That's bound to be a red flag for the Hearst newspapers and the goddamned Bible Belt crusaders who are already whining about 'Hollywood's shocking morals.' So you want my advice? Don't get into the subject matter. Just say it's about a missionary and a native girl who fall in love in the South Seas, period. The last thing you and me and the studio need right now is to get on the wrong side of the press."

"If you're so worried, why this circus?" Sloane asked. "I'd be just as happy to slip off without a word."

"Because any movie that costs a million bucks is gonna need a hell of a lot of publicity if it's ever gonna make its money back. *Good* publicity, that is." He glanced around and saw Liana standing there. "And you. No mention of that little Gloria Swanson stunt, you hear?"

With that he stalked off.

"Charming fellow," she murmured.

"Don't mind him," Sloane told her. "He's just burned because he has no real control over us."

She hadn't been alone with him since that night in his hotel. He'd communicated with her through studio underlings, passing on his instructions for a series of makeup tests, costume fittings, and interviews with the publicity department who were eager to give her the star buildup.

"You've been avoiding me," she commented. Now that the dust had settled, she could begin her campaign.

His gaze traveled slowly down the length of her and back again. She'd worn a new dove grey chiffon dress, the latest word in chic, bought with an advance on her new—and uncontested—salary. She caught his glint of arousal, as if remembering every curve of her body underneath. Delighted with the expected reaction, she chuckled low in her throat.

He hardened his gaze, masking the liability. "I was under the impression that's what you wanted."

She grinned and said in a sultry voice, "It's a woman's prerogative to change her mind."

His eyes crinkled, as if trying to decide what she was up to. But before he could respond, Greenburg's impatient voice from the doorway interrupted.

"Let's get going," he demanded. "We haven't got all day."

They walked in single file down the hall toward the reception room where the contingent of press waited. A hundred faces turned as a door opened and five figures took seats at a long table that faced the crowd. Liana felt a flutter of trepidation as she found herself the focus of so much public attention. It made her feel starkly alone. With Nelson away on location, working on the new Gloria Swanson picture, she had no ally in attendance to give her a sense of comfort.

Tod Perkins stood and began to introduce the panel. But he was immediately drowned out by a chorus of questions. Sloane rose and pointed toward Adela Rogers St. Johns of *Photoplay* magazine.

"Mr. Sloane, is what they're saying true—that this will be the most expensive photoplay ever made?"

He gave one of his tight-lipped smiles. "Upwards of a million dollars. It will be a small price to pay if we get what we're after up on the screen."

"But where is all that money going?" someone asked snidely. "The director's salary?"

"We've hired the best technicians, rented the most advanced equipment, and are paying top dollar for our stars. Unlike the usual two cameras, we're taking along five. We intend to shoot untold thousands of miles of footage using the new and more expensive panchromatic film—stock that will give us the contrast and visual perfection we're seeking. We'll build lavish sets, re-create a tropical hurricane, and mount a spectacular battle sequence. This will be no less than the most ambitious movie location expedition ever undertaken. We're committed to doing whatever it takes to capture the magic, the romance, and the ultimate desecration of

Polynesia on film. And that, as I'm sure you understand, will cost a pretty penny."

A man from *Bioscope* called out, "Do you intend to shoot all your footage in the South Seas?"

"All of it. We'll remain as long it takes to get the footage we need. Even if we have to stay for six months."

Another reporter shouted above the others, "Do you think the world is ready for million-dollar pictures?"

"It's inevitable," Sloane said. "Audiences are tired of small, unambitious pictures. The nickelodeon era is over. Already ground has been broken in numerous cities for what will be luxurious movie palaces. These grand theaters will demand even grander pictures. And by that, I don't just mean grand in visual scope, but in theme. Motion pictures can do more than just entertain. They can inspire and elevate us. They can show us worlds and ideas we haven't considered before."

As more questions were fired at him, Sloane turned to Liana. "I'd like to take this opportunity to introduce my star." He pulled her to her feet. "Liana Wycliffe."

She smiled as a round of flashes from the photographers blinded her. The loudest voice in the blur before her cried out, "How does it feel to be picked for such a big part out of nowhere?"

"A bit like Cinderella," she gave the expected reply. Then added, "A Cinderella who's spent four years kicking around this town waiting for her fairy godmother to get on the stick."

This elicited a wave of appreciative laughter.

"Was the story true that you initially turned down the role? And *that's* why production was halted?"

She glanced at Greenburg and caught his warning glint. Evasively, she asked, "Is everything you print in your papers true?"

Greenburg groaned, but the reporters responded with a collective chuckle.

A man from the side asked, "Why did you decide to change your name from Veronica Dare to Liana Wycliffe?"

"That's my real name. Besides, I wasn't having much luck as Veronica."

"I saw you in *They Won't Laugh*. I thought you were terrific."

"Thank you." She began to relax in the wake of such appreciation. This wasn't so bad after all.

Hobart Farnsworth stood and struck a pose. "Perhaps you'd like to ask a question of *me,*" he suggested dramatically, clearly annoyed at being ignored.

Liana moved to sit down, but then a man called to her, "Miss Wycliffe, I'm Roger Hampton from the *Mendocino Record.* The press release says you grew up in Mendocino. Are you the same Liana Wycliffe who's the daughter of Richard Wycliffe and Christina Wentworth-Gibbons, who lived in Mendocino around the turn of the century and who were later executed in England?"

All at once, the color drained from Liana's face. She'd told the publicity department nothing about her family background. When they'd continued to hammer away at her, insisting that they have something, she'd thrown them a bone and mentioned that she'd grown up in Mendocino. It had never even occurred to her that anyone would put it together, or that a reporter from that small and isolated settlement by the sea would be present here today.

In that instant, Liana saw her worst fears realized. She felt the blood rush to her head and swayed slightly, touching the table with her fingertips for balance.

Dan Kincaid of the *Los Angeles Times* surged to his

feet. "Was that the notorious Christina Wentworth who authored *The Lady and the Highwayman*?"

It was happening again. The old nightmare coming back to haunt her. "She never wrote that for publication," she cried heatedly. "It was her private journal."

"Wait a minute," another voice called out. "Isn't that the book that's been banned everywhere? Why, it's supposed to be pure smut."

"That's a lie!"

She turned to Sloane. Like the rest of the panel, he was staring at her in shock.

"I read that book in Paris," still another reporter declared. "Olympic Press, plain brown wrapper, sold under the table. It's beyond racy."

A few feet away, Greenburg was whispering frantically in Tod Perkins's ear.

"I remember now! Your mother was that duchess who scandalized all of England by joining up with a wanted criminal and later running off with him. Romanticized him as a highwayman. Are you their daughter?"

"My father wasn't a criminal. He was—"

"Not a criminal! He was hanged by the neck until dead. Right beside his paramour in crime—your mother."

"They were betrayed—" she tried to explain.

But they weren't interested. They crawled over one another to shout their questions, like sharks roused to a frenzy by the smell of blood.

Liana stood in the midst of the clamor as the past came rushing back to her. Those awful days in the orphanage after her mother's private journal was published and the scandal was on everyone's lips. The endless gibes from those horrid girls who viciously called her "duchess" and sang as she passed, "Your mother was a bandit's whore." Lunging at them and beating them senseless, one after the other, in a blind fury, until she was forcibly pried loose to be locked in a dark closet with her tears. Happening again and again until it had driven her so mad that she'd risked poverty and starvation to escape. Hating them all for turning something beautiful into something ugly and obscene. Hurting for her parents' violation when for years they'd led a secret, private life so no one would know. Thanking God they hadn't lived to see the besmirching of that which they'd held sacred and pure.

By now, Greenburg's face had turned purple. He glared in horror at Sloane and lurched to his feet. "Ladies and gentlemen, this press conference is over."

His words barely penetrated the uproar. The gathering had burst into a free-for-all as each reporter remembered some aspect of the legend of *The Lady and the Highwayman*.

"Wasn't your mother once the lover of King Edward the Seventh?"

"When they ran away from England, did they come to America?"

"Why did they go back to England when he was a wanted man? Wasn't that what led to their hanging?"

"The Dirty Duchess's daughter. What a story this will make!"

Perkins stood and tried to quell the mob. But nothing could turn the tide.

"How old were you when they died?"

"Did you see the hangings?"

"My God! Did Paramount know about this when they hired you?"

Liana's anger was so intense that she trembled with it. As Perkins tried to out-shout the reporters, she turned and stumbled from the room.

She pushed her way out onto the dock, where the S.S.

Catalina was firing its engines in preparation for departure. A tall crane was lifting a seaplane onto an upper deck. She watched bleakly, knowing the ship wouldn't sail.

Then the door flew open and a stampede of reporters nearly trampled each other in the rush to file their stories. Behind them, Sloane and Greenburg emerged. As they drew closer, Liana heard Greenburg say, "She's off the picture as of now. You call a halt until we find a replacement. I'll call Swanson. No, she's off on another picture. Nita Naldi, then. Or Blanche Sweet. *Anyone* else, for Chrissake. I'm gonna cable Zukor right now. And *this* time you do it my way."

He stormed off down the pier, where his chauffeured Hispano-Suiza idled.

Liana had to fight to keep her voice from quivering as she turned to Sloane. "Well, that's that, isn't it? It seems you've gone to all this trouble for nothing."

He turned to look at her. "Why didn't you tell me?" he asked softly.

Her humiliation, and her anger, nearly choked her. "I thought it was all behind me. It never occurred to me that anyone would—" She stopped and met his gaze with burning eyes. "And anyway, when did we ever tell each other anything? Wasn't it you who said, 'Let's not talk about our pasts?' Who didn't even bother to tell me your name? You made it clear you didn't want to know anything about me. Besides which, if you can't understand me, you'd never understand my mother. Well, to hell with you. To hell with all of you. I don't give a damn what any of you think. But just for the record, I loved my parents. I'm proud of them. And I'd give up everything you could ever offer me to have them back."

She was about to leave when Sloane blocked her path. "Tommy, come here."

Despairingly, his friend stepped over to join them. "I can't believe this is happening again."

Ignoring him, Sloane asked, "Is everything ready to go?"

Gaping, Tommy cried, "What are you talking about?"

"You heard me. Is everything loaded?"

"The crew is all aboard except for us and Farnsworth. We might as well go up and make the announcement."

"There's nothing to announce."

"But . . . you heard Greenburg . . ."

"Until Zukor says otherwise, I'm still in control."

"As soon as Greenburg gets on the horn to New York, you won't be."

"Which is precisely why we're leaving now."

Tommy sputtered, "You mean you're just gonna leisurely sail away?"

For once, Sloane's mouth crooked in a hint of a wolfish grin. "Not leisurely."

Planting his feet on the ground, Tommy glared at his friend and partner. "Ace, you can't do this again. Paramount won't stand for it."

"They'll have to."

"It was one thing to call it off completely, but to hijack the picture from the studio—it's insane! For God's sake, get another actress. At this point, it's not even important who."

Sloane fixed him with a steely gaze. In a deceptively soft tone he said, "It's important to me."

"Ace, listen to me. This time they won't just cancel the picture, they'll take it away from you."

"They can't. I insisted on the money up front. Most of it's already spent. And what I need for expenses in Tahiti is on the ship."

Tommy's shoulders slumped. "You're committing suicide. And you're taking all of *us* with you."

"You leave that to me. Where's Farnsworth?"

"He's back there, sulking."

"Go get him."

Reluctantly, Tommy left and Sloane turned to Liana. "Get on board."

"It's a waste of time," she told him. "Zukor will radio the ship."

"The ship's radio is on the blink. I'll make sure of that."

"They'll send someone after you."

"By the time they catch up to us, it'll be too late. We'll be too deep into production."

"With this kind of publicity, they'll never release it."

"It'll be so good they'll *have* to release it."

She stared at him incredulously. "You're fooling yourself. I want no part of this. I'm leaving."

He captured her gaze with eyes that blazed like backlit gems. In a silky tone, he said, "I want you, Liana. I'm not going to let you go."

"Oh, no? Watch me."

She turned on her heel. Sloane made a swift survey of the scene to see Tommy and Hobart already at the top of the gangplank. An instant later, he moved with the stealth and speed of a panther, once again stepping in her way. He took her shoulders in both hands and forced her to face him. "I swear to you, Liana. I won't let them hurt or humiliate you again."

She stared at him, dumbstruck.

But he didn't seem to notice. Without another word, he grabbed her and threw her over his shoulder like a sack of booty and carried her on board.

7

Liana stood alone at the rail. All around her was the vast blue of the Pacific, steeped in the gentle hues of twilight. The end of a day that had at first devastated her, and had then left her strangely confused.

She recalled the way Sloane had swept her up into his arms like a marauding pirate.

I want you, Liana. I'm not going to let you go.

His swashbuckling insurgence had thrilled her. She told herself it was nothing more than illusion. But as he'd carried her up the gangplank, she couldn't help but relive the time in the Pigalle dance hall when he'd gallantly whisked her out of harm's way. The woman in her responded to the wildly romantic gesture. And once again she saw him as a man afraid of nothing and no one. Who created his own law and took destiny into his own hands. A man much like her father.

Have I been wrong about him? Have I misjudged him?

A sound behind her brought her out of her reverie. She'd lost all track of time. The sun had disappeared, to be replaced by a smattering of stars in an inky purple sky. She turned to see Sloane closing the door behind him. He wore white trousers with a blue shirt, rolled up at the sleeves, with no tie. He joined her, resting his elbows on the rail.

Did he have to look so maddeningly handsome, standing there in the starlight, his hair glinting like California gold? She caught his distinctive scent on the breeze, clean and masculine, and her knees felt weak.

He said nothing. And because he offered neither banal conversation nor cryptic repartee, the silence took on a benevolent air. Companionable. Intimate. Seeming to invite confession. As if he waited patiently, with an open heart, for whatever she might want to say.

Lulled by the lapping of the froth against the ship, she, too, rested her arms on the rail and leaned out into the darkening night.

She began to speak. Not in the breezy tone she normally assumed, but softly, in the more refined manner of the household in which she'd been raised. Not in the guise she showed the world, but as her real self. "My mother was a duchess in London back in the eighties. She was a part of the fashionable and shallow crowd around the Prince of Wales, and was something of a scandal even in *that* decadent set. She'd buried two husbands by the time she was twenty, one of whom she'd married for his title. But her frivolous life changed forever when she was abducted by, and fell in love with, Richard Wycliffe, an Irish patriot who robbed the English nobility on the road at night to send money to Ireland to aid their cause. My mother, being of a highly romantic nature, saw him as a dashing highwayman."

He said nothing, so she continued.

"He stopped her coach one night and took her back to his camp to hold her for ransom. In the process, they fell madly in love. She joined him in his daring holdups, even planned some of them herself. Being who she was, it particularly outraged the aristocracy, who were determined to bring them to the gallows. But my parents escaped, married, and eventually came to America."

"Where you were born, I take it."

"Yes. They settled in Mendocino. He bought a schooner and became a ship's captain. Doctors had told my mother she couldn't have children, so she always called me her miracle. It was the three of us against the world. Mother and I traveled with father everywhere he went. They used to tell me stories of the old days, and they'd laugh thinking how they'd outwitted their pursuers. Oh, those were happy times. But then something happened . . ."

"The diaries?" he prompted when she'd drifted off.

"Yes, the diaries." She pressed her hands together at the painful memory. "My mother had kept a journal chronicling her abduction and the intense love affair that followed. One day, when I was thirteen, she read in the San Francisco papers that a London publisher had obtained a copy of the journal she'd left with a friend in England. That he intended to publish it under the title of *The Lady and the Highwayman*. He was planning to publicize it as the scandal of the century. My parents secretly went back to try and stop the publication. For the first time, they wouldn't let me go along, as if they'd had a premonition that they'd be caught. Which, of course, is just what happened. They were betrayed and captured. And sent to the gallows for their crimes of over a decade before."

"That must have been horrible for you."

"It was . . . beyond horrible. But even worse is the

way my mother has been portrayed since her death. She never intended for her journal to be published. But there was nothing in it that she was ashamed of, or would even be embarrassed to have me read. In fact, it set down her philosophy of life and love. She believed, and taught me, that women are empowered by their sexuality. That it was something that could be wonderfully liberating on every level. The intimacy she attained with my father was her greatest achievement in life. She believed this with all her heart. And she taught me to believe it.

"She was a marvelous woman. Elegant and sophisticated. Nothing like the tart she was made out to be by the wags who'd only read a passage here and there of her journal, and who wouldn't have understood it if they *had* read it all. She always said it took a highly enlightened man to accept a truly liberated woman."

In the silence that followed her confession, she could hear her heart pounding. *I can't believe I've actually said it. All of it.* It was such a relief that she felt herself soaring with the sheer exhilaration of it, with the anticipation of this confession drawing them closer, creating an understanding between them that had never existed until now. An understanding that could be the basis for a whole new future for them. All she needed was a word from him, a gesture that indicated he had, indeed, understood.

The sounds of the sea enveloped them. And as they did, she began, slowly, to notice the shift in mood. The silence was no longer companionable, welcoming. The exhilaration slipped from her. Her racing heart slowed to measured dread.

She turned to him. His face was set, as if etched in stone.

"You know, Liana," he commented at last, "no one can damage us like our parents."

He tipped his head to behold the sky, sniffed the air, then added as he left, "It's been a long and trying day. We'd better get some rest."

She stood in the wake of his departure, trembling uncontrollably, feeling exactly as she had that morning in Paris when she'd held his dismissive letter in her hand. Cheap. Rejected. Ashamed.

She didn't know how long she stood there, pulsing with pain. But eventually the air cooled, the breeze on her fevered face bringing her back to where she was. And she knew that, in order to survive the ordeal of making this film, she must put it all behind her. She couldn't look to him for understanding, or hope, or help. She must realize that this longing was nothing more than a moth's attraction to the flame. Repress this treacherous weakness, harden her resolve. Find a way—God help her—to turn this debacle around and make it work for *her*. To beat him at his own game. And, yes, she thought, with quivering breath . . . to make him pay.

That night, alone in her cabin, she began to dread facing the rest of the company the next day. She felt much the way she had as a young girl in the Mission Street Settlement House. The object of salacious curiosity. Shunned and ridiculed by outsiders who would never—*could* never—understand her family. She told herself she must be strong, take a deep breath, and meet them all with her head held high, with her customary show of reckless nonchalance. As if the censure of what she held most dear was nothing to her.

She spent the remainder of the night preparing herself. But in the morning, as she entered the main lounge, she was startled to find herself greeted by a company giddy with fascination. They rushed to her in an eagerly inquisitive mass, firing questions in rapid succession.

"Your mother was a duchess?"

"Was she really the lover of the king of England?"

"A highwayman for a father! It's just *too* romantic!"

"Hanging—together in death as they were in life! It's too much!"

"What a scenario this would make!"

She was too stunned to answer. She'd hidden this skeleton in her past for so long, she couldn't quite adjust to the fact that this revelation was suddenly lending her an aura of glamorous intrigue.

The only sour note was sounded by Hobart Farnsworth, who was every bit as stunned by their reaction as Liana. He'd spread the story of what happened at the press conference verbatim, with the intention of stirring up animosity for the woman who'd so spectacularly stolen his thunder. His contempt for their unexpected reverence broke through the jubilant barrage.

"You ignorant pups! Don't you realize what a rash act this has been? We've been all but shanghaied aboard this vessel. When Zukor hears about it, the good Lord only knows what his reaction will be. Not to mention that this prurient scandal could outrage the picture-going public and ruin a career that *Photoplay* once called 'a meteor streaking across the sky of the cinema.' "

"Like a falling star," one of the cameramen muttered.

"Why, you young hooligan!" Farnsworth cried. "Apparently, you haven't read the reviews of my last two pictures. Robert Sherwood said I absolutely *stole Winds of Fate* from Lillian Gish."

"Oh?" One of the makeup girls giggled. "Was it *Winds of Fate*? I thought it was Windbag *of Fate*!"

In an attempt to placate the irate star, Tommy quickly interceded. "Don't worry, Farnsworth, old boy. This picture is going to be so good, it'll keep that meteor streaking for years to come."

Farnsworth forgot the fray and peered at Tommy thoughtfully. "Do you really think so?"

"I guarantee it. My camera's gonna make you look like such a handsome devil among all those palm trees that the women will be lined up all the way to Tijuana."

Farnsworth was stopped cold. As they all watched, he noticeably puffed up, raising himself to his full height and screen grandeur. "In that case, I shall, as always, give the picture the benefit of my artistic dedication. I am, after all, from the school that believes the show must go on . . ."

When he'd pranced off, Tommy drawled companionably, "You know something, kids? The amazing thing about that old ham is that on screen, he's almost as good as he thinks he is."

One of the grips muttered, "Ham is still ham, no matter how you package it."

Liana joined in the collective laughter.

"Now, get out of here, all of you, and let the lady eat in peace." As they reluctantly drifted off, Tommy added to Liana. "Jokes aside, I believe everything I said. This picture is gonna be like nothing Hollywood's ever seen before. And you're gonna be sensational in it."

"That's not what you said on the dock," she reminded him.

His round face flushed. "I was worried about the studio's reaction. I never was as brave as the Ace. But he knows what he's doing. Now that it's done, I'm glad. So if Hobart tries to upstage you, which he probably will, just remember you have a friend behind the camera."

She felt warmed by the sincerity of his words. Perhaps, after all, she did have a friend on this shoot. An ally she'd need if she was going to succeed.

And maybe it had been a mistake to hide herself for so long, to shun friendship as a way of keeping her secrets. Being around Ace again had made her realize something she'd ignored too long: She was desperately lonely.

She could use a friend.

The sky was clear and the weather balmy over the next few days. The passengers quickly settled into a pleasant shipboard routine. The circumstances of their brazen departure had taken on mythic proportions, adding to the adventurous spirit of the expedition, and bonding them into a family of renegades.

It wasn't a large crew: the director and two stars, a handful of cameramen and carpenters, a production manager who doubled as art director, two lab technicians, three makeup and wardrobe girls, one hairdresser, four musicians to provide mood music during filming, and only three laborers, as they intended to hire the rest of the cast and crew from the local population. Only twenty or so in the entire group, so it wasn't long before they felt they knew each other well. Mornings were spent lounging on deck in the warm Pacific sun. Afternoons, they played pinochle or mah-jongg. At night, after dinner, the musicians played ragtime while the company danced and partied until late. Knowing the expedition would become grueling once they reached Tahiti, they seized the occasion to have a jolly good time, treating the voyage as a holiday.

Liana basked in the conviviality of it all, enjoying their company, joining in the fun. Despite her conflict with Sloane, she felt strangely renewed. The roll of the ship and the slap of the sea breeze reminded her of the happy voyages she'd taken with her parents—to Australia, to South America, even to China when she was twelve. Since they'd died, she'd endlessly repeated the details of those voyages in her mind like a mantra—all she'd experienced and everything she'd learned—so she would never lose the gift her parents had given her by taking her along. Sometimes, standing alone at the rail, she could almost feel their presence with her now.

This helped fuel her new desire to open herself to the possibility of deeper friendships, particularly with Tommy. When he wasn't holed up with Sloane for story conferences, he spent much of his time with Liana. Sometimes he studied her to determine her best photographic angles, but often they spent lazy hours sunning themselves. At first he just chatted about the events of the day, or gossip he'd picked up from others in the company. But when he discovered that Liana was an attentive and sympathetic listener, he began to reveal bits and pieces about his past.

He came from a long line of Scots-Irish farmers who'd moved from Tennessee to Kansas before he was born. It wasn't long before he realized he had no aptitude for the mundane life of a farmer. While blundering through his chores, he used to daydream about his grandfather, who'd run off to the "War Between The States" at the age of twenty-two and had died a hero on Shiloh's bloody ground. "From what I heard, Grandpa Rafe had less of a calling for the family profession than even I did. Ran away from it the first chance he got. But every cousin of mine from South Memphis to Topeka regards him as a cross between Ivanhoe and Davy Crockett. Thinking on it, I knew I wanted to be just like him."

So he, too, had gone off to war. "I was the first hayseed in the state of Kansas to sign up for the Escadrille.

I went to France with dreams of shooting Heinies out of the sky like ducks over a pond." But his physical revealed that he was nearsighted, so instead they made him a mechanic. "Truth be known, I wasn't much better at fixing engines than I was at farming. But since I was a boy I'd messed around with cameras and such. When the Ace saw some of my pictures, he put me in the back of his plane and said, 'Go to it, boy.' That's how it all started for me."

As the days passed in a haze of sea and sun and pleasant deck-chair conversation, Liana saw little of Sloane. For the most part, he spent his time in his stateroom, working on the scenario, conferring with the location director, discussing shots with Tommy and the other cameramen. For Liana, this was a blessing. She needed the time to crystallize her plan. To use whatever means available to undermine his manipulative intentions. To make the character of Tehani her own. And to make him suffer. She'd subtly build his desire for her so she could use it against him; show him up for the hypocrite he was in wanting her sexuality, then condemning her for its existence. She'd show him what it was like to long for something he couldn't have, to want it so badly he tossed the night away in sweat-soaked sheets until he felt he'd give anything, do anything, just for one small taste. One instant of relief to make the waiting, and the suffering, bearable.

To suffer as she had.

Toward this goal, she used the sea voyage to slowly set the stage. Making sure, when he made one of his rare appearances in the dining room or in the lounge after dinner, that she was at her most appealing. Wearing the clothes she'd bought with her advance in salary to her advantage. Brushing past him in an insouciant manner, just close enough for him to catch a whiff of her perfume. Seizing opportunities to show a bit of leg or a carelessly bared shoulder before slowly replacing the strap. Nothing overt. Just enough to tease him without letting him know he was being teased.

While pursuing that part of her plan by night, she spent her days learning everything she could about Tahiti—the first step toward putting her stamp on this nebulous role. There was no scenario to be read since Sloane hadn't shared it with them yet. He'd told them earlier that he wanted the actors to experience each scene spontaneously and without preparation so they would be living the moment, not acting it. Don't anticipate, he'd said. But Liana felt the need for preparation. The artist in her feared being so completely the director's puppet—particularly *this* director. So she read all the books Sloane had taken along for reference. She attended all the afternoon orientation lectures Ted Ames, the production manager, had arranged as a way of preparing the actors for their roles, and often collared him for individual sessions. In the course of this quest, she learned a great deal about the isolated and romantic corner of the world where they would spend the next few months of their lives.

Tahiti, some three thousand miles from Los Angeles, was the largest of the Society Islands. It wasn't until two hundred fifty years after Magellan "discovered" the Pacific that England's Captain Samuel Wallis happened by in 1867 and laid claim for King George III. Captain Cook followed several years later, as did the ill-fated Captain Bligh with the mutinous crew of H.M.S. *Bounty*. By the 1800's, it had become a battleground between Catholic and Protestant missionaries, and it was to protect the Catholics that the French landed in 1836. When the British seemed unwilling to fight for this lonely outpost of the Union Jack, the French laid their own claim and had ruled ever since, making it the administrative capital of French Polynesia: a vast conglomeration of islands that stretched across an expanse of the South Seas as wide as the entire United States.

The natives of Tahiti were descendants of ancient mariners from Southeast Asia who'd made successive waves of emigration across the Pacific as long as five thousand years ago. The British had organized the Tahitian tribes under a single ruler, King Pomare. After several unsuccessful wars of rebellion, the Pomare kings gradually gave in to French power and were loosely allowed to reign under the French tricolor.

Tahiti and its surrounding islands were the most stunning in all the Pacific, some said in all the world. Its people were the most gentle and, to Western sensibilities, the most beautiful. The women welcomed the foreign ships with an open, charmingly natural, and unembarrassed sexuality that astonished men accustomed to the restraints and moral judgments of their homelands. But beyond this, an intangible spirit, an inexpressible magic, seemed to permeate these islands. Anyone who'd experienced it never forgot it. Almost from the outset of European discovery, a legend began to spread. That legend became mythic in the writings of Melville, Stevenson, and Jack London, until the name of Tahiti came to embody the very essence of romantic escape to a weary, war-torn world.

Ironically, this myth of paradise had brought the rush of beachcombers, adventurers, and profiteers who were now despoiling the islands.

Five days into the voyage, after reaching the official point of no return, Sloane assembled the company in the lounge and finally told them what they were breathless to hear: the story of *Tehani of the South Seas.*

"I know you all have questions," he began. "You've

come a long way and put a great deal of trust in me, and for that I thank you. Now I'm going to be frank with you. You've all heard the rumors that this picture has a daring, antimissionary theme. Those rumors are true."

The mood sobered. Big-budget Hollywood photoplays simply didn't take on such controversial subjects. Rumors were one thing, but now, faced with the reality, they began to shift uneasily in their chairs.

"Our picture is going to be no less than the definitive depiction of the violation of paradise by monsters masquerading as the hand of God."

This statement was stronger than anything they'd expected. No one seemed to know how to react.

"For the past seventy years and more, the islands of the Pacific have been the playground for these false prophets—Catholic, Protestant, and Mormon alike. They have decimated the population with their diseases, stripped the natives of their culture and their ancient religions, sold their children to blackbirding slavers. The most entrenched and abusive of these groups is the Boston Missionary Society. An American Protestant organization, its practice was to install a pastor on an island who would eventually come to rule it like a feudal lord. He would recruit religious police—called wardens—who would enforce his law with clubs. In Samoa, these wardens were known to actually beat the natives to death for minor religious infractions. In Fiji, under the guise of enforcing chastity, they would take native women at their whim for sexual use. In Tonga, they tortured small children for laughing during services."

They were all riveted. Some were shocked, some moved, some frightened by the enormity of it all.

"And in Tahiti, what they've done is almost beyond belief. They've taken away their land and forbidden them the use of their own language. Their power throughout Polynesia is unchallenged. Until now. Our picture will expose this sacrilege to the world."

Hobart Farnsworth stood with a flourish, clasping his hand theatrically upon his chest. "And I'm the man who is going to save the beautiful Tehani from the clutches of the evil missionaries!" He took a bow and some of the group applauded appreciatively.

Sloane gave a closed-lipped smile. "Actually, Farnsworth, you *are* the evil missionary. The villain. There is no hero."

Farnsworth stood frozen, his hand still on his heart, shock transforming his matinee idol's face. "*I* . . . play the villain?"

"You'll not only play him, you'll play him magnificently."

"But . . . I don't play villains! I've never played a villain in my life!"

In a mild tone, Sloane said, "Then let's just see what kind of actor you really are."

"But, sir . . . I protest!"

Sloane approached the outraged actor. "Farnsworth, when I get through with you, you're going to play this villain so convincingly that audiences will weep. You're going to show them, like no one else can, the horrors we depict. The entire picture rides on your ability to personify this evil. And in the end, you'll become a hero such as you've never played on screen. You'll be the man who gave the world a glimpse into the inner sanctum of depravity and hypocrisy cloaked by missionary robes. They'll hail you for your great service to mankind, as they hailed John Barrymore for playing Mr. Hyde."

As he'd spoken, with such passion, such conviction, Farnsworth's face had altered by degrees. "It's true," he murmured now. "*Jekyll and Hyde made* Barrymore. Very well, Sloane, I shall play your villain. To perfection."

"But tell us, Mr. Sloane," a cameraman called from the back. "What's the story about?"

After a pause for dramatic effect, their director began: "It's the tragedy of Tahiti embodied in the downfall of one heroic but doomed Tahitian woman."

Pausing again, and feeling their rapt attention, he went on: "It's the story of Reverend Wendell Slocombe, a graduate of Harvard Divinity School and member of this same Boston Missionary Society—a widower with a small son—who, in the year 1912, comes to Tahiti to serve God and the people of the islands.

"From Tahiti he's sent to the distant island of Pukapuka in the Tuamotus, where he's to set up a new outpost of the B.M.S. He's essentially a good man, who wants to help the unfortunates of the world. But our story chronicles how those good intentions, compounded by certain character flaws within himself, are corrupted by the missionary mentality.

"Pressed by the B.M.S. elders to make the mission self-sustaining and even profitable for the Tahiti headquarters, he gradually succumbs to evil. He steals the islanders' possessions. He sells off the hardier men to work as slaves in distant sugar plantations. He eradicates all their cultural traditions, one by one. And finally, he destroys the innocent Polynesian woman who has come into his household to raise his son.

"This woman—Tehani—is our symbol of everything that is clean and pure in the world. She gives the islands a face. Through her, we feel an emotional stake in the fate of her native land. It isn't just paradise that's imperiled: It's the fate of a lovely young woman with the power to break our hearts. She loves the missionary's child as her own, loves God, and wants only to do good. But her state of grace is no match for the missionary's evil. When Tehani resists his advances, he takes her the only way he can. Corrupt now beyond redemption, he ravishes her."

Hobart blanched.

"The climax of the picture comes with the beginning of the war. When the French government seeks to correct some of the abuses by the society, Slocombe, now head of the B.M.S. in all of Tahiti, conspires with the Germans to seize the islands. We will recreate the 1914 shelling of Papeete by German cruisers. Tehani, having discovered the missionary's treason, alerts the authorities in time for them to defend the port and blunt the invasion. But the vengeful Slocombe finds out. With bombs exploding all around them, he chases our fleeing heroine and kills her just as the French repel the cruiser and the colony is saved. Thus she becomes a martyr to, and symbol of, the rape of Polynesia."

A numb silence followed in which the group inwardly digested the immensity of this undertaking which they'd blindly assumed.

"I won't deceive you." Sloane continued. "This will be a dangerous venture. Though we'll take security and safety precautions, word of what we're doing in the islands *will* leak out. And when it does, the current B.M.S. leadership will do everything in its power to stop us. The civil administration has pledged to help us, but this sinister society is a government unto itself, and in many ways more powerful. I can't stress this enough. Once they realize the threat we pose to them, they will go to any lengths to put obstacles in our path."

Hobart called out, "Are you implying, sir, that our lives will be in danger?"

Sloane fixed him with a steady gaze. "I'd be lying if I blithely dismissed the possibility. But I want to assure you that we'll do all we can to make sure that doesn't happen. The governor, Philippe Vidal, is an old war buddy of Tommy's and mine."

The name jarred Liana back to her time in Paris, when a charming, towheaded liaison officer named Philippe had told her one night that Ace was the Tom Mix of the skies. A chill ran through her. How long had they been planning this?

"Hobart, Liana, Tommy, and myself will be staying at Philippe's gated compound in Papeete, the capital. The rest of you will stay under guard at a hotel in town. Philippe has arranged for a detachment of French Foreign Legionnaires to accompany us while we're filming there and on the surrounding islands. If we stay together as a group, there should be no problems."

Sally, the hairdresser, piped up, "I, for one, want a big hulking *brute* of a Foreign Legionnaire to protect *me*!"

This elicited some laughter, and helped to dispel the somber mood.

In this spirit, Sloane added lightly, "So if anyone wants to go back, a lifeboat will be lowered in one hour. And you can take your chances with the sharks."

Tommy said, "Sounds to me like there are enough sharks in Tahiti. With turned-around collars."

They began to drift off, relaxed now, exchanging jokes, Tommy at the center of it all. Liana kept herself apart, feeling as if she had lead weights slowing her steps. Far from reassuring her, this briefing had only served to confirm her worst fears. The part of Tehani was even more of a one-dimensional victim than she'd suspected. But this quest to immortalize her on film was so thoroughly thought out, and, if what she was beginning to believe was true, had been years in the planning. How could she possibly divert such a juggernaut to her advantage?

8

It was almost unbearable. Never in his life had Sloane experienced such sweltering heat. It was three in the morning and he still hadn't been able to sleep. He'd tried to work but had ended up pacing his stateroom instead. So he'd stepped out on deck seeking relief. He'd found none. Not a breath of a breeze. Not so much as a sigh. No respite from the fever that gripped him.

Frustration curled his hands into tight, clenched fists. After ten days at sea, they'd finally arrived in Tahiti. But, delayed by a storm, they'd come to the main port of Papeete just an hour before, when the small city was asleep, and there was no pilot to guide them through the reef. So the captain had dropped anchor a half mile out to sea, intending to dock in the morning.

Now Sloane stood on deck, peering into the darkness, trying to determine if the jagged silhouettes in the distance were really the mountains of Tahiti or just a figment of his imagination. There were no lights on the island, nothing to serve as beacon. Only the moonlight spilling over the sea, illuminating the crystal-clear water all around him but leaving the distant island cloaked in the mystery of night.

So close and yet so far. He cursed the captain unreasonably for the delay. If they'd arrived as scheduled, they'd be on land now, away from the close confines of the ship. Away from the ragged torments of his mind.

He tried to calm himself. Standing alone in the humid night, the ship eerily motionless, the light of the full moon streaming down from an inky sky, he felt the spirit of the place seep into his soul, the lure of the tropics casting its spell. There was in the air an imperceptible aura of romance, laced with something bolder and more intoxicating. It pulsed all around him, like the steadily increasing throb of a heartbeat, seeming to grow stronger with each breath he drew, like a promise of magic in the air. Alone in the night, surrounded by darkness and the unsettling stillness, it was easy to believe that he was the last man on earth, a man standing on the threshold of paradise with no one to share the enchantment all around him. The loneliness was almost as crushing as the heat, leaving him with the edgy sense of a promise impossible to fulfill.

He shook himself to dispel the mood. He'd been alone most of his life. He'd chosen a solitary existence, locking away his past and his more vulnerable core. Sharing himself had never come easily. How could he expect others to understand what he couldn't fully comprehend himself? He'd decided long ago that there was no point. And so he'd accustomed himself to being alone.

Alone, but not lonely.

It was the heat, he told himself. That and the god-damned stillness, as if the whole world throbbed with a tension that set his teeth on edge. As if the sultry silence was but a prelude, a warning of danger in the air.

He had to put it out of his mind. Concentrate on the task at hand, this epic undertaking that was the summation of his whole life. Tomorrow he'd be off this ship and then, he promised, he'd lose himself in work.

But what about tonight? Tonight his body screamed with need.

He took a steadying breath and contemplated the bower of stars that glistened in the vast, dark sky. Swallowing his restlessness, he called forth the spirit of Tehani, willing her to bring him solace in this seemingly endless night.

Suddenly the hush was broken by the sound of an opening door. Not wanting to be disturbed, he stepped back into the shadows—and saw before him the source of all his turmoil. The woman who was crucial to his mission, but who threatened his peace of mind. Liana.

She was wearing a long robe that glinted white in the moonlight. On bare feet, she glided slowly along the deck, gazing out across the expanse of sea like a sleepwalker, called forth by the primeval forces that orchestrated the destiny of the night. She took a trembling breath as if she, too, could feel the romance, the promise, the ache of experiencing such an evening alone. She seemed small and fragile as she lifted her face to the moon—the face that had first captivated him in Paris: faintly exotic, yet so pure, so innocent, so softly vulnerable that the sight of it made a man want to risk his life to protect her at all costs.

The ache intensified until he could feel his heart thundering in his chest.

When she moved, it was with the motions of

someone in a trance. She crossed the deck, detached a section of the rail, then dropped a rope ladder over the side so it splashed lightly in the water below. Then, in one lithe movement, she untied her sash and let her robe drop to the deck.

Sloane watched, transfixed, as the robe seemed to fall in slow motion, baring her shoulders, her back, the softly rounded buttocks, the long line of slim yet shapely legs. Exposing a vision of sumptuous naked flesh. Baring herself to the homage of the moon's caressing rays.

She graced the ship like a figurehead. Then, raising her arms, she dove in a symmetrical arc into the water, barely making a ripple. Leaving him stunned, as rigid as stone, as the effect of it swept through him. As his erection swelled in response.

More than a week had passed since their last confrontation, when she'd shared with him her dangerously salacious views, bent on invading his resolve. When he, with his intrinsic sense of self-preservation, had symbolically slammed the door in her face. Knowing all too well the hazard of letting her in.

Since then, he'd taken pains to avoid any personal interaction, confining his communication with her to business. But whenever he turned around she was there, just out of reach but tantalizingly alluring. A siren beckoning him toward the rocks. Smelling faintly of French perfume and looking like an enchantress unconscious of the hazard of her appeal. Now, seeing her, unknowing in all her naked glory, brought his defenses crashing down. Everything he'd been trying to push to the recesses of his mind all came rushing back: How her presence had kept him walking a tightrope. How every time he saw her, the shock of it hurtled him once again to those early days in Paris. The face of the woman he'd thought he'd known. The mirage.

He'd succumbed to that deception so completely that the wonder of it had pierced his disillusioned soul. He'd always avoided romantic entanglements, seeking women only as a means of releasing sexual tension. They'd been happy enough to comply. But every encounter had left him feeling hollow inside.

Until he'd met Liana. Until he'd seen in her shining, vulnerable face all he'd been questing for without knowing that he had. She'd seemed, from the first, like a gift to be treasured and treated with care. A woman so hauntingly close to his ideal that he'd seen in her another chance at life.

From the start, his impulse had been to protect her, as he'd failed so miserably to protect Tehani. To make up for the past by lavishing Liana with all the tenderness and solicitude that a woman such as she deserved. He'd even kept his real name a secret as a form of preserving her from harm, in case he was killed in the air. But even as he'd withheld his identity, he'd found himself sharing pieces of his soul—the Gauguin paintings, his love of moving pictures—honoring her for the gift of making him feel there was a purpose to life, after all.

It was meeting her that had convinced him that he could someday put the story of his past on film. That she was an actress seemed a miracle. Already, he could visualize her playing the part, working with him to bring his vision to fruition. But he'd wanted more. He'd wanted to share with her, should he survive, all the good, clean things he'd lost faith in so long ago. To share his dreams. . . .

In the midst of the horrors of war, she'd made him feel young again, cleansed of the ugliness of his past and the senseless misery all around him.

But then, in one bold stroke, she'd destroyed the illusion. She'd shown herself to be not the gentle soul in need of his protection, but just another woman who couldn't wait to get him into bed. Throwing herself at him like all the others who were dazzled by his uniform or his reputation or the outward appearance of a man who seized the world by the tail. Knowing nothing of the longings of his wounded heart.

He'd fled from the truth, his mind reeling, still not wanting to believe that this delicate creature who'd looked at him with such trust and childlike joy—this woman he'd held above all others as something pure and noble—was just like all the rest: the wanton women of a war-torn city, sharing themselves with a succession of soldiers under the guise of patriotic duty, but really expecting favors in exchange. But even as he'd reviled her deception, he couldn't stay away. She'd unleashed the weakness in him with her touch and her kiss. His mind, still mourning the loss of his ideal, was suddenly at war with a body too long starved. He'd tried to get drunk, to drown out his need, never wanting to see her again. But the feel of her was burned into his soul.

And so he'd gone to her in a fury of passion and confusion, bent on punishing her for defiling something he'd thought beautiful and innocent. To have sex with her as he had had with countless other women. To abate the lust pulsing in his veins and once and for all put her out of his mind.

To leave and never look back.

But once he'd given in to her, he'd found himself more disconcerted than before. Because sex with her had been so much more than just a melding of bodies to satisfy carnal need. The sense of completion, of satisfaction and peace that had come over him shocked and frightened him. He'd never felt such a thing before. He didn't understand it. Perhaps it was the alcohol, playing tricks with his mind. She wasn't the sort of woman he could love—he knew that now. And yet . . .

It had scared him so much that he'd had to prove to himself—and to her—that what they'd shared had been the sating of his lust and no more. He had to end it in a way that would close the door on any tender memory. So he'd left the letter.

And it had worked. He'd put all thought of her behind him. Until he was finally ready to make *Tehani of the South Seas*. Until he realized that only she could do Tehani justice. She, who'd so convincingly fooled *him*.

He'd gone about it with businesslike efficiency. When she'd refused, he'd even decided to seduce her to convince her to take the role. What difference did it make? She was just another actress, after all. And she'd already proved her own weakness in such matters.

But his plan had backfired on him once again. He hadn't counted on how she would feel in his arms. Or how desperately he would want her in his bed. When he looked at her, he saw once again the girl he'd first seen in Paris. But when he came near her, he was struck by a wave of such desire that it was painful to be near her. Her face might speak of innocence and purity, but her aura was blatantly sexual. Feeling her allure and forcing himself away was creating a distracting tug-of-war between his body and his mind.

Against his will, he crossed the deck to the rail. Below him, in the moonlight, he could see brief glimpses of her as she swam. Flashes of silvery flesh made him shudder with lust.

He gritted his teeth, telling himself it was just sex he wanted from her, nothing more. Not the abatement of his loneliness. Not the need to share his dreams and his soul. He'd rebuffed her efforts to share herself with him because that self was antithetical to everything he believed and everything in her that he wanted to capture on film. It was a formidable enemy, because here he was, feeling the torment of its seductive power.

He tore himself away and stepped back into the shadows, lighting a cigarette. He noted with annoyance that his hands were shaking.

He'd smoked only half the cigarette when he heard a small splash below. He stared at the rope ladder, knowing she was coming, willing himself to leave, yet unable to take a single step. In another moment, she appeared, rising naked and dripping to the deck, her sumptuous flesh shimmering in lush, jiggling curves. As he stood stock still, barely breathing, she wrung out her long hair and bent to retrieve the robe, walking naked toward the door with the garment trailing behind.

But suddenly her steps slowed. She smelled the smoke, lifted her head, and caught the faint red glow of the tip of his cigarette. Slowly, altering her course, she approached, not bothering to cover herself, her breasts rising proudly as she came forth, unashamed. It infuriated him. For all she knew, he could be *anyone* standing in the shadows.

A foot before him, she stopped and saw who he was. Her eyes flicked over him in contemptuous amusement, as if she could read his every thought, could feel the straining bulge against his pants. "You know, *Captain*," she said in a deceptively sweet tone, "the more you disapprove, the more *fun* it is for me."

Holding her gaze locked with his, she slipped into the robe, covering herself unhurriedly, defiantly, denying him the sight of the body he hungered for but wouldn't allow himself to have. Then, with a last taunting glare, she walked away. He heard the door close behind her.

With a savage gesture, he flung the half-smoked cigarette over the rail.

Liana awoke with a start, a shaft of sunlight warming her face. After a night at anchor, the ship's engines had rumbled to life, taking them into port. Rising quickly from her bed she saw through her porthole a breathtaking display: a jagged, lushly green, cloud-wreathed mountain rising up from turquoise waters.

Excited, she threw on her clothes and ran up the outside steps to the promenade deck. There, she found herself surrounded by the most incredible, epic scene. To her left was the ramshackle cluster of white buildings that was Papeete, the capital of the beautiful main island of Tahiti. On the right, in the distance, was its even more spectacular neighbor, the smaller island of Moorea. The sky was a topaz blue. The morning was already hot, but a fresh breeze cooled her face.

On the deck below the doors burst open and the rest of the company began to float out into the morning, some dressed, some still in robes, squinting at the already intense morning sun, then gasping in wonder at the astonishing panorama before them. She joined them and before long was surrounded by the entire group, all exclaiming their amazement in a bubbling rush, voices tumbling over one another.

Noting Sloane's absence, Liana finally spotted him above on the bridge with the captain and a shirtless Polynesian man who she assumed was the pilot, guiding them into the harbor. Sloane appeared tired, but seemed alert and focused, humming with the same excitement that had gripped them all.

She hadn't slept well the night before, fretting in damp, tangled sheets. She'd purposely taunted Sloane with her brazen display. But she hadn't counted on her own reaction to the hunger that had leapt into his eyes. The sexual tension had vibrated between them, compelling her toward him as if he were a magnet whose pull had been fashioned for her alone. She'd never imagined that she would toss and turn the night away, remembering how his heated gaze had flicked over every inch of her exposed flesh, in a fever of wanting the very thing she'd used as an instrument of torture, wanting more than breath itself to rise from her solitary bed and go to him, to satisfy her own need. Gripping the sheets in tight fists, willing herself to be strong. But the truth was, she'd played a dangerous game with him. Because despite the resolve of her mind, her body still wanted him more than ever.

She shook off these thoughts and concentrated on her new surroundings. The setting, alien but strangely beckoning, was reviving her senses. In all her travels with her parents, she'd never witnessed such a charming scene. All of it seemed to offer up a buoyant welcome. The blue lagoon whose waters reflected green hills, palms, and fancifully shaped clouds. The copra schooners moored to the quay. The outriggers in the lagoon from which sun-bronzed men were diving for pearls. The whitewashed buildings of the little town along the lagoon. The flowers, aptly called flamboyants, brilliantly scarlet against the azure sky, like come-hither lipstick on a woman's mouth, sensual but unashamed. The crowd along the wharf, noisy, cheerful, bustling, coming out to greet them. The heat and colors dazzling.

Once they'd docked, they were met as they descended the gangplank by lovely Tahitian women dressed in bright, colorful but voluminous Mother Hubbards, a far cry from the saronged beauties who'd met the sailors of the last century. They placed leis about the necks of the newcomers made up of delicate white flowers called *tiaré tahiti,* which enveloped them with the succulent scent of gardenias. Nearby, a small group of Tahitian men, their saronglike pareus wrapped about their waists, torsos bare, played native tunes on concertinas and a variety of drums, one of them made from an old gasoline can. The music was mesmerizing, carrying them through customs in a state of dreamy suspension. They had, quite literally, stepped from the ship into a different world.

They were met outside by a rush of giddy children hawking leis and cheerfully asking for handouts of chocolates and cigarettes. Adults followed, gathering out of curiosity and smiling greetings to the newcomers. They stared at Liana, some even coming up to touch her sleek Dior dress in fascination. While the sight of Western men was commonplace on the big island, Western women were a novelty. She returned their smiles and patiently allowed them to indulge their curiosity.

Out of this melee, Philippe Vidal appeared. He'd put on some weight since the war years, and it suited him. His once fair skin was deeply tanned and his hair bleached white from the sun. Clean-shaven when she'd last seen him, he now sported a splendid blond mustache. His position in the islands had matured him. He assumed an unruffled ease, radiating in every way the confidence of a competent colonial administrator.

He grabbed Sloane and Tommy in an affectionate embrace. "Here they are, Patrick Garrett and Billy *L'enfant*. Ready to fight the desperadoes, eh?" He reached over and pinched Tommy on the cheek. "And you, my fine country bumpkin, do you still have manure on your shoes?"

"We may have manure on our shoes in Kansas,"

Tommy countered cheerfully, "but by golly, we don't eat frogs."

Philippe wagged his finger at him playfully. "How many times have I told you? We only eat the legs."

"Oh, I forgot. It's more civilized to eat the legs!"

He turned then to Liana. "Ah, there she is!" With a flourish he bowed and kissed her hand. "*La Belle de Paris*. How well I recall seeing you in a performance of Monsieur Wilde's *Lady Windermere's Fan*. A delightful diversion from the carnage of the front. How desperately we needed to be uplifted in those sad days. And how fortunate we all are to have you as the star of this groundbreaking landmark of the *cinéma*. Welcome, welcome."

There was nothing flirtatious in his manner; rather it was one of charm and admiration.

When he'd exchanged pleasantries with Hobart he addressed Sloane once again with a mock frown. "I have in my possession five angry cables from a Monsieur Adolph Zukor in New York City. It would appear that our old *capitaine* has been a very naughty boy."

Standing at the side of the pier, Sloane took the cables, then opened his fist and let them flutter into the water on the breeze. "How clumsy of me," he said. "But I suppose if it was important, he'll cable me again."

"Same old Rough Rider Sloane. Charging up San Juan Hill, laughing in the face of danger." Having said that, Philippe sobered. "But I must tell you, *mon ami*, that word of this picture has reached the missionary powers. We must be on our guard every minute."

He dispatched a group of laborers to begin the process of unloading the seaplane, the food, generators, wind machines, cameras, editing tables, construction equipment, and the many boxes of delicate film and developing chemicals, most of which would be stored in a government warehouse at the end of the dock. This would serve as their headquarters: office space, darkroom, editing and screening facilities. Across the street was the small hotel where most of the crew would be housed, complete with its Legionnaire defenders. "Despite the threats and the inconvenience of having to be guarded, we want your stay to be as pleasant as possible," Philippe told them. "You will find, for the most part, that we enjoy a gracious style of life here in the islands."

A government limousine—the only one in all of French Polynesia—whisked them through the dusty, heavily potholed streets to the Arué district some miles south of town. Along the way they passed a smattering of modest copra plantations, the houses roofed with red tile, tucked here and there in small clearings off the road. Most of the island was covered with natural vegetation. There were so many types of trees and foliage, all intermingled, that it created a luxuriant visual tapestry. Every shade of green imaginable, light against dark, displayed interesting contrasts. The leaves were so varied in size and shape—minuscule, gigantic, smooth, fringed, long and extended, delicate as lace—that Liana felt she'd never really noticed trees until this day. Flowers of every color grew wild along the way: hibiscus, bougainvillea, camellia, red ginger, orchids, jasmine, scenting the air sweetly with their fragrance. And everywhere there were birds, in the cloud-softened sky, in the trees, on the grass, their songs offering a lilting cadence.

Occasionally they were forced to swerve to keep from hitting donkey carts laden with vanilla beans, coconuts, or pineapples. Women walked along the road carrying babies and balancing bundles on their heads, each with a freshly baked baguette tucked under her arm. On their left were the black sand beaches of Matavai Bay, and on the right, staggering views of the jagged green mountains surrounded by valleys of an even deeper green, nearly black in the shadows cast by the morning sun. Every once in a while they could see a waterfall cutting a path down a heavily wooded hill, its dancing waters casting off prisms of light like tiny rainbows.

Before long they veered off the main roadway that Philippe told them circled the island, and climbed a steep slope that rose to the top of a hillside overlooking Point Venus, where Captain Cook had first dropped anchor. Ahead were tall wrought-iron gates that the guards opened to admit them. Within was an immaculately landscaped government compound that would be their living quarters while on the main island.

Philippe's home—officially the governor's mansion—was a sprawling open abode with ironwood-paneled walls fronting the bay below. Banana, mango, and papaya trees grew wild among the frangipani and elephant ears, bushes whose crimped leaves grew two and three feet in diameter. Sprinkled among this explosion of tropical splendor were bungalows where each of the four guests—Liana, Sloane, Farnsworth and Tommy—would stay.

"Tonight," Philippe proclaimed, "we will have a modest fête to celebrate your arrival."

It was, in reality, a lavish dinner party with cuisine that would be the envy of the finest Parisian restaurant. Champagne flowed freely throughout the evening. The entire crew had been brought from the hotel to share in the festivities. The other guests were mostly French colonial officials who spoke little English, giving Liana an opportunity to brush up on her French. But there was a smattering of Americans and other expatriates who'd been lured by the legend of Tahiti.

Liana had never thought much about Philippe, but in the course of the conversation, she learned a bit about his background. A native of Marseilles, he'd first come to the Pacific as a member of the Foreign Legion and had stayed on to work his way into the Colonial Office. He'd managed to climb the ladder of success as far as lieutenant governor before the war took him back to France. After the Armistice, he returned to Tahiti and, after the death of the governor last year, was appointed to the top spot.

After the other guests had left, the veterans began to reminisce about the war years. The company gathered round, eager to hear their stories.

"Shall I tell you the sort of man your illustrious director is?" Philippe asked.

Through her lashes, Liana studied Sloane. He'd been fairly quiet all evening, as if his weariness was beginning to catch up with him. He seemed happy enough to be in the heady male company, but let the others do most of the talking, as if a part of his mind were elsewhere. Now he squirmed in his seat and said, "I wish you wouldn't."

But Philippe ignored him. "In the second week of June, 1917, this man downed ten enemy planes. Ten! In one week! A record that is unmatched in aviation history. Not by Rickenbacker, not by the Red Baron, not by anyone. Ace Sloane," he said admiringly, "the *real* Devil of the Air!"

As the guests issued admiring gasps and comments, Sloane said, "Let's change the subject, shall we? Old war stories only bore those who weren't there."

Philippe smiled at the company at large. "He is too humble, *non?* It is no surprise to those of us who knew him then that he became a director of motion pictures. I shall never forget how he used to speak on the subject.

'The motion picture camera,' he told us, 'is just a machine, like the planes we fly. But it will do more to change the world than these planes ever will.' "

Tommy took a sip of his drink and quoted, " 'No machine ever invented has the power to touch the hearts and souls of humankind like the motion picture camera.' "

"Exactement!" Philippe paused to stroke his sumptuous mustache. "Of course we all thought he was mad. But he showed us, did he not? Did you know the extraordinary aerial footage used in *Devils In The Air* was real, shot by the Ace himself during the war?"

"You *must* be kidding!" Hobart choked.

"Au contraire! I shall never forget that spring dawn when he told Tommy to grab the Bell and Howell and get in the plane. They were going, he said, behind the enemy lines to survey their troop strength all the way back to the German border. Naturally, we thought he was bluffing. But we soon learned that our *capitaine l'Amérique* never bluffs. With a thousand German guns blazing at him every inch of the way, and the Red Baron's entire squadron trying to shoot him out of the sky, he flew like the eagle he is and shot the footage that single-handedly allowed us to blunt the Hun advance of 1917. I tell you, my friends, it was the single most heroic act any of us ever saw in the war. Naturally, he was awarded the Croix de Guerre—the highest military honor France can bestow."

As the company murmured their appreciation, Tommy rose and fixed himself another drink, then proclaimed, "I propose a toast, gentlemen. *And* ladies. To Captain Sloane, the greatest ace of them all."

It seemed to Liana that Sloane flinched. As if feeling her gaze, he lifted his lashes and met her eyes. Embarrassed to have been caught staring at him, she raised her glass mockingly and said, "Captain." But she didn't drink.

As the rest of the guests joined the toast, she took the opportunity to slip out onto the patio and into the night. She could hear the sounds of clinking glasses and raucous laughter, as if coming from some other world. But she wasn't a part of it.

She didn't want to remember him as the dashing war hero she'd fallen in love with. Seeking escape, she wandered out to a path that meandered through the gardens. Out here it was quiet. A slight breeze off the ocean brought relief from humid heat. Palm leaves caught the filtered moonlight, casting fanciful silhouettes on the path before her. Gigantic elephant ears created a bower overhead. But as she strolled out into the open, she could see the ebony sky alive with a dazzling display of stars. In the distance, the sound of lapping waves hummed a lullaby. It seemed to her that there was something here, something approximating peace. But just as she was taking a deep breath, wanting to draw it in and make it a part of her, she heard a heavy step. Wheeling, she saw coming toward her a uniformed guard with his rifle unslung and pointed her way. When he saw her, relief eased his stern expression. But his voice was adamant as he told her in French, "It is best not to wander from the house, mademoiselle."

The sense of freedom she'd just barely glimpsed was dashed. *It's like a prison,* she thought. The last thing she wanted was to go back to the party, to have her nose rubbed in the fawning over Sloane. So she pacified the guard by pretending to walk the way she'd come. But when he'd gone, she changed direction and headed instead for the viewpoint Philippe had earlier shown them.

Here, on the crest of the hill that towered above the

bay, she could see the moonlight spilling over the black sands of the beach. The sound of the surf was more pronounced, thundering below with cosmic rhythm. And once again, she began to feel the pull of something deep, exotic, mysterious. Something that called to her like the promise of something rare. Something that gave her an awareness of self such as she'd never experienced before, as if the moonlight shining down was a spotlight fashioned just for her. Something that made her tingle with a desire so potent that it throbbed in every pore.

It seemed to her that the Tahiti beyond the gates and guards of this opulent fortress was summoning, beckoning her to soar into the unknown like a bird freed from its cage. The island whispered that here, all around, was something she'd been searching for all her life. That all she had to do was have the courage to embrace it, and it would be hers.

A rustling behind her jarred her from the magic of the moment. Annoyed, she whirled toward the intruder, expecting the guard. And froze when she saw Sloane.

He spotted her and stopped short. She waited, cloaked in shadows, a dim figure, mysterious as a phantom. The air was hushed, throbbing with the presence of something too tumultuous to be contained. She heard him breathing. Then he stepped into the patch of moonlight. Gleaming like a god.

It seemed that they stared at each other for an eternity, neither of them knowing what to say. As if they'd each stumbled across the last thing either had expected or wanted to find.

Finally Liana spoke, tartly because she felt so exposed. "Did you get your fill of adulation?"

"I came to get away from it."

"Oh? I should think it would be delicious, having everyone worship the ground the great hero walks on."

"I'm not a hero," he said quietly.

"I suppose those ten planes just fell out of the sky."

"Is that what you think makes a hero?"

"Most of the world does."

"What do I care what the world thinks when I know it's a lie?"

"You mean you *didn't* shoot those planes down?"

He looked up at the starry sky as if seeking help. Then he blurted out, "Those planes were nothing! It took nothing on my part. Just sheer animal instinct. It happened during a period when I really didn't give a damn whether I lived or died. You think I went to war to be a hero? I went for the adventure. To . . . escape. But it wasn't adventurous. It was miserable. The senseless slaughter—for what? It sickened me, all of it. Every time I went out, a part of me wanted to die. It wasn't until . . ."

His words seemed to hang in the air between them. When he didn't continue, Liana prompted, "What?"

He sighed heavily. "It wasn't until I found the cinema, until I got my hands on a motion picture camera, until I made that wild dash behind enemy lines to film the German troop movements . . . only *then* did I feel there was a purpose to any of it. I found a means to fulfill a higher calling. So whenever they say I'm a hero, it sets my teeth on edge."

"What calling?" she asked.

But her question seemed to break the flow of his words. His pained expression shut down and his features become inscrutable once again. "You wouldn't understand," he said simply.

It was true. She *didn't* understand him. Indeed, she

realized from this halting encounter, that she'd never known anything about him. Who was he? What exactly was this "calling" that was so important to him, he would defy the fates, mow down anyone in his path, and bring her, against her will, to the very end of the earth?

9

Within three days, Liana was chafing under the imposed restrictions. The day after their arrival, Sloane and Tommy took the seaplane to shoot various exteriors and establishing shots around the islands. On their return, they would cast the child actor who would play the missionary's son from a group of candidates Philippe had selected from among some of the local French families. Meanwhile, the construction crew would be building several standing sets on some of the outlying islands: Moorea, Huahine, Raiatea, and Bora Bora.

It was a relief to have Sloane gone, but that left Liana with nothing to do. She didn't have Tommy for company. Hobart took no interest in his surroundings other than to enjoy the bountiful stock of cognac and imported wines, and to tell his life story and backstage experiences to a fresh audience. Liana thought she'd go out of her mind.

A local guidebook she'd found in Philippe's library had placated her for the first two days, but after committing it more or less to memory, her natural restlessness began to assert itself. She couldn't walk about the grounds without a guard hindering her. More and more, despite Philippe's gracious hospitality, she felt herself the inmate of a very real prison. And yet she was standing in the heart of a paradise that had inspired dreams in poets, painters, and adventurers for more than a century—all of it just out of reach.

As she stood at the promontory staring longingly at the turquoise waters sparkling in the sun, and at the graceful curve of land on her right reaching to Point Venus, she remembered the first time her mother had told her about the spirit of place. She'd been standing with her parents before a lost city of Inca ruins in the Peruvian Andes when her mother had said, "If you close your eyes and open up your heart, you can experience the unique vibrations that make this unlike any other place on earth. Every spot has a spirit all its own, an energy that comes from the earth itself, but is flavored by history, by the sum of all the human experience for which it has been the stage. If you're very quiet, you can absorb that energy, and it will stay with you. Not until you've felt that spirit have you transcended the experience of the typical tourist and made that place a part of you forever."

Liana couldn't yet define the spirit of Tahiti. It was more elusive than anything she'd felt before. She only knew there was a whisper on the breeze that seemed to call her name. And she must follow wherever it might lead.

She went to Philippe. "I've got to get out of here," she exclaimed. "I'm going stir-crazy."

He smiled sympathetically. "Ah, you impetuous

Americans. Always on the move. The spirit that won the west, no?"

"I can't just stay bottled up on this mountaintop. I'm expected to portray a Polynesian woman, but I've hardly even seen one except in books and briefly on the roadside. I need to mingle with people. Study them. Find out what makes them who they are. An actress *has* to do that if she's any actress at all."

Philippe nodded. "I can understand that. But what can I do, *ma chérie?* Your director would have my head. He would skin me alive."

"My director's not here."

"Which puts me in the unfortunate position of being his surrogate. Should something happen to anyone else, it would be unfortunate, certainly. But *you* . . . you are the star! If harm should come to you, it would be the end of the entire project. And the missionary powers know this. Thus, you would be their prime target. You can see my position, no? But perhaps tomorrow, we might take you out with an escort."

"An escort is just what I don't want," she insisted. "I want—I *need*—to be anonymous."

He considered this with a small sigh. "I appreciate your dilemma; believe me, I do. And it may be that all my precautions for your safety seem to you somewhat . . . ridiculous? But you must understand that this project profoundly threatens the missionaries' power and I have no idea to what extent they will retaliate. It is not just my responsibility as governor of these islands, but am I not also an old and trusted friend of Ace? Therefore, I would prefer to err on the side of excess protection, rather than not enough. You understand?"

She did. She understood that Philippe felt his responsibility keenly, and wouldn't waver. She would have to find an escape hatch on her own.

She found it just after lunch. On a walk to study the grounds, she reached down to stroke a stray cat the guards had adopted. Spooked, it shot toward the bushes that lined the fence. A moment later, it was staring at her, tail riding high, from the other side of the barbed wire barrier. On closer inspection, she discovered a patch of earth that had been dug away underneath. Retrieving a large oyster shell from a pile behind the kitchen, she dug away at the loose dirt until the opening was wide enough for her to slip under the fence.

It wasn't until she'd made it to the main road and hopped on the back of a horse-drawn lorry filled with breadfruit that she finally allowed herself to realize she'd made her escape. She was free! She dangled her legs gleefully from the back of the lorry, feeling the exhilaration spill over in a giddy mood.

At last she would be able to observe the people of Papeete up close, even talk to them. Perhaps even learn from them what this indefinable spirit of Tahiti was—a spirit that, somehow, she must embody in the character of Tehani.

As the lorry reached the outskirts of the small town, she was bursting with questions. But to her dismay, she found not a bustling seaport, but a village deep in the slumber of its noontime siesta. Slipping from the lorry as it passed by the huge *marché* that was the center of town, she found herself engulfed in funereal silence. All around her, as she walked the narrow hodgepodge of streets, her feet kicking up dust, she saw the very people she'd hoped to study lying sprawled in hibernation. They lounged in the doorways of closed shops, and beneath the cooling shade of plantain, mango, and casuarina trees. Indeed, it was the shade that determined their positions, away from the merciless glare of the midday sun which spilled in enervating pools, hot, heavy, eerily still. Only the pounding of the surf on the reef beyond and the chime of the bell in the cathedral clock tower, striking the quarter hour, broke the pervasive tranquillity. But it, too, passed as if it had never pealed, dissolving once again into the languid heat. Not a breath stirred as she made her way toward the waterfront where here, too, the people slept, on the decks of schooners, and amongst the hibiscus and frangipani that decorated the facades of the public buildings along the quay. A cluster of Chinese fruit vendors dozed against their stands. A young Tahitian man lay flat on his back in the shell of his outrigger, a red-and-orange pareu draped like a tent to shield him from the sun. The lorry she'd come in was parked by the dock, the driver snoozing atop the breadfruits, as if he'd been there the whole time.

She stood in the middle of the empty street, feeling as if she'd stepped into another world, a world of enchanted slumber, and she a sleepwalker, drifting through it like a dreamer who left no footprints in the dust. She'd come full of vitality, but now her senses felt languorous, succumbing to the lull of her surroundings and the breathless shimmer of the heated air. She was beginning to wonder if she *was* dreaming.

As she gazed about, she noticed the dockside Hôtel de Paris where the rest of the movie company was ensconced. It appeared as sleepy as the rest of the town. Even the three armed legionnaires that guarded it were resting against the front wall, only half awake. The sight of them reminded her that she was a fugitive. She couldn't even run up and visit the company without the guards likely carting her back to the fortress on the hill. She turned to head off in the other direction, and nearly bumped into someone standing behind her.

He'd come from out of nowhere: a young, dark-skinned

Tahitian man wearing flowered trousers, with an intricate display of tattoos covering both bare arms and forehead in the Polynesian fashion. *"Bonjour, mademoiselle,"* he greeted her. *"Voulez-vous un guide?"*

"Non, merci."

"Oh, you are one of the Americans!" He instantly switched to English. "My name is Charlie. I'm the best guide on this island. I speak English like President Wilson."

The absurdity of it caused her to laugh. "Well, thank you, Charlie, but I don't need a guide."

She began to walk away. Remaining at her side, he persisted. "You speak Tahitian, maybe? How come you think you need no guide?"

"I just want to experience things on my own. I speak French, so I'll get by just fine."

"Your boss, he go away on big airplane, yes? You gots nothing to do. I show you Tahiti. Good price. Twenty-five francs for all day. Take you anywhere you want to go."

"Not today, Charlie." She smiled and increased her pace.

He stayed with her. "Don't you want to see the *Bain Loti*? The famous Pierre Loti's pool?"

Pierre Loti was the pen name of Julien Viaud, the French author whose book, *The Marriage of Loti,* described the love affair of a Frenchman and a Tahitian girl. The book was a tremendous success in the late 1800's and helped to create the legend of Tahiti as the Island of Love. It was this book that inspired Gauguin to go to Tahiti.

The pool where Loti first saw his Tahitian beauty was several kilometers up the Fautaua Valley. The only way to reach this fabled spot was by a narrow trail up the mountains that surrounded Papeete to the south. Liana *had* hoped to see it as a source of inspiration.

"You take that trail yourself, you get lost plenty fast," Charlie told her, seizing the interest he detected. "It's high in the mountains and very cool. Not like this sweatbox here."

Still, she hesitated.

"Last year I take Mr. Somerset Maugham and his friend up there. You know Mr. Somerset Maugham?"

She laughed. "Every guide in French Polynesia must make the same claim."

"No, lady. I got written recommendation. You wait here, I go get. It say, 'To whom it may concern, my friend Charlie . . .' It signed 'W. Somerset Maugham.' It say *my friend* Charlie."

She was beginning to like him. "You don't have to go get it. I believe you."

"Then we go, yes?"

The tactic had struck a chord. She'd probably never find the place on her own. And perhaps Charlie could answer some of her queries along the way.

When he saw that she was wavering, he added, "I give you my *best* price. Fifteen francs. Okay, ten francs."

"Done," she told him. "But let's go ahead and make it twenty-five francs. Mr. Somerset Maugham's guide deserves nothing less."

They set out on foot. The trail began where the southern edge of the town butted against the plush green of the mountainside. The bare dirt track was narrow and twisting, offering spectacular views of the harbor and Moorea in the distance. As the elevation increased and they reached the summit of the mountain, the air lost its sweltering grip and a refreshing sea breeze cooled them.

After walking another two kilometers or so, the path began its downward descent into the river valley.

"Where did you learn to speak English?" she asked him.

He flung his arms wide. "Missy, I speak five languages. I been all over the world. I work as merchant seaman. I fight with Tahiti corps in France. A thousand of my people fight in trenches. Three hundred buried there." He turned and showed her, on the back of his left shoulder, a scar that he'd received from a bullet wound in the Battle of Verdun. "I learn to speak English, but not as good as French."

"I was in France during the war, too," she told him.

He gave her a baffled look. "I never saw you."

Soon they heard the gentle rush of the river below them. Unlike the dusty town of Papeete, this valley, protected from the ravages of summer hurricanes, was rich with ancient vegetation. From every direction, she found herself surrounded by ripening fruit: banana, mango, custard apple, guava, lime-green grapefruit, papaya, pineapple, watermelon, and a hundred more. The air was redolent with the bouquet of tropical blossoms. "This flower here," he told her, pointing to a yellow blooming bush with blossoms much like a hibiscus, "turns three colors in a day. Yellow, pink, and white. And at night, it falls to the ground and dies."

He snapped one from its stem and added, "If a woman is taken, she puts a blossom behind her left ear; if she's still available, behind the right."

"And what about you, Charlie? Do you have a sweetheart?"

He grinned widely. "I have two, missy."

She returned the smile. "Your women . . . what are they like?"

He considered. "Well, missy, in some ways they're freer than you. In other ways, not as free."

"In what way are they freer?"

He just smiled.

In the ensuing hush she felt once again the tantalizing sensation that had captured her on her first night here: indefinable, intangible, but as real as the flowers surrounding them. "Tell me, Charlie. There's something in the air here . . . a feeling I can't quite put my finger on. It's different from any place I've ever been. What is it?"

He shrugged. "Why, missy, it's the spirit of love."

He said it matter-of-factly, as if everyone should know. But it hit her like a blow.

"Come, I show you."

Once again she followed him. Presently, the path ended at the base of a small freshwater pool, in its pristine state except for a bust of the author of the romantic legend, which the French community had erected.

"This place . . . " he began, but then switched to French in order to express himself more easily. "Loti first saw the lovely Rarahu bathing just there," he told her, pointing to a spot a few feet away. "He was captivated by that spirit you talked about. Later he had to leave Tahiti, but he never forgot her. And never experienced such powerful love again in his life. That's the legend of Tahiti. Love is all around us, even in the air we breathe. That's why it is called the Island of Love. Because no one can come here without falling under its spell. Loti found with his beloved Rarahu the kind of . . . passion he could find with no European woman. *That* is why our women are freer than you. Because they love without censure or fear."

She thought of the stories she'd read of half-naked women greeting Captain Cook's ship with open arms; of the men of the *Bounty* who'd mutinied so they could stay with these women who embodied a sexual freedom unknown in the West.

"Are your women still like that?"

"The first missionaries tried to scare it out of them, and believed they had succeeded, but it is still there, under the surface. In our culture, love is something to be given without reservation or limit. It is the thing we value above all else. It is the very essence of life."

His words resounded in her with the ring of truth. *This* was what she'd been feeling. Not just the spirit of love, but of true passion, raw, primordial, more powerful than any force on earth. And it had been calling to her.

She thought of her character, Tehani, who was the antithesis of this spirit. She'd hoped to come to a better understanding of the character she was to portray. But Charlie's words had left her with more questions than they'd answered. Every instinct told her that at the heart of this project—and Tehani—something was drastically wrong.

Her thoughts were interrupted by Charlie's voice, speaking once again in English. "I show you something else now."

She suddenly realized how much time had passed since she'd left the compound. No doubt her absence would have been noticed by now. "Thank you, Charlie, but I think we'd better head back."

"No, no, I show you. Come, please."

Without waiting for her response, he walked toward a trail that branched off from the pool. Reluctantly, she followed, wondering at his insistence. This trail was narrower and less trodden than the other. Occasionally, she tripped over giant roots and fallen trees. They were heading deeper into the rain forest until the sun was cut off almost completely by the overhanging canopy of vegetation. Only the shrieks of mynah birds broke the jungle stillness. Charlie quickened his pace as he walked, leaving her to struggle to keep up.

"Charlie, I think we should go back."

"It's not far now."

"What is it?"

"You see, missy."

He increased his stride. Briars scratched her as she strained to keep pace. She called to him, but he didn't answer, just kept plunging ahead through the ever-thickening brush.

The stillness and density of their surroundings began to assume a menacing face. Where was he taking her? Why was he suddenly so determined? She felt an impulse to stop and turn around, to head back for Papeete as quickly as possible. But there were so many turns and forks in the trails, she would surely lose her way.

When Charlie glanced back at her, his countenance only added to her growing alarm. He seemed furtive now, not the accommodating guide, but a man possessed by a fierce determination.

Then, all at once, they came to a clearing where the sun once again beat down on them. As abruptly as he'd taken off, Charlie stopped and allowed her to catch up with him. "We're here."

"Where?"

"This a place for lepers."

In the clearing stood four or five open, thatched huts where some dozen older Tahitian women were weaving straw hats. Then she saw him. A tall white man with greying hair and beard, wearing a turned-around collar.

A missionary!

As the man came their way, he smiled, extended his

hand, and said, "Miss Wycliffe. Welcome to our little community."

So this had been a setup all along. And she'd waltzed right into it!

"You were expecting me," she said tightly.

"I'm truly sorry to have to resort to this little subterfuge," he replied. "I'd have come to you, but I'm quite certain the governor would object."

"The governor would assume you'd come to cause me harm."

"The governor is overly dramatic at times. I am Reverend Dale. I represent the Boston Missionary Society on the island."

Philippe's warning came back to her. *They'll do anything. . . . If they get rid of you, there's no picture. . . . You can't be replaced. . . .*

Dale said, "Thank you, Charlie. Why don't you go get yourself some guava juice and relax." Charlie nodded and left. "He's a good man," the reverend added.

"What are you going to do with me?" Liana demanded.

"Do? Why, nothing. But I *would* like to show you around, if you'll allow me."

Just then, a small boy came up, his skin swollen by his disease. He carried a bouquet of hibiscus and orchids.

"These are for you," the reverend explained. "Please don't be afraid to touch them. I assure you Simon is in no way contagious."

She took the flowers and smiled down on the boy's shining face. "*Merci.*"

Reverend Dale proceeded to show Liana around the open-air hospital. "Leprosy has long been the curse of Polynesia. It brings out the worst in people, I'm afraid—not the patients, but those around them, who have little understanding and a great fear of the disease. Most of the patients are kept in the Orofara Leper Colony on the north coastal road. Only the most advanced cases wind up here."

Beyond the hospital perimeter was a circle of huts used by the families when they came to visit the patients. They were currently occupied by a dozen Tahitians who seemed to have formed their own little community and were in the process of making tapa—the clothlike substance hammered out of tree bark from which they made their traditional clothing.

The reverend introduced her as a cast member of the motion picture that was to be filmed in the islands. They'd all heard of it and made a huge fuss over her, plying her with questions in French. She answered them as best she could, and in return, asked questions of her own about their daily life. Before she knew it, an hour had passed and she realized she'd learned more from this impromptu exchange than from all the books she'd read about Tahiti. She was actually enjoying herself. But before long, they began to praise Reverend Dale and his efforts with their family members and she began to tense.

Seeing this, he broke things off, suggesting the Tahitians go off to begin the lengthy process of preparing the communal dinner. When they'd wandered away, Liana turned to the reverend and asked, "Is that the reason you brought me here? So they could sing your praises to me?"

"No, Miss Wycliffe, I thought you might gain a different perspective if you had a chance to talk to some of the local people. I understand you've been fairly isolated."

"You'll forgive me, I'm sure, but isn't it possible

you've coached the people here to tell me what you wanted me to know?"

"If I told you I hadn't, would you believe me?"

"You can tell me anything you like. That doesn't mean it's true."

"Which is why I won't bother. I read in the Papeete paper about your visit here. I don't really know the nature of the photoplay you've come to make, but from what I understand, Mr. Sloane isn't here to film a typical South Seas fantasy."

Cautiously she prompted him, "And . . . ?"

"Allow me to ask you something. How much has Mr. Sloane told you about his upbringing?"

Her eyes narrowed suspiciously. "What does that have to do with anything?"

"Did he ever mention living in Hawaii as a boy?"

She recalled the afternoon in the Louvre when he'd first shown her the Gauguin paintings. A lifetime ago. "Once."

"Did he say anything about his father?"

"His father? No. Why?"

"Let me ask you something else. Is it fair to say this picture doesn't portray the missionary community in a flattering light?"

Her patience finally snapped. "If you want to know about this movie, why don't you ask Mr. Sloane himself?"

"I would, but I doubt very much that he'd see me."

"Reverend, I don't mean to be rude, but you took the trouble to bring me here under false pretenses, so why don't you just tell me what's really on your mind?"

"Miss Wycliffe, you're obviously an intelligent, thoughtful, feeling woman. And you've obviously been indoctrinated to believe certain things about this project with which you're involved. If I told you all I know and asked you to see things in a different light, you would surely reject the suggestion, so I won't. All I ask is that you go back, look around you, and see if it's possible that this entire enterprise is based on a lie. And perhaps that Mr. Sloane's animosity toward missionaries is nothing more than a . . . personal grudge."

"You're actually trying to tell me that Sloane is making this picture out of some sort of vendetta?"

"I'm asking you to look around you and see if it isn't possible."

"How clever of you. You don't want to antagonize me by blackening his character outright, so instead you slyly insert a seed of doubt in my mind."

He smiled thinly. "You've found me out, I'm afraid. Have I succeeded?"

"I—don't know."

"Then I'll call it a success." He signaled for Charlie, who came rushing forward. "Now, my child, you had better head back. It gets dark fast in the tropics once the sun starts to go down."

As she reached the crest of the hill, she looked back to see the reverend staring at her. For the life of her, she didn't know what to make of this experience, or whether this man of the cloth was a benevolent Saint Francis . . . or a diabolical Cardinal Richelieu.

A crowd had gathered on the waterfront to watch the seaplane land. While the few automobiles of the French administrators and plantation owners were an increasingly familiar sight on the dirt streets of Papeete, an airplane was still a distinct rarity. The mob of children and shop owners who'd hastily left their establishments stared at the great mechanical bird that soared down from a sunset sky in a splash of spray and foam.

As it tied up to the company dock, Sloane leapt out with a Douglas Fairbanks flourish. He was dressed as an aviator in jodhpurs and high gleaming boots, light jacket and scarf. On his head he wore a leather cap and goggles which he yanked off and tossed to Tommy, who replaced them in the plane. The very vision of the adventurous aviator.

Philippe was on his way to meet him when he spotted Liana. He came rushing up to her. "Thank God you are safe!" he cried. "We have worried ourselves nearly to death. We've scoured the entire mountainside. *Please,* I beg you, do not do this again! You will make me old before my time!"

"I'm sorry to put you through that, but I just had to get out. And as you can see, I'm perfectly fine."

"Well, in any case it is done. *C'est fini.* As you say, you are fine, and for that I am thankful. I shudder to think what the *capitaine* would think of me should I allow harm to come to you. Unfortunately, I feel it my duty to tell him what happened. You understand?"

"I'll save you the trouble," she told him in a kindly tone. "I'll tell him myself."

As if on cue, Sloane appeared. If he noticed anything amiss, he gave no indication. His eyes were gleaming and his body hummed with excitement. "Unbelievable!" he exclaimed to Philippe with more enthusiasm than she'd ever seen in him before. "These islands are even more gorgeous than you boasted. And Bora Bora! It must be the loveliest spot on earth."

Tommy, juggling the canisters of exposed film in his arms, passed Liana and beamed a greeting. "Wait till you see this footage, Li. I'm going to develop it right away."

Sloane's gaze turned toward her. But just then Hank,

the chief grip, came up and handed Sloane a small pouch. "Here's your mail, boss."

"From Paramount, no doubt."

"No, it's all local."

"Local? I suppose the bills are already piling up. Just throw them in the office."

"Speaking of Paramount," Philippe interjected, "you received a cable from a Monsieur Elkins of the Honolulu office. It appears he has been empowered by Monsieur Zukor to close you down. He will arrive on the Friday steamer and has ordered you to cease production immediately."

"I never got that telegram," Sloane said pointedly.

"Certainly not. Such a pity, no?" Philippe smiled conspiratorially.

After a pause for thought, Sloane said, "Tell me, old friend. What would happen if I were to take the crew off to the outlying islands without telling you where I'll be filming?"

Philippe caught on at once. "Ah, *mon ami,* in that case I should have to guess as to your whereabouts, and send this Monsieur Elkins out accordingly. Is it my fault if my guess is not . . . how shall we say . . . *accurate?* We can stall him for weeks, chasing from one island to another, eh?"

Sloane slapped him on the back. "Good. You keep him on a wild-goose chase and buy us some time before he can catch up to us." That taken care of, he turned to Tommy. "I'll help you in the darkroom. I want to screen this as soon as possible."

With that he strode off toward the company's dockside headquarters. Liana had come with the intention of telling him about her strange meeting in the jungle. But this wasn't the right time. He was churning with energy and so eager to see the footage that there was no room in his mind for anything else. Better to wait until after the screening, when he might be more relaxed and receptive.

The footage was everything Sloane and Tommy had promised and more. The image of the South Seas captured by the silvery black-and-white photography was utterly magical, as if they'd caught the essence of a dream. The pièce de résistance was an extraordinary shot in which the camera zoomed in on Bora Bora from the air, just a distant speck at first, but filling the screen more and more as it drew closer, then rose over the palms of the central island to give an exhilarating introduction to the glory of Polynesia. The cinema had never seen anything like this before and—proud of being a part of such a staggering innovation—the company rose to its feet and descended on their director in a burst of elation.

Tommy broke out some cooling bottles of Dom Pérignon and a party was soon in full swing. Liana was no less enchanted than the others by the footage. For the first time, she realized this picture could be something trailblazing and magnificent, but only if its visual splendor was matched by the depth of characterization needed to turn a melodrama into a work of art. The realization buoyed her, gave her confidence for the confrontation ahead.

When Sloane left the party to tend to accumulated business in his office, she waited a few minutes, then followed. As she reached the doorway, she could see him half sitting with one leg hooked about the edge of his desk, reading his mail in the meager light of the kerosene lamp. His shadow loomed up one wall and onto the ceiling overhead, giving him a potent presence. She watched as he read one letter then tossed it to his desk before ripping open another and repeating the process.

He was so virile and appealing, his rugged face burned from sun and wind, lending him a robust glow. Memories flashed like lightning through her mind. The way his kiss overpowered her, making her wet with need. The way he captured her gasp with his mouth, their breaths becoming one. The way he lifted his head now and peered at her so intensely, so starkly, as if trying to convince himself he didn't want her; knowing he fought a losing battle.

Her legs felt weak. *It's the illusion,* she told herself. *Nothing more than this damnable spirit of Tahiti. The spirit of passion . . . of love.* Charlie's words returned to her: *No one can come here without falling under its spell.*

That spirit consumed her. She wondered then: Did Sloane feel it, too?

A deep longing fluttered through her, causing her to draw shaky breath. Digging her fingernails into her palms, she fought for control. She'd intended to taunt him with his desire for her, to use it as a weapon to help bend him to her will. But all she really wanted now was to go to him. To pull him slowly to his feet. To whisper to him, "Kiss me." That damned, haunting kiss . . .

Stop it, she scolded herself, dragging her gaze away. *It's this island that's doing this to me. It isn't real. But I'm not going to give in to it. I'll fight it, just as I'll fight him. And I'll beat them both, if it's the last thing I do.*

He cleared his throat, breaking the spell. Then slowly, as though forcing the effort, he dropped the letter to the desk.

"I hear you took a little stroll by yourself today," he said mildly.

She welcomed his words. They reminded her why

she'd come in the first place. To talk business, nothing more . . .

"*Quite* a stroll," she told him, assuming an airy tone. "It turned out to be something of an adventure. I ran into one of those missionaries you're so afraid of."

"You . . . what?" he choked.

She told him her story. Charlie, the pool of Loti, the leper colony, Reverend Dale.

Sitting rigidly erect, Sloane listened to the end. But she detected the twitching of a muscle about his mouth. Finally he said disgustedly, "Dale!"

"So you *do* know him."

"I know him. The Reverend Jeremiah Dale of the Boston Missionary Society."

"He sounded like he knew a lot about you."

A long pause stretched between them. He lowered his head and looked up at her with an intense blue gaze. "What did he tell you?"

"He asked if I knew about your father."

In a rage, he shot to his feet. "The bastard!"

His outburst startled her. "He didn't seem like such a bastard."

"*Of course* he didn't. These missionaries excel at charm and ooze credibility. I can't believe that bastard is here. Once he did all he could to destroy the culture of Hawaii, he's moved on to a new place to make a fast buck."

This struck her as extreme. Sarcastically, she said, "Main Line Philadelphia is just full of millionaires who made their fortunes off helping a band of outcast lepers."

He flared. "Let me ask you something. Ever hear of the Hiali Pineapple Company? It's the fifth richest company in the Hawaiian Islands. Know who owns it? The Boston Missionary Society. You know how they got it?

They stole it from their trusting flock. And did any of the locals ever see any of the profits? Not a penny. Now, would you like to know who ran this booming capitalistic concern for over fifteen years? The Right Reverend Jeremiah Dale."

She digested this for a moment. "Look, I don't know what the missionaries here are doing and I don't know if this man is what you say he is or not. All I know is he said I should keep my eyes open. That the situation around the film might not be what it appears. And that your perception of missionaries might be—"

He cut her off. "So the situation isn't as it appears, is it? Well, let me show you something."

He grabbed the stack of letters and threw them before her. Slowly, she picked each one of them up. There were three in all, one for each day they'd been here. The messages were scrawled in large print.

"Leave Tahiti at once or suffer God's retribution."

"Death and eternal damnation is the fate of those who besmirch the Lord's messengers."

"The motion picture camera is the eye of Satan and will not be allowed to defile God's island kingdom."

Sloane was glowering at her with angry satisfaction. "As you can see, these people are fanatics. And a fanatic who thinks he's in the service of God is capable of *anything.* Remember the Spanish Inquisition?"

Seeing the letters, she felt a little foolish. "All right. I admit that puts a different complexion on things. So let's forget the missionaries for a moment. What is this about your father?"

He stood towering above her, his face raw with fury. "Forget it," he growled. "He's just trying to stir up trouble."

She stared at him, flushed with frustration. "That's

right," she said quietly. "The great Captain Sloane never reveals anything about himself. Why should he begin now?"

He slumped wearily. With a sigh he said, "Get some sleep tonight. We start shooting in the morning. I want you fresh."

It infuriated her that he could so easily dismiss her. But his reaction to her questions made her think he was hiding something—something Reverend Dale had implied could be skewing his perception of the film they'd come to make. Something that might help her in her fight over Tehani's character. Well, he wasn't going to get away with it. Whatever the big secret was, she was bound and determined to find out—with or without his help.

10

At dawn the next morning they traveled by oxcarts along the coastal road for several kilometers, then deep into the interior of the island, passing a few sleepy French plantations on the way. Stray dogs came out to greet them. They were encompassed on all sides by the intoxicating aromas of exotic fruits and flowers. The morning was fresh, clean, serene. This being the first day of shooting, everyone was either nervous or gathering their concentration, and there was a noticeable lack of idle conversation.

The sun was well risen by the time they reached their location, but from some faraway haven, a rooster crowed incessantly as if, mindless of time, he felt compelled to herald another gorgeous day. The oxcarts came out of the thick forest and into an open glade. And there before them, trickling down the rocky black mountainside, shaded in rich greenery, was a waterfall spilling majestically into a large pool, the splash of it a cool, beckoning melody in the gathering heat of the day. Palm trees swayed lazily in the morning breeze.

Tents had been erected out of camera range. Tommy and his assistants began setting up their cameras at different angles while Sloane moved between them, giving instructions.

At any other time, Liana knew, the setting would be a place of peace. But after the threatening letters he'd received, Sloane had increased security. A squad of legionnaires accompanied them, standing about the set with rifles at the ready. It made her nervous. The others, too, were self-conscious at being watched so carefully yet dispassionately.

The night before, they'd finally cast the boy. His name was Alain and he was the son of a French coconut plantation owner. He was a beautiful child of ten with a large mouth and a shy, ingratiating manner, who'd developed an instant crush on Liana.

Inside one of the tents, Sofie, the head makeup woman, worked on Liana. As a parting gift to her, Nelson had developed a stain for her face and body that would take the place of makeup and, he boasted proudly, would last a week, giving her a more natural appearance and saving them the three-hour process of applying body makeup on a daily basis. Before leaving Los Angeles, Sloane had ordered screen tests using the stain on an extra and had been pleased with the results. Sofie applied the pigment, then, while it was drying, made up Liana's face to Nelson's specifications. At first, Liana had been wary of Sofie's ability to duplicate Nelson's artistry, but it soon became apparent that she'd worried needlessly. Sofie was a pro, and, sensing that Liana needed quiet to build her focus, worked without the usual gossipy chatter. Just as they were finishing, Tommy called from the tent flap, "Are you decent?"

"That's a matter of opinion," she retorted. "But come in."

He did so, beaming at the transformation. "Lordy hallelujah! If you're not the picture of a Polynesian Juliet waiting for her Romeo."

"Martin Luther, more likely," she retorted.

Adding the finishing touch, Sofie said, "You're all set, kiddo. Break a leg."

When she'd gone, Tommy rounded Liana, putting his hands together to form a makeshift frame, studying her through it as if inspecting her through the eye of his camera. "Do you mind?" he asked, tilting her head first one way then the other. "I don't think you *have* a bad side. That's damned rare. And if I didn't know better, I'd swear you really were Tehani."

Outwardly, she imagined she could easily pass for Tahitian. But inside, something was missing. She wasn't ready.

"By the way, I heard about your run-in with that missionary yesterday. How you stared into the eye of the enemy and lived to tell the tale."

"The funny thing is, when I was with him, he didn't seem like such an enemy."

Tommy shrugged. "Well, Li, what do I know? I'm just a country boy. I stay out of politics. I don't live here, so I don't really know what's going on. But Philippe does. And the evidence he's gathered would curl your hair. I know Philippe. In the war, you get to know men, what they're like way down deep. You share the battles, the waiting, the fear, the death of your buddies. And I'm telling you, if he thinks this turned-around collar is up to no good, I *believe* him."

"I suppose you're right. But . . . I don't know . . . something just doesn't seem right."

She read behind the sheen of his glasses his affection and concern. "Li, I know this is hard for you. I know you didn't want to come with us in the first place. And I know it can't be easy, being around the Ace like this. But we're here. And we have a chance to do something important. A lot of folks don't get that chance." She was about to say something, but he continued quickly. "Aside from all that, I like to flatter myself that we're becoming friends. I worry about you. Call me a cow-milking rube, but there it is."

"I'd like to think that we're friends, too," she told him. "I haven't had many real friends in my life."

"Then I'm beholden. And as your friend, I don't want anything to happen to you. So promise me something, will you? That you won't pull any more crazy stunts like that. Just so I can sleep nights."

She took his hand and squeezed it. But before she could reply, Sloane stuck his head in and asked, "Are we ready?"

Liana gave herself a final glance in the mirror, feeling her nervousness flutter inside. She turned to Sloane, but forgot what she was going to say when she saw his face. He was staring at her with haunted fixation, as if seeing her made up as Tehani in the flesh had shaken him. He didn't speak. He just stood there regarding her as if momentarily immobilized by the transformation.

Clearing his throat, Tommy left, murmuring something about giving last-minute instructions to his cameramen.

Liana began to chafe beneath Sloane's penetrating gaze. "Well?" she asked.

His throat moved as he swallowed hard. "You're perfect," he told her, his voice husky in the heightened stillness left by Tommy's exit. Then, as if reminding himself why he was here, he shook his head and asked, "How do you feel?"

"A bit skittish, if you want to know the truth."

"First-day jitters. That will pass."

"I may look the part, but I don't *feel* right. I don't know my character. I don't understand her."

"I understand her," he assured her. "Just remember that Tehani is the very essence of purity. She's been untouched and therefore uninfluenced by man. She's as natural and unaffected as the day she was born. Untainted. Keep that picture of pristine innocence in your mind. And I'll be there to help you, if you'll let me."

Instead of consoling her, his words unsettled her all the more. Purity . . . innocence . . . untainted. Everything Liana wasn't. Everything Sloane had wanted her to be.

He led her outside and then to the edge of the pool, where he had her kneel beside a large shell. At his signal, the musicians behind the cameras began to play a pastorale to help create a soothing mood. But Liana felt tense and uneasy, gearing herself for battle, distracted by the armed legionnaires, who'd perked up considerably when she'd come out dressed only in her pareu.

Sloane sat in a director's chair across the pool from her, leaning forward, his elbows resting on his knees. "Roll film."

As the cameramen cranked the cameras, Sloane began to speak in a low, whispery tone, meant only for her. "Now, I want you to lose all track of yourself. You're not Liana Wycliffe. You're Tehani, the most beautiful and sought-after *vahine* on the island of Tahiti. You're a child of paradise, a product of the tropical beauty all around you. You've awoken to a lovely day. You kneel before this charmed pool. The sun bathes you in splendor. You're surrounded by palm trees that sway gently in the breeze. You know each leaf like an old friend, every grain of sand on the beach. The pulse of the sea and the lushly wooded hills beat in your blood. You're alone and free in a world of tranquillity such as few people have ever known. You feel it, glory in it. You reach over and pick up the shell that lies beside you. Gently, reverently. You worship nature in all its forms. You dip the shell in the water and move it slowly to your lips. That's it. This is a daily ablution, a time spent communing with the ancient gods. The day is hot, but the water is cool and clear. You sip it . . . slowly . . . feel it cool your throat. Feel it nourish you."

His voice, so velvetly hypnotic, began to weave an unexpected spell. She felt it all through her, guiding her, lifting her to a place of heightened reverence. She drank as he'd coaxed her to, feeling the pristine water trickle down her throat. She *became* the lovely island girl before the waterfall and palms. And then his voice drifted off. There was nothing but the music and the splash of the water and his unspoken encouragement. An electric current passed between them, a mystical communication without words. She *felt* what he wanted, and her body responded to the image in his mind. Moving for his eyes alone, leisurely, lulled by his trance, she took the shell in both hands and dipped it in the water until it was filled to the brim. Then she raised it and, tipping back her head, feeling the flow of hair brush her naked shoulders, let the refreshing liquid spill down her face, her chin, to cascade to her half-exposed breasts. Her lips parted, her eyes closed. She felt the rapture of it fill her with desire.

And when she opened her eyes, she looked up languorously. Not at the camera, but at Sloane, who watched her with an ardent, arrested stare. It was just the two of them now, in the palm-strewn glade by a sweetly flowing fall of water. She was his creation, the vision of his midnight dreams. But it wasn't the vision she'd expected. And she understood in that moment that she'd misjudged him. What he'd brought out in her was so much more than what his words had led her to suppose. And because it was, she felt her resistance vanish. With her talent, with her body, with her very breath, she gave herself to him completely.

She was so enraptured by the experience that it startled her to hear the sound of applause coming from the crew. She'd lost all track of who she was, where she was, even of those around her. It had just been she and Sloane working together with such harmony that it had felt like making love. She'd never had such a transcendent experience before a camera. She'd never known it was even possible for an actress to feel in such consummate rapport with her director.

Throughout the day she felt an astonishing artistic satisfaction. Marveling at the intimacy that seemed to envelop them, cushioning them from the world around them. Aware only of Sloane's voice, comforting, coaxing, carrying her, bringing out the best she had to give.

By late afternoon, when they began to lose the sun, it all seemed like a dream. Only when they packed up the equipment to return to their lodgings—and once again the legionnaires closed in protectively around them—did reality begin to pierce her intoxicating sense of communion. She realized with a jolt that she'd forgotten all that lay between her and Sloane. There was still a mystery at his core that she hadn't come close to touching, a motivation propelling all his actions that she couldn't begin to comprehend.

But what was it?

* * *

This feeling of communion persisted over the next three weeks as they moved around various picturesque locations on the big island of Tahiti. Sloane was concentrating on the scenes between Tehani and the boy, who had to go back to boarding school in France in another month. The boy's crush on Liana had deepened, and she found herself feeling a great deal of affection for him. She discovered that Sloane was unusually relaxed around the boy, even teaching him the rudiments of baseball in the off-times when the crew was setting up shots. The filming itself seemed effortless. With the string quartet playing in the background, Sloane's whiskey-tinged voice guiding her, and little Alain worshipping every move she made, it didn't seem like acting at all. Here, she *was* Tehani: loving her charge like a son, frolicking with him, tucking him in bed at night and singing him to sleep.

Once these scenes were completed to Sloane's satisfaction, they geared up to film what would be one of the most complicated and spectacular scenes in the picture: the devastating hurricane in which Tehani risks her life to save the child. Aside from the daring rescue, the hurricane would destroy an entire village that the carpenters had spent two weeks constructing on the deserted west coast of the island. A dozen giant palm trees had been uprooted from the coastal highway and shallowly replanted around the faux village so they could be pulled into the air by cables, giving the impression of being swept away by the storm. The logistics of positioning and repositioning the mammoth wind machines—which kept breaking down—to convincingly obliterate the village proved a nightmare. The storm would comprise only twelve minutes of screen time, but even working up to twenty hours a day, it took them two full weeks to complete.

As difficult as it was, Liana enjoyed every moment of

it. She found the challenges of the special effects fascinating. And with Tehani the center of the sequence, she relished the physical action and the touching heroism of her character. But she also found an immense satisfaction in being part of the filmmaking team. She stayed at Sloane and Tommy's side through the whole ordeal, watching when they filmed scenes with Hobart and the extras. Once, when she suggested that she and the boy leap from the limb of a tree just before it was swept away, she was amazed to find that Sloane seized upon it, immediately calling orders to the crew to set up the shot. Encouraged, she began to offer more ideas as they came to her, and was equally surprised to find a receptive audience in Sloane. For the first time, it seemed to her that he was accepting her as an equal. Unlike so many directors, his ego never kept him from considering the suggestions of others. Indeed, his respect for her judgment seemed to be growing daily.

The morning after the hurricane scenes were completed, Sloane moved the entire company to the neighboring island of Moorea, twelve miles across the sea but a whole world away. With the good weather holding, he wanted to film the scenes establishing Tehani's idyllic early life and upbringing against the island's unspoiled beauty—scenes he considered especially important to impress upon his audience what would later be lost.

With no docking facilities on the sparsely settled island, the company and its equipment—minus the cumbersome wind machines—were carried in a convoy of outriggers rowed by Tahitian men. As they rowed, the early morning clouds gave way to gentle sunrise. Carnation light suffused the crystal air. In the distance the water was a deep viridian green rimmed with turquoise, but as they crossed the passage in the island's enveloping reef, the water was shallow, so clear they could see every crack and crevice of the rocks and coral below. Ripples of pink and yellow sunlight formed a sparkling canopy for the vivid assortment of fish that darted in their wake: black-and-white bodied with bright blue fins, deep canary yellow, and pastels of aquamarine. A group of children, swimming naked in the shallows, waved.

Unlike on Tahiti, the beach here was white sand, nearly blinding in the sun. The shore was lined with coconut palms, some lying on their sides, parallel to the water, as if too lazy in the tropical heat to stand upright. Beyond the shore, the serrated hills were a luxuriant green, seemingly covered in thick moss. Jagged peaks appeared black in the distance, rising like prehistoric monoliths, nature's tribute to ancient Polynesian gods.

The carpenters had already erected a small village and extras had been hired from among the locals. When Liana was made-up and ready, Sloane joined her.

"What I want you to do is this: Take as much time as you need and make yourself comfortable in this setting. Get to know the people who will be your family. Take part in the food gathering and the cooking of meals. Explore the rain forest. Feel yourself part of the rocks and the trees and the spirit of the island."

She met his gaze for a moment and a current ran through her. The spirit of the island . . . the spirit of love . . .

"Yes," he murmured. "That's the look I want. What I'm going to do is follow you around with Tommy and his camera. At first it might seem awkward, but soon you won't even know we're there. We'll be capturing Tehani in her natural environment. Occasionally I'll give you direction, but what's important here is that you *become* Tehani. If I shoot twenty-five hours of film and get ten minutes that are honest and pure, I'll be happy."

She tried to do as he'd requested. At first it *was* awkward. She didn't know the villagers and they didn't know her. But, prompted by Sloane, they showed her how to do the things they did every day: preparing food, making baskets, creating tapa cloth from the bark of trees. Soon they were laughing at her attempts, and she joined them. It seemed to take no time at all for them to accept her, their initial wariness giving way to a touching sort of protectiveness. They were so helpful, so ready to laugh, that she found herself loving them and feeling, as the day progressed, that they were, indeed, like family.

They filmed her in various locales and moods: using coconut oil to give a village elder a *lomi-lomi*—the traditional Tahitian massage; knee-deep in the lagoon, spearfishing against the verdant backdrop of Mount Mouaputa; frolicking with a band of village children as they leapt barefooted amidst the mammoth roots of a banyan tree.

Gradually, as the days passed, Liana, Sloane, and Tommy began to work so agreeably that they seemed almost to be of one mind, united by a singular vision. Tommy worked quietly, unobtrusively, until she *did* begin to forget that he was there. Sloane directed her gently, and only when necessary. But she found herself wanting to hear the seemingly omnipotent voice that always seemed approving, even celebratory, of her actions. A voice that was like a kind of music that often made her feel that they were the only two people in the world. There was no hint of a harsh word. The euphony of it carried her along, as if she were floating in water with the sun bathing her face with warmth and appreciation.

It was the most satisfying experience she'd ever had as an actress. She'd never felt so outside herself, so at one with everything around her, so completely absorbed by her character. It was like the ultimate escape that all actors secretly longed for in their hearts but rarely found. She didn't want it to end.

At night, alone in the hut the carpenters had built for her, she could still hear his voice in her mind. Those nights seemed endless.

As their stay on Moorea drew to its close, she felt this spirit ever more strongly and profoundly. She wondered, lying alone during the long nights, if he felt it too. How could he not?

On their last evening on the island, she lay on her pallet feeling a sense of loss. She couldn't sleep. It seemed to her that the night was beckoning. Some force seemed to be pulling at her, a force that couldn't be ignored.

Eventually she gave in to it. Wrapping her pareu about her body, she left the hut and walked on bare feet toward the beach. The makeshift village was deep in slumber. The only sounds were the surf on the reef and an occasional call of a night bird. The moon gleamed on the water with a seductive, silvery luminescence. Stars sparkled in a low, onyx sky. On the beach, the water lapped against the shore.

She trod along the soft sand, skirting palm fronds and bits of coral, absorbing the melody of the night. Feeling the force all around her, all through her, saturated by the palms, the sea, the heated breath of the night.

And then she saw him.

* * *

He was sitting and smoking on a large rock at the edge of the sea, absorbing, as she was, the beauty and loneliness of the nocturnal somnolence. She stopped and watched him, her heart aching.

He lifted his head and saw her standing alone on the moon-drenched beach like a goddess bathed in silver. He said nothing. No word of greeting, no obligatory remark. He just sat where he was and watched. Waiting.

Slowly, she approached him. It seemed she could feel every grain of sand beneath her toes. The breath of the sea seemed her own.

She stopped and stood before him, as wordless as he. It seemed inevitable that she should find him here, waiting for her. That the power of the island had called them both to this.

She reached down and took the cigarette from his hand. After an instant of surprise, he relinquished it, watching her closely. She put it to her lips and took a puff, relishing it, then blew the smoke into the night. Never once taking her eyes from his. Watching as recognition registered.

I only smoke when I'm having sex . . .

He stood. Reclaimed the cigarette and tossed it aside.

And then, without knowing how it happened, she was in his arms and he was kissing her hungrily, passionately, as if every ounce of resistance had burst free and dissolved in the dreamy night.

He held her so tightly that her breath was cut off, his arms pinning her to him, crushing her. His erection jutted up against her, hard, demanding. Her body melted beneath his masterful kiss, her hands shaping themselves to the granite contours of his chest. Her longing for him consumed her. Her body was clay beneath his hands, molding itself to his unleashed passion. Coiling inside with desire that flickered to life and leapt to meet his flame, she returned his kiss with a welcoming cry.

Still kissing her fiercely, he lowered her into the sinking refuge of the sand, his hands ripping at the pareu that stood as barrier to his desire. His mouth tasted of her with an urgency that knew no denial, demanding complete surrender from her with his lips, his tongue, his insistent palms. Tearing at his clothes as if they burned his flesh, oblivious now to the moon and the lapping tide, to the gently swaying palms overhead. Needing only her.

She met him with a ferocity all her own, hungry with unashamed arousal, moaning her pleasure, urging him on by wrapping her legs about him. Crying out under the delicious friction of him filling her completely, his mouth at her nipple, causing purls of rapture to arch her against him and meet him stride for stride. Showing him, in her eager surrender, all that a woman—a *real* woman—could be.

And when the mad passion had spent itself, they lay in each other's arms, cradled by the sand, the sweat from their exertions cooling slowly, gazing up at a frothy cloud backlit by the moon, its edges rimmed in light so that they shimmered like glinting gold. Still not talking, as if words would spoil the majesty of the moment, and all that had passed between them. And in that moment, Liana knew finally what she should have known all along.

She loved him. She'd never stopped.

11

She awoke the next morning feeling as if the world had been born anew just for her. Stretching luxuriously, smiling to herself as she recalled the perfection of the night. She could still taste Ace's kisses on her lips, kisses like no other man's, kisses that even now spurred a rush of arousal.

She relished this new awareness of herself. Her denial of her love for him had been the greatest of all her self-delusions. Now, her heart was nearly bursting with her recognition of that love. She felt the impulse to sing it out, to embrace everything and everyone, to transmit to all the world the exuberance she felt inside.

Ace, she thought dreamily, realizing this was the first instance when the old nickname hadn't brought a stab of pain. She felt lighter than she had in years, as if some great burden had been lifted. The burden of keeping her feelings for him hidden, even from herself, had vanished in the night. So, too, had her doubts about the dream her mother had given her. Because she remembered now something she'd forgotten. Her mother had said that a sexually fulfilled woman was the most liberated and happy of all. But, she had added, that fulfillment reached its peak within the security of love. That's why every other encounter had left her feeling empty inside. That's why only Ace brought her bliss.

She stretched again, feeling the relief of it, as if the tension of all the days and nights without him had seeped from her at last.

When she hurriedly dressed and left her hut, she saw Sloane drinking coffee and gazing out over the beach where they'd spent their night of love. When he heard her footfall he turned. He was so handsome and fresh in the morning, rested, energized, the very vision of her hopes and dreams.

He wasn't alone—Hobart and Tommy were chatting beside him—so she gave him a conspiratorial grin as she accepted a glass of pineapple juice. Raising it in a toast to him, she asked in a deadpan voice, "So . . . how did you sleep last night?"

A hint of a smile touched his lips. "Remarkably well. And you?"

"Like a baby. Funny . . . until last night I was having trouble getting to sleep."

"Maybe you're not used to sleeping in the wild."

"But I slept in the wild last night."

"So you did. Perhaps it was the alignment of the stars, then."

"And the moon. Did you notice the moon last night?"

"No," he answered with an uncharacteristically wicked gleam in his eyes—a gleam that thrilled her to her toes. "I was . . . distracted by other things."

"Pleasant things, I hope."

For once he smiled openly, showing straight white teeth, and flushing just the slightest bit. She found it utterly charming. Briefly, she caught a flash of the man he'd been in Paris, his face more boyish, his manner more relaxed. But before he could say anything, Hobart interrupted, proclaiming, "I, for one, don't see how the two of you could sleep at all. The mosquitoes bit me the whole night long."

Ace and Liana exchanged glances and all at once burst out in laughter. She realized in that happy instant that she'd never seen him really laugh before. It warmed her heart that it should be because of her. She drifted away with a last, secret smile for him, but couldn't resist throwing back over her shoulder, "I think I *was* bitten last night. But not by a mosquito."

She floated through breakfast in a mist of rapturous emotion, not wanting to leave this enchanted island where everything had changed. But before long they caravanned back to the landing where the outriggers took them back to Papeete. From there, they boarded the *Catalina* and steamed the hundred miles to the island of Huahine, where the carpenters had constructed the breakaway sets for the missionary's house and a mock-up church in the clapboard Colonial style. Not wanting to film the more provocative scenes between Tehani and the missionary under the ever-watchful eyes of the B.M.S., they'd chosen this more isolated island.

It was a glorious voyage. The sky was a tapestry of puffy clouds, the water calm, the seascapes staggering. Ace showed no outward signs of affection. Liana understood this. He was a private man and would naturally keep his feelings from showing. But he was also a savvy enough filmmaker to know that a romance between a director and his star could be disruptive to the psychology of a company on location. It didn't matter. It seemed to her that when he glanced at her, in the midst of conferring with Tommy about the upcoming scenes, she saw not the haunted coldness she'd come to know, but something of the tenderness he'd shown in Paris. For now, that was enough. As she leaned over the rail and lifted her face to the kiss of the sun, she felt she'd never seen a more beautiful morning than this.

But late that afternoon, as the island came into view, storm clouds gathered on the horizon. Since the pass into the lagoon was shallow, the *Catalina* had to anchor outside the reef. By the time they'd taken a series of landing craft into the town of Fare, it was pouring rain. The shower was warm, but heavy enough that they had to wait it out under the row of palms that lined the beach. Liana stood by Sloane, wishing they were alone so she could kiss him beneath the palms and the rain.

When the downpour slackened briefly, they made a dash for the Pension Enite at the end of Fare's main street, next to the open field where the sets had been constructed. Liana bided her time impatiently through the activities of the evening: checking into the pension, being shown their rooms, dinner with the proprietor who was full of curious questions about the expedition, drinks and cigars afterward. The minutes seemed to creep by. She found it difficult to keep from pacing like a caged cat. All she could think of was being alone with Ace once again. And yet the company lingered. So much talk about such nonsensical things. Why didn't they all just go to bed?

Finally, as if he felt it too, Sloane rose and stretched. "It's late," he said in his best director's voice. "We shoot in the morning. I want you all rested and ready."

"We shoot if it stops raining," Tommy reminded him.

Hobart added dourly, "Rain is always a bad omen."

But he headed for his room and the others followed. As Sloane passed Liana, he gave her a brief, blazing glance.

She waited as long as she could stand it. Listening for the sounds of activity to die down. Brushing her hair heedlessly as she estimated how long it would take the others to fall asleep. Finally, she could bear it no longer.

After scanning the hallway to make sure the coast was clear, she crept to Sloane's room. She knew it would be unlocked, so she needn't disturb those in the adjoining rooms with a knock. She opened the door to find him waiting for her.

They flew at one another with animal passion, clutching each other madly, drowning in heated kisses and hot, impatient hands. Ripping at clothing. Falling onto the bed in a tangle of quivering limbs. So lustful that preliminaries were forgotten in the crazed rush to join themselves. He thrust into her with an erection like steel, his hand clamping over her mouth to stifle the moan of ecstasy so others wouldn't hear. Making love in a fever, as if starved beyond endurance. And finally . . . finally . . . falling back into sweat-dampened sheets to gasp in astonishment, willing the calming of their racing hearts.

Liana lay in his arms as the room slowly stopped swirling. Luxuriating in the feel of his chest against her cheek, she was so happy that she was consumed with the need to voice her feelings aloud. *I love you,* she wanted to say. *I've always loved you.* But it was too soon.

He raised himself up on one elbow and smiled down at her dreamy face. Trailing a finger along its contours, he said gently, "If you don't get some sleep, the camera will show it tomorrow."

Feeling that a door of intimacy had been opened, she, too, leaned up on an elbow, facing him.

"I'd like to tell you a story," she began.

"I haven't been told a bedtime story for some years."

"It's about my mother." She waited for disapproval and found none, so she let her mind drift back to the past. "Most people would call her a Bohemian," she admitted. "She wasn't conventional in any way. She'd been raised in luxury, among a fairly decadent set. She didn't cook or clean or do any of the things other mothers do. But she had an amazingly perceptive mind, and a thirst for knowledge."

He nodded, signifying that he was listening, so she continued.

"But one day she decided to plant some white roses in a patch of ground outside our home in Mendocino. I was about twelve, I think. My father and I watched in amazement as she rolled up her sleeves and started digging up the ground, ridding it of weeds. After a while she called me to her. I assumed she was tired of the hard work and wanted me to take over. But she sat me down beside her in the dirt and said she wanted to show me something. She told me that at first she'd just started pulling up the weeds, impatient to plant the roses. But soon she began to realize what an intricate root system the weeds had. That by pulling them up quickly, she was only breaking the surface, not getting to the core of the roots. So she began to take the roots and follow them patiently, moving the dirt aside, until she finally reached the core. She told me that what had begun as a haphazard uprooting had in fact become a sort of Taoist meditation."

She paused, trying to gauge his reaction. He was watching her intently, wondering where this was going, but feeling himself drawn into the story by her soft, earnest voice. "How did an English duchess know about Taoist meditations?" he asked.

Pleased by his interest, she explained, "She was a student of all the cultures and religions of the world. She said the only way to truly understand the world we live in is by traveling and keeping our minds open to new ideas. Taoism appealed to her because it was all about finding your own unique path to God. Anyway, she had me take a particularly long root in my hand and follow it along its natural path. I pulled too hard and it broke off, so she had me find what was left and follow it to its source. Then she told me this lesson in nature could be applied to everyone and everything. That in order to truly understand a person or a situation, you must be patient. You can't just assume you've found the root of the problem and tug at it too quickly, or you'll never find the source. Do you understand?"

"I think so," he said carefully.

It felt good to talk to him this way, without antagonism. "That's what I do as an actress. In order to understand a character, I have to keep digging until I find the true essence of her, not just the surface."

"Why do I get the feeling you're trying to tell me something?"

"I want to see if I can't understand what you're trying to say in this picture about the missionaries. Not just the blanket statements. I've heard all that. But what's at the heart of the conflict between them and the people of these islands? Outwardly, they've conformed to Christianity. But they still secretly pray to their old gods. They practice the old rituals. So my question is: Why have the missionaries found their task here so difficult? Why did they have to resort to brutal tactics to enforce their views?"

He peered at her as if he were now the one trying to gauge the depth of her interest. "You really want to know?"

"Yes. If *you* know."

She became aware of the rain beating against the tin roof, gushing through the downspouts. It felt muggy inside the room, the heat damp and still. But gradually, the mood began to shift. She felt his wariness give way to wonder, as if both surprised and impressed by the workings of her mind. Shifting slightly, he told her, "The missionaries came to the islands with a single purpose and message: to bring the natives out of the darkness of their so-called ignorance and into the light of the one true religion. But they never took the trouble to try and understand the Polynesian culture they were trying to change. Because to Polynesians, the darkness is the realm of the spiritual. Their gods live in the darkness, which they call *po*. The womb is the dark from which creation is formed. To them, the light is the world where humans live. When they die, they return to the darkness, or the spiritual world. So to take them from the dark into the light is to take them *away* from the spiritual. It doesn't make sense to them. Their entire culture is based on reverence for darkness. They're even a nocturnal people. They sleep in the heat of the day and fish at night by torchlight. But the missionaries never bothered to learn this. So the people of the islands pay lip service to Christianity because their lives suffer if they don't. But their hearts are with their own gods who dwell in the dark."

"So the missionaries were attacking the roots without finding the core."

"Exactly. And when they couldn't convince them with talk, they resorted to harsher methods. Anything to force their own will on the people."

Liana gazed at him consideringly. "Did Tehani love this missionary?" He blinked, taken aback. "Because if she did, wouldn't she have tried to explain this basic difference to him? Try to help him understand what he was doing?"

"Of course she didn't love him," he snapped. "And even if she tried to explain, he wouldn't listen."

"But if he loved *her,* wouldn't he want to try and understand her point of view?"

He sat up in bed abruptly and swung his legs over the edge, turning his back to her. "He *never* loved her," he said, with a vehemence that startled her. "He wanted her. He was obsessed by her. His need to bend her to his will was symbolic of what he was doing on a larger scale. His mission was conversion, not understanding."

"I see," she said. But she didn't. Not completely. Her instinct told her that his vision of the missionary—and of Tehani herself—was incomplete.

It seemed that Hobart's prediction was coming true. From the inception of their stay, they were plagued with a swarm of unforeseen troubles. The gentle rain that normally passed within the hour evolved into a deluge that lasted three days, washing away the sets that had taken a week to construct. When it finally stopped, the single street of Fare was ankle-deep in mud. In the wake of the rain, the mosquitoes—barely noticeable on Moorea—took to the air with a vengeance. The sun returned, but the cooling breezes disappeared, leaving behind an atmosphere of debilitating heat and humidity. It was so hot that the carpenters had to work at night to rebuild the sets. During the days, the cast and crew slumped in the wicker chairs of the pension with tepid highballs dangling from limp hands, almost too lethargic to brush aside the insects. When Mr. Nihau, owner of the pension, began to string ornaments in preparation for Christmas, no one lent a hand. "Christmas in this heat," Hobart complained. "Surely you jest."

To add to their troubles, they began to notice that their supplies had been steadily dwindling due to petty theft. Cans of food, minor props, bits of costumes, film, strings for the quartet's instruments . . . anything that could easily be carried off. At first Sloane suspected sabotage by the missionaries. But gradually it became clear that the culprits were their Tahitian hosts and the crowds of children that good-naturedly followed them around all day like an entourage. Ted Ames, the production manager, shrugged it off philosophically. He told them at dinner one night, "Unlike us, Tahitians have a god of thieves, called Hiro. He's one of their most important deities. When I catch someone with his hand in my pocket, he just smiles and says, 'Hiro's doing.' Apparently, there's no shame involved."

Mr. Nihau, a Tahitian himself, was listening with a grin. "Before embarking on a theft, we have a prayer: 'Oh, my god, I am going to steal; do not heed me; do not notice me, O god.' "

Hobart glanced up from his *mahimahi* and *miti-hue* sauce to favor Liana with a raised brow. "Your father said that same prayer before his midnight rides, I'll wager."

She stuck her tongue out at him.

When they finally resumed shooting, they found the inner mechanisms of the cameras had mildewed in the muggy aftermath of the storm and had to be painstakingly stripped and cleaned. By now tempers began to flare. Hobart threw a tantrum when the hotel generator broke down and the ceiling fans no longer worked. The heat was so intense that the company abandoned their western clothes and "went native," the men shirtless with pareus loosely knotted about their waists. Every movement seemed an ordeal. Shade was such a scarce commodity that fights broke out for a meager patch of it. Even Sloane, who'd struggled to keep up some semblance of morale among his steadily sinking troops, was beginning to show his frustration over the endless delays. He was so consumed by the company's deterioration that he drifted away from the intimacy he and Liana had shared, spending every waking hour trying to deal with the morass of problems. Seeing that he needed it, Liana left him alone.

Just when the sets were finally ready, the cameras made operational, and Hobart coaxed into his makeup and heavy Prince Albert coat, a schooner appeared in the harbor carrying a rat-faced man in a white suit and matching Panama hat. J. J. Elkins, Paramount's Honolulu branch manager, had arrived at last—and he was none too happy about the wild-goose chase he'd been led on before finally tracking them down.

Production ground to a halt once more as Elkins and Sloane argued and threatened with increasing animosity.

"You have no idea what's going on back in the States," Elkins seethed when Sloane showed no signs of backing down. "The Hearst papers have been having a field day with that woman's parents. They've even reprinted censored versions of her mother's smutty diary. The Mothers for Decency are on a vendetta against Zukor, who is now claiming we have nothing to do with this. He told *The New York Times* you're a renegade, and if he could reach you, he'd fire you. So, as his representative, I am hereby terminating your employment. I'm ordering you to hand over the entire operating budget you've withdrawn."

Expressionless, Sloane listened, then softly ground out, "Get off my set."

"This is *not* your set," Elkins raged. "It belongs to Paramount. I have a paper here giving me authority to—"

"If you don't get off my set," Sloane repeated, his voice dangerously low, "I'm going to throw you off."

The executive blanched. "You're bluffing."

With the spring of a cobra, Sloane shot to his feet, grabbed him by the collar and pants of his spotless white suit, and sent him crashing down the front steps of the pension and into a pile of discarded coconut shells. "I *never* bluff."

Horrified, Elkins cried, "You're crazy! You're a madman!"

"That's right, you son of a bitch," Sloane said in the same deadly tone. "You tell Greenburg that."

He took another step toward him, but Elkins wasn't taking any chances. He scrambled to his feet and ran back to his launch as if fleeing for his life. But once he was safely out of reach, he wheeled and yelled, "You won't get away with this. Zukor will cable the French ambassador in Washington. He'll dispatch an army of Pinkerton agents to seize your film and close you down."

In the wake of this, the company—who'd gathered outside—gawked at Sloane. Liana felt as shaken as the rest. She was grateful for his support, but to go out of his way to assault this envoy who might have been wooed to their cause did, indeed, seem irrational. It brought home once again the depth of Sloane's obsession and his unyielding determination to dominate the situation—no matter who tried to get in his way.

"I think he means business, Ace," Tommy said. "You can't just ignore this."

As if he hadn't heard, Sloane stalked off into the surrounding jungle.

No one dared make a move to follow him. So they waited, not sure if they would work that day after all,

Hobart's makeup sweating off his face. They spoke in whispers as if their irate director might suddenly reappear and overhear their reactions to what he'd done.

"He's done it now. Nobody spits in Zukor's face and gets away with it. Even if the Pinks don't find us, Paramount's army of lawyers can tie up the picture's release for the next twenty years."

"We might as well pack our bags and go home."

"It's this damned heat. It's enough to make anyone balmy."

"I'm hot, too. But it hasn't made me crazy enough to bite the hand that feeds me."

Grim-faced, Tommy paced back and forth in the pension's dirt forecourt until he'd worn a dusty path. Liana sat off to the side at the base of a slender *mape* tree, thoroughly mystified.

So deeply were they entrenched in their own musings that Sloane's reemergence from the jungle caused a guilty start. If he'd gone away to cool off, it clearly hadn't worked. If anything, he appeared more tense than when he'd left. His jaw was set, his eyes a scalding blue. Without preamble he strode over to Tommy and asked, "Have you been printing duplicate copies of everything we've shot?"

Disconcerted, Tommy replied, "Yeah . . . sure. Just like you said."

"Then put together a reel of some of the best stuff and send it to Zukor in New York. That should shut him up and make him call off the dogs. But not now. I want you all ready to shoot."

Ted Ames stood and said wearily, "All right. Everyone back to the village."

"Forget the village," Sloane countermanded. "We're going directly to the church."

The company exchanged baffled looks. Tommy glared

his disbelief. "Ace, it's taken us all morning to get ready for this scene. We're got twenty costumed extras waiting on the set. Not to mention—"

Curtly, Sloane cut him off. "Just do it." When he saw Tommy's crestfallen face, he added less forcefully, "You saw what happened today. There's no way of knowing what Paramount will throw at us next. I want to get the trickiest scene in the can before I have to deal with them again."

Tommy gave a rueful smile. "That's why you're the boss and I'm just the cameraman." To his assistants, he added, "Let's head 'em up and move 'em out, boys."

The others began to follow. Sofie picked up her bulky makeup kit and teased Hobart, "Come along, Hoby old boy, let's get those wrinkles patched up again, shall we?"

Hobart was too drained from the heat to make his usual retort.

Once everything was in ready, Sloane gathered his two stars before the breakaway church for a conference. He was all director now. And when he addressed Liana, it wasn't as the woman he'd made such passionate love to just nights before, but as her character.

"Tehani, you've been living with this man for some months now. Taking care of his son. Sweeping his floors. Doing his laundry. Making his meals. What you haven't done is pacify the lust you feel growing in him. You've rejected a series of advances that have escalated in intensity. But it's getting to the point where you're frightened. It's the rainy season. The storms rage outside. It's hot and muggy. You're confined with him in a small space. Wherever you move, you catch him watching you with increasing hunger."

"You mean I've been leering at her?" Hobart asked.

"That's precisely what I mean. We'll film those close-ups of you later. But right now, you've just made your strongest play for her. She's run to the safety of the church. She's weeping in fear, on her knees praying to the God you've given her. You burst in the door. She's too frightened to look at you. You simply cannot contain yourself any longer. You *must* have her. Unbeknownst to you, your son has followed you. We've already filmed his reaction shots. But you don't know he's there, and you're so enflamed that you probably wouldn't care if you did."

Hobart quailed. "I'm not sure I like where this is going." He glanced at Liana, but she was watching Sloane intently.

"Don't think," Sloane snapped. "Just feel. I'm going to guide you through this."

"Through what?"

"You're going to burst in the door. You're going to grab her and throw her down and take her like the animal you are."

Hobart stood gaping at him. "In a *church!*"

"Can you think of a more appropriate place?"

All around them, work had stopped.

"And me . . ." Liana choked. "What am I doing all this time?"

"You're fighting him off with every ounce of your strength. Fighting to protect your honor."

She raised her chin.

"You have a problem with this?" he ground out.

"Yes, I do."

Taking her arm, he steered her off, leaving Hobart and the curious bystanders behind. "Because it takes place in a church? You never struck me as someone who balks at controversy."

"I'm not. But I do balk when I'm asked to play a dishonest scene." She lowered her voice so those standing about couldn't hear. "Ace, I know you're upset. I know you feel like you're being hounded from all sides. But please don't let it cloud your judgment. For the sake of the picture, we have to be reasonable."

In a clipped tone, he said, "I wasn't aware that I was being unreasonable."

"This whole business with Tehani and the missionary doesn't make sense. You said it yourself: She's lived under his roof, she's cared for his son, she's seen that he's a good father. He may be a zealot, but he's still an attractive man. If this were some prim and proper old maid from Boston, I'd say yes, he'd probably have to rape her. But this is a child of nature, as you called her, who's grown to womanhood on the Island of Love. Whose culture embraces sexuality. He wouldn't have to rape Tehani. She'd go to him willingly."

"Tehani isn't like that," he insisted. "She's a shy delicate creature who—"

"Everything I've learned about South Seas women says that's wrong. What about all those bare-breasted beauties who met Captain Cook's ship? These women weren't ashamed of their bodies. They didn't hide in church to keep from—"

He cut her off in a rage. "I'm not creating a stereotype here, some sailor's fantasy. I'm depicting a very real human being. A woman whose destruction was fueled by that ugly image invented by randy sailors and hypocritical missionaries."

"Stereotypes come into being because they have a basis in reality," she insisted. "You say you're creating a real human being, but real women have more than one dimension. Tehani is Polynesian. You have such a grasp of their spiritual culture, yet you have a blind spot about this."

His face had progressively hardened as she'd spoken. "I *know* Tehani," he said, angry now. "She'd never give in to this vile man willingly."

She felt floored by his epic stubbornness. She recalled the first scene they'd shot at the pool, when it seemed their visions had merged and become one. Now she could see they'd had completely different readings of that scene, after all.

"I can't believe this!" she cried. "You listen to suggestions about everything else, but when it comes to Tehani . . . it's like you have blinders on. You lash out. Why is this so personal to you? If you tell me, maybe I can help."

"I don't need help," he growled. "I know what I'm doing. This is my picture. Just turn off your mind and play the scene the way I tell you."

Needing to reach out to him, to try and close the gap between them, she gently took his arm. "All I'm asking is that you reconsider this," she urged. "Explore it some more before you commit it to film. Just listen to what I have to say. Please?"

As she pulled him closer, his arm grazed the soft mound of her breast. She hadn't intended it, but he jerked away as if she'd deliberately set a trap. "If you think you can seduce me into changing my mind, you're sadly mistaken."

She was so wounded by the contempt in his voice that she dropped his arm and stepped away. It was true she'd tried to use her wiles to sway him in the past. But the woman who'd done that seemed like someone else. She'd reached out to him now sincerely, with all the love she had in her heart. Wanting to help, to heal. And once again, he'd rejected her.

She lost the will to fight. Feeling as shocked and betrayed as Tehani did in the scene, she went along, wanting to get it over with. But Sloane wouldn't get it over with. He kept filming again and again, until she was numb, throughout the rest of the day and long into the night. He was adamant that they keep the momentum, rebuffing all suggestions to continue the next day, insisting on setting up the lights and forging ahead. They shot the violent scene again and again, from every conceivable angle. Close-ups of Liana's face, her hands gripping the altar above her. Long shots, medium shots. Over and over, until they were so exhausted they could barely move. Liana used her pain throughout the filming, channeling her despair into the character of Tehani so that the scene was infused with all the shattering authenticity that Sloane had been seeking. The tears she shed were real, the violation she felt genuine. She couldn't have felt more abused if the rape had been real.

When it was finally over, long after midnight, the depleted crew stood watching her in utter silence, too moved by the depth of her performance to say a word. Liana slumped back against the makeshift altar and put her face in her hands, feeling ravaged.

Presently, she heard a muffled step and felt a presence before her. It took every ounce of strength she possessed to lift her head and face Sloane, who stood before her, his face expressing a mixture of emotions: crushed by the experience as if it had been real, yet visibly awed by her ability to bring his vision to life.

"You were wonderful," he said softly, as if their earlier confrontation had never happened. "Thank you."

He held out a hand to help her up. But she ignored it, instead struggling on trembling legs to stand by herself. She met his gaze and, with the last of her energy, told him tonelessly, "I never thought you could hurt me more than you did in Paris. But you have. You think you know what you're doing. But you don't understand a thing."

12

The squeak of the screen door as Sloane pushed it open broke the heavy stillness all around him. He stepped out onto the rough planks of the pension's front verandah. Before him, the sun was sinking over the sets that had stood empty since production had ground to a halt after filming the last of Hobart's scenes three days before. Behind him, the idle crew, waiting to go in to dinner, milled about the lobby in the awkward uncertainty that had engulfed them since Liana had walked off the film and left Huahine a week ago.

Seeking escape from the oppressive air, Sloane strode out into the brilliant twilight. Slashes of reds and oranges painted the clouds in fiery brushstrokes. The crunch of his feet on the coral sand heightened his sense of isolation. Land crabs scurried out of his path as he wandered through the false fronts of the colonial village, past the breakaway church, the missionary's house, the *gendarmerie*. Before long, the sky turned a deep purple, the shadows lengthening over the empty set. A ghost town. And then, with the suddenness of the tropics, he was enveloped in darkness. And still he stood alone amidst the wreckage of his dream.

He lit a cigarette, seeking some solace in the glow of its brightly burning tip. But nothing eased his troubled state of mind. For a moment, he stared at the lighter in his palm.

What next, indeed?

The morning after filming the rape scene, they'd discovered Liana was gone, without so much as a note of explanation. After a thorough search of the island, they'd learned that she'd hopped the morning mail boat for Papeete. She'd checked into the Hotel Tiara and was waiting for passage back to the States. He'd cabled Philippe, who'd frantically reported back that she was adamant about leaving, but would offer no explanation. So he'd sent Tommy to appeal to her, knowing of the friendship that had grown between them. But even Tommy had met with a wall of resistance and a refusal to explain herself. She was leaving the picture. That's all she had to say.

It was this refusal to justify her defection that unsettled him the most. She wasn't a woman given to martyrish silence. She'd had no trouble voicing her objections every step of the way, standing up for herself with a determination that matched his own. So what accounted for this drastic shift in behavior?

He had to get her back. Tehani was central to every scene that remained to be filmed. Without her, there was no movie. He was at her mercy.

Philippe, and even Tommy, were insisting that she should be forced back. But for some reason, he couldn't bring himself to do it.

I never thought you could hurt me more than you did in Paris. But you have . . .

Her words haunted him. Try as he might, he couldn't shake the image of her shattered face. Why had this rattled him so? So much that, for the first time, his urgency to make the picture that had been the single driving force of his life seemed a secondary consideration. What was happening to him?

He threw the cigarette to the ground, stepped on it, and walked further into the night. He'd hurt her. It was what disturbed him most, the sense that he'd caused her pain. This realization had smashed the image of her that he'd carried with him all these years. The image of a woman ruled by superficial carnal desires, incapable of being hurt. Incapable of . . . love.

Without realizing it, he stopped in his tracks. He was a director. It was his job to put a face to human emotion. And what he'd seen in Liana's face that night had devastated him. Because it hadn't been acting. It had been the face of wounded love.

Had she *ever* been acting? Or was it possible that her expression of love for him in Paris had been genuine? And if that was true, what did it do to everything he believed? About Liana, about Tehani, about women . . . What a week ago had seemed so certain now suddenly seemed muddled and confused.

Was it possible that Liana really loved him? That he'd misjudged her so completely? Obviously he had, but to what extent? He didn't know. All he knew was that his smug little world had suddenly been turned upside down.

There was only one thing to do. Go to her and tell her the truth. Not just a piece of it. Not just enough to make her want to come back. All of it. The pain, the betrayal, the open wound he'd kept hidden from the world. He'd have to reveal himself in a way he never had before. Expose himself completely. *Trust her.*

It wouldn't be easy. It might be the hardest thing he'd ever have to do in his life. He'd be sailing into uncharted waters without any guarantee of an outcome. But he had to do it.

For the first time, he felt he owed it to her.

Liana spent her days locked in her room, waiting for the next ship back to the States. Her only desire was to be left alone, but it was not to be fulfilled. Philippe had come to see her so shortly after her arrival that she wondered how he'd known she was there.

"You do not understand how important this picture is," he'd stressed. "Not merely important to you as filmmakers, but to Tahiti and its people as well. The evil of this Boston Missionary Society is even greater than you know, or than the picture shows."

"I don't care about this," she'd insisted.

"Perhaps you will care when I tell you how Reverend Dale is stealing from the people of these islands."

"Stealing? What is there to steal?"

"Why, the black pearls, *chérie.* Pearls are the only valuable commodity these islands have to offer, and black pearls are the most precious of all."

The hair tingled on the back of her neck. She, too, had been robbed of black pearls. Pearls that had been *her* only valuable possession. Even now she recalled the pain of it. . . .

"The good Reverend Dale has been seizing them from the natives under the guise of taking them for the glory of God. This is the sort of systematic theft that has made his evil society wealthy, and bought them the power to corrupt everything around them and compromise even the authority of the colonial government."

This backed up what Sloane had told her about Dale's involvement in the pineapple company in Hawaii, how he and his fellow missionaries had used the company to rob the people of the islands. But she was sick of it all, and so she said, "If that's the case, the making of a movie isn't the way to stop them. You have the power of Paris behind you. Arrest him, bring him to trial, and send him to Devil's Island. I don't care what you do. Just leave me out of it."

But Tommy's visit was more difficult. He arrived the next day full of concern.

"Listen, Li," he told her. "I understand what you feel a lot more than you think I do."

"Then you know why I have to leave."

"The worst of your scenes is over. All you have to do is grin and bear it for another couple of weeks and you'll come out of it a star." He softened his tone. "I've seen the Ace since you left. He's distraught. Don't you think you could give him another chance?"

"How *many* chances, Tommy?" she cried. "I gave him another chance. I went to him out of love. I thought he—" She broke off. She felt too frayed to say it aloud. *I thought he loved me, too.* Gulping air, she went on. "But he still thinks I'm a two-bit whore who uses sex to get what I want. That wasn't Hobart who raped me in that scene, it was Sloane. Don't you understand? I can't do it anymore. I have to get away from him."

"Then do it later. People are counting on you. We've come a long way and taken a hell of a lot of risks to make this picture. Please don't stab us in the back."

Of course he was right. She *was* being selfish. Tommy had stirred her guilt, but her sense of self-preservation was stronger. She knew that, in order to survive, she had to get away, as surely as she'd had to escape the orphanage. So she shut herself away, not answering when anyone knocked on her door unless she was expecting the waiter with her meals.

She was booked to leave on the Friday ship to San Francisco. It seemed fitting that by Thursday, the last of the stain that had turned her into Tehani had worn off. She would take nothing of Tahiti with her.

After dinner that evening, she packed her things; then, feeling restless and edgy, she went out to walk along the waterfront. The night was hot and humid, but the ever-present breeze brought relief, carrying with it the twang of steel guitars and string instruments from the thatch-hut bars along the quay. The ship that would take her away rode in the harbor with the bobbing of the tide. Sailors from the ship wafted through the night with Polynesian women on their arms, their faces radiant, inviting. A festive mood seemed to carry on the breeze with the music.

What a fool she'd been. She never should have come at all. The instant she'd found out Sloane was directing the picture, she should have stuck to her guns. She'd have saved herself, and everyone else, a great deal of trouble if she'd listened to her instincts.

But even then she'd still loved him. And had foolishly hoped for a new beginning.

She felt the old impulse return—the need to do something supremely self-destructive. It was like an addiction, wanting to fill that emptiness at any cost. Like a hunger that couldn't be satisfied, a thirst impossible to quench.

She found herself standing before Quinn's Bar—the legendary watering hole of the Pacific. It would be so easy to step inside. To lose herself in the freewheeling merriment. To drink herself into oblivion. To kick up her heels and wear herself out in a night of frenzied dancing, letting the music and revelry carry her away. So easy.

But when the night was over, where would she be? Back where she'd started. She'd have filled the emptiness with the shame, regret, and self-loathing that comes from doing the very thing you swore to never do again. No, there was no escape there.

She returned to the hotel with the conviction that there was no help for her at all. Climbed the stairs to her room as if each one were coated with molasses, weighing down her steps. Opened the door with hands that seemed too tired to turn the key. And flicked on the light to find Sloane slouched in a chair.

It was eerily reminiscent of the night, months before, when she'd found him waiting in her Hollywood apartment. But this time the arrogance that had slapped her in the face was missing. The details of his appearance spoke of a personal torment: The tumble of his hair as if he'd done nothing more than rake a hand through it. The stubble of whiskers on his jaw. The rumpled state of his clothes. The way he slumped in the chair, arms draped limply over the armrests, a drink dangling from one hand. The bleary lassitude in his eyes as he raised his gaze to hers—a flash of jaybird blue—before squinting them against the glare of the light.

He seemed the physical embodiment of all her defeat and despair, as if she were seeing her inner self reflected in a mirror.

Slowly, deliberately, as if every action cost him effort, he sipped from the glass, then let his hand drop back to once again dangle negligently over the side.

"Turn off the light," he said in a voice that sounded rusted from disuse.

"Why should I?" she asked, trying to make some

sense of his presence here, in this condition, at this late date.

"Because I have something to tell you, and I can't do it with that goddamned light in my eyes."

Wearily, she told him, "If this is another ploy to convince me to stay, you're wasting your time. You've run out of weapons."

His reply was equally drained. "I didn't come to use weapons against you. I came to tell you the truth."

Don't listen. You've been fool enough for one lifetime.

"You're bluffing," she accused. Then corrected herself in a sarcastic tone. "Oh, *that's* right . . . I forgot. The great Captain Sloane *never* bluffs, does he? So you must have an ulterior motive." She cooed at him sweetly. "What's the matter, Ace? Did you realize on your own that you'd run out of tricks? You can't threaten me with never working again, because I won't, regardless. What's left, then, but to violate your own stubborn refusal to share even a scrap of yourself with me? Throw the silly actress a bone. Let her think you're baring your soul and she'll come crawling back. Is that it?"

He peered up at her. "I want you back, there's no question of that. But I'm not telling you this to try and convince you. I just . . . want to tell you."

"Why?" she demanded.

He scrubbed his face with a rough hand, struggling to understand it himself. "Because what you said about Paris has thrown me. I can't stop thinking about it. I haven't slept for a week. I've barely been able to work. Every time I tried to concentrate, I kept hearing your words. Haunting me. In the end, all I knew was that I had to tell you the truth. That I *wanted* to."

She could hear the sincerity in his tone. She stood rooted to the floor, knowing she'd never been in more danger than she was at this moment. Knowing she should turn and run. Now, before it was too late.

But all she could do was stand there, her heart hammering in her breast.

"Are you going to turn that light off or not?"

She felt herself bend to his will. As if in a trance, she went to her bedside table and struck a match to light the candle that served when the electricity failed. But her hand shook so much that the flame disappeared. She took another, but after three fumbling strikes, couldn't manage to ignite it. Exasperated, she flung the box to the table and stood there, breathing hard.

"Try this," he suggested.

He reached into his shirt pocket and thrust something toward her. She crossed the room and took it, then stopped cold. It was the gold lighter she'd given him in Paris, all those years ago, worn smooth from use. She turned it over and saw the engraved nameplate: *Ace.*

She remembered the night in the Hollywood Hotel when she'd asked for a light. He'd instinctively reached into the pocket of his robe, then hesitated and gone for the lighter on the table instead. Not wanting her to know he still carried the gift she'd given him.

Touched, bewildered, she lit the candle then crossed the room again to snap off the light, needing the darkness now as much as he.

She walked back to him cautiously and handed him the lighter. Then she sat at the edge of her bed, facing him.

"I've never told this to anyone," he began.

Liana gripped her hands together. She didn't know which was worse: the absence of hope . . . or hope itself.

In a single swift motion he raised his glass and drained it, as if gulping courage. For the first time she realized he was afraid. He, who'd never seemed afraid of anything. Who'd faced death repeatedly with a come-and-get-me resolve.

"Tehani isn't a fictional character," he confessed. "She was real."

Liana's hands were clenched so tightly, the fragile bones threatened to break. "And you loved her," she choked out, recalling what he'd said to her at the Louvre before the Gauguin paintings.

You remind me of someone I used to know.

A girl you loved . . . ?

"Yes. I loved her. But not in the way you think. As you suspected, this is more than just a picture to me. The boy in the film—Daniel—is me. Tehani was the woman who raised me in Hawaii."

The grip of her hands slackened in astonishment. "Tehani was your *mother*?"

"A stepmother of sorts. And the missionary—the man who rapes and destroys her—is . . ." He paused. When he spoke again, his voice rasped with hatred and an anger amplified by years of secret suffering. "My father."

Liana winced. The explosive information made her feel as if she were sinking in quicksand. As if nothing before this had been real.

He was breathing deeply now. "We lived in Maui. My father was with the Boston Missionary Society in the Hawaiian Islands. Dale was his colleague and head of the company the society ran. The same breed of Bible-thumping hypocrite. My mother had died giving birth to me, so it was just the two of us. I was a lonely child. My father didn't show much interest in me except to periodically beat the fear of God into me.

"Then one day I met Tehani. She was several years older than I was but I fell in love with her at first sight. I discovered that she took the same walk every day, by the sea. So I began to go and wait for her. At first I'd just hide and watch her. But she caught me one day and chided me playfully, telling me that if I was going to come here every day anyway, I might as well join her. I used to run to meet her and we'd walk and talk. Sometimes we'd lie on the edge of the cliff and she'd read poetry to me. I was . . . enchanted. There was something about her that seemed luminous. As if a light shone from within her. As if she was the very definition of joy. I was only a boy, but when I was with her, I walked tall. Like a man."

He let his mind wander back for the first time in many years. Liana watched him, waiting.

"For a long time, she was my secret. But my father began asking where I went at the same time every day. He insisted that I show him. He was sure that I was up to no good. I didn't want him to know, so I did all I could to deflect his interest. But finally he beat me down and I had to give in." His brow creased in painful memory. "The minute he saw Tehani, I knew it was a mistake. He didn't care that in my mind she was mine—my cherished secret. He didn't even see. I was just a boy and my feelings didn't matter. He wanted her and he took her. He was old enough to be her father, but that didn't stop him. He brought her into our home under the pretense of being a servant, my governess. But all along, he just wanted her for himself."

He raised the glass to his lips again but, finding it empty, set it aside. Liana watched, saying nothing, not wanting to interrupt the flow of his words. Words that had been bottled up for much too long.

"Tehani was every bit as wonderful to me as she is to the boy in the picture. She saved my life. She was the only person I ever loved. And my father—that animal, that hypocrite—forced himself on her. He never even bothered to marry her. He just kept her in our house as a slave and used her to satisfy his own filthy needs. He made her do . . . *perverted* things."

He was trembling now with rage. "I saw them once," he told her in a haunted tone. "I'd been asleep, but I heard her cry out. I crept through the dark house toward the sounds and opened the door to his room. He'd tied her to the bed and was—"

He stopped and put his face in his hands as if trying to block the vision. Liana slipped from the bed and knelt on the floor beside him, placing her palm on his leg to offer warmth, comfort.

"I didn't know anything about sex. I was too young. But I knew what he was doing wasn't right. I flung myself at him, beating him with all my strength, screaming at him. All the time he was preaching about morality, he was doing—*this* to my beautiful Tehani.

"He must have known what my witnessing this could do to him. He didn't beat me the way he used to. Instead, he took me to my room and told me it was all right. That I was to forget about what I'd seen. And then he went back to her. I cried myself to sleep that night. If only I'd been older—just a little older—I'd have killed the son of a bitch."

A tear splashed on her hand and Liana realized with a shock that he was crying. She reached up and stroked his hair as her own tears filled her eyes.

"The next morning she told me that I must never go to my father's room at night again. When I tried to argue, when I told her I wanted to rescue her, she just smiled and said what a brave little man I was. She pretended to me that it was all right. She never once let on what her real feelings were. But I knew. I knew she hated the touch of him so much that he had to tie her up and force her. And the more she hated it, the more it excited him. I could see it in his eyes when he looked at her. *Lusted* after her. After that, I heard her cries at night, but I'd promised her I wouldn't go in, and I never did. A few months later, she died. Of influenza, they said. But I knew better. I knew my father killed her. He'd broken her with his defilement and her spirit had withered away and died."

He was sobbing now. She reached up to take his head in her hands, to draw him close. But he shoved her away and stood abruptly, struggling for control.

"The worst of it," he said, bitterly now, pacing the room like a restless beast, "is there's a part of me that's just like him. He was sick, and I inherited that sickness. I didn't want to do to any woman what he'd done to Tehani. So I avoided sex as long as I could. But the need would build up until it was like a fever eating at me. I took care of it by sleeping with women who didn't matter to me. One-night stands. No involvement, no chance that they might be hurt. And then I . . . met you."

He let out a slow breath. "And you were so much like her. You had that same quality, as if some inner light shone brightly. It seemed to say, 'In this light, you'll be healed.' It scared me. I didn't want to get close to you because I was afraid that I might do to you what he'd done to her. So I didn't even tell you my name. I meant to stay away, but I couldn't. Because I'd never known anything like it before."

He began to pace again, the despair overtaken by restless energy. "I wanted to cherish you, as I had Tehani. To talk to you, hold your hand, show you the things that were special to me . . . even as I was afraid to. I fought back whatever sexual urges I had. I didn't want to ruin things by provoking something that could turn ugly. I knew myself too well. I couldn't do that to you."

"And then I forced the issue."

"Yes. You brought to the surface all the feelings I'd been battling. The feelings I couldn't afford to give in to. Not with you. So I ran. Again, I tried to stay away. I told myself that I'd been wrong about you. That you were just another of those women I'd spent no more than a few hours with—women who wanted sex and nothing more. That I wanted you the same way I'd wanted them. It confused me, because I didn't want to think of you that way. I wanted a relationship with you that, for once, was pure and untainted.

"But once you'd opened the floodgates, there was no turning back. I had to have you. I got myself drunk trying to resist. But I couldn't. The fever was back. So I went to you with the intention of putting out the fire and nothing more. You'd be like all the rest, after all. But it was . . . different. So different. At the end of it, I didn't feel empty and sick. I felt so . . . complete . . . that it scared the hell out of me. I didn't know how to handle it. So again, I ran. And I left you that note because I had to. Not because I hated you. But because I hated myself. Because I'd allowed my own sickness to spoil the only clean relationship I'd ever had. It never once occurred to me that you could have . . . loved me."

Slowly, Liana stood, her legs aching from kneeling by his chair, looking at him in the hushed aftermath of his confession.

"What have I done to you?" he whispered.

All resistance melted. She rushed to him and clutched him close, feeling him tremble in her arms. "It's all right," she murmured soothingly, stroking his hair. "You couldn't help it. You had a beautiful boyhood crush on Tehani. But your father made her a substitute mother to you, so you didn't know *what* to think. And when you saw them together like that, it confused you even more. In a way, you've never gone beyond that episode. And you're making this movie to get back at your father."

He straightened from her embrace. "I *have* to. To get revenge for her. To somehow make it up to her that I allowed her to live and die like that, without lifting a finger . . ."

She stroked his face tenderly, feeling the bristle of beard along his jaw. "You *will* make this picture," she promised. "And I'll help you."

He blinked. "You won't leave?"

"No." She smiled. "I won't leave."

"I didn't tell you this to make you stay."

"That's why I'm staying."

He let out a breath and rubbed his eyes. "Christ, I'm tired."

"Stay with me. It's all right. I'll just hold you as you sleep." When he peered at her uncertainly, she added with a sheepish smile, "Don't worry. I promise to behave."

She undressed him, because it became apparent that the last of his energy had been spent in pouring out his tale. She settled him under the covers then quickly changed into a nightgown. By the time she slid in beside him, he was nearly asleep.

She took him in her arms and gently laid his head on her shoulder, cradling him protectively. Feeling the warmth of his body like a soothing balm. Thinking of all the pain he'd kept locked inside, with no one to share it with. Until now.

He felt her tears on his cheek and shifted slightly. "If I said anything to hurt you . . ." he began, but she put her fingers to his lips. She was crying because of what he *hadn't* said. What she'd never known, but knew now.

The real reason he'd come to her and told her everything. The reason even he himself didn't fully comprehend.

"Sleep, Ace," she told him, kissing his cheek. "Just sleep."

13

For much of the night, she didn't sleep. Occasionally she would doze a bit, but always she awoke with the same realization. This wasn't a night for sleep. This was a night to savor.

It seemed such a wondrous thing to lie, for endless hours, with Sloane in her arms. To feel the warmth of his body against hers, the tough sinews and firm, sculpted torso relaxed and trusting in the haven of her embrace. To feel the occasional bristle of his jaw against her shoulder when he stirred in his sleep, the steady rise and fall of his chest as she listened to the rhythmic measure of his breath. It was something she'd never even hoped to have again: an entire night entwined with him.

He slept like a man who hadn't closed his eyes in days—deeply, with the kind of peace that comes from the final shutting down of the unsettled mind. Like a man who felt instinctively that he was safe.

But every once in a while his body would pulse with a life of its own, disconnected from the quandary of intellect or the dictates of conditioning. Those were the times when he shifted and his cheek came to rest on the pillow of her chest. When he drew a long leg across hers and she felt the swell of his erection. When his hand sought her other breast, to find it covered by the nightgown, to begin a voyage of its own, seeking a path inside.

It was so unexpected, so at variance with the tender solicitousness of her mood, that it elicited a gasp of surprise. She lay completely still, afraid to move lest she awaken him. But as his large hand roamed over her, her breath caught in her throat. Her flesh, made suddenly sensitive, began to quiver beneath the pilgrimage of his fingers. And when he found the gaping neckline and plunged his hand inside, when he found naked skin instead of concealing cloth, she was wracked by a shudder of desire.

And then he was still again, his hand still clutching her. But gently, tenderly. As if a part of him, the part hidden even from himself, needed the contact that the conscious will denied.

She lay with him, deliciously aroused but reminding herself of her promise to be good. This night had taught her many things. And his sweet and trusting attraction to her, while sleeping, furthered her understanding still. There was nothing ugly or perverted about his desire. Even in the throes of what he'd called his fever, sex with him had been lovely and life-affirming. The ugliness, the perversion, was caused by his gazing into the fun-house mirror within his own mind, a mirror that twisted and reshaped reality because it was reflecting impressions of a little boy who'd seen what he couldn't possibly comprehend. That experience had festered within him like an open wound.

Not only had that wound twisted his life, but it had come close to destroying hers. This night had been a new beginning. It had convinced her that everything she'd longed for—the love, emotional security, and sense of belonging—was within her reach. But before they could find that consummate fulfillment, there remained a difficult task: finding a way to heal the wound that had dominated his life.

But how?

She thought about it through the long hours of the night. She thought of all that had happened, and all he'd told her. What was the key? It seemed to her, as she pondered, that something was struggling to surface from the depths of her mind. Some memory . . . something someone had said . . .

At some point she must have slept, for when she awoke the sun was shining. Ace continued to sleep soundly, as if making up for lost time. His arm, flung across her, was heavy, but she welcomed the weight. She stroked the hair on his bronzed forearm with fingers that could never get enough of the feel of him.

But after a time, her quandary of the night before came back to her. And as it did, she remembered what she'd been struggling to recall. Reverend Dale had said Sloane was using the picture to perpetuate a lie. She'd assumed that he was referring to Sloane's views about the missionaries. Yet his father's treatment of the real Tehani certainly justified those views. And she knew in her heart that all Sloane had told her was the truth.

What, then, was the lie?

There had to be more to this. Yet, the only man who could tell her was Reverend Dale. A man both Sloane and Philippe had damned as a liar and thief. A man who was a friend and colleague of Sloane's sanctimonious and deceitful father. A man who might very well be dangerous.

* * *

She rose with care, slipping her body from beneath his arm. She held her breath as he stirred briefly, but settled back into slumber. Dressing soundlessly, she penned him a note and left.

It was nearly nine o'clock by the time she made her way out onto the street. Not certain where to find Reverend Dale, she went in search of Charlie. She finally caught up with him in the *marché,* where he told her the missionary could be found in a soup kitchen just off the dusty waterfront street that was grandly called Pomare Boulevard.

She made her way down to the waterfront, past the block of honky-tonk sailor traps, to a makeshift pavilion—just a canvas roof propped up on four wooden posts—where a line of parishioners were queued up for a free breakfast. She could see Reverend Dale patiently ladling out the porridge and handing each a portion of French bread. Keeping well out of sight, she watched him for a while. The way he seemed to be enjoying his duty, taking the time to smile and give each recipient a friendly word, teasing the children so that she could hear their squeals of laughter. Could this possibly be the monster Philippe had described?

As she stood pondering, an elderly Tahitian man scooted past her and bucked the line to approach the reverend, excitedly thrusting forth a small leather pouch. Quickly covering it with his hand, as if trying to hide it, Dale motioned for the man to follow him, then called an assistant to take over his duties.

As they came her way, Liana crouched behind a stand of coconut-scented soaps and oils. Moving to the other side of the pavilion, away from the line, the two men stopped short. There the reverend took the pouch from the man, opened it, and let its three objects drop into his palm. Black pearls! As big as marbles.

So it was true.

After studying them, Dale slid them into their pouch and the two men headed off together down the tree-shaded road. Dazed, Liana followed at a respectable distance, careful to stay within the morning shadows. They continued for nearly a mile north of town before coming upon a solitary, dilapidated building, apparently an abandoned warehouse. Its lopsided wharf stretched out over the water atop a series of pilings. The men disappeared into the building.

Breathing heavily, Liana paused outside the door, wondering whether or not to risk entry. Unable to resist, she carefully inched the door open and, finding the coast clear, stepped into the dim interior. A strong fish odor assaulted her. As she adjusted to the darkness, she spotted coils of rope, old nets, and an assortment of wire baskets similar to crab traps. Oyster shells littered the floor.

Across from her, at the other end, another door stood ajar, letting in a patch of sun. Through it, she could see that the two men had walked out onto the wharf. She quickly crossed the room and peered around the corner of the doorjamb, watching. Dale and the Tahitian crouched on their haunches at the end of the pier as the Tahitian began to hoist a chain out of the water. At the end of it was one of the wire baskets, dripping as they set it on the pier beside them.

A hand on her shoulder made her swing around. As she did, she was grabbed by two male Tahitians. She tried to struggle, but was quickly subdued.

"Get your hands off me!" she demanded.

One of her captors called out to the reverend.

Liana renewed her struggles as he approached, but

the men held her fast, dragging her out onto the pier. As Dale came before her, his puzzled frown hardened into a cautious glare.

"They were right about you all along," she spat out at him, trying still to wrench her arms free.

"About what?" he asked.

"I saw that man give you the pearls. You're doing just what they say you are. Stealing from the people who trust you."

The grip on her arms tightened convulsively. She jerked at them and asked, "Now that I've caught you red-handed, what are you going to do with me?"

Dale studied her as if trying to decide what to do.

"It's quite a dilemma, isn't it?" she persisted. "Maybe I left word where I was going. Maybe Philippe and his legionnaires will come bursting through that door any minute. You don't know, do you?"

At this empty threat, one of the men gave her a rough shake.

Dale's eyes flared. She waited for him to snap at her. But instead, he said to the men, "Let her go."

Reluctantly, they obeyed. Liana was wondering what trick he was up to when he added, speaking to her now, "You'll have to forgive them. We try to work in secrecy here. They've been warned to watch out for spies. They're a little overzealous."

Irritably, she brushed herself off. "You're telling me."

"Would you walk with me? Perhaps I can try and explain a few things." In Tahitian, he dismissed the men, then gestured for her to accompany him to the end of the pier, where the pearl man stood by the raised basket, warily watching their approach.

"Explain . . . or justify?"

With a quiet word, he asked the Tahitian to leave

them alone, then turned back to her. "Perhaps you'll understand when you've heard the whole story."

She wasn't sure what to make of either this man or the situation. Was the dismissal of his thugs indication that he was going to free her, or just a temporary delay? Stalling for time, she said, "By all means."

"First let me ask you a question. What do you know about black pearls?"

"I know they're valuable. My mother had a black pearl necklace. It was my inheritance, but it was *stolen* from me and sold to pay off debts." She gave him a pointed look.

"I'm sorry to hear that," he said, ignoring her implication. "A necklace of the right sort of black pearls, perfectly matched, could indeed be deemed priceless. Black pearls are some of the rarest gems on earth. And they're found only in this region. So those who control the market stand to make a considerable fortune. A fortune that could well save the native population and their culture, which is rapidly disappearing, by decreasing their dependence on the French government."

"And that's always been a big concern of you missionaries, hasn't it? Saving their culture."

He met her sarcasm with an unfazed smile. "We deserve that, I suppose. My brethren and I have made mistakes in the past. But some of us have come to realize the error of our ways and are struggling to rectify the damage."

"And just how are you doing that?"

"When I came here, three years ago, I learned that there is an organized network of corrupt officials within the government. This gang of thieves and their Tahitian toadies have concocted a loathsome conspiracy to control the black pearl market and rob the natives of their birthright. When pearls are found by the population, they're instantly confiscated. If any of the natives discovers a black pearl and tries to keep it for himself, he and his family are killed as a warning to others."

"You're can't be serious!"

"I'm deadly serious. The people know this, so they give up the pearls out of fear. For the past few years, they've been living under a reign of terror. And nothing has been done to stop it."

"You forget. I saw you with the pearls."

"What you saw—and what you see here—is a longstanding experiment of ours. What we're trying to do is develop a process of artificially cultivating black pearls."

"Cultivating?"

"Yes. The Japanese have pioneered a process of inseminating an oyster with the irritant around which the organism develops a pearl. The resulting gem is every bit as real, but the process can be controlled. The Japanese have succeeded sporadically with white pearls, but—"

"You're trying to do it with black pearls."

"Exactly." He opened the pouch he still carried and dropped the contents into her palm. They were gorgeous, a deep black with a lustrous undertone of peacock blue. "These are the best we've produced. For the first time we have a marketable commodity. Think of it, Miss Wycliffe. What if we could create a cultured black pearl industry in these islands? Controlled by the natives, not the government. Think of what it would do for these people. And think of what it would do to the ongoing conspiracy that has lined the pockets of all these corrupt colonial officials."

Or what my discovery could do to the lining of your *pockets,* she thought. But she continued to play along. "They know what you're trying to do?"

"Of course. It's a grave threat to them because our

success would dramatically increase the supply of black pearls in the world market and thus decrease the value of the market they control."

"This is all very interesting, but I know what you people are capable of. I read the threatening letters you wrote."

He froze. "I wrote no letters."

"Someone in your society did. I saw them myself."

The gaze he turned on her was faintly piteous. "My child, there *is* no one else. I *am* the Boston Missionary Society on this island. We have five other pastors on the far, outlying islands, but they know nothing of your picture."

"Are you seriously trying to tell me the government had us guarded day and night to protect us from *one man*?"

"No. I'm telling you that they used their troops not to protect you from me, but to isolate you from me to keep you from learning the truth."

He was good, she'd grant him that. He sounded as if he actually believed this preposterous tale. "Then explain this: If the government here is so murderous, and you pose such a threat to them, why don't they just kill you?"

"They may yet. But they know the society would just send someone else to take my place."

"But they're the government. Why don't they just kick the Boston Missionary Society off the islands?"

"They'd dearly love to, but they can't. You see, my child, the French are Catholic, but the Tahitians are overwhelmingly Protestant—stubbornly so, because the first missionaries here were British. In recognition of this, the French government made an agreement with our brotherhood five years ago. They gave us the missionary 'concession,' as it were, in exchange for staying out of French Canada. This agreement still has twenty years to run. So they can't kick us out. But they can discredit us. And what better way than with an epic Hollywood motion picture that would blacken our face before the entire world? That's the real reason why the government has been so eager to have this picture made."

"Come now, Reverend, that's too absurd even for you."

"Think about it. Does this photoplay flatter our islands? Will it make people want to come here as tourists?"

"Philippe Vidal was the one who encouraged the picture."

"That's because Philippe Vidal is the head of this conspiracy."

She glared at him. "That's impossible."

"Is it? What do you really know about this man?"

"I know he's been nothing but gracious and helpful. And I know he's Sloane's friend."

"Or *pretends* to be."

"Pretends . . . why would he do that?"

"He hatched this plot himself as a junior member of the government before the war. By the time he was lieutenant governor, he was confiscating pearls at the rate of a hundred a year, and using the profits to create his own private army and reign of terror. We realized what he was doing and convinced the governor to call a halt to his activities. That's when he left the islands to go off to war. But no sooner had he returned than the governor died in a mysterious boating accident. Philippe, his disgraced assistant, pulled strings—and no doubt paid huge bribes—in Paris to have himself appointed his successor. The fact that the islanders believe Philippe killed his predecessor adds to their fear of the man."

"Why would he do all this? Greed?"

"Greed, yes. But not for money. For power. I've spent many months trying to understand what drives Philippe Vidal. And I believe it stems from his father's loss of the family fortune when Philippe was a child. He harbors a deep-seated bitterness, and he dreams of revenge. I believe he wants to use the money from his pearl monopoly to create a foundation of power from which to launch his true political career. I've been told he dreams of being no less than president of France."

"To dupe Ace and Tommy . . . his best friends! I can't believe . . ."

"They are *not* his friends. They are loathed marionettes in a puppet show of Vidal's making."

"Loathed?"

He took a breath. "When I began to gather information on Philippe Vidal, I wrote to an old friend living in Paris and asked him to find out what he could. He was able to locate some people who had known Philippe in his younger days. Apparently, Philippe made no secret of his hatred of Americans. It was American businessmen who talked his father into a consortium that failed. The Americans escaped unscathed, but Philippe's family lost everything. His father became a bathroom attendant at a Marseilles hotel. Knowing human nature as I do, I suspect the indignity of this has never left Philippe."

"But I saw them together in Paris. They were like the Three Musketeers."

"A charade on Philippe's part. What better way to study the enemy? An enemy whose face must have assumed even more sinister proportions in his mind during the war. Bad enough the American pilots of the flying Escadrille became mythic heroes. Philippe had to live among them but, not being a pilot himself, had to sit back and watch while they tasted all the glory. But when the United States came rushing in at the final hour to save France, he may well have taken it as a personal humiliation. In his mind, it no doubt appeared to the world as if his homeland was so pitiful that the brash young Americans had to come to her rescue. Dignity is important to Frenchmen, but to Philippe it seems to have become an obsession. And finally, the last straw: Even the missionaries who uncovered his conspiracy, and who continue to plague him, are American. I believe, in a way, that this is the consuming focus of his life."

"Are you trying to tell me that Philippe was plotting this movie from the moment he met Sloane?"

"Of course not. When they first met, he no doubt saw in Spencer Sloane an opportunity that would never come again: not only to observe his enemy at close range, but to intimately study the best of them under the guise of friendship. To discern his weaknesses. And perhaps, if he was clever, to find a way to humble him. He had the best entrée imaginable, a shared past in the Pacific. But it was not until much later, when *Devils in the Air* became a hit, that it must have all come together in his mind. The perfect plan. To manipulate a great American hero into using American movie culture to destroy his American missionary enemies. He knew about Spencer's hatred of his missionary father. He knew of his great talent as a filmmaker. He knows the power of the Hollywood cinema to mold world opinion. Spencer must have seemed like a godsend to him."

"But even if they discredit you, you still have an agreement to be here for twenty more years. Even if the picture hurts your image, the public's memory is short."

"I agree. There is an element to their motivation that I don't understand. There has to be something more specific to their intentions, in the manner in which they hope to use this photoplay against us. But I don't know what it is."

She'd heard enough. "You've thought this out to the last detail. And I have to admit, if I'd sent down to Central Casting for someone to play this role, they couldn't have found a more convincing actor. But I'm afraid there's one little detail you've overlooked."

"What's that?"

She faced him squarely. "I know all about the Hiali Pineapple Company. How you and your so-called saviors kept the profits for yourselves and robbed the population of what you'd no doubt call their birthright. I imagine you were just as convincing then."

She was watching his face carefully and saw the flush of color. He lowered his gaze from her scrutiny and thought for some time before answering.

Go on, she thought. *Come up with an excuse for* that.

Finally he spoke. "I've already told you that we made mistakes. You're absolutely right. I'm guilty of everything you say. We all were. I carry the shame. For many years in Hawaii, we missionaries behaved despicably. We stole the land and gathered riches for ourselves. Some of my predecessors even left the ministry to become wealthy land holders. It bothered me at first, but I was schooled in obedience and I did as I was told. Gradually I, too, began to look the other way." He looked up and met her gaze. "But I was changed by the example of . . . a remarkable man. It was because of this man that I and my fellow brethren in the Boston Missionary Society came to see how grievously we'd erred. I came to Tahiti for a fresh start, to use what I'd learned to help the people here, not harm them."

"Just like that."

"Evidence to the contrary, people are capable of learning from their mistakes. With some, it takes a lifetime.

For others, once they've been shown the light, they no longer wish to be a part of the darkness, particularly if that darkness has brought them pain. Once a person is able to ask with horror, 'What have I done?' change can occur very quickly. That was the case with me. I knew what I was doing was wrong, but it took seeing myself as others did to change me. Once I was able to see clearly, I could no longer stomach my past actions. I decided then and there to change."

Against her will, she was touched by his story. But she remembered Sloane's warning about his ability to charm and convince. "Some might say this conversion is a bit too convenient. How do I know the B.M.S. isn't planning to keep the profits from the pearls for itself?"

"Because we severed all ties to our company in Hawaii. Its stock has reverted back to the people of Maui. That was my final act before leaving. But I don't expect you to take my word for it. It's easy enough to verify. When you get back to your hotel, send a wire to the *Honolulu Dispatch,* the most antimissionary newspaper in Hawaii. They'll confirm what I say."

She blinked. "You mean I'm free to go?"

"Of course you are. Find out for yourself."

Now she didn't know what to think. He could be telling the truth, after all. Or he could be bluffing, thinking his offer to provide proof would be enough to keep her from sending the wire. She considered him and as she did, remembered why she'd come in the first place. "Is this the lie you spoke of before? What you've told me today?"

He hesitated briefly. "First go find out if I've told you the truth about my past. Then come find me and I'll tell you the rest."

"The rest of what?"

"What you wanted to know initially. About Spencer Sloane."

The next night Liana and Charlie were quietly creeping through the brush outside the governor's compound. The sun had gone down around six o'clock, and clouds covered the moon. A perfect night for mischief, her father would say.

She put a hand on Charlie's arm to caution him. "Be as quiet as possible," she whispered. "There are guards everywhere. Try and blend into the surroundings as much as you can."

"I know, missy." He grinned. "I go on night maneuvers in the war. I move like ghost."

Silently they picked their way through the brush across the hill and along the fence. In the dark, Liana had to feel her way to the opening she'd discovered the day she'd made her escape from the compound. She finally found it and Charlie wiggled under, then pulled her through. They paused, regulating their breath. Liana knew the level of security only too well. If one of the guards were to discover them, they'd lose their only chance to learn if Dale's accusations were true.

She'd returned to Sloane the morning of her meeting with Dale with a loaf of bread and some papayas as an excuse for her absence, having stopped off along the way to send the wire to Hawaii. He'd just woken up and had no idea how long she'd been gone. Though she was tempted to tell him everything, she was loath to disturb the peace they'd found. Better to find out for herself what merit there was to Dale's story . . . if any. So she'd spent the day with Sloane, biding her time until she heard back from the *Honolulu Dispatch.* Today, when he'd said he wanted to meet with Philippe to let him know their plan to resume filming, she saw her chance to learn the level of Philippe's culpability, suggesting Ace take Philippe out to dinner to help make up for the trouble she'd caused. Armed with the certainty that the governor would be out of the house tonight, she'd found Charlie and had laid out her plan. He seemed trustworthy, and she would need a helper in this caper.

Now they made their way through the gardens, their ears tuned for any sound. It was remarkably quiet. Only the distant wash of the sea and an occasional night birdcall disturbed the tropical hush.

Charlie motioned for her to stay where she was, and crept around the side of the house. Liana waited impatiently, willing him to be cautious, planning what she'd say should they be caught. Finally, he returned. "No guards, missy."

"No guards? How can that be?"

He shrugged and repeated, "No guards."

That was odd. She thought back on what Dale had said: *The guards are not to protect you, but to keep you from learning the truth.* Still, it didn't prove anything. There was a lot riding on this night. If what the reverend said was true, Ace could be in serious danger. But before she could bring herself to believe it, she'd need concrete evidence.

Still, if there were no guards present, this might be easier than she'd hoped.

The house was dark. She led the way to the French doors in back to find them unlocked. She frowned, puzzled. It wasn't the custom in Tahiti to lock doors, but if Philippe was so worried about safety, surely he'd take better precautions.

Once inside, Charlie asked, "What we look for, missy?"

"I don't know. Anything that might implicate the

governor." When he gave her a blank look, she repeated it in French, then reiterated, "To prove he's bad."

"Oh, he bad, missy. He put my uncle in jail."

"What did your uncle do?"

"Well . . . he stole a goat. But not a very big goat."

She smiled with him. "We'll need more than that, I'm afraid. From now on, I'm taking no one's word for anything. I want to see for myself. You look upstairs and come and get me if you find anything suspicious. And be careful."

"Yes, sir, missy."

When he'd gone, Liana turned on the flashlight she'd brought and shielded the light with her hand, looking around the shadows of the living area. She had no idea what to search for. If Philippe was as treacherous as Dale made him out to be, he wasn't likely to leave any incriminating evidence lying around. She went to the library where she'd spent so much of her time while staying here, wondering if he could have hidden anything in one of the hundreds of books. It was too daunting a prospect. She tried to recall the things her father had told her about where people hide things. Often, their choices are obvious.

Look for the obvious.

Her gaze fell on the desk where she knew Philippe took care of his correspondence. A quick perusal through the drawers uncovered nothing of interest. She reached for the bottom drawer. It was locked.

Taking a pin from her hair, she quickly picked the lock and opened the drawer. Inside was a stack of writing paper. She lifted it out and stared in consternation at the empty cavity. Nothing.

But as she was replacing the stack, the bottom pages fluttered, revealing several pages of writing. She took them in hand and read them, one by one. There were five in all, written in bold ink—stumbling drafts of letters she'd seen before.

"God will punish."

"Your redemption is near upon you."

She stood staring at them in shock, realizing the implication. Philippe had written the damning notes. And if he had—

Suddenly she heard a noise from the front hall. She cursed Charlie's carelessness, but in a moment heard the front door open. Then Philippe's voice saying, "Come in, please." And an answering voice she recognized at once: Sloane's.

Her heart hammered in her chest. Where was Charlie? She quickly snapped off the flashlight, took one of the letters, and replaced the stack in the bottom drawer. A light came on in the front hall. Her hands shaking, she worked the pin, trying to relock the drawer. She was too panicked. She had to calm down. She drew a breath and tried again. This time it locked.

"Come into the library and we'll have a drink to celebrate," Philippe was saying.

They were coming in here! Liana glanced about in renewed panic. Another few seconds and she'd be discovered. There was nowhere to hide.

In a rush, she ran to the window and shoved at it. It was stuck. She could hear their footsteps crossing the hall. She tried again, pushing all her weight into it. This time it opened. She succeeded in leaping out into the night just as light flooded the library.

She was about to flee when once again she heard Philippe speak. "How very peculiar. I do not recall leaving this window open."

She flattened herself against the dark outer wall. From the corner of her eye she could see Philippe's head pop out and look around. She held her breath, her pulse racing. She fully intended to tell Sloane everything. But not here. Not in the presence of this evil man. Should Philippe know she was on to him . . .

She didn't even want to think what he might do.

The seconds ticked off in her head as her lungs began to burn. But finally, Philippe withdrew his head and lowered the window.

Like a shot she ran, hiding herself in the foliage as much as possible. Just as she reached the opening in the fence, she heard a sound. She whirled with a gasp. But it was only Charlie. "No luck, missy," he said, breathing as hard as she from having climbed down the side of the house.

Sighing her relief, she hastily folded the letter and tucked it into her blouse. "We've had luck, Charlie. But whether it's good or bad remains to be seen."

When she arrived back at her hotel and was about to go upstairs, the concierge called out to her. "A wire came for you, Miss Wycliffe."

She opened it and glanced at the contents. It was from the *Honolulu Dispatch.* But she didn't have to read it to know that everything Reverend Dale had told her was true.

She found him the next morning at the small church where he was preparing his Sunday sermon. He looked up and read everything in her face.

"Can you forgive me, Reverend?"

He smiled, put down his papers, and came to her, his shoes sounding on the rough wood floor. "There's nothing to forgive, my child. Your loyalty would naturally be to your company and your director."

"I found this hidden in Philippe's desk." She showed him the damning missive.

"So that explains it."

"Which means that a man I love very much could be in danger because of someone he mistakenly thinks is his friend."

"Spencer?"

She nodded. "Who has good reason not to trust anything you say."

His gaze softened in sympathy. "Come. Sit with me."

They settled themselves in the last pew, Liana sitting stiffly straight. "He's arranging for transportation back to Huahine so we can resume filming. I don't have much time. And I don't know what to do."

"Perhaps I can help."

"He told me about his father and what he did to Tehani. He told me everything. Please don't try to tell me it's a lie. He poured his heart out to me. I know acting when I see it, and he wasn't acting."

"He believes it. But it's not the truth."

She sighed in frustration. "Reverend, the time for riddles is past. I came to you because I want to help him. And I can't do that unless I know everything."

"I promised to tell you and I shall. If you love him, you have a right to know."

In the stillness and comfort of the church, he began to tell her a story. As Liana listened, the pieces of the puzzle finally fell into place. For the first time, everything made sense.

When the tale was finished, he added, "But the fact that Spencer has told you his version makes me think he may finally be ready to hear and accept the larger truth. How do things stand with the picture now?"

"We have a few more scenes on Huahine with Hobart, then we move on to Raiatea."

"Raiatea . . . perfect!" He actually looked mischievous.

"What are you thinking?"

He nodded as if unfolding it in his mind. "Your finding this letter of Philippe's has given me an idea. It's risky. There's a good chance Sloane may think you betrayed him. But it just might be the shock he needs. Shall we take the gamble and see?"

"I'll do anything," she vowed.

"Good. I'll need some time to wire Hawaii and have something sent on the next ship. It may take a week or even two. By then you should be well established on Raiatea. There's a place there to which I'd like you to take him. When you hear what I have to say about it, you may think it strange that I would suggest this, being a Christian minister. But there's a power there. I don't understand it; I can't explain it in the context of my beliefs. I can only say I've come to accept it. I know that power exists and I know it's integral to these islands. And this place may be just the right setting for what you have to do."

14

Where are we going?" Ace asked as they followed the narrow path through the thickening rain forest in the late afternoon shadows.

Liana brushed aside some jungle growth and spotted the sign Charlie had left, pointing the way. "A very special place," she told him.

"What do you know about special places on Raiatea?"

"You'll see."

She spotted the purposely bent branch of a pistachio tree and headed off in the direction indicated. But before she'd taken many steps, she felt Ace's hand on her arm. She turned to find him peering at her warily.

"I'm not crazy about surprises," he warned.

She could feel the sweat on her palms. This would either be the most enlightening experience of his life, or it would effectively end any chance she had of sharing a future with him.

They were on the island of Raiatea, twenty-five miles west of Huahine. Nearly three weeks had passed since her meeting with Reverend Dale, weeks in which she'd begun to execute the first steps of their audacious plan.

She'd returned to work, finishing up the rest of the scenes on the Huahine sets before they set out for Raiatea. Suddenly, everything was going smoothly, as if the clearing of the air between them had cleared the way for everything else. The weather was cooperating. A cool trade wind lessened the heat and humidity. The spirits of the company began to rise, most of the tension of the past weeks vanishing. The change in their director was apparent to everyone. They wondered at first what had inspired it, but it soon became evident. By the tender way he took her hand after each take. By his smile when she glanced his way.

It warmed Liana's heart. In his own way, without actually saying so, he'd made a commitment to her and didn't seem to care who knew it. It was so wonderful that often, alone at night in her hotel room, she trembled with trepidation. Because she now had something to lose. She was risking everything she'd ever hoped to have for the sake of helping him to heal. Once it was done, there was a good chance that he'd hate her for her duplicity. But she had to take the risk. If she were to have him, it had to be the whole man, not the wounded shell.

Yet here he was warning her that he didn't like surprises. Having no idea of the immensity of the surprise in store for him.

She took his hand. "Think of it as your Christmas present," she said. "And if you want to give *me* one, give me your trust."

His gaze never left hers. "I don't have a lot of experience with trusting women," he admitted honestly.

"I know. I'm not in the habit of trusting men, either, but I'm trusting you."

She realized only too well how much she was asking of him. *Please let me be doing the right thing.*

It seemed an eternity before he answered. Finally he said, "All right. Since it's your Christmas present, I'll try."

"Good. We're almost there."

They continued their journey through the brush as the sun began to drop low in the west, Liana following the trail Charlie had laid out. Then, stepping through a cluster of Tahitian chestnuts, they came out onto a clearing.

Spreading out before them was a flat, sandy promontory between two bays. A disorderly multitude of rocks covered the sand, as if the area might have once been paved with them. A few lonely ironwood trees had sprouted up here and there like weeds in a garden. There was about the place the feeling of a Roman ruin—decayed grandeur amidst a sprawling, open space situated to offer a spectacular view of the eastern coast of the island. A sense of history and pageantry. The sensation that those who'd come here down through the centuries lingered still.

Off to one side was an enclosure rimmed with huge, squared-off rocks forming a rectangular outer border. Inside, overgrown with tangled vines, was a stone platform that had once served as an altar.

"This is a *marae,* an ancient temple," she told him. "The most sacred temple in all Polynesia. It's called Taputapuatea. *Tapu* means forbidden, right? Europeans changed it to tabu."

"And *tapu-tapu* means doubly forbidden." He was examining his surroundings, clearly wondering why she'd brought him here.

"That's right. Because it's so sacred. This spot is the very heart of all Polynesia, the cultural and spiritual center of all the islands. From here, canoes were sent out to colonize other islands in the Pacific, including Hawaii. In fact, the original name for Raiatea is Havai'i."

"Sacred Island," he murmured.

"Yes. Legend has it that it's the birthplace of the gods. Any marae built in Polynesia had to begin with a stone from this most sacred of maraes."

"I know some of this from living on Hawaii. But why did you bring me here? Why now? You said it had to be today."

"It's from this spot that the purest energy can be felt. The true spirit of Tahiti. There's magic here. Tonight is Christmas Eve, which is special in itself, but it's also the full moon, when the spirits are most active. When you can feel the energy—the magic—most intensely."

"You believe in these—spirits?"

"As a child, I traveled a great deal with my parents. My mother taught me to feel the spirit of place. She said you can learn everything there is to know about a land and its people—intellectually. But until you feel the spirit of the place—the *real* spirit—you'll never understand a thing."

"And what's the spirit of Taputapuatea? The . . . magic?"

"See if you can feel it."

Thoughtfully, he wandered off by himself, stepping from stone to stone, letting his gaze ramble over the large area, lighting here, lingering there, as he strolled, resting on the main altar, roaming beyond the coral wall that protected it from the sea. His back to her, he lingered over the process as Liana watched, her heart pounding rapidly now that the dreaded confrontation was upon her.

Eventually he turned to her with a puzzled expression on his face. Turned to find Reverend Dale standing beside her.

Hidden behind the main altar, he'd stepped out to join Liana when he was sure Sloane's back was turned. Now he stood as she did, still, waiting.

Sloane froze. His shocked expression, as it flicked from the missionary to Liana, altered as a flood of stark emotions passed across his face. Confusion. Comprehension. Bitterness. Anger.

Betrayal.

Liana saw his Herculean effort to control those emotions in the clenching of his fists at his sides. In the straightening of his shoulders before he began the journey back to them, his steps slow, measured, his stance rigid. His gaze of mounting hatred fixed on Dale as he approached.

They stood and let him come.

When he was within speaking distance he stopped, tearing his gaze away with effort to sweep incredulously over Liana. "You'd—do—this—to—me?" he growled. Every word labored, as though his anger, his recognition of her treachery, was too deep for mere histrionics. His pain raw on his face.

It was Reverend Dale who spoke. "Liana brought you here because this has gone on too long. Because she—and I—felt you were ready to hear the truth."

"Truth," Sloane spat out. "You'd choke on the truth."

His voice shook as he said it. But still he was eerily controlled, as if afraid of what might happen should he give vent to his actual feelings. His fists were so tightly clenched that his knuckles showed white beneath his tan. She glanced at the reverend helplessly. *We've lost.*

But Dale faced Sloane's leashed fury serenely. "What you perceive to be the truth is, however well-meant, a lie. I know what you think you saw between your father and Tehani. But you're wrong. I knew your father. I knew Tehani."

"I knew them, too. And I know what I saw."

"You were a child," Dale insisted kindly. "You had no idea what you saw. You witnessed something you weren't prepared to understand and imagined the only thing of which you were capable."

"Did I imagine her screams?"

Dale hesitated. Liana could feel the tension crackle between them. She knew what was coming and unconsciously held her breath.

Finally, with great care, the reverend said, "What you heard, my son, were her cries of pleasure."

The words lashed Sloane like a whip. "You sick, demented—"

"I was Tehani's spiritual counselor. She told me everything. How you saw her and your father . . ."

The color drained from Sloane's face. "She . . . *told* you?"

"She was concerned that you'd misconstrue what was going on. Which you did."

"You expect me to believe she'd go to you—a man of the church—and confess something like . . . *that*?"

The reverend had been standing with his hands behind his back. Now he brought them forward and showed a black, leather-bound book. On the front, in peeling gilt letters, were the initials *B.M.S.*

"It's all here. I'm sure you'll remember that your father, like many of our brethren, kept a daily journal. This is one of the volumes for that critical year. It was in the society's archive in Honolulu. I sent for it."

"I don't believe you."

"I think you'll recognize the handwriting." He held it forth.

Sloane just stared at it. "I won't read it."

Reverend Dale set the journal on the low wall that surrounded the marae. "Read it or don't read it. But the truth is in those pages. Before you read it, I want you to know that your father was a changed man. He saw his mistakes and learned from them. And he influenced me, and others like me, to learn from our mistakes as well. I owe him a great deal. I'm hoping this will help me repay him. If you'd stayed with him longer, instead of running away as you did, you might have seen those changes for yourself. He tried to find you after you'd gone. He died wishing the breach between you could have been mended."

He turned to Liana. "I must go back now while there's still a little light." He took her hand, felt the iciness of it, and gave it a reassuring squeeze. To Sloane he added, "I hope for nothing more than that you may open your mind. And your heart."

With that he was gone. His footsteps crunched on the coral gravel along the path, then died away. Already streaks of orange and violet light were heralding the setting sun.

Sloane didn't even glance after the reverend. He stood staring at the journal as if it were a draft of poison he'd been invited to drink.

The silence stretched between them. He never looked at her. For all she knew, he might have forgotten her existence.

Or chosen to ignore it.

The sun slipped lower. A brief, glorious sunset and then, quite suddenly, it was dark. Still he didn't move.

Liana went behind the altar wall where Charlie had left supplies for the night. She lit one of the tall torches, then took it and stuck it in the ground so its light shone on the journal. Sloane seemed not to notice. He was locked away in a world of his own thoughts, his own torment. Where she couldn't reach him.

"Don't be afraid of the truth," she coaxed. "It can't hurt you. It can only help."

"Truth?" he snarled. "From that villain? Didn't Philippe tell you how he's stealing from his own parishioners? And enslaving them in the process?"

She steeled herself for his wrath. "That morning in Papeete, when you wondered where I was? I followed that man you call a villain because I wanted to know for sure. That *villain* is trying to save these islands."

Carefully, she explained about the pearls and told what Reverend Dale had related about Philippe. When she was finished he said, "This is madness!"

"It's Philippe who's trying to enslave these islands, not Reverend Dale."

Her hand shaking, she retrieved the letter she'd found from her bodice and showed it to him.

"Where did you get this?" he demanded.

"In Philippe's desk drawer. I was there the night you took him to dinner. That's why he came home to find the library window open. I was hiding outside."

He stared at the letter in horror.

"All those guards of Philippe's—they're not there to protect us from the missionaries. There *is* no threat from the missionaries. The guards are there not to keep them locked out, but to keep *us* locked in. So we won't find out what he's really been up to."

She could tell by his face that she'd struck a chord. While it seemed he was looking at her, he was in reality gazing down the road of the past, looking at Philippe's actions in a new light.

She pressed on. "It was my finding this letter that

gave Reverend Dale the idea to send for your father's journal. He went to a great deal of trouble to help us. It wouldn't hurt to read it, would it?"

The book still lay where Dale had left it, inanimate, but seeming to radiate a life of its own. Determined to disregard its summons, Ace turned his back on it.

She left him. For a long interval, he continued to struggle with his own mind. But finally, reluctantly, he gave in to the inevitable and picked up the journal. Then he took the torch and carried it to the edge of the sea. Sticking it in the sand, he sat beneath it and slowly opened the book that would help decide the course of the rest of his life.

Liana made a little sanctuary for herself, spreading out the colorful sheets of tapa cloth Charlie had left for them, surrounding them on four corners with glowing torches, unpacking the hamper of food. She drank deeply of the wine, her nerves throbbing, her discomfiture growing. She caught the flare of Ace's lighter as he lit a cigarette, then turned the page.

What was he thinking?

I have to believe in him.

She poured another glass of wine and took it, with the bottle, across the long expanse of clearing, to him. He sat with the light from the torch spilling onto the page he read, the water lapping serenely just inches from his feet. She held the glass out to him but he didn't even glance up. She fought to calm her breathing. Had she lost him because she'd sought to set him free? Placing the bottle in the sand beside him, she put the glass in his hand. He drank absently, his hand poised between sips as if his mind were too occupied to notice what he was doing. Silently, she left him.

As time passed, the moon rose high, a full, frosty orb that silvered the sand, the sea, the sacred stones, seeming to cast upon them rays of filtered, benevolent light. The only sounds were the kiss of the sea upon the sand, the whisper of the breeze, the occasional call of one night bird to another, seeking a mate in the sweet and sultry night.

She knew when he was finished reading because she saw him set aside the book. Still, he sat where he was beneath the beacon of the torch, knees bent, elbows resting upon them as he sipped the wine she'd brought him and gazed out at the moon-drenched horizon.

She had to gulp down her own wine to keep her impatience curbed. Everything rested on the next few minutes. It was all she could do to keep from jumping up and running to him. To shake him out of his reverie and beg him to speak his mind. But of course it wouldn't do. He had to come to her.

At last he stood stiffly, picking up the torch, and made his way back to her, journal and wine in hand. She'd been lying on her side, head propped in her palm, but now she rose up on her knees and watched him come, aware of the flickering golden flame of the torches, highlighting her face with its unashamed hope and fear.

When he reached the edge of the tapa sheets he stopped, suspended in his own thoughts, looking at but not seeing her. The torment had been washed clean from his face. In its place was an expression of profound bewilderment.

She said nothing. Let him drop to the blanket before her. Let him find his own words, in his own way. Knowing all that he'd just read, but waiting to hear it from him.

He began haltingly, as if still struggling with what he'd learned. Running his finger absently along the rim of his wineglass as if needing some small action to make it easier to speak.

"My father . . . I always thought he took Tehani against her will . . . that he seized her as a possession . . . his dirty little secret . . . But he loved her. I didn't want to believe it—I never *would* have. But the way he writes about her . . . it isn't sordid or dictatorial. He writes as a man who could never quite bring himself to believe his good fortune in having such a woman. He fought his love for her for as long as he could. He knew he was renouncing all he stood for by falling in love with her. He hid it from his colleagues in the B.M.S. Decided never to see her again. It was Tehani—" He nearly choked on the words. "Tehani who went to *him.* She knew he needed a governess and made certain she was the one chosen. Even then he was determined to avoid her. It was her subtle advances that convinced him. *Hers.* She let him know from the minute she was in our house that she wanted him. He tried to fight it off, but finally found himself so helplessly in love with her that he—what did he say? He had to *express* it. So he finally submitted and it was . . ."

"What?" she prompted.

He gripped the glass. "Wonderful, my father said. And as the months passed, it was more and more wonderful. He was always concerned about me, so he hid it from me. He wanted to marry Tehani—he says so repeatedly—but marriage wasn't a prerequisite for love in her culture and she didn't feel the need. She thought it would spoil their love if they married to satisfy the expectations of others. At first he felt guilty about breaking all the Christian conventions he'd been espousing. But as the intensity of his lovemaking with Tehani increased, he . . ."

Again he stopped and again she pressed him. "He what?"

He turned a blank gaze on her. "The way he puts it, it was all so different from what I thought. She must have instigated all of it. That night . . . when I saw them together . . . she must have asked him to tie her up. Because she . . . enjoyed it. He doesn't actually say so, but he keeps talking about her 'playful encouragement,' he calls it. He refers to the games they played, says they brought him out of his prison. Says they *liberated* him."

"Liberated," she repeated, savoring the promise of it on her tongue.

"He says her natural and accepting attitudes about love invalidated so much of his life. Laid waste to his whole idea of changing natives; as it turned out, they possessed more wisdom than he did. He says that instead of foisting one-sided views on them, he instead learned from them. About what love—including love of God—was all about. He says his love for Tehani changed him forever."

He understands, she thought.

"So Dale was right," he continued. "It *was* a lie. My whole vision of Tehani as someone good and innocent . . . she wasn't either of those things. All the years I spent revering her—wanting to avenge her—and all the time it was *she* who provoked it all."

"Provoked?" Her hopes came crashing in around her. She saw herself as from above, kneeling pitifully before him, waiting . . . her future hanging in the balance, praying for the golden words that would transform her life—waiting, in essence, for him to rescue her from her purgatory. Like one of the damsels in distress she so despised.

In a rage, she snatched the wineglass from him and

flung it so it shattered against the low wall. "You pig-headed bastard!"

He jerked, shocked out of his contemplative rumination, darting his startled gaze toward the smashed glass then back to her face again. Staring at her as if she'd now, truly, lost her mind.

15

She was so outraged that she couldn't stay kneeling before him. Shoving herself off the tapa, she stood trembling with anger. Her shadow, cast by the torch behind her, engulfed him.

"What's wrong?" he asked, sincerely at a loss.

She glared down at him. "Do you think I went to all this trouble—put myself on the line like this—plotted to bring you here—risked your everlasting *hatred*—all so the only thing you'd get out of this is that Tehani was a scheming little *whore?*"

He just stared at her, too startled to speak.

"Did you understand *anything* your father said?" she cried in exasperation. "Or are you so consumed by your own delusions that nothing penetrates? You're a man of vision, for God's sake! But is it only *your* vision that's allowed? Is everyone else's vision brushed aside like so many pesky mosquitoes?" When he continued to stare at her, she sighed irritably and pushed on. "How can such a brilliant man be such an idiot? Tehani wasn't good and she wasn't bad. She just *was*. And who are you to judge her anyway? Are you so perfect that no action of yours could ever be wrongly judged by others? Because that's what you've done. You've judged her wrongly. *Both* times."

She turned her back on him, so discouraged she wanted to weep. *All for nothing . . .*

But then he said softly, "I don't understand."

And suddenly, through the craze of anger and incredulity, she realized that it was true. He didn't.

It seemed to her that the night breeze stirred. The hostility drained from her. Instead of listening to the recriminations of her own mind, she listened to the breeze. To the earth. To the sea. And felt, once again, the true spirit of Polynesia flow into her. To fill her, consume her, overflow from her. She lost track of the seconds as they ticked by. She just stood listening. Feeling. The music that was Tahiti.

And suddenly she knew she could get through to him. That somehow, in *this* mystical night, she'd been empowered by the spirits and shown the way. As if she'd been called to this hallowed ground because only here, only tonight, could she work the miracle. She'd been granted a window in time through which she could step, leading him through with a gentle hand.

The knowledge caused her to tingle with new awareness. It seemed to her that suddenly she was one with the goddess of love, sharing the munificence of her silver light. That in this moment of this night, she was the essence of all the women who had ever lived and learned and loved.

She dropped down beside him on the tapa and took both his hands in hers. "Ace, listen to me. Tehani wasn't a saint and she wasn't a sinner. She was just a *woman*. She loved your father as a woman. Not grudgingly, not in return for favors, not because it was her duty. Because it was her joy. You weren't completely wrong about her. Her love of sex with your father *was* innocent and child-like and natural. Because it carried within it no guile."

"That still doesn't explain what I saw. Or . . . thought I saw."

"Reverend Dale said your perceptions were based on a lie. But the lie wasn't about whether or not the missionaries were evil. It wasn't about the sort of woman Tehani was. It wasn't about your father's intentions or actions. The *real* lie was your expectations of women. You built this fantasy in your mind that no woman could possibly live up to. She doesn't exist because she's not based on what women really are. You think no good woman could enjoy making love. You've thought of sex for so long as something dirty, and women who love it as being cheap. But, knowing now that some of your perceptions were skewed, what if you did something really novel? What if you revised everything you once thought was true? What if you began to view sex as a creative expression—a *celebration* of love?"

"A celebration . . ." he repeated, as if he'd never considered it before. "What you're suggestiong . . . would mean letting go of everything I've ever believed to be true."

"But those things you believed were instilled in you by your father, and he ultimately rejected those things. If you hadn't run away from home, you might have seen this on your own. But now you have the next best thing, your father's own words, attesting to the fact that those beliefs are empty and false. All you need is the courage to see that and let these things go. I read somewhere once that whenever we learn something, it seems at first as if we've lost something. But once we let go of those chains, we're free."

He glanced about him, as if seeking guidance from the night, before returning his gaze to her. "How do I do that?"

"Are you sure you *want* to?"

His hands still in hers, he pulled her to her feet. "You said it yourself. You went to a great deal of trouble and risk to get me here. And I don't just mean today. You've fought me tooth and nail every step of the way. But you weren't really fighting me, were you? You were fighting *for* me."

Tears welled in her eyes.

"No one has ever cared enough about me to go to that much trouble. To risk so much for my sake, with no guarantee of anything in return. No one has ever—loved me that much."

Choking on the words, she said, "You're right. No one ever *has* loved you as much as I do."

His gaze softened on her face. He wiped the tears from her cheeks with the pad of his thumb. "Come," he said with the assurance of command in his tone. "Let's show you that I'm worth the effort, shall we?"

She beamed. Suddenly she felt like a girl again. Standing at the beginning, on the threshold of discovery, with no expectations. Just waiting with baited breath to see what would come. Lost in the blue fire of his eyes.

"What do we do?" he asked.

Quickly, she gathered her thoughts. "They have a ritual here that will help us put all of this in the past. First you write on a piece of paper everything you want to get rid of. All destructive emotions, harmful habits, unhappy memories, self-doubts. Misconceptions. Anything and everything that you want to disappear. No matter how small, or how many pages it takes." She reached into the hamper and withdrew the writing implements she'd asked Charlie to bring. "I'll do it, too. Just write for yourself. When we're done, we're going to burn them. No one will ever see what you write."

They sat side by side and made their lists. As he wrote, occasionally pausing to formulate his thoughts, Liana was seized by a wave of curiosity and the urge to glance at his paper and see what he was writing. But this ritual was private, and to peek would be profane.

When they were done, she took one of the torches and led him to the main *marae.* "Now we burn them. As we do, the spirits take them and we're liberated from everything we wrote down. A clean break from the past. But you have to believe. You can't do it halfheartedly or skeptically. In order for the catharsis to work, you must have complete faith. This isn't a game. This is sacred."

He nodded his understanding. Together they knelt before the marae in the gleam of the full moon. She held her papers to the flame of the torch, then passed it to him and he did the same. As one, they laid the burning pages on the altar, watching them blacken and curl, following the flight of orange sparks as they drifted skyward then disappeared into the night. Finally nothing but ashes remained.

He took her hand. "Can you forgive me for being such a—what was it?—pigheaded bastard?"

She smiled but said seriously, "There aren't many men who can admit they're wrong. Or that they need help understanding why. They think it's weakness, when really it takes a great deal of strength. But to do something about it—to actually change because of it—that takes true courage."

"I *am* going to change," he vowed. "I know that everything I've believed is wrong, because I was so wrong about you. I knew it that night when I first realized you loved me. It hit me as if I'd been shot—the way only the truth can. I knew then that I'd been a complete idiot. I didn't even know why. But what you've said tonight has made it clear to me. I held you up to this impossible ideal, and never saw what you were offering. Never understood that—frankly—"

He broke off, searching for the right words.

"Righteousness isn't much bloody fun?"

His smile was self-deprecating, and all the more charming for the humility it contained. "I never thought of sex as being fun."

His manly helplessness melted her heart. "How could you?" she asked gently. "Your father taught you that passion was evil. So when you saw him with Tehani, you jumped to the only conclusion you could. But the glory of life is that we can learn to see things in a whole new way. Your father did and Reverend Dale did. If you want to enough . . . if you're sick enough of feeling miserable . . . you can, too."

He mulled this over. "I *am* sick of it. I *want* to change. But . . ." He paused, looking at her. "Will you help me?"

A warm breeze sighed, rustling the leaves of the trees, flickering the torchlight. Again, it seemed to her that she heard the whispers of the night, of the consecrated stones, of the moon and stars and sea, guiding her. "Come with me."

They stood and walked slowly hand in hand. The whispers were all around her now. The languorous breeze moved over her, through her, touching her like a lover's caress. Making her aware of every movement, every brush of her clothing against her skin, every graze of her hair against her cheek.

As they walked she said, "When I was twelve I went

to China with my parents. It was the last trip we took together. Did you know the Chinese character for crisis is the same as the character for opportunity? You've faced a crisis, but you've also been given an opportunity. To relive that scene in your mind. To see it, not as a child, but as a man. To be happy that Tehani and your father found a rare love. And to realize that Tehani asked for what she did that night because it was *fun*. Because it added spice to her love."

He stopped and took her shoulders in his hands, turning her to face him. "I love you, Liana. I always did. I knew I loved you in Paris. But it wasn't fun. It was torture. It scared the hell out of me. It scares me now."

"That's because you were trying to control it. And the more you tried, the more it controlled *you*. You've held yourself from me with an iron hand, only coming to me when you felt your demons eating you alive, and you had to let off steam. But even then you were trying to control things. Your feelings, me . . . everything."

"I couldn't give in to it."

"Why? Love isn't something you can regulate the way you direct a picture. It just *is*. What if, for once, you let down your guard? Stop trying to manage it. Just let your feelings take you where they will. Without judgment or censure."

"How do I do that?"

"By realizing—by *feeling*—that everything two people do to express their love is beautiful and good. That it doesn't demean us, it elevates us. Do you honestly think that anything I do to show my love for you could be shameful or wrong?"

He grinned sheepishly. "Not anymore."

She led him back toward the flickering torches that formed a square of platinum light around the tapa sheets. Once there, she sat down upon them and pulled him down beside her.

"You were afraid of me . . . of loving me. But what, exactly, were you so afraid of?"

He seemed surprised, as if he'd never asked himself before. But as his gaze roamed her face, he found the answer. "I didn't want it to be ordinary between us."

She smiled tenderly. "Darling, don't you know it could never be ordinary between us? We were made for each other. Every touch, every kiss, everything we do is extraordinary. Because no one can satisfy us the way we can satisfy each other. On every level. That's why my body feels as if it was made for you. Because it was."

"Do you really believe that? That we're made for each other?"

"I knew it in Paris."

He smiled. "Just like that?"

"No. When you rejected me, you made me doubt it. I cursed myself for being such a fool. To believe something so ridiculous. But it was true. No matter how we've tried to deny it, we belong together. Nothing can be done about it. It's as if—" She glanced at the hamper by her side, where the paper they'd used was fluttering in the breeze. "As if you and I had been made from a single sheet of paper that was torn in two. Only when we put those pieces together do we have a whole."

Mulling it over, he said, "After tonight, I don't know much of anything. I just know I don't want to lose you."

"If I have anything to say about it, you never will."

"I want to believe that."

"Then open yourself up. Don't think about it. Let the spirit of this place tell you what's true."

He looked at the marae where once pilgrims had come to worship. "In this temple?"

"It's true, this is the most sacred spiritual temple.

But, for the Polynesians, the spiritual and physical are closely linked. Physical love was often used as a form of worship—as a way of attaining oneness with the gods. For hundreds of years, supplicants would come here and offer themselves in sexual rites that celebrated the gods of love. Reverent. Joyous. Unashamed. It was all about the beauty of the human body and the privilege of sharing it with another. *That's* the true spirit of Tahiti. That's why Tahitian women met foreign sailors with no thought to covering their breasts. There was no shame in sharing one's self—only joy. That's what happened to your father. He yielded to the intoxication of the islands and found that it was pure and perfect, that guilt had no place here. *That's* really why Tahiti is called the Island of Love. That's the gift Tehani gave him. The Chinese would say it's the balancing of the yin and yang—the female and male energies. The two separate energies coming together to create a balanced whole. Without one, the other is incomplete. Like us." She paused, then added, "Maybe the torture we felt came from not accepting something that was obvious from the start."

She caught his flash of comprehension. "Lie back," she suggested. "Close your eyes and see if you can feel that spirit. Let it speak to you in its own way. Just see what happens. Let it take you on a voyage of discovery."

She did just that. She suddenly felt drained from talking. She wanted to just turn off her mind, to float seamlessly as on a soothing wave, to lull herself into absence. Absence of thought, emotion, fear. Emptiness was what she sought. She'd done all she could. The rest was up to him.

But now that she'd said her piece, the old fear crept back into her heart, making it ache with dread. She'd said they belonged together. But was it just that she wanted it to be so? All her life, she'd sought the sense of belonging she'd felt with her parents as a child, that almost-forgotten comfort of being loved for herself alone. Of being held and cherished for no other reason than that she was adored. Now, she knew, she wanted to belong to him. But could wishing make it so? Could he set aside the scars of the past and be reborn? Accept the love she had to offer, as unconventional and fearsome as that love might seem? Or had she, once again, merely set herself up for colossal rejection? A rejection that at this stage, she knew, would leave scars that couldn't heal.

But it was *his* scars she sought to heal. She felt his struggle and his pain. And she knew if she could take his distress upon herself, she gladly would. If she could absorb it all, to free him from it . . . even if she suffered as a result . . .

She prayed to all the spirits that seemed to linger in the shadows. *Please help me take away his pain. . . .*

She heard the dry rasp of palm fronds on the ancient stones as the warm breeze stirred. Behind her closed lids, she could sense the brief flare of torchlight. The sea beyond lapped against the embracing sand. And then the breeze died, as suddenly as it had come, and all was still.

And in that stillness she heard his breath beside her. The hasty intake of air gentled by degrees until he began to breathe deeply, slowly. She matched her breath to his, willing the pounding of her heart to find a peaceful rhythm. Drawing in the breath he exhaled so it became her own, mentally absorbing, with each new breath, more of his distress, more of his fear. *Give it all to me,* she beseeched him silently. Surrender . . . The word sprang to her mind like a mantra. *Surrender* . . .

She felt him shift beside her, but she didn't move, didn't want to see what might be revealed in his face. As he leaned toward her, she caught his scent. Warm. Musky. Mingling with the salty tang of the sea.

And then she felt his mouth on her forehead, imparting a gentle kiss. His lips soft, his kiss as delicate as the brush of a butterfly's wing. They lingered only fleetingly, but in that time she felt her love for him shudder through her, filling her, consuming her, until the force of it was so great, so unbearably sweet, she felt she couldn't contain it all. Swamped by emotion, she felt the rise of tears at the back of her throat.

He kissed her again with heart-melting tenderness. The back of each eyelid. The tip of her nose. Her cheek. Her chin. She couldn't move.

Then she felt his hands opening her clothes. As he did, he continued to trail kisses along her body, in the wake of his hands. The hollow of her throat. The arch of a shoulder. The breeze touched her naked breasts and she shivered. But in an instant, his mouth was on her, warm, moist. Tasting of her flesh. Flicking his tongue over a nipple until it hardened in his mouth. Touching her now as if he'd never touched a woman before. Not timid or self-conscious, but with extravagant appreciation, as if exploring a treasure he esteemed beyond measure. As if each touch, each ardent kiss, was a discovery all its own. Paying tribute to her with masterful hands and scorching tongue.

Reverently, he took her hand and pressed it to his lips. She drew a ragged breath, striving desperately to fight back the tears that threatened to spill from her tightly sealed eyes. He moved lower and lower still, each touch a worshipful caress. Without realizing how it happened, she was naked, her body radiating the soft glow of flickering flame, his lips relishing her flat belly, the pliable curve of her hip. And then he was running his hands up her legs with loving strokes, parting them with a gentleness akin to devotion, opening her to his eyes. She felt his tongue at her inner thigh and a wave of sumptuous desire tingled up her spine.

He kissed and licked and nipped, moving inexorably toward the heart of her need. He parted the lips with his fingers and his mouth descended on her, finding her core, exploring it with such exquisite ardor that her rush of emotion spilled over and she began to cry.

She'd never cried while making love before. But she wanted so desperately, with all her heart and soul, to ease his pain, to drain it from him and replace it with the balm of her love. Hot tears bathed her cheeks, even as she tried to still their flow. She had to stop. This was the first time he'd come to her like this, openly, willingly, with all barriers and defenses dissolved. As vulnerable as she. What would he think if he found her blubbering like a baby? She put a hand to her mouth to muffle the sobs that wracked her body.

He moved away. She thought at first that he'd noticed her crying and was distressed. Then she heard the whisper of cloth against skin, and his mouth was on her again. But this time, as he lowered himself, his erection jutted up against her mouth. Velvet and steel. Smelling intoxicatingly of sex. With a gasp, she opened her lips and took him in, feeling him swell at the touch of her tongue. And as they feasted on each other, their bodies fused in timeless veneration, a burst of joy drove away her tears. All was forgotten as a ripple of sensual delight coursed like heated wine through her veins. She felt in the shared giving of pleasure a communication so deep, so profound, that she knew at last where she belonged.

He stirred again, turning himself so he faced her now, covering her trembling body with his own. His skin was rugged and thrillingly masculine against her yielding female flesh. Taking her face in his hands, he said in a husky whisper, "You're achingly beautiful."

She lifted her lashes and saw his beloved face in the honeyed gleam of the surrounding torches. Reflecting back to her all of the adoration she felt inside. Appreciating her as he'd never allowed himself before. She saw the acceptance—the celebration—she'd so desperately coveted. And knew it was he who was really beautiful.

Her heart bursting, she pleaded breathily, "Kiss me."

He obliged. As his mouth met hers, she knew this was what she'd been waiting for all her life. A blinding kiss that stole her consciousness as it stole her breath. A kiss that merged their souls. She wrapped her arms about him, pulling him closer, as she felt his hand between her thighs. His tongue, playing with hers, caused her to shiver with desire. Succulent longing combined with fulfillment so intense that her senses roiled. Against his hand, she was wet with unquenchable need. She felt deliciously juicy inside, felt herself open and blossom beneath the warm radiance of his sun. Every nerve and fiber throbbed, gushed, burst forth like a storm-swollen river crashing through a dam. Shuddering with heat, she drowned in his kiss, molding her body to his until she felt that they were one. Waves of feral love swept her upward in an ever-tightening spiral. Panting into his mouth, their breaths indistinguishable, her moans came fierce and wild. Her loins convulsed in shock waves of shameless, unapologetic lust. Hungry . . . ravenous . . . instatiable . . . Wanting it to never end. And then delicious shivers until her heart-swell of passion exploded and she came gasping into his mouth.

He gentled her, stroking her hair. But she heard the wonder in his voice as he said, his mouth at her ear,

"You're the only woman who has ever come while kissing me."

Her flesh tingling, she murmured with panting breath, "No woman has ever loved kissing you as much as I do."

He laid his cheek against hers as if savoring the words, his tenderness unbearably sweet. But even as he did, she felt his erection leap against her stomach. He kissed her lips, briefly now, and pushed himself up, positioning himself between her out-spread legs. Taking her knees in his hands, he thrust them back. She felt him against her, stiff as iron against her dewy flesh. Entering her slowly, luxuriating in each sensation as she welcomed him inside. And for a breathless instant, he held himself there, imbedded deep within her. As if allowing himself the luxury of experiencing the soundless communion that flowed between them like a physical force. As if the pleasure, as their bodies became one, was too intense to move.

She felt more attuned to him than she ever had. As though, in the act of entering her, he'd truly become a part of her, and she of him. As though joined together they'd become more than the sum of their parts. Feeling it deeply, she wanted to know if it was the same for him.

"How does it feel?" she asked.

He stayed still for a moment more, his pulsing erection fitting as if it had been fashioned just for her. Taking a slow, rasping breath, he whispered, "Like coming home."

It was what she'd known he would say.

"Kiss me," she sighed, the words sounding to her ears like a heartfelt plea.

He bent and kissed her again, pushing her legs back so that he was lodged even deeper. She gasped just before his mouth found hers. And then he was moving, thrusting into her with mounting desire. Banishing the emptiness she'd carried like a cross. Completing her. Making her whole.

She understood through this union that miracles did exist. And that she'd been granted one in the form of this extraordinary man.

16

They lay in each other's arms through the night, feeling the peace and quiet steal over them. Feeling that they were truly one. No more secrets. No more conflict. No more separation.

For Liana it was heaven. But the next morning when she awoke and saw Ace's face, so peaceful in slumber, illuminated by the first gentle rays of the sun, she felt a glimmer of trepidation. What if last night hadn't been real? What if he'd merely been swept away on a tide of passion? Was the mana of this place so powerful that it could change the entire course of a man's life in a single evening of revelation?

As if he felt her staring at him, even in sleep, Ace's eyes fluttered open. Liana's heart beat faster, wondering what his first words would be. Would they repudiate all he'd promised the night before?

Sleepily, he murmured, "Merry Christmas."

"So far, it's been the best Christmas of my life."

"I don't have a present for you, except . . ." He gave a sheepish smile. "Except that . . . I love you."

He said it as if it was a confession he'd wrested from the depths of his soul. She laughed and, when he blinked surprise, told him, "It's no big secret, you know. I've known it since the night you told me about your past."

"You have?" His face, usually so guarded, broke into a grin.

He reached up to cup her head and bring it closer for a kiss. His mouth locked with hers, he made love with her again, showing her the depth of his feelings without the use of words. Banishing the remainder of her fears.

When she was once again lying in his arms, gazing up at the freshening morning sky, she teased, "I was afraid I'd wake up this morning to find that the prince had turned back into the frog."

"Your sorcery is too strong for me."

"My sorcery, as you call it, just set the stage for you to hear your father's truth."

Serious now, he said, "If my father could be changed by the love of a woman, how could I not at least try? You wouldn't believe what a pompous, self-righteous son of a bitch he was. Always quoting the Bible's fire-and-brimstone passages to scare the hell out of everyone around him. It wasn't so much that he believed he was an instrument of God. I honestly think in his twisted mind, he thought God was *his* instrument. That God meted out punishment or compassion at my father's decree. But Tehani changed him. The man who wrote that journal wasn't the man who raised me. I can see now that he'd changed, that he was trying to mend the rift between us. But I didn't understand it at the time, because I saw him the way he'd always been. We don't expect people to change, and if they try to tell us they have, we don't believe them, do we? When Tehani died, I thought he'd killed her and I ran away. Stowed away on the first boat to the mainland. He died within the year. I hated him so much that when I got word of his death, I didn't even go home. Now it seems it was he, not Tehani, who died of a broken heart."

She felt awash with pride. "Reverend Dale told me your father didn't just change personally. He also helped change the direction of the Boston Missionary Society to a more enlightened point of view. Once he realized his mistakes, he did everything he could to make up for them. Today the Hawaii missions are completely different than they were. They're a force that's trying to preserve Hawaiian culture, not destroy it. All because of your father, and the things Tehani helped him understand. Reverend Dale is trying to live up to your father's legacy, continuing his work here. That's why the French hate him so much."

"Which brings us to Philippe."

He said it so tonelessly that she couldn't tell what he was thinking. "What *about* Philippe?"

"My old friend Philippe," he said bitterly. "Who listened so sympathetically when I drunkenly blurted out the pathetic story of my past . . . who after the war followed my career with such relish . . . who wrote me all those glowing letters about Tahiti . . . who said he could open up the doors here that would allow me to make the movie of my life . . . who played on my mistrust of missionaries to make damned sure I'd never listen to Dale . . . It would be so easy to just take a gun and shoot Philippe. But that's not good enough. There's a better way out of this."

She turned on her side. "What are you thinking?"

The bitterness had been washed from his face. "You've really changed me. I feel like . . . I don't know . . . like I won't ever be the same again. You've given me such a gift. But it isn't enough to tell you that. I'm going to show you."

She grinned saucily. "I thought that's what you'd just done."

"I'm serious. We're going to make a different film, with a different vision. Not my vision, but *ours*. We'll make it together, every step of the way. A labor of love that will say to the world, 'This is what we are and what we believe. This is the true expression of us.' We're going to make the kind of film you always wanted it to be."

She was so startled by his words that she sat up straight. "What do you mean?"

"We're going to make a film that's the exact opposite of what Philippe expects. Instead of what we've got now, we're going to tell a story that reflects the truth. How the limited vision of the missionary was changed and expanded by the love of this remarkable woman—not my misconception, but the *real* Tehani. Instead of morbid and downbeat, it will be beautiful and inspirational. And buried within the story will be Dale's vision for saving these islands. It will glorify him and what he wants to do with the pearl industry. We can do all of this using what we've already shot. We'll scrap the rape and replace it with the most honestly passionate love scene Hollywood has ever seen. We'll come up with a transcendent ending and rewrite what we haven't yet shot."

"He'll try to stop us."

"He won't know. No one need know except those necessary to the scenes: you, Tommy, Farnsworth, and myself. As far as Philippe is concerned, we're making his picture just as before."

"So we don't confront Philippe?"

"We'll assume he has spies planted and be careful. No crew, no extras, no musicians, no cameraman but Tommy. No legionnaires. We'll let it be known that we're shooting the more intimate scenes and want privacy for your sake. If Philippe comes around, we treat him exactly the same as we always have. We get the footage we need, then get the hell out of here. Once we're out of his reach, there's nothing he can do."

"Will you be satisfied with that? Will it be revenge enough for you?"

"If this picture is released in all the capitals of the world and has the opposite effect of what Philippe wants, and if it's our vision, that will be more than enough."

"You really *have* changed."

"Before last night, I probably would have killed the bastard. But it doesn't matter now. I have a future now that I can care about. And I want to spend that future with you. There's been too much wasted time between us. From now on, the most important thing in my life is you, and our working together to express ourselves on film."

She couldn't believe what she was hearing. "That's what I've always wanted. But I've never had the chance."

"You're going to have that chance from now on. You remember that story you told me about your mother's garden? I wasn't sure I understood your point at the time, but I do now. That's exactly what I was doing. I thought I was using this film to tell the truth. But I was only yanking at weeds without getting to the core. I was met with pain and resistance every step of the way because my vision was a lie. The whole point of art is to find the truth of the piece and be faithful to that truth. Otherwise, what's the point? Now that I know what it is, we're going to express that truth. And make a wonderful picture in the process."

Elated, she threw herself at him so they tumbled backward together. Wrapping her arms about him, she rained impulsive kisses across his face, his shoulders, his chest.

When he could finally surface, he rolled her over so that he was lying on top of her. Brushing back her hair with both hands, he studied her face. "I just realized what it was."

"What was?"

"Why you reminded me of Tehani."

She sobered. "Why?"

"You don't resemble her exactly. You're not Polynesian. But there's something about you . . . something about the way you seem to light up from within . . . the way you look so pure, yet exude sensuality from every pore—I never realized it until just now, but *that's* what I saw in Tehani. That's why I couldn't accept any other actress but you to play her. Because I've only seen that quality in one other person. You."

"And just what is that quality?"

"An innocence that comes from a childlike joy of . . . love."

"Of *sex,* you mean."

"Okay, of sex."

"I just love a man who can admit he's wrong."

"I admit it," he said with a laugh. "You've made me see the light."

"Then give me one more Christmas present. Kiss me and show me you mean it."

She reached for him but instead he took her hand and pressed the palm to his lips. "Thank you," he said simply.

* * *

In a burst of creative energy, they returned to Uturoa, Raiatea's sleepy administrative center on the northern tip of the island. Questions about their mysterious disappearance were explained by the announcement that they'd found a fabulous location they wanted to integrate into the film. Instead of shooting the climax as planned, a skeleton crew would return with them to this location. The rest of the company could relax in the comfort of Uturoa over New Year's. Tommy was stalled while Sloane and Liana holed up in his tiny hotel room putting down the specifics of the new scenes on paper. When they'd finished, they called Tommy in and spread the idea before him.

He listened, taking in the glow of the effervescent couple, then said, "You're both nuts."

Unperturbed, Sloane told him about the events of the last two days: Reverend Dale, his father's journal, the awakening from a lifetime of delusion. But the explanation did nothing to assuage Tommy's doubts.

"But all our plans . . . Philippe—"

"Philippe is a scoundrel."

"I don't believe it. He's our friend!"

"He's just been using us," Sloane told him. "The man is a monumental villain."

Tommy's eyes flicked to Liana, as if wondering if she'd cast some spell upon her director. She answered his unspoken question with a serene smile. "It's all true." She touched his arm. "Don't fight us, Tommy. Join us. We can make this picture into so much more than we ever dreamed when we left Hollywood."

"You've always trusted me," Sloane urged. "Don't stop now. I've never been more sure of anything in my life."

Tommy removed his glasses and wiped them with his

shirttail, as if weighing the pros and cons of the new concept. Finally he said, "Well, Ace, no one's ever been able to tell you anything."

Sloane clasped his shoulder in a gesture of camaraderie and said, "Then let's make a movie."

The rest of the company was happy with the hiatus. Hobart, told of the new direction, was delighted to once again be playing a noble character. "I always knew such a rogue was beneath my talents!" he proclaimed. Tommy apparently set aside his doubts; he became so enthusiastic that he came up with new ideas to augment their plan, ways of capturing the mood they wanted in inventive ways that had never been tried before. To facilitate this new vision, he sent one of his assistants back to Papeete to gather some filters he'd left behind that were more conducive to the aura of sensuality that would permeate every shot of the redesigned sequences.

On New Year's Eve, Ace and Liana slipped away together on donkeys, loading a third mount with a camera, generator, lights, and film. Wandering along the coast, they found a particularly picturesque cove where the beach was ringed with palms and a profusion of flowering brush, the leaves varied in size and texture, offering a rich tapestry to dazzle the camera's eye. There, over the course of the afternoon and into the night, Ace filmed a series of intimate shots himself. Liana walking barefoot in the sand, her nude body glistening, holding in her outspread arms a gauzy see-through pareu that fluttered in the breeze, alternately revealing and disguising her so that she appeared like a mirage. Flashes of her naked form through the fringe of leaves, the glimpses so fleeting, it was hard to discern if what was being seen was real. Swimming naked by moonlight through a school of fish, the ripples of the water distorting her image like a floating phantom. His camera saw her now as he did, with a loving, impassioned eye.

At midnight, they drank a toast together to the new year. A new concept, new dream, new love. It was the first time in years that either had faced the turning of the year with a sense of hope. Then, as the camera lay forgotten, and the burros grazed among the leaves, they made love in the starlit sand.

When the filters arrived, Sloane and Liana hiked back to Taputapuatea with Tommy and Hobart, accompanied only by the donkeys to carry the equipment. For three days, they filmed what would be the love scenes in a frenzy of passionate creativity, re-creating in the exquisite pantomime of film the miracle they'd experienced. Hour after hour, Liana and Hobart lost themselves in their roles as two people discovering the birth of passion in the midst of the sacred shrine. Even Farnsworth became intoxicated with the special spirit of the place, surrendering his ego and turning in a performance that communicated a transcendent passion. A reluctant Adam melting before the unashamed exuberance of his Eve. Sloane's hypnotic voice weaving the spell, laying down a path for them to follow, a song for which their contribution was the harmony.

For two more weeks they moved about the island, out of touch with the rest of the company, filming the scenes that would radically change the concept of the picture. Liana worked as she never had before, feeding off it, energized by it, needing neither sleep nor food. She hummed to the tuning fork of her lover's voice, until Farnsworth disappeared and the scenes became theirs, hers and Sloane's, an ode to their love and unity.

The atmosphere, in fact, was so highly charged, so intensely focused that when the intruders came, it was difficult to adjust. The armed legionnaires that flooded their Eden didn't seem real. It wasn't until the soldiers parted and Philippe strode angrily toward them that they began to realize the extent of the threat that now faced them.

"Ever the hero, *mon ami,*" Philippe greeted with a sneer. "Fighting the forces that oppose you. It becomes a habit, does it not? A habit that needs to be broken."

Cautiously, Sloane scanned the perimeter of the clearing, gauging the extent of the danger. The legionnaires outnumbered them fifteen to one, and each carried a carbine. An overwhelming force. Stiffly, he said, "I seem to recall a little matter of an agreement between us. No interference from the government. Your presence here smacks of interference, *mon ami.*"

"Oh, come now. The cat is out of the bag, so to speak. I think we both know where we stand. There need be no pretense between such old and trusted comrades."

"Trust. An odd word, coming from you. While I was trusting in the bond of old friendship, you, apparently, were trusting that you could dupe me forever."

Philippe shrugged philosophically. "It was a good plan. *Formidable,* in fact. But alas, one cannot foresee every bend in the river. Who could have predicted that this woman would fall under the sway of Père Dale to help turn your head?"

"She did more than turn my head. She's given me a new life. And a new vision."

"Which you intend to immortalize on celluloid."

Sloane frowned. "How do you know all this?"

But Hobart interrupted. "What goes on here?" he asked.

Philippe turned to him with an ingratiating smile. "Merely a difference of opinion. Nothing of import, I assure you." He motioned to one of the soldiers, who snapped to attention. "Corporal Lyon has a flask of the finest cognac. Why not take a little walk with him, while we discuss these pesky details?"

After weeks in the wild, Hobart was eager to oblige.

Once they were gone, Philippe turned to Sloane as if he'd never been interrupted. "How sad to have to throw water on your burning artistic passion. But that is exactly what I must do."

"Our association is finished."

"Oh, no. Not *nearly* finished. You, my old *capitaine,* will return to the original scenario and finish the picture we agreed to make."

In a mild tone, Sloane said, "I think you know me better than that, Philippe."

"It is precisely because I know you as well as I do that I say this."

"What are you going to do, force me? You can't kill us; that won't get your picture made. You could torture us, but you need a healthy director, star, and cameraman. Face it, Philippe. You have no leverage."

"Do I not?"

His hand extended to a large banyan tree up the path. So signaled, a guard disappeared, then returned with a battered figure bound with ropes.

Reverend Dale.

Philippe gave another signal and the beefy legionnaire put his foot on Dale's back and shoved him so he stumbled toward them, tripping over the ropes at his ankles and landing at their feet. With an anguished cry, Liana rushed to him. He was bruised and bloody. In fluent French, she cursed their brutality.

"Yes," said Philippe, unruffled. "I fear my men, in their enthusiasm, were *un petit peu* too hard on him. But then, they are dedicated Catholics. And since he is not a Catholic priest . . ." He drifted off with a shrug.

In his tempered voice, Dale said, "Don't give in to

them. No matter what they do to me, don't let them use me to force you to do their evil work. I'm not important. Others will follow me."

"Ah, but *mon père,* you sell yourself short. Such modesty does not become a man of your standing. Who could they send who could readily duplicate your advances in the cultivation of black pearls? And thus have the means of saving these islands from the clutches of scoundrels such as me?" He cackled, clearly pleased with himself.

"You're saying if we don't make the film your way you're going to kill this good man." It wasn't a question.

"Very slowly. In the manner these legionnaires have learned in their conflicts in North Africa and Indochina. Not a pretty sight, I assure you."

Sloane and Liana exchanged glances. Without a word between them, they realized that they had no choice but to bend to this vile blackmail.

Liana saw no hesitation in Sloane's decision. Just days before, he'd loathed Reverend Dale and everything he'd stood for. And yet, he was now willing to sacrifice himself and his own integrity for this same man. It made her realize how far he'd come. Her heart overflowing, she stood and took his hand.

He squeezed it—whether seeking or giving comfort, she couldn't be certain.

Philippe continued. "You have only the climax to film. The rest of the cast and crew will be present, but will be unaware of what is really going on. Understand that if you mention any word of this to them, you will be signing their death warrants. Understand also that if I find you are not giving the scene your absolute best efforts, I will begin removing the good reverend's bodily appendages one by one."

"Where will the rest of the company be?" Sloane asked. "I want a guarantee of their safety."

"They will remain on the *Catalina*. And as long as you do as you are told, you have my guarantee."

Sloane was watching Philippe thoughtfully. "You must have known about our change of plans for a while now. Almost as long as I have. To find Reverend Dale, make this trip from Papeete . . . How did you possibly—"

Suddenly it dawned on him. He cocked his head at Tommy, who was standing stoically beside his camera. "The man you sent back . . . *You* told Philippe . . ."

Philippe grinned. "A deduction worthy of Sherlock Holmes," he drawled. "It took me several days to track you down, but here I am."

Sloane's eyes never left Tommy. "You betrayed me. Why, Tommy?"

Tommy's face had become a mask of bitterness. "Because I hate your guts. And you're so wrapped up in yourself and what *you* want that you never even noticed it."

17

Liana looked in distaste at the sodden floor of her cramped cell in the fortress surmounting the village of Uturoa. Built in 1887 to help put down the island's ten-year war of resistance to French annexation, it stood over the harbor as a grim reminder of that country's determination to dominate its Pacific possessions.

Philippe had brought the three prisoners here that afternoon. Reverend Dale had been placed in the building's dungeon. Sloane was locked in the cell next to Liana, but he hadn't spoken for hours. Dried bloodstains left by previous tenants added a grotesque touch to the decor.

With an entire regiment of legionnaires now ensconced in the town, Uturoa had become an armed camp. Outside in the corridor and adjacent hallway, their gruff voices could be heard. Periodically, one of them would come in with food or water, and to make sure no escape plan was in motion. Philippe wasn't about to take any chances that the threat to Reverend Dale would alone ensure Sloane's cooperation.

As the hours dragged by, Sloane sank deeper into despondency. Tommy's defection had been a devastating and completely unexpected blow that took the heart out of him in a way that nothing else had done. Liana felt his withdrawal. Every attempt to encourage him was met with wordless resistance, as if telling her she wouldn't understand.

But she understood more than he realized. Stretching her hand through the bars of the cell, she was barely able to touch his fingers. When his hand flinched slightly, she made a greater effort and clutched it with tender force.

"I know this is awful," she told him. "I know it seems like the end of our dreams. You've been betrayed by not one but two people you thought were friends. I know you don't understand what happened to Tommy, and the need to know is eating at you. But, Ace, if you withdraw from me now, they've won. We've come so far. We've finally reached a point where we can be honest with each other, no matter how much it might hurt. Please, for both our sakes, don't go back. If we lose that, we've lost everything."

"We've lost everything anyway. Just when I finally realized what this picture could be—what it *must* be—they're forcing me to make a film that perpetuates the old lies. I can't make a picture I no longer believe in. Yet, trapped like this, how can I not?"

"We can find a way. I know we can."

He turned glacial eyes on her. "They're going to kill us, Liana. They're going to watch us like hawks until we finish making their film, and then they're going to make sure we die—most likely in what they'll later call a 'tragic accident.' Along with Reverend Dale. They can't afford not to."

"Not if we keep our wits. Together, we can find a way out."

He let out a ragged breath. "I can't stop thinking about Tommy. I never even guessed . . . I don't know. It's too much."

"Those sound like the words of a man who's given up."

"What else can we do?"

"We can fight them."

"With what? How? We can go through the motions and make the picture they want to keep ourselves—and Dale—alive. But once the picture's finished, it's over for all of us. The best we can do is drag out the filming somehow and stall for time. But even that's useless in the end."

She'd never seen him like this, so sick with defeat that he hadn't the will to go on. Watching him thoughtfully, she said, "When you heard about Philippe's betrayal, it made you strong. It brought out the best of you. But Tommy's betrayal has shut you down completely."

"Tommy was like a kid brother to me. Like a puppy scurrying after me, just happy to follow my trail. No matter what happened, he was always there, believing in me. And now . . . to find out it was all a sham . . . I don't even know when it started. When did he change? Why?"

"I know it's hard. And baffling. But you have to think of the future. Think of a strategy."

He dropped his head back against the wall in a weary gesture. "What would you suggest? We're sitting here in a prison, guarded by a gang of cutthroats. Even if we could escape, where would we go? And how would we get there?"

"I don't know," she admitted. "All I know is there must be an escape for us. There *has* to be. We didn't learn all we have and come all this way for nothing."

He angled her a bleak look. But before he could say anything, they heard footsteps coming down the stone corridor. A key creaked in the lock and the metal door swung open to reveal Tommy standing before them with a victorious sneer.

"Ready to go over the notes for tomorrow's filming?" His voice seethed with sarcasm. He was here to gloat. When Sloane didn't answer, he took a step closer and paraphrased, "Oh, mighty Caesar, how low you've sunk."

Sloane looked at the iron bars that caged him. "How could you do this?" he croaked. "We were friends."

"Friends!" Tommy barked a laugh. "That's the bunk! We were *never* friends. You saw something in me you could use, and you recruited me into your service."

"Tommy," Liana cried, "you know that's not true! You know how much Ace cares about you—"

Tommy cut her off with a snarl. "I pity you. You're as wooden-headed as I used to be. You think he loves you. But he doesn't know *how* to love. He's the center of his own little world, and what anyone else wants or needs just doesn't enter into it."

"Have you gone mad?" Sloane asked.

Tommy whirled on him. "You don't even know you do it! That's why we take it for so long. 'Cause you don't have the faintest idea of how you hurt people. How you use them to get what you want." Once again he spun toward Liana. "Did he ever tell you how he got to be such a big-shot director in the first place? All he had at the end of the war was a hero's medal and the footage *I* shot.

But he says to me, 'We're goin' to Hollywood. We're gonna make pictures.' I told him, 'You're nuts. We're nobodies. The money boys in California will throw us out on our ears.' But ole Ace, he tells me, 'All we need is nerve. A wink and a smile and ice water in our veins.' " He glanced at Ace contemptuously, then back to Liana. "And you know what? Damned if it didn't work. They took out their checkbooks and said, 'Go ahead, boys, go make *Devils In the Air.*' And what happened? It was a smash. All over the world. Why? 'Cause people were blown away by the war footage. 'The most daring and realistic portrayal of aerial combat . . .' And who got the credit? Me? The guy who *shot* that footage? Fat chance. The Great Ace got it. Director extraordinaire. It turns out a director doesn't really need confidence in himself—just confidence in his ability to use other peoples' talents."

"That's what a director does," Sloane said through gritted teeth. "He uses his organizational and leadership ability to put the components together. And make all of you shine in the process. That's what I did when I put you in that plane with that camera during the war."

"You didn't even ask me if I wanted to go!"

Tommy had bellowed the words so they echoed, in all their anguish, throughout the cold stone cavern. Words ripped from the soul of a profoundly troubled man. As one, Sloane and Liana sat staring at him, watching the play of suffering etch deep lines in his face.

His breath was coming hard. But when he spoke it was in a defeated tone. "I never wanted to be a cameraman. But you never even asked me if I did. You just tossed me your goddamned charity like you'd toss a bone to a dog."

"If you never wanted to be a cameraman, why didn't you quit after the war? Why make these pictures?"

Tommy blinked, thrown off by the question. "Because I'm a damned good cameraman. I can't do anything else. And because I couldn't be what I really wanted to be. I had to do something."

"What *did* you want?" Sloane asked, too late.

Tommy's hatred seemed to seep out of every pore. "I wanted to be a hero."

"A *hero*?"

"I wanted to be what you were."

Sloane blinked, then asked harshly, "What did Philippe offer to get you to betray me?"

Tommy straightened, squaring his jaw. "What I should have had in the first place. What I deserve, dammit. The Croix de Guerre."

Sloane stared, incredulous. "Because you didn't get a medal—*a hunk of bronze*—you'd do all this? Why didn't you just tell me? I'd happily have given you mine. It meant nothing to me."

A sneer twisted Tommy's face. "Don't you get it? I don't want yours. I want my own. I deserve it. You may have flown the plane, but it was *my* footage that revealed the enemy position and got you that medal. Philippe will arrange for me to have one because he knows I deserve it."

"Tommy, I always felt that medal belonged to both of us. We were both in the plane. We were partners. You were like my brother."

"Is that why it's *your* name on the citation?" Tommy cried. "Is that why the medal hangs in your office, not mine? I wasn't your brother. I was your *toady*! Do you have any idea what it's like to live in the shadow of a man like you?"

"I never claimed to be a hero," Sloane said quietly.

"It doesn't matter what you *claimed*." Tommy was all but screeching now. "Everything you *do* makes you a hero. You roll out of bed in the morning and find some heroic way to go about your day. You don't even have to *try.* Is it supposed to make me feel better that you never wanted it? When I've spent my life struggling for something you throw out like old bath water? Well, screw you, buddy!"

In the stillness that followed, Liana thought back on all the occasions when she'd heard Tommy refer to Sloane as "the Ace." Not Ace, as a friend might, but *the* Ace. She realized now that far from being a sign of respect, it had signified a hidden contempt.

Sloane, too, had been replaying all the shared scenes of their past life together. Suddenly he looked at Tommy intently. "I don't believe it. I don't believe you did all of this out of jealousy. There's more. What did I do to you?"

It was Tommy's turn to blink. Evasive now, he muttered, "What difference does it make?"

"It matters to me."

Still Tommy hesitated, as if this were territory he didn't want to tread.

"It's time for truth, Tommy."

"Truth! Since when have you ever cared about the truth?"

"Try me."

He said it quietly, calmly. But the words carried within them the old spark of leadership that was impossible to ignore. His narrowed eyes blazed at Tommy like blue ice, compelling him to obey.

Tommy crumbled. Hollowly, he said, "Marie."

Sloane frowned. "Marie?"

"You don't even remember her, do you? She was nothing to you. Well, she was something to me."

Sloane was clearly at a disadvantage, and looked blankly at Tommy.

"Marie Ardent! My girlfriend in Paris!"

"What about her?"

"She was the only girl I ever loved. I wanted to marry her. I knew I'd never find anyone like her again. And I haven't."

It came back to Sloane now. "And I talked you out of it."

"You told me she was a tramp. 'My God, Tommy,' you said, 'you don't marry someone you meet in a bar. Can't you understand these women are all whores?' "

"Tommy, I'm—"

"I listened to you. I believed you. I cut her off like a ten-franc Pigalle hooker. Just like my hero the Ace told me to. And you know something, Mr. Hero? That 'whore' was pregnant with my child. And you want to know something else? A week after I dumped her, she slashed her wrists and bled to death in her bathtub."

Liana's legs felt weak so she sat down on the bunk behind her. She thought about the vivacious French girl who'd romped with her before the camera in Paris that long-ago day. Who'd gazed at Tommy with such devotion that it had distracted his concentration. That radiant young woman who'd bubbled with life . . . dead by her own hand.

Tommy was breathing hard. Sloane watched with a stricken face.

"She was everything to me," Tommy raved. "Everything I've ever wanted or ever *will* want. The only person in my whole miserable life who loved me for myself. Who saw me as the hero I wanted to be. For her, I could have been. Without her I was lost, and I knew it." His voice choked and he took a shaky breath. "But I listened to *you*! You ruined my life that day, you smug son of a bitch. I swore to get even with you if it took the rest of my life. Philippe just gave me the chance."

In the interlude that followed, Sloane began, "Tommy, I'm so sorr—"

But Tommy spun on his heels. "You can just go straight to hell."

He left a resonance of pain in his wake. Liana felt it deeply, felt her heart throb. Tommy had told her about Marie, but he'd tossed it off as if it hadn't mattered, as if Ace had done him a service by saving him from a costly mistake. How it must have hurt him to deny his true feelings.

And Ace . . . Just weeks before, he might have sloughed off Tommy's accusations, finding ways to justify himself. But now, having traveled his own rough journey of the soul, she knew he couldn't turn away from the bleak truth he'd never before wanted to see.

She ached to say something that might absolve him. But it was he who must speak. And so she waited, when all she really wanted was to go to him and hold him close.

When he spoke at last, the words sprang forth as from some deep well, hollow, strained. "My God, I can't believe the damage I've done. It's true. Everything he said is true. My twisted view of women has hurt everyone I've ever loved. Him . . . you . . ."

She started to speak, but checked herself, waiting to see where this realization would take him.

"I thought I understood everything you'd told me earlier. But the truth is, it wasn't until Tommy told me about Marie that I really saw what I'd been. I think back on how I hurt you . . . and *why* . . . Can you ever forgive me?"

It was gratifying to hear him say it at last. "You know I do. And if Tommy's helped you to really understand, maybe some good can come of this, after all."

He rose from the bunk. "I have to make it up to him. I got him into this mess and, if possible, I have to get him out. He's been nursing a grudge that he has a right to nurse, but he's not evil. Tommy's impressionable. He's been influenced by Philippe the way he was once influenced by me. If we can help him, there may be hope for him yet. I won't give up on him."

"I hope you're right. I know there's good in Tommy. I just hope it isn't too late."

He turned to her. "But it isn't just Tommy. I want to make it up to *you*. Find some way to make the film we envisioned in Taputapuatea." He shook the bars between them. "But first we have to get out of here."

She caught his fever, realizing the significance of it. The old wound was finally healed. At last he'd put aside his despair and was ready for action. Excited now, she told him, "My father escaped Newgate prison after they'd beaten him senseless."

"How did he do that?"

"By coming up with a brilliant plan, then throwing his captors off guard. He told me once, when you're faced with an impossible situation, it's not the half measures that will get you out of it. It's the unexpectedly bold stroke. He said let them think you're giving them what they want, then turn it on them."

He was nodding thoughtfully. "So that's what we have to figure out how to do."

She continued her circuit of the cell, chewing her lower lip in concentration. Then, suddenly, she began to smile.

18

Tommy strode purposefully down the single street of Uturoa. Its dozen clapboard buildings had been augmented with twice as many false-front structures to re-create prewar Papeete. Anchored in the lagoon were two war-surplus cruisers which had been left in German Samoa at the armistice and requisitioned for the film. All around him were clusters of legionnaires, movie extras, the other cameramen, and those involved in staging the picture's show-stopping climactic scene: the shelling of Papeete by the German navy in 1914.

Where the main street ended at the wharf, Tommy climbed a flight of outdoor stairs leading to the second floor of a white colonial building with an expansive view of the lagoon and the German cruisers. He opened the door and entered the harbormaster's office, which Philippe had made his headquarters on Raiatea, to find the governor in discussion with a gaunt, bearded French officer.

Referring to the telegram the officer had delivered, Philippe said, "They will be arriving on the twenty-third of February, approximately one month from today. The party will consist of five dignitaries, headed by Monsieur LeGrand, the High Commissioner for Colonial Affairs himself. He is a meticulous man, so everything must be just so. Only the best French wines. The services of a mademoiselle may be required. His quarters must be spotless. But most importantly, the projection equipment must be installed in the auditorium of the town hall at least one week before his arrival. I want no slipups in this matter."

"I will see to it myself, *mon gouverneur.*"

He dismissed the man and, seeing Tommy, waved him over. "It is all set, *mon camarade.* The commissioner has given us a firm date for his arrival. Now all we have to do is make certain the picture is completed and edited before that time. I have also received a wire—for Sloane, of course—from Paramount. They have seen the footage we sent back and are delighted with the results. There will be no more studio interference." Noting Tommy's troubled expression, he added, "There is a problem?"

"I've just come from Sloane. He says now that he doesn't need all this for the scene. He says he can do it with half the men and a third of the explosives and finish it in a quarter of the time."

"*Magnifique!* We need to save some time. One month, as you have said, is not long to edit an entire picture. Especially since Ace is now almost guaranteed to be dragging his heels."

"Don't worry about the editing. I can take care of that myself if I have to. I'm sending everything back to

Papeete to be developed and printed, so all the footage we've shot will be ready by the time we get back. But you're missing the point. We need that big set piece. To be a big, successful Hollywood movie, to have the kind of worldwide impact you're talking about, it needs that one epic scene the audience will never be able to forget."

"But we have the hurricane, don't forget."

"It's not enough. To really damn the missionaries, we've gotta do more than just show them mistreating a bunch of natives. That might rile up some folks, but not everyone. You show them collaborating with the Germans and you'll have the whole world hating them. That's why we planned this scene in the first place. But in order to work, it has to be really spectacular."

"Then you direct the scene yourself."

Tommy sneered impatiently. "You don't know anything about pictures. I'm not a director. I don't have that kind of vision. If I did, we wouldn't have needed the Ace in the first place. We do need him. But he's up to something. I can feel it."

Philippe stroked his mustache thoughtfully. "You think perhaps he is trying to sabotage the scene?"

"What else? It's the only thing he can do to fight back. Make a mediocre picture. Lessen the impact."

"You are correct, of course. The High Commissioner must be convinced that this is going to be a huge international success." Philippe paced thoughtfully around the desk, mulling things over. "In that case, we will refuse to play his little game. In fact, we will double our efforts to make this the most extravagant scene ever. Go back and tell him we will use twice as many extras, have twice as many explosions, and spare no expense. Tell him that when I view the daily footage, if what I see is not the most thrilling and convincing sequence imaginable, I will put a bullet in the Reverend Dale's head."

"I'll tell him."

He turned to leave, but stopped short in the doorway, his hand resting uncertainly on the frame.

"This does not reassure you?" Philippe asked.

"I was just thinking. What if this is what he wanted all along?"

"What he wanted, how?"

"We both know the Ace. He's a great strategist. He may just be trying to manipulate us into botching the scene. Or he may be trying to heap another manipulation on top of the first one. A manipulation upon a manipulation."

"Meaning?"

"What if he's up to something? What if he *wanted* us to make this decision?"

"To what end? Escape?"

"Possibly."

"But that is madness. We will have him surrounded by legionnaires. Even if he were to escape, we still hold Dale. It would be for nothing."

"Maybe."

"What matters is that we get this scene on film and finish the picture in time."

Tommy nodded, but his frown increased. "Still, I reckon I'd better keep an eye on him."

Later that morning, Tommy stood with his Tahitian assistant atop a large wooden camera platform that held a panoramic view of the town and harbor. Four other cameras were positioned in strategic places to catch different angles of the action about to take place.

The sequence would crosscut the German shelling of Papeete with a frantic chase through the chaos as Tehani tried to escape the evil clutches of the crazed, traitorous missionary. In the distance below, he could see Sloane giving last minute instructions to one of the camera operators. He watched him with a careful eye. Sloane had received Philippe's decision with a resigned shrug, as if it didn't matter to him one way or the other. But once he'd begun to work on the scene, the artist in him seemed to have taken over. As always when he was intensely involved, he seemed possessed, the consummate director, completely absorbed with the task of capturing the scene on celluloid. But was he really? Or was he, as Tommy suspected, feigning the role with some ulterior motive in mind?

But what motive? Escape was impossible. Uturoa was an armed garrison. And even if by some miracle he was able to outwit them and get away, Tommy knew him well enough to know he wouldn't leave Dale behind. Time and again in France, he'd seen Ace risk his life to go back after pilots under heavy fire rather than leave them behind to die. Once he set himself up as supreme commander, Sloane took care of those he considered to be in his charge.

At Philippe's suggestion, the legionnaires had taken the extra precaution of removing Dale from the Uturoa jail and placing him under heavy guard on board the *Catalina,* anchored in the harbor to help re-create the flavor of the larger port of Papeete. If Sloane *was* planning a foolhardy rescue, he'd show up at the jail to find an empty cell.

Nervously, Tommy glanced at his watch. This was the most complex scene he'd ever photographed. It had taken a week just to set it up, to rehearse the action and choreograph the special effects. With split-second timing so vital, and five cameras covering the action, they'd had to hire extensive help among the local population. Fortunately, most of the workers had turned out to be diligent and eager to please. His own assistant had proved to be particularly helpful. Having fought with the Tahitian Brigade in France during the war, he'd learned all about explosives. He spoke passable English, and knew the back-door ways of getting things done on the islands. Tommy turned to him now.

"Are you sure the explosives are timed right?"

"You bet, boss."

"Each of the five explosions has to be bigger than the last. Savvy?"

"No problem, boss. One stick dynamite in first explosion, five sticks in last. Building, building. Big bang at end." He pantomimed a massive explosion.

"But the timing's gotta be just right with the woman running through the town. We don't want our star to get blown up."

"Mr. Sloane, he got it timed to the second. He don't want nothing happen to the pretty lady."

"And the smoke canisters. They need to be released just as we rehearsed. Too much smoke will ruin the scene."

His assistant held up five fingers. "I got it, boss. Five smoke canisters, each release five seconds after explosion. Mr. Sloane, he say that give scene compo . . ."

"Composition?"

"That's it, boss. Composition of 'terrible beauty,' he say."

Once again, Tommy looked down at Sloane, who was now conferring with Hobart. Clearly, the director *was* caught up in the creation of his spectacle. Tommy was grateful for the reassurance. This assistant was proving to be more than just a competent technician. He was soothing Tommy's frazzled nerves as well.

"You're a handy man to have around, Charlie," he

said now. "By the way, you never told me. Where did you learn your English?"

Charlie beamed. "Why, boss, I'm a first-class guide. I guide tourists all over these islands. I was the guide to Mr. Somerset Maugham!"

Liana, her skin newly stained, stood in costume just below the camera platform, awaiting her cue. Her breath was coming in short gasps. The plan was complicated. Timing was crucial. There were so many ways it could go wrong. But despite the dangers, she was tingling with excitement. This was just the kind of gamble her parents had relished in their youth, the kind of desperate adventure they'd told her about time and again. But this time she wasn't merely an audience to their tales. This time she was a featured player in a real-life drama about to unfold.

They were nearly ready. Above her on the high platform, Tommy was double-checking the settings on the camera that would film the entire scene in long shot. Hobart, dressed in his heavy missionary costume, was behind her, out of range of the cameras, doing his deep breathing exercises while an assistant fanned him. All during the week of rehearsals he'd been disgruntled and perplexed because the scenario and direction of the picture had changed yet again. He'd filmed so many conflicting scenes, he had no idea if he was the villain or the hero of the piece.

Sloane was several hundred yards away, down by the wharf, holding a large megaphone. Liana took a breath and tried to bring her focus back to the task at hand. Before they could carry out their plan, she had to get through the filming of a scene that offered dangers of its own. She would have to run across the hot dirt streets of this imitation Papeete, recently watered down to make them tolerable to her bare feet, through an obstacle course of successive explosions. They'd rehearsed her run all day yesterday to make sure there would be no slipups. But Sloane had warned her that dynamite was tricky, and the size of the explosions always somewhat unpredictable.

Through the megaphone, Sloane's voice bellowed out. "Is everyone ready?"

All over the set, people stopped what they were doing and turned their attention to the director.

"Okay, let's do this in one take. Roll film."

Swallowing her nervousness, Liana waited for his signal, then burst forth like a horse out of a gate. When she'd run about twenty feet, she heard Hobart start after her. She glanced back and saw him already covered in sweat, very much in character, yelling, "Stop, Tehani! Stop!"

The first explosion erupted to her left, shaking the ground beneath her and spraying her with dirt and debris. She could feel the blast of heat. Her ears were ringing in the wake of the shattering sound, much more intense than she'd expected. She'd have to be careful to stay farther away.

A hidden technician had released the first smoke canister. She ran on. Hobart, jarred from the impact, spooked briefly before regaining his composure and continuing the chase. After another hundred feet, the second explosion rang out, behind her this time, between her and Hobart. Then, only seconds later, the third one, an equal distance in front of her. As rehearsed, she fell to the ground right in front of the first concealed camera crew. Momentarily, Hobart was upon her. They struggled as two more smoke canisters were released. She shoved him away and he tripped and fell backward to the ground.

Through the megaphone, Sloane's voice boomed out

over the clamor. "Farnsworth, you're angry now. You're furious. You'll do anything to stop her."

Hobart's face transformed itself into an animal snarl. Feigning horror, Liana ran on. Another hundred feet and the fourth explosion rang out before her, more powerful than the others. Once again she fell to the ground, covered with debris. As the fourth smoke canister was released, she swiftly leapt to her feet and ran on. As she approached the wharf, the final and most spectacular explosion shook the earth and a fifth canister of smoke was let loose.

She heard Sloane's voice, barely audible now. "Don't stop, Tehani. He's still after you."

Out of breath now, her side aching, she continued the journey. Only five explosions had been planned. But suddenly, all hell broke loose. One after another, five unexpected blasts caught the startled crew off guard. As Liana turned, she could see that three of the blasts had leveled the legionnaires' barracks and armory, while the other two had completely destroyed the sandbagged gun emplacements Philippe had established to watch over his puppet show. Almost instantaneously, the smoke from a dozen more canisters began to fill the air from all directions. Soon the smoke was so thick Liana could only see a few inches in front of her face. Her eyes began to burn and tear. All around her she could hear cries of surprise and panic as chaos and confusion reigned. As the smoke thickened, enveloping the entire scene, the cries were replaced by deep, wrenching coughs. Liana held her breath as Sloane had instructed. But the smoke was so dense that she'd lost all track of her bearings. She turned in a circle, disoriented, not certain which way to go.

Then she felt a hand grasp her arm.

19

It was Sloane. He pulled her toward him and gave her a hasty kiss. "Now for the hard part."

"I can't see. Which way is the jail?"

"He's not in the jail. They moved him this morning. He's on the ship."

She heard running feet behind them, then a rush of air, and Charlie, with Hobart in tow, was at their side. Breathlessly, Charlie said, "My spies say they have the reverend tied up in the ship's lounge. But the place is all full up with legionnaires. We'll never be able to get to him."

"What the devil is going on here?" Hobart demanded. "Every time we try to shoot a scene—"

"The scene's finished," Sloane told him. "We're getting you back to Tahiti. Don't ask any questions. Just do what Charlie tells you." Turning to Charlie, he asked, "Is everyone else on board?"

"Everyone but the cameramen. My people are leading them there now."

"Good. When we get to the top of the gangplank, you go to the bridge and tell Captain Morris to make preparations to sail. Leave the rest to me." Turning to Liana, he added, "You stay here until I'm sure it's safe."

"Not on your life. I'm coming with you."

He arched a questioning brow. "You're taking a big risk," he warned.

"No," she corrected. "*We* are."

After a brief hesitation, he nodded decisively. Reaching behind him, he withdrew something he had earlier secreted beneath his shirt in the back waistband of his pants: a bundle of dynamite with a six-inch fuse. Then he took his lighter from his shirt pocket. But just as he was flipping the lid open, Liana put her hand on his. "Let me do the honors," she said. She took the lighter, flicked the wheel, and watched the flame ignite. On her way to lighting the fuse, she paused. "Kiss me," she urged. "A *real* kiss."

Her cupped the back of her head with his hand and yanked her close. This time he kissed her as if he meant it. "That's more like it," she said with a smile. And lit the fuse.

A guard stood sentinel at the top of the gangplank. But as the two figures emerged from the smoke, Sloane holding in his hand the threat of total annihilation, the guard, already flustered by the unexpected havoc and blinding smoke, just stood helplessly staring as they charged past him. But by the time Charlie and Hobart joined them, the startled sentry found his wits and fled down the gangplank toward safety.

Charlie sent Hobart to his cabin, then went to the bridge while Sloane and Liana headed briskly for the lounge. Gathered before its entrance was a cluster of legionnaires staring incredulously at the burning fuse that was fast approaching. In an instant they measured the danger and with cries of alarm, leapt over the side to splash into the water below.

Sloane didn't so much as pause. Moving with that same marching gait, he thrust the dynamite behind his back, flung the door open, and stepped inside. Hurriedly, Liana followed. The scene that greeted them was an ominous one. Reverend Dale was tied to a chair in the center of the room, flanked by a semicircle of heavily armed guards. Behind him, Philippe stood with a pistol pointed at Dale's temple. He bestowed Sloane with a knowing smirk.

"Very clever, *mon ami,*" he greeted. "But, unfortunately, not clever enough. You see, I expected an extravagant escape attempt from someone such as yourself. I even expected that you might figure out where we had stashed your newfound friend. But you've done all this for nothing."

"It seems you were one step ahead of me the whole time," Sloane said.

"Sadly for you, it is so."

"But there's one little thing you *didn't* expect."

"And what is that?"

"This."

He brought his hand from behind his back to reveal the deadly sparkler. Philippe and the guards gaped, paralyzed.

"Think fast, Philippe. This is a quick fuse. There are only seconds left—"

In a burst of panic, the guards bolted, scrambling for the door. "Fools!" Philippe screamed after them. "Shoot him!"

"Too late," Sloane said in his calm, whiskey voice.

"You're bluffing!" Philippe snarled.

But Sloane stood his ground, staring the Frenchman down. "I don't bluff. You know that."

Philippe directed his attention to Liana. "You may kill me and the reverend, and even yourself. But you wouldn't kill her."

As Sloane glanced her way, Liana tucked her hand through his arm. "If he dies, I die with him," she pledged.

His gaze darting furiously now, the Frenchman cried, "You're both mad!"

"Wasted words, Philippe. Time's almost up."

The fuse had nearly burned to the quick.

Philippe, struggling to control his rising terror, fixed Sloane with an accessing gaze, as if trying to peer into his soul. Suddenly, he muttered, "No, you never bluff, damn you. And you're just stubborn enough to blow yourself to hell."

With a curse, he burst from the room, and flung himself over the ship's rail.

An instant later, Charlie came running in with Captain Morris in tow. Spotting the burning fuse, the captain cried, "Good God!"

He braced himself for oblivion and watched helplessly as the flame reached the end of the fuse. But instead of causing the expected explosion, it merely fizzled out.

Liana laughed delightedly. Sloane tossed it aside and grinned at her. "Don't worry, Captain," he said. "It was only a bluff."

The moment of triumph was broken by the sounds of gunfire. Sloane went to the rail to see what was going on. The smoke was clearing. Philippe and his drenched legionnaires had crawled onto the pier. The ship's gangway had been hoisted and Tommy was directing several of the marksmen to fire at the ship, as if to frighten it into submission.

Sloane turned to find the others at his side. Charlie had untied the reverend, whose wrists were raw from the ropes. His voice was apologetic as he said, "That was a brave act, Spencer. But I'm afraid I've caused you more trouble than you bargained for."

"No more trouble than I've caused you," Sloane told him sincerely.

A sudden volley of bullets ricocheted off the side of the ship. Captain Morris, clearly shaken, said, "This isn't a battleship, you know. We can't take much more of this."

Sloane commanded, "Get this ship out of here as fast as you can."

"And go where?"

"Back to Tahiti."

"To do what?" the captain demanded.

"Go to some remote corner of Tahiti-iti, the lower portion of the island, and let Charlie and the reverend off. Charlie, you and Reverend Dale head for the leper colony. If there's any way I can get back to you, I'll meet you there. Captain, once you've deposited Charlie and the reverend, take everyone else back to Los Angeles."

Before the captain could respond, Liana proclaimed, "I have no intention of going back to Los Angeles without you."

Sloane noted the stubborn tilt of her chin and realized that it was useless to argue. "Go with Charlie and Reverend Dale, then. But be careful. Charlie, you take good care of her."

A second volley of gunfire riddled the ship, cutting off Charlie's reply.

"Tahiti be damned," Morris thundered. "I've had

enough of this. You chartered this ship to make a moving picture, not fight a war. I'm heading straight back to the States."

Liana put her hand on his, gently persuasive. "We're counting on you, Morrie. The reverend has to get back to Tahiti, where he's needed. His work is vital and must continue."

The captain glanced from her to Sloane, who added, "Don't worry. There's no danger. Philippe doesn't have anything fast enough to overtake you. He can't use the German cruisers because they're mostly gutted. Besides which, as soon as you get free of the harbor, I'm going to have you lower the sea plane for me."

"Lower the sea plane? What on earth for? That will only slow us down—"

"Think about it. If I take off in the direction of Bora Bora, they're going to come after *me,* not you."

Morris glanced back to see the rest of the regiment lining up on the pier, getting into position to start firing. "All right, Mr. Sloane," he relented. "Whatever you say."

They steamed out of the harbor in a hail of bullets. But it wasn't long before the ship had outdistanced the range of the marksmen. As it turned about to lower the plane, Sloane took Liana's hands in his. "Charlie will make sure you're safe with the reverend," he told her.

She arched a brow. "Oh, will he, now?"

"I'll meet you when I can be sure of not being spotted."

"You won't have far to go."

"What do you mean?"

"I mean I'm coming with you."

He stilled. "Forget it. It's too dangerous."

Still humming from the exhilaration of their grand

bluff, she assumed a teasing tone. "Since when have I minded a little danger?"

"Liana, listen to me. Taking you on board with me with a bundle of dynamite I know isn't going to explode is one thing. But this time I have no guarantees."

"It isn't an adventure if you have guarantees."

"You're not listening."

"I'm listening, darling. I just don't agree."

"Here's what I've got to do. First I'm going to buzz them—a pass so low, so cheeky—"

"I *adore* cheeky!"

He gripped her arms, as if trying to get her to see reason. "—So cheeky that it will enrage them. So they'll forget about the ship and come chasing after me in the opposite direction—toward Bora Bora."

"I'm *dying* to see Bora Bora. Charlie says it's the most beautiful island in the Pacific."

"But before I get there, I'm going to crash the plane on the reef. So when it washes ashore, they'll believe—or at least strongly suspect—I'm dead."

She smirked. "You're the greatest pilot of the war, and Philippe is going to believe you crashed on a routine run to Bora Bora?"

"That's what makes it so dangerous. I'm going to fly low enough to take a couple of hits. They'll think they punctured my fuel tank and I ran out of gas trying to make the lagoon."

"Perfect! Then they'll think we *both* died."

His mouth tightened. "You're not being very helpful."

"I was under the impression I'd been an enormous help. Wasn't it my idea that got us free in the first place?"

"Will you be serious?"

"No. This is *fun* for me. I haven't had such fun in I don't know how long. I gave you the setup. You can't deny me the final act. Besides, what's the finale without the leading lady?"

She put her hand to his face and said softly, "Ace, we were separated for far too long. From now on, we work together. For better or worse. Come what may. Danger be damned."

He chewed his inner cheek thoughtfully.

"Okay," he said finally. "Get in the plane."

They climbed in, Sloane in the front, Liana in back. He tossed her some goggles, which she put on while he did the same. When he saw that she was ready, he signaled the captain. Winches attached to the plane's front and rear slowly hoisted the craft into the air, then down into the water. As the plane bobbed in the waves, Sloane crawled forward and aft to loosen the winches, then regained his seat and started the engine. The plane began to move forward cautiously, then gradually gathered speed, sending a spray of sea water in all directions. Liana felt a surge of excitement as they left the cradle of the water and zoomed into the air.

She'd never been in a plane before. But as they gained altitude and made a wide arc in the sky, her heart lifted with it. She felt like a bird, set free from the world and its shackles of gravity, high above a breathtaking spectacle: the islands of Raiatea and its neighboring Taha'a; the circular outlines of the coral reef beneath blue-green waters that caught the sparkle of the sun, sending out prisms of dazzling light, and the sapphire blue of the Pacific on the epic horizon all around them.

As he completed the arc, they were now pointed squarely in the direction of the still chaotic village of Uturoa. Coming closer, they could see that remants of the special-effects smoke lingered. Here and there small patches of fires still burned. Near the pier, legionnaires were dashing wildly about, many of them piling into smaller ships to make chase. And in the middle of it all, Philippe, having grabbed the discarded megaphone, was bellowing orders to them all.

He stopped short as he heard the plane's engine. As he stared in disbelief, Sloane dropped into a nosedive and bore down on the scene as if he were a bomb and Philippe the target. It happened so quickly that no one on the island had time to react. They stood where they'd been, staring into the air, transfixed. On and on the plane came, veering straight for Philippe. But just when they were close enough that the two men could see the whites of each other's eyes, Sloane jerked back the stick and pulled out of the dive.

As he headed off to the northeast, he tipped the wing back and forth in a gesture all veterans of the war would recognize as a sign of contempt: thumbing one's nose at the enemy. Over her shoulder, Liana caught the mix of wrath and humiliation on Philippe's face and laughed into the wind.

Regaining their wits, the soldiers began firing a furious fusillade. Liana felt several bullets whiz by, but only the tail was hit and they were soon out of range. Nevertheless, Sloane immediately dropped some fuel from the tank to produce an oil slick below them and make it appear that they'd taken a critical hit. And as they made their twenty-five mile journey, he periodically dropped more fuel, so their pursuers could follow a trail of lost fuel.

It wasn't long before they could see the fabled island of Bora Bora rising out of the sea like an enchanted kingdom in some fairy tale. Liana had only seen it in the silvered images Sloane had captured on film when he'd gone with Tommy to shoot exteriors. Now, the colors dazzled her eyes, greens and blues in the richest shades imaginable, like liquid turquoise, sapphires, and emeralds melting into the horizon. Charming thatch-roofed huts extended out over the water on stilts. The island itself, moss green sheer-cliffed mountains topped with a collection of puffy, white, cotton-candy clouds in an otherwise royal blue sky, was almost completely surrounded by a string of *motus* along the circle of the coral reef. These small islets of dazzling white sand and lazy palms were completely deserted, beckoning a tropical welcome, like smaller offshoots of the larger jewel in its midst. Heaven on earth.

As they came closer, they could see the frothy white spray of the surf breaking on the reef. Sloane pointed to a minuscule, palm-covered motu in the lagoon. "That's our destination," he called against the wind. "Once we're free of the plane, we'll swim for it. There's only one passage in the reef, about two miles from the motu. We'll jump into the water before we reach the reef, so we won't be cut by the coral. Then we'll swim through the passage, into the lagoon, and then to the motu. When I give you the signal, we'll jump. Be sure to go in the water feetfirst."

Before she had time to think about it, the island was looming before them. Sloane dipped the plane so it was on a collision course with the reef. Holding the stick back with one hand, he stood on the seat and pulled her up, and they climbed precariously onto the wing. He waited until they were just a few feet over the water then, calling, "Now!" let go of the controls. Together they jumped and plunged into the open sea below. The water, as it enveloped them, was warm but intensely salty. In that same instant, they heard the crash as the plane met the reef. The fuel tank exploded in a blaze just before the craft broke into a shower of splintering pieces and began to wash in toward Bora Bora with the surf.

Liana felt herself being towed by the current toward the reef and its razor-sharp coral. But Sloane guided her in the opposite direction, toward the passage, fighting the tide. When she'd adjusted to the current, she swam by his side. From here, the motu they were heading for was too far off to see, so she relied on him to guide her. The crystal water sparkled all around them in the sun, so clear she could see the bed of assorted coral far below.

Once they were through the passage, the lagoon waters were calm and increasingly shallow. When they were still a good distance from the motu before them, Liana felt her bare foot scrape the bottom and winced. Below she could see the varied shapes of coral, some branching out like stag horns, some shaped like oversized mushrooms, some assuming the contours of giant human brains. All of it white or grey in the surrounding bed of sand, creating a moonscapelike vista. Dozens of long, stringy bunches of kelp swayed toward her in unison, giving the impression that they were coming after her. Through this, small colorful fish darted out of their path.

Spooked, Liana stopped and dog-paddled to keep her feet from touching the coral. Sloane noticed and came to her rescue. He walked across the sea bed, swept her into his arms, and carried her toward their island refuge.

20

It was a postcard vision of the ideal tropical paradise—a tiny island dense with swaying palms and thick vegetation, rimmed with pristine white coral sand. Set in the loveliest lagoon on earth, the island welcomed them with the promise of intimacy and utter privacy beneath the brilliant caress of the sun.

"It's like a whole other world," Liana sighed in wonder. Once he'd set her down, she turned a circle to take in the panorama of Bora Bora's craggy wooded peaks across the eastern side of the vast lagoon, and procession of larger motus to the north and south.

"It's called Motu Tapu," he told her.

"What's a *motu*?" she asked.

"All these islands in the Pacific began life as volcanoes. Over the centuries, the volcanoes became extinct and began to sink back into the ocean. At the same time, reefs were rising up around the dying volcanoes. As these fringing reefs neared the surface of the water, sand and other debris gradually accumulated on them, forming islets—called motus. In time, the high islands disappeared completely, and the motus connected, forming the flat, circular atolls. They're scattered all over the Pacific."

But this motu was little more than a dot in the tranquil blue expanse of the sea, small enough and far enough from its neighbors that it couldn't be seen from any of them. "Tapu . . . that means it's tabu."

"It belonged to the old royalty of Bora Bora: their sacred picnic grounds. For anyone else to set foot here meant a horrible death at the hands of the gods. That tabu holds to this day. One thing the missionaries have never been able to eradicate here is the power of tabu. Polynesians cherish their superstitions."

She scanned the horizon and the larger, more prominent motus of the circular chain. "But this motu is so small. It gets lost among the rest of them. How did you know about it?"

"Charlie told me. He thought it might be a good place to hide. The French don't have a presence on Bora Bora. Philippe's only been in these parts once or twice. When I was coming here to shoot exteriors, he couldn't even tell me about the area. He suggested I hire local guides, which is exactly what he'll have to do, if he doesn't believe we're dead and decides to make a search. Not only won't those guides bring him here, they won't even mention its existence. It's small enough and far enough away from the pass that they'll never see it unless someone tells them it's here and they come looking for it."

"So we're safe?"

"Safer than we'd be on Bora Bora, which is the first place they'll look. But we still have to be on our toes."

They walked the circumference of the island—easily

accomplished in five minutes. The beach seemed decorated for a party with palm fronds, fallen coconuts, and stunning fragments of snow white coral in the shape of intricate tree branches, some the size of a human hand but many larger, exquisitely sculpted, lying unbroken and undisturbed by the tramp of intruding feet. Nearer the center of the island, breadfruit and massive bunches of small, thick bananas hung heavily from the trees. And all around them was a balmy stillness, a peace, serenity, and beauty that was entrancing. The isolation was so resplendent, so complete, that it seemed they were the only two people on the face of the earth.

But it didn't last long. Soon there was a dot on the southern horizon. One ship, then two, then an entire flotilla approached like an invading armada. Sloane led Liana to a patch of shrubbery at the water's edge, where they crouched, watching the show in the distance. Their pursuers sailed through the pass in single file, and began inspecting the wreckage of the plane, which by now had scattered as much as a mile in every direction. Fanning out, they gradually widened their search, obviously hunting for bodies. But at this distance they looked like mere specks on the horizon.

One of the ships sailed back out of the passage to examine debris that was washing out to sea. Finding no trace of their prey, they returned to the lagoon to reconnoiter with the others. For some time, there was no motion among the distant figures. Then, what appeared to be three squads of legionnaires were dispatched to the main island of Bora Bora.

"They'll ask if anyone saw the wreck or any survivors. Eventually, when they get no indication that we're there, they'll do one of two things: either assume we're dead and give up, or continue their search and possibly come this way. We'll just have to wait and see.

Regardless, it will take some time for them to search Bora Bora, so for now we can relax."

Night fell swiftly on the heels of a glorious sunset, the reds and golds and violets reflecting on the surrounding waters and deepening them to magical hues. They feasted on ripe bananas and coconuts, drinking the milk, toasting one another as if with the finest champagne. Their escape had left Liana feeling giddy, the triumph of it pumping through her veins. As the sky darkened to a rich midnight blue and the clouds drifted like lace before the moon and stars, they lay back in the sand at the edge of the island to watch the sky. The water lapped against the shore gently, creating a lullaby in the splendor of the night.

"It's so quiet here," she sighed after a while. "It's almost as if nothing exists but the two of us. As if we had no problems, nothing to worry about. Just endless peace."

He took a lock of her unbound hair and thoughtfully twisted it around his finger. She could feel the steady hum of his heart against her ear.

"Your plan worked brilliantly," he told her. "It was so crazy, I wasn't sure it would."

"The crazier and more daring a plan, the more likely it is to work. Catching people by surprise. Taking what they expect of you and twisting it on them. Philippe knows you never bluff, so it wouldn't occur to him that you would. Did you see his face?" She laughed. "He was livid! And soaking wet, to boot." She took in a breath of the fragrant air. Then, turning her face to his, she added, "You were wonderful. Even Hobart couldn't have played the part as well."

He flashed a wry smile, then went back to toying

with her hair. "I'd never even have thought of it, if it hadn't been for you. Not just the idea. You gave me the courage to fight them when I needed it most. Your everlasting faith in me. You were the one who was wonderful."

"It isn't much of a feat to have faith in you. You've proved to me that you're worthy of my trust."

He digested this in silence.

"How did you like doing it?" she asked.

He thought back on it, then grinned. "It was great fun."

"Getting the best of hypocrites and stuffed shirts is always fun."

Again, he was quiet. She felt his head shift, as if allowing his gaze to roam the night sky. "Tell me something," he said at last.

"Anything."

"How did you come up with that crazy plan?"

She shrugged. "Oh, that was easy. I grew up listening to my parents' escapades. I remembered something they'd done once, and rearranged it to suit our circumstances, that's all."

"Tell me about it."

Once again she turned to him. His face, so often grim and foreboding, was relaxed and inviting. No trace of censure or judgment. "You really want to know?"

"I really do."

She lay back again, nestling into the folds of the sand, settling her head cozily in the crook of his arm.

"You know my mother was a duchess, right? And she gave it all up to be with my father. You also know that her parents were Derk and Sasha Wentworth. They were actor's actors. You know, the bigger-than-life kind they parody in satires. But because they were also nobility, they were terrible snobs. My mother didn't get along with them. In fact, she hated them."

"Why?"

Like the actress she was, Liana let her voice take on a tone of intrigue as she told the tale. "She'd inherited their flair for drama in *life,* but none of their acting ability. That went to her twin sister, who died young. My grandparents blamed my mother for it. They never showed her any affection or approval. Treated her like hired help. It was one of the reasons she was so happy to run off with an Irish rebel—to get back at her parents."

"And to romanticize him as a highwayman in the process."

"She *was* a romantic. She liked to think of him that way." She sat up, warming to her story. "Anyway, my father's grudge was really against the Prince of Wales. The prince was a friend of my grandparents' and had been a lover of my mother's. When my father started robbing all the prince's friends, it caused a howling scandal, as you can imagine. My grandparents—consummate impresarios that they were—decided they could make a fortune by putting on a play about this notorious bandit and the mysterious lady who rode by his side . . . never guessing that the mysterious lady was their own daughter. Mother was livid. So my father came up with a plan. The two of them, in costume, with my mother masked, would rob the theater during one of the performances of the play about them."

"You're kidding."

"Not at all. It was really dangerous, too, because the prince was up in arms and had police everywhere." She stood now, and began to act out the scene with gestures of her own. "So Father used that against them. He dressed his own men in policemen's uniforms, and stationed them at the theater. Then my mother sneaked him backstage. Just when my grandfather, as the highwayman, was holding up a coach during the play, my father swung down onto the stage. The *real* bandit showing the impostor how it was really done." She pantomimed the flourish of her father's swirling cloak as he'd landed on the stage. "You see how delicious it all was? My mother joined him at stage right, the fake police locked all the doors, and my father calmly sent his men up and down the aisles to rob the patrons of their coin and jewels. Taking them, needless to say, completely by surprise. It never occurred to anyone that he'd have the audacity to show up at a play that was making fun of him, and *rob* the audience in the process!" Delighted with her re-creation, she laughed, then fell back onto the sand beside him once again. "Utter genius. And a great gift to my mother. Father's way of repaying her parents. Not just for defaming him, but for being so mean to *her*."

"And they got away with it?"

"At first. Although they were captured later, and Father was sentenced to hang. That's when he escaped from Newgate, with my mother's help."

"Tell me more," he invited.

She'd never had the luxury of speaking openly about her parents. As she did, she felt a great sense of relief. All the things she'd bottled up inside all her life came tumbling out.

"The awful irony is that my grandparents ended their play by having the highwayman and his lady swing side by side from the gallows. My parents couldn't have known it, but that's exactly what was going to happen to them. When they went back to England to try and stop publication of my mother's journal, they were found and betrayed. They hanged together. Life imitating art in the worst way."

"It must have been awful for you."

"It was more than awful. But don't you see?" She sat up again, swinging her legs around and crossing them in front of her. "The outrage of it all is how the world twisted and misunderstood everything they'd done. My father wasn't a common thief. He was fighting for the Irish cause, using the money he stole to help people in need. He'd never have considered himself to be noble, but he was. And my mother was rebelling not just against her parents, but against the hypocrisy of her times. She did what she did out of love for my father, but also as an expression of her own beliefs. They *lived* what they believed. And yet the world sees them as nothing more than a thief and a whore. It's the greatest sorrow of my life. Worse, even, than losing them."

He sat up and put his arm around her, holding her close, as if to protect her from the pain of the memory.

"But loving you makes up for all of it," she added.

He stroked her cheek, then lay back once again. "I'm glad you're here with me," he said, stretching his arms back over his head. "Despite the danger, and the uncertainty, it's good not to be alone."

She rolled onto her stomach. "I want so much to help Reverend Dale. When I learned it was black pearls he was fighting for, I realized that I had to try and help. My mother's black pearls came from these very seas. They seemed to me like . . . the symbol of everything she was. I wish you could have seen them, Ace. Three strands, each pearl exquisite and perfectly matched. They were fastened with a platinum catch that was as beautiful as the pearls: a stylized *W* set in elaborate scrollwork. As a child, I used to hold them in my hands and dream about the day when they'd be mine. I didn't know it, but I had a connection to Tahiti even then. But they were stolen from me, just as Philippe is stealing *these* pearls. If I can help stop that, maybe, in some small way, it'll make up for what I lost."

He nodded his understanding. "I'll help you if I can. But I don't know what the future holds. Today was fun, a triumph. But we've just won the battle. I'm not sure where we go from here. As much as I'd like to promise that we'll win the war, I can't. The odds are stacked against us, I'm afraid."

"I don't care about the odds," she said heatedly. "I know you doubt yourself at times. But I believe in you. I believe in us, in our ability to work miracles together. I *have* to believe."

"Then we will."

She flopped onto her back into the sand. "If you believe we belong together, that's all I need. I don't want to think about the future. For once, I just want to live for the present. We're here together, that's all that counts. Just the two of us in paradise. Whatever happens in our lives, we'll always have this one moment of perfection. This will never come again. I want to enjoy it while I can."

"You're right," he agreed. "The future be damned."

"I read a legend once," she told him, gazing at the stars. "About the butterfly lovers. A man and a woman loved each other so much that even in death their hearts were faithful to each other. The gods saw their devotion, and to honor it, they changed them into butterflies and let them come back together in life after life. I want to be like them. Two butterflies, flitting around this perfect island, glorying in our beauty and the beauty all around us. Free to fly away, but choosing to stay." She paused. "They can't see or hear us, right?"

"They're two miles away. You saw for yourself when we were swimming. Unless you're in a plane, this motu is all but invisible."

"Good." A sudden impulse sent her scrambling once again to her feet. She stood before him and with a single motion, untied the pareu and let it drop to her feet. He sat up, mesmerized, watching as she spread her arms to the majesty of clouds and stars in the midnight sky, beneath the moon that cast its sterling light on her womanly form. She danced in circles, throwing back her head so her dark curtain of hair flowed like a waterfall down her shapely back. Frolicking beneath the heavenly skies, sending a laugh like a melodious chord into the night. She held her arms out to him and said, "Come, my dearest love. Come be a butterfly with me."

She thought his dignity might keep him rooted in the sand. But he found her so bewitching in her pagan gaiety that he couldn't resist. With a sudden flash of white teeth, he threw caution to the wind. He pitched aside his clothes as carelessly as she had, then marched to her and grabbed her waist with strong hands, thrusting her high. A tribute to the perfection of the night. He twirled her round and round until they were both laughing. Gradually he lowered her and, breathless now, she collapsed into his arms. They stayed just so, locked together, laughing to show the watching fates that they felt no fear. Only love. Only joy. Only contentment in this splendid night, where time seemed to stop and wait for them.

And then, with an impulse as sudden as hers, he bent and put his shoulder to her waist, hoisting her up and carrying her, laughing, into the sea. The warm water enveloped them, washing them clean. They cavorted like children, splashing each other, dunking their heads below the surface, until they were dripping with droplets that sparkled in the light of the moon. Liana realized how seldom she'd heard him laugh like this, like an innocent youth, stripped of pain and fear and dread. His merriment was all the more precious for its scarcity. She looked at him, his hair plastered against his head like a Roman statue's, his torso leanly muscled. A man who'd transcended his imperfections and had been reborn, stronger, more gentle, more compassionate. A man she could trust her life to, as well as her heart. Awash with adoration, she went to him and kissed him, feeling free, feeling that the two of them, naked beneath the starry night, were a part of all the magnificence around them.

He held her close, his arms powerful, kissing her lusciously. She felt herself lifted in his arms, her feet dangling in the lapping water below. Desire mingled with her love, coiling within, filling her with such a sense of well-being that even as she kissed him, a giggle bubbled from her throat. She wrapped herself around him, her arms about his neck, her legs hugging his waist. He took them deeper into the surf, still kissing her, chuckling as he did. They stayed there for a time, bobbing in the hospitable tide, kissing like teenagers who'd just discovered bliss. His kiss elevated her until she couldn't discern if the sensation of floating came from the motion of the sea or from the touch of his lips against hers. When she finally wrested her mouth from his, it was to take in the perfumed air with a sigh. "You see? It's fun being butterflies," she murmured, feeling dreamy.

"I don't feel like a butterfly," he said.

"Oh? And what *do* you feel like?"

She caught the lusty gleam in his eyes. His grip tightened and he carried her through the water and onto the beach. There, he deposited her in the sand and fell on top of her, his body heavy and warm. Catching her hands in his, he raised them above her head, pinning them as he leaned over her. "I feel like a pirate who's stolen the lovely princess and carried her off to his island hideaway, like a prize."

She recalled the way he'd snatched her and carried her like a sack of booty up the gangplank of the *Catalina.* "This is a *recurring* fantasy, I see."

Ignoring her as any self-respecting pirate captain would, he lowered his head and began to feast on her flesh with a ravenous mouth, wandering, exploring, finding spots that blasted through her dreamy state and jolted her with passion. She squirmed beneath him, seeking to free her hands, wanting to run her fingers through his hair and guide his head where she wanted it. But he clenched her tight, pushing her arms back into the yielding sand, holding her down. "You can't escape me. While you're on this island, you're mine to do with as I will."

Pinned down as she was, with his hard-muscled body pressing into hers, she felt a thrill sweep through her. "And if I don't comply?" she teased.

"You have no choice. There's nowhere to run, nowhere to hide. You're my prisoner. I've brought you here for my use. And I'll use you any way I please."

Again she tried to move, and again he held her down, sucking on her breast until she was arching against him, her breath coming in small, gasping pants. Everything in her was swimming with lust, ripe, juicy, the game enflaming her senses, leaving her hot and wet. "And if I rebel, as any princess worth her salt would? Will you make me walk the plank?"

"No," he said, drawing out the word. "I'll fuck you senseless. Until you're so drained you won't have the will to fight me. And then I'll fuck you again and make you love it, until you're begging me for more. Until I've made you mine completely."

"In that case, I'll do all I can to resist."

She struggled beneath him, the conflict inciting her, the crush of his overpowering arms making her feel deliciously helpless. He took her hands and, angling her briefly, thrust them behind her back, imprisoning them in the grip of one mighty fist. Then he rolled her onto her back again, so the pressure on her arms intensified. With his other hand he touched her between her thighs and she cried out, electrified by a fierce current of desire. His fingers played with her mercilessly until she was moaning with impassioned pleas, her breath scorching her throat, her arms struggling to be free. Then he took his stiff erection in hand and plunged inside.

She felt wild with lust, his power urging her higher, wracking her body with shudders of startling pleasure. He took her as he'd promised, like something he'd stolen and claimed for himself. As she felt herself roaring toward climax, she lifted her head and pleaded desperately, "Kiss me."

With the flat of his hand, he gave her face a gentle smack. "I'll kiss you when *I'm* ready. Not when you want me to."

His denial made her want it all the more. She sought his mouth with hers. But he clamped his lips on her nipple and thrust into her with renewed force. Her body exploded in wave after wave of delirious shivers, her moist tunnel convulsing on him, clutching him like a vise. She felt light-headed, as if she were soaring to the heavens, drifting back to earth at a leisurely pace, languorously fulfilled. Her body tingled with stark awareness, his erection still raging hard within her.

She gave him a radiant smile. "You misled me. You *do* know how to play."

He grinned in return. "You're right," he admitted. "This *is* fun."

"Bravo! Then play the game, and glory in it." Then she added in a tigress growl, "I just *adore* having a big brute of a buccaneer in my bed."

She felt his erection burgeon inside her. "Shut up, wench," he ground out through his teeth. Then he gave her what she wanted, kissing her blindingly. Pinning her to the soft coral sand, he unleashed his lust and plundered her body with such exquisite skill that she began once again to soar.

21

She awoke with a jolt. Sitting up, she wondered what had shaken her from sleep. The scene around her was tranquil and full of beauty. The sand took on the colors of the dawn.

She recalled the ecstasy of the previous night and stretched voluptuously. Then she spotted Ace a few feet behind her, sitting rigid and alert, his attention riveted on the horizon.

She felt his urgency and knew it must have roused her from slumber. "What is it?" she asked.

"I think they're checking the motus."

She followed his gaze and could see a trio of small boats rowing in different directions toward the larger surrounding islets, still distant but close enough by now to make out what they were. Obviously, they'd been under way for some time. "Are they coming here?"

He watched for several minutes with crinkled eyes, then said, "I think they might be."

Alarmed now, she asked, "What do we do? There's no place to hide."

"If they do come, we could jump them, but if they don't return to the ship, the others will know something's up and come in force." He chewed his lip, considering. "Maybe this is an opportunity."

"A fine time to play the Pollyanna."

He continued to study the approaching rowboat. "There are three imperatives here: escape, get back to Tahiti, and derail Philippe's plans, whatever they are."

"And how do we do all that?"

He pierced her with a keen glance. "Didn't you tell me your mother used to dress as a man and play pranks in London?"

"All the time."

"Then that's what we're going to do."

He hurriedly outlined his idea. As she listened, excitement quickened in her veins. "It's awfully daring. But if it works, what a coup!"

"Good. Let's get going, then. We haven't got much time."

He moved to leave, but she held him back. "Kiss me," she petitioned. When he pierced her with a glare, she added, "For luck."

He took her face in his hands and brought her close for a searing kiss. She smiled dreamily against his lips. "Now I can do anything."

They took their places: he behind a dense clump of plantains, she seated cross-legged in the sand at its side, strategically close to a small pile of driftwood. Then they waited as the minutes dragged by.

Eventually the boat drew up and two legionnaires jumped out and pulled it onto the beach. One was a tall Frenchman, the other a short, swarthy Annamese, one of the many legionnaires recruited from French Indochina.

With rifles out-thrust, they began to comb the island with the attitude of men who assumed their mission was a waste of time, but were cautious nonetheless. When they came upon Liana sitting in the sand, they stopped abruptly.

She let them make the first move.

The Frenchman quickly perused the island with his eyes. In French he asked, "Where is the man?"

"Il est mort," she replied. "Dead."

This threw them. They glanced uncertainly at one another.

"Where is his body?"

"Washed out to sea."

"Make a search," the Frenchman said to his partner, who took a swift circuit of the tiny island. When he returned, he said, "I saw nothing."

The Frenchman lifted his rifle in the air. Liana realized he was about to fire a signal to the ship that she'd been found. With no time to think, she grabbed a piece of driftwood, sprang to her feet, and broke it over his head. The rifle fell, unfired, to the ground and the man crumpled in its wake.

Shocked, the Annamese roused himself and rushed her. But before he reached her, Sloane leapt from the bushes and tackled him to the ground. They struggled in the sand until a powerful blow rendered the intruder unconscious.

Breathing hard, Sloane marveled, "That was quick thinking. That one shot would have done us in."

She took a bow. "An outlaw woman doesn't wait to be rescued."

He rose and shook the sand from himself, then took the bayonet from the unconscious Frenchman and began cutting long strips of burro bark from a nearby tree. As he did, Liana worked at removing the legionnaires' uniforms. When the men were stripped to their underwear, Sloane used the bark he'd cut to bind their hands and feet, then dragged them into the shade.

"Are you sure they'll be able to free themselves?"

"We'll tie them tightly enough that they'll stay put for now, but loosely enough that they'll be able to work free in a few hours."

"You should have told me last night that there was rope on the island," she teased. "We could have had even more fun than we did."

He shot her a wry look, then glanced down at the unconscious Annamese. "This couldn't be more perfect. With your dyed skin and small stature, you should be able to pass for this little fellow. There's only one problem. What do we do about your hair? Even if we tuck it up under the cap, it won't be convincing."

"That's easy." She bent to retrieve the bayonet in the sand. Without hesitation, she took a hunk of hair in her hand and severed it at chin level with a single slice of the razor-sharp edge.

The color drained from Sloane's face.

"Don't worry," she assured him. "It'll grow back."

With that she completed the job, hacking off the rest of it. "This will have to do for now. If we manage to survive this, I'll try to make it a bit more stylish." Her task accomplished, she asked, "What do you think?"

He was still staring at her in shock.

She laughed. "You men. You never want a woman to cut her hair."

"It isn't that," he said, finding his voice.

"What, then?"

"I was just thinking it's a damn good thing we finished shooting your scenes."

She went to him and put her arms about his neck,

kissing him lightly. "Always the director. Very well, Master Director, what's our next scene?"

The true danger of the situation didn't really hit Liana until they'd rowed out into the lagoon and were nearing the ship. Philippe himself might be on deck, anxiously awaiting the report of the real legionnaires. He'd recognize Sloane in an instant.

Ace rowed slowly, trying to time their arrival with that of the other two boats, so they could blend in with the returning soldiers. Anxiously, Liana scanned the deck. She could feel the sweat trickling down her sides. After the light pareu she'd been wearing, the heavy wool uniform felt stiff and oppressive. She had to forcibly resist the urge to squirm within its chafing confines.

As the first boat approached the ship, Ace pulled in behind, so there would be legionnaires before and after them, and their presence would be less conspicuous. Still, when her turn came to climb the ladder to the upper deck, Liana felt so hot and nervous that she had to pause halfway up to take a steadying breath. Their perilous game would come to a crashing conclusion if their identities were discovered. Philippe had no more need for them: Tommy could edit the film. And they'd unwittingly given Philippe the perfect cover for their own murder. He could say they'd died in the plane crash, and who would contradict him? Enough wreckage had washed up on the Bora Bora beach to satisfy any investigator.

She was trembling with dread. But when she reached the top, she was relieved to find that neither Philippe nor Tommy were on deck. The sergeant at arms said, as he had to those before her, "Nothing, eh?" Liana shook her head and he added, "So, they must have died in the crash."

His contention eased her trepidation and made her feel bold. Deepening her voice, she asked in French, mimicking the accent of her Annamese counterpart, "Will we be leaving, then?"

"As soon as the last of you are aboard. I'll send word to the governor. You men go below and get some food."

Sloane stepped on deck then, averting his head. She now felt reasonably secure in her disguise, but they would have to find a way to keep him out of sight.

Dutifully, they went below to the galley. Its only inhabitants were two men playing cards in the corner and the Tahitian cook, who was uncorking a bottle of wine and cutting up baguettes to arrange on a tray.

As inconspicuously as possible, they sat down and began to partake of the bread and cheese left on the table. Liana found to her amazement that she was hungry. Just then she felt the motion of the ship. They were on their way.

No one paid them any mind. The cook called to one of the men playing cards. "The governor's tray is ready, monsieur."

"Not *now,*" the man cried. "I'm finally winning!"

The losing soldier grinned. "The governor is not one who likes to be kept waiting."

"One more hand and I'll go. It's a sacrilege to break a lucky streak like this."

"All the more reason why you should go now," said the loser, still grinning widely.

On impulse, Liana said, in her husky voice, "You stay and play. I'll take it for you."

Sloane was shocked. But suddenly Liana was enjoying herself. This was the perfect opportunity to get close to Philippe. The challenge of boldly walking into the lion's den was just too delicious to resist. *Let's show him what kind of actress I really am!*

She answered Sloane's fierce frown with a hasty smile of reassurance, then rose and took the tray.

"Why, that's good of you, my little friend," said the man relieved of the duty. "May the god of gamblers smile on you."

"De rien," she replied, with a dismissive shrug. "Where is the governor?"

"In the captain's cabin at the end of the passageway."

She left the galley alone, but felt Sloane on her heels. "I can't let you do this," he whispered urgently.

"You want to know what Philippe's up to, don't you? What better way to find out?"

"And if he recognizes you?"

"He won't."

"You can't be sure of that."

"Ace, just go find a place to hide and let me do this. Have some faith in me."

He studied her determined face. "All right," he said at last. "But I'm going to be right outside the door. If you get into trouble, scream."

She smiled at him tenderly. "Those protective instincts die hard, don't they? Very well. Guard the door, if you insist. But I won't need it."

"Let's hope you don't."

They made their way down the passageway. At the door, she glanced at Sloane, who was still frowning, as if not convinced. But as she knocked on the door and prepared to enter, he detained her, giving her a kiss and whispering, "Break a leg."

She winked at him, then, schooling her face, went in.

The room reeked of cigar smoke. Philippe was sitting behind a desk, across from a man with his back to her. Three henchmen were sprawled in chairs surrounding a circular table. As Liana entered, one of them shoved some papers aside, making room for the tray. The man across from Philippe turned and she caught the glint of his glasses. Tommy!

She quickly moved so her back was to him and placed the tray on the table. As she unloaded its contents, Tommy and Philippe continued the conversation she'd interrupted.

"They must be dead, then."

"Most likely. But I left a platoon on Bora Bora to continue the search, just in case."

"The sight of that wreckage makes me feel sick to my stomach," Tommy said, leaning his head into his hand.

"This is no time for a weak stomach, *mon ami,*" Philippe warned. "This is an auspicious development for us. Now we do not have to kill them ourselves. And we can still blame it on Dale, as we originally planned. We have only to tell the world we hold irrefutable evidence that he sabotaged their plane."

"Will they believe it? He's a missionary, after all."

"But a corrupt missionary," Philippe grinned. "A missionary who has been stealing the precious black pearls from his parishioners. Who would do anything to cover up his dirty little secret. And the newspapers will eat it up. What a world!"

"Isn't it bad enough we have to do it?" Tommy muttered. "Do you have to gloat about it, too?"

"Be not a hypocrite, *mon ami.* In any case, there is no time for recriminations. There is still too much to do. The High Commissioner will be here in less than a month. That film must be completely edited and ready to show him when he arrives."

"Ace has been editing as he goes along. I only have to do the climax, then cut the negative. I think I can get it done in time."

"Do not think. Be sure of it. But do not be sloppy about it. This film must be devastating. When the High Commissioner sees it, it must shake him to his core. He must realize that it will make him appear an incompetent fool in the eyes of the world, especially given that the star and director have been murdered by the villains depicted in the picture. He is the only person who has the power to abrogate the agreement with the B.M.S, but only if he has evidence that they are engaged in criminal conduct. We must present him with a spectacular *fait accompli*. The movie, the murder of its director and star, the potential for a vast, international scandal, and the only means of averting it: summarily throwing the B.M.S. out of Polynesia forever."

"What about Dale? He'll be on Tahiti by now. Word of the High Commissioner's visit has already been announced there. He could figure out what we're up to and make trouble."

"The good reverend and any of his supporters will be arrested on sight, and will be shot while attempting to escape."

"He has a lot of support among the natives. What if there's an uprising?"

"If there is, it will be put down." To make his point, he crushed the cigar in the ashtray at his side. "All you have to worry about is making that film as effective as it must be."

Having heard what she'd come for, Liana picked up the now empty tray and started for the door. But Philippe called, "You! Stop!"

She froze. Steeling herself, she turned slowly to face him. *"Oui, monsieur le Gouverneur?"*

She stood before him, trying not to tremble. Keeping her eyes lowered to hide their blazing green.

It seemed that he'd study her forever. She could

scarcely breathe. No one had noticed her before, but now they all swiveled toward her. She felt that every one of them could see through her disguise.

Would he never speak? Never break the suspense?

At last he said, in a voice seething with contempt, "Take these empty glasses with you. This place is a pigsty!"

The rest of the trip was uneventful. The legionnaires, with nothing to do until they landed, spent the day-long voyage scattered about the deck basking in the sun, playing cards, shooting craps, and idly exchanging war stories. Liana and Sloane kept to themselves, pretending to snooze in a remote corner of the deck, their caps angled over their faces as if to protect them from the sun, their rifles lying in their laps, ready to be used should their deception be discovered. But no one bothered them. She'd let him know with a nod that she'd found the information they sought, but it was too risky to discuss it now.

When they docked in Papeete, they found that patrols of legionnaires were on every corner, on the lookout for Dale or any hint of a demonstration from the local population. Philippe had obviously wired ahead from the ship.

They weren't far from the dock when they heard the sound of running feet and a voice crying out, "*Monsieur le Gouverneur*, an urgent message!"

A corporal of the guard rushed through the crowd to thrust a cable into Philippe's hands. Tommy, coming up behind him, asked, "What's up?"

"It's from Bora Bora," Philippe ground out. "They weren't killed. They were on one of the motus after all.

They tied up two of the men we sent to search and made their escape."

"Escape . . . where?" Tommy asked.

"They took the uniforms. They must have disguised themselves. They were probably on this very ship!"

Sloane grabbed Liana's arm and said, "Let's get out of here."

Philippe began to bark orders. In a minute, there would be no avenue of escape. Her impulse was to run, but he cautioned her with a firm grip. "Walk with determination, like you know where you're going, but don't run. Do nothing to alert their suspicions."

At Philippe's shouted order, the legionnaires began to scatter. Liana and Sloane were walking away when a bull-headed sergeant with a scar across his nose blocked their path. They stopped short. Beside her, Sloane slowly bolted a bullet into the chamber of the rifle he still carried.

The man inspected them for a moment. Liana's hand convulsed on the rifle she, too, carried. She wondered, if it came to that, if she could actually pull the trigger.

"The Americans . . ." he said.

Cautiously, Sloane began to raise his rifle.

". . . They're loose in the city. They may be disguised as legionnaires. But they should be easy to spot. One of them is a woman."

It took a moment for Liana to realize they hadn't been caught after all. But Sloane had the wits to say, in passable French, "Don't worry. We'll find them. I know a woman when I see one."

"The order's been given. Shoot to kill."

"The woman, too?"

Disgust flashed across the sergeant's face. "I like it no more than you. But orders are orders. Get going. I have to pass the word along."

He left, and Liana allowed herself a sigh of relief.

As they hurried away, Sloane asked, "Can you find your way back to the leper colony?"

It was late by the time they'd made the trek over the narrow mountain trail through the jungle. As it had grown dark, Liana had lost her way several times. But once they found Loti's pool, she was able to re-create the steps she'd taken with Charlie months before. Along the way, she told Ace what she'd overheard between Philippe and Tommy on the ship.

When they finally reached the isolated clearing, steaming in their heavy uniforms, they found it deserted. But the air smelled of a recent fire, quickly extinguished.

"Someone was here," she said. "But they—"

Suddenly she remembered they were dressed as legionnaires. Any observer would assume they were the enemy. Through the still night, she called out to Reverend Dale, to Charlie, to anyone who might hear, identifying herself. The only answer she received was a bird call somewhere in the distance. To more clearly show themselves, Sloane took out his lighter and used the flame to illuminate them. Liana doffed her hat. Presently they heard the rustle of bushes. Charlie stepped into the clearing, followed by Reverend Dale. Liana rushed to embrace him. "Thank God you're safe."

Breaking the embrace, Dale peered at her and asked, "What have you done to your beautiful hair?"

Liana had all but forgotten about it, but before she could reply, Charlie slapped Sloane on the back and crowed, "We showed 'em, didn't we, boss? They never guessed the servant boy they hired was first-class, A-number-one spy!"

"You foxed them, all right," Sloane agreed. "We're in your debt. But the question is, what do we do now?"

"You're safe here," Dale assured them. "Philippe sent a patrol, but we melted into the jungle and they were afraid to stay for long—even though the patients had been removed to another location. Papeete, on the other hand, is another story. It's an armed camp."

"We noticed," Sloane murmured.

"The French High Commissioner is coming. I suspect his visit has something to do with what's been going on, but Charlie hasn't been able to find out what."

Sloane filled him in. "Philippe is going to show the commissioner the recut film. This was his plan all along. That, and to murder us and blame it on you."

Dale sighed. "Now it becomes clear. The High Commissioner has the power to cancel any agreement made by the Colonial Office." He ran a weary hand over his face. "I should have figured it out. He sees the movie, and summarily outlaws the B.M.S. forever, as a self-protective measure, *before* the film opens worldwide. It's perfect: the one quick, sure way for Philippe to solve all his problems."

"None of us knew," Sloane said.

"There's no use castigating ourselves, I suppose. There's nothing we can do now."

"I can't live with that," Sloane snapped. "I've been manipulated into making a false statement to be used for evil purposes. If there's even a chance of stopping them, I have to take it."

"But how?" the reverend asked. "It seems they hold all the cards."

Sloane addressed Liana. "Any words of wisdom from your highwayman father?"

She'd been mulling it over as they talked. "What is

the very last thing they'd expect you to do at this point?"

Sloane frowned at her thoughtfully. "You tell me."

"I have an idea, but you'll probably think it's crazy. It's even bolder than the last one. But it could be just the thing to catch them by surprise."

"Didn't your father say the bolder the advance, the more likely it was to succeed? What's your idea?"

She gave a sly look. "Reverend, you might want to cover your ears."

He looked baffled. "Why?"

"Because I think we should start by saying a prayer."

Dale offered, "Then I'll lead the prayer."

"Not *this* prayer." Liana grinned. "It's to Hiro. God of thieves."

22

Three weeks later, the newly whitewashed town hall was decked out in French tricolors. An army band stood ready to play *La Marseillaise* when the High Commissioner and his entourage arrived. A platoon of sentries in dress whites with fixed bayonets stood in stiff formation. A red carpet led a path to the entrance.

Philippe paced the gravel driveway out front, glancing at his watch. Tommy joined him. "Everything's ready inside. The projectors are all set up. The film arrived this morning. I ran the opening scene. The print looks swell."

Pinching him on the cheek, Philippe crowed, "Ah, American efficiency. There is nothing like it. What did the world do before there was an America?"

"Has there been any word on Sloane and Liana?"

"Not yet."

"I still say it was a fool thing to do, announcing their death when we know they're still alive."

"It was the only way. We had to explain their absence, did we not? And it has added to the mystique of the picture, just as we planned. When I told him the story, the High Commissioner was enthralled. He actually put his hand on his heart and said, 'They gave their lives for the cinema.' " He chuckled sardonically, but had the presence of mind to keep it low enough that no one else could hear.

Tommy shifted irritably. "But where are they now?"

"Hiding in the interior, no doubt. But they cannot hide forever."

Just then the government limousine rounded the corner on the boulevard and the band leader waved his baton. The car drew up and the commissioner stepped out, followed by his entourage. The band began to play. Philippe saluted the attractive elderly man with close-cropped grey hair and a pencil mustache. His chest was heavily laden with medals. He stood at attention, listening to the strains of the French national anthem, then shook Philippe's hand. "I have been awaiting this most eagerly," he said, "however saddened I might be that it had to come at the cost of such a tragedy. The loss of young life is always unsettling, in war or in peace."

"Yes, it is a tragedy. But at least the work they gave their lives for was completed and will stand as a testimony to their courage and dedication to justice."

Beside him, Tommy squirmed.

Philippe led the way to the reception line where he began the process of introducing the commissioner to various members of his staff. They were halfway through when a late arrival pulled up, the sound of the tires crunching on the gravel attracting their attention. A large Citroën stopped at the foot of the carpet.

"Are you expecting someone else?" the commissioner asked in a clipped tone. Clearly, he was annoyed with the breach in etiquette. He should, by rights, be the last to arrive.

Philippe didn't know what to say. He was as surprised as the commissioner. Which of his underlings would dare? A head would roll for this faux pas.

All eyes turned as the Tahitian driver came around and opened the back door. A long, shapely leg appeared. A woman's leg, showing a tempting glimpse of a black silk stocking almost to the thigh. As they stared, it stepped delicately to the running board. A female hand came next, lightly taking the outstretched arm of the driver. Then the woman herself rose from the shadows and stood before them like a diva making her grand entrance. The crowd caught its first glimpse of the new modern woman of the 1920's, her dark hair and bangs cut short and bobbed, her grey sequined dress shorter than they'd ever seen, showing a shocking amount of leg beneath. The commissioner, his entourage, and the governor's staff were riveted.

But Philippe and Tommy paled. Because the woman was Liana.

She moved aside and Spencer Sloane stepped out. Immaculately groomed and dressed in black evening finery, he was every inch the handsome and cocksure director. He took Liana's hand and together they stepped toward the gawking assembly.

No one uttered a sound. Coming up to Philippe, Sloane arched a brow and said smoothly, "Have you no word of greeting for an old *friend*?"

Philippe was clearly at a loss, so Sloane spoke to the commissioner. "I'm the director of the picture you're about to see. And this lovely woman is my star."

All at once the commissioner understood the sense of

shock that had gripped the governor and his staff. "But monsieur, they told me you were dead!"

"The news was premature, I assure you. Our plane did, in fact, crash. But as you can see, we're alive and well."

"Mon Dieu!" cried the Commissioner. "A miracle has occurred." He addressed Philippe. "It is wonderful news, is it not? And just the thing to make of this night a true celebration."

Philippe's gaze never left Sloane's. What could he do? Call them impostors and arrest them? No. It would soon be apparent that Liana was the star of the film. His mind struggled to accommodate this shattering turn of events. Why were they not crying foul? Why were they going along with the premiere as if nothing untoward had happened?

Sloane saved him the trouble of a reply by telling the commissioner, "I, for one, can't wait to see the finished product." Turning to Tommy, who was as white as Philippe, he added, "We put our hearts and souls into this one, didn't we, Tommy?"

Coming to his senses, though taut with suspicion, Philippe found his voice. "This is quite a shock. Perhaps we should postpone this for another time."

"Nonsense," Sloane said, slapping him on the back. "There's no reason to delay."

Liana flashed the commissioner her most beguiling smile. "If Your Excellency would do me the honor of escorting me inside . . ."

The Commissioner flushed. "With the utmost of pleasure, mademoiselle. I have never before had the privilege of watching a moving picture with its charming star at my side."

She took his arm and they moved en masse into the auditorium. As she passed, Liana caught a glimpse of

Tommy's face, his lips trembling ever so slightly. His wide eyes, behind the glasses, twitched from her to Sloane and back.

Once they were seated, the lights dimmed and the buzz of conversation died. A square of light hit the screen. An ensemble of Tahitian musicians, situated up front and off to the side, proceeded to play.

The story began to unfold in silvery chiaroscuro, so lush, so exquisitely capturing the visual splendor of the South Seas that it took the audience's breath away. Gasps of awe and wonder mingled with the haunting wail of steel guitars.

Tommy, frightened and perplexed as he was, nevertheless began to lose himself in the beauty of his own photography. Gradually, magically, he, too, was seduced by the saga of the narrow-minded missionary and the tragic goddess of the South Pacific. But before the first act was finished, he realized with a jolt that this wasn't the picture he'd edited. It was a completely different story, with a different sensibility—not the expected tale of the innocent island girl debauched by the evil missionary, but rather, a parable of redemption, in which the missionary, through Tehani's influence and sexual expansiveness, comes to see the true evil of the land: the colonial government's theft of the islands' precious black pearls.

Philippe sat, stunned, watching every image with nails digging into the armrests, in agonized anticipation of what treachery was to come. His spine stiffened as he began to realize the unexpected twist the narrative was taking. And as it hit him that the reworked film was an indictment of his administration and a salute to a selfless missionary bent on developing a cultured pearl industry for the natives, he knew he had to end this madness at all costs. Trembling with rage, he shot to his feet and shrieked, "Stop the film!"

As the lights came on and the puzzled dignitaries waited for an explanation, he glared at Sloane who was sitting back in his seat with an ankle crossed over his knee, a slight smirk on his face. "How did you do this?" he demanded.

Sloane shrugged airily. "A little breaking and entering. A little creative editing."

Actually it had taken quite a bit of doing. To steal into the waterfront warehouse in the early hours of the morning three weeks ago and take the necessary supplies. The duplicate footage. The editing materials—scissors, magnifier, and glue. To carry it all back to the abandoned leper colony. Then to edit the finished product under the most primitive of conditions, and with precious little time. And finally, just before dawn this morning, to sneak back into the headquarters and replace Tommy's edited version with his own.

"And the original print," Philippe was asking now. "Where is it?"

"In a safe place."

"The negative as well, I suppose?"

"Naturally."

The commissioner stood. "What is the meaning of this interruption? May we not continue with the film?"

"This screening is over," Philippe announced.

"But monsieur, this is most frustrating. I demand an explanation."

Philippe's rising panic was evident in the compulsive throbbing of a vein in his temple.

Tommy came to his side. Quietly he said, "This is bad, Philippe."

The governor, in his rage, snarled, "Fool! Do you think I do not know that?"

Liana, watching them, caught the nonplussed flush on Tommy's face.

"What are we going to do?" Tommy persisted.

Arching a brow, Sloane drawled, "Yes, Philippe, what now?"

Philippe said nothing, frantically weighing his options. Suddenly his darting gaze hardened on the commissioner. "Arrest them. All of them."

Tommy balked. "All of them?"

"At once."

"Even the commissioner?"

"Especially the commissioner."

From her cell, Liana could hear the enraged voice of the High Commissioner, demanding to be released. He'd been bellowing his protests for nearly an hour, and the unrelenting sound of his voice was beginning to grate on her nerves. Her head began to pound.

But the commissioner's shock was no greater than her own. The last thing they'd ever expected was for Philippe to take such a suicidal measure. Imprisoning the High Commissioner! The man who administered France's entire colonial empire. What could Philippe possibly hope to gain? Did he think he could take on the entire power of France itself?

She paced the cell in a fever of agitation. What had Philippe done with Sloane? He hadn't brought him with the rest of the group to this cell block. Stark images flashed through her mind—Sloane being savagely tortured in some dark and filthy dungeon; being dragged, beaten and bloody, out to the jungle in chains and shot through the head.

The sudden clang of the iron door made her jump, echoing the gunshot in her imagination. Philippe and

Tommy entered the cell block. The commissioner, seeing them, began to spew curses on their heads. But Philippe ignored him and led the way to Liana.

She gripped the bars and told Philippe, "You've just made the stupidest mistake of your life. Do you think the commissioner is just going to go back to France and forget this little episode?"

Philippe snarled, "He is going nowhere. And neither are his men. Tragically, they are going to die in a shipwreck. How distressed I will be to have to report to Paris the grievous loss of my good friend, *monsieur le Commissaire.*"

"You can't possibly hope to get away with this. Word will leak out. The legionnaires—"

"Do you think me such a fool? Only my most trusted men know of this. I have promised them favor once I've secured political office in France in exchange for their silence. They are ambitious men and loyal to one who can further those ambitious. I assure you, *chérie,* they will say nothing."

"But you yourself said the commissioner is the only one who can cancel the treaty with the B.M.S."

He peered at her strangely, then a smile of comprehension curled his lips. "*You!* You were the little Annamese with the tray . . . very clever, indeed. And yes, what you say is true about the High Commissioner's power. But he will have a replacement, no? And when his successor sees the original film, and I suggest to him the vile missionaries may even have been instrumental in the unfortunate demise of not only the director and star, but of the High Commissioner *himself* . . ."

"But you don't have the film."

"Oh, but I will. I have just released our heroic Ace and given him until dawn to bring back the original print and its negative."

"You're mad," she spat out contemptuously. "After all he's done to stop you, do you seriously believe he's going to waltz in here and just hand it back to you?"

"Let us see, shall we? Let us just see what he values most: the fate of Tahiti . . . or you."

"Me?"

He formed an ugly grin, stroking his lavish mustache. "Oh, did I neglect to tell you? If our brave champion does not meet my demands, you will die at the stroke of dawn."

"You were going to kill me anyway. Ace knows that."

"Plans change, do they not? I told him I would let you go."

With a knowing smirk, he left. Tommy remained behind, staring at Philippe's retreating back as if realizing for the first time the malignancy of his partner in crime.

Seizing the opportunity, Liana said to him, "My God, Tommy. He's insane! Surely you can see that. Who but an insane person would arrest the High Commissioner and his party, then kill them and claim they died in a shipwreck? He says he trusts his men, but what if he crosses one of them down the line the way he crossed Ace? What if one of them talks? Sooner or later, word of this is bound to get out. You'll be haunted by this the rest of your life. Philippe's crazy, Tommy, but you aren't. You can stop this."

He said nothing. He was still staring after Philippe.

She pressed on. "Are you going to stand by and let him do this? For what? For pearls? For greed?"

He turned to her then. "I don't care about pearls, or missionaries, or even Philippe," he said. "All I care about is making the great Ace pay for what he did to me. To Marie."

She grabbed his wrist through the bars and said earnestly, "I know how you feel. You know that's true,

Tommy. You recognized it yourself, that day you came to convince me to take the role. You saw that we were alike, because we'd both been hurt by him. That's why I can't blame you for what you've done. I know better than anyone how Ace can break your heart. But he's truly sorry. He never understood what he was doing. People *can* change, Tommy. Ace has changed. *You* changed him. *You* made him understand. And now he's doing everything he can to make it up. He believes that underneath all of this, you're still good at heart. Think about it. You thought Ace used you as a puppet. But is Philippe doing any less? Can't you see Philippe is using you for evil? Ace wants to help, if you'll only let him. You can get out of it before it's too late."

She thought from his expression that she'd reached him. But he shook his head. "It's already too late."

It was nearly dawn. Liana hadn't slept. She'd spent the night pacing her cramped cell. Afraid, not for herself, but for Ace. But underlying her fear was a painful sense of guilt. Her grand idea had backfired. She and Sloane had expected the all-powerful High Commissioner to see their version of the film and realize what Philippe's corruption was doing to these islands. Instead, they'd walked into a trap. Even knowing what Philippe had done so far, they'd underestimated his diabolical mind. Now there were no options left.

Her only hope was that Ace would have the courage to *not* return the film. But it was a paltry hope at best. He was being asked to choose between the two things he held most dear: his artistic integrity and her. There was a time when she'd known exactly what he would do: He'd have sacrificed anything for his cinematic vision. But that was before he'd changed . . . before *she'd* helped to change him. In a spiritual sense, he'd already made that choice, vowing to her that nothing in life was more important to him than she. Now he was being asked to give concrete proof.

But if he chose her, it would be for nothing. She didn't believe for a minute that Philippe would let her go. And so she prayed that Sloane would have the strength to do what must be done. To save himself. To prevent Philippe from using the film to continue to exploit the people of Tahiti. To somehow get away and tell the world what was really happening to this enslaved paradise. By choosing to save Liana, he would be proving his love to her, but it would be a selfish choice, and would ultimately come to no good end. But if he denied Philippe the film, he would be serving a higher good.

And he would live.

She would willingly sacrifice herself for that.

Please, she prayed to him, *realize there's nothing you can do to save me.*

But as the first pink light of dawn showed through the bars of her window, she heard an ominous sound. Footsteps in the courtyard below. Then Sloane's voice calling, "All right, Philippe. I'm here. I've got the film and I'm ready to make our deal."

Liana raced to the window and peered down. She saw him standing in the courtyard, accompanied by Charlie and three other Tahitians, each holding four large reels of film: sixteen in all, the negative and positive versions. They stacked them in two columns in front of Sloane, then left at his command. Her heart sank. He'd done what she feared he would. She loved him for it, desperately, but wished he'd had the strength to resist. And yet he'd never looked stronger, standing there in the meager dawn light, his hair tousled by the morning breeze, his face impassive. He put a cigarette in his mouth and, leisurely, as if he didn't have only minutes to live, took out the lighter she'd given him and lit it.

The door opened behind her and Philippe reached in to pull her out by the arm. "It is time for your little rendezvous with destiny," he sneered.

Tommy stood behind him. So her plea to him hadn't affected him at all.

Holding a pistol to her ribs, Philippe shoved Liana down the outer steps and into the courtyard. Sloane looked up and their eyes met. In that instant, they were the only two people in the world. She was so in love with him that her body ached. She started to run toward him, but Philippe yanked her back.

"Okay, Philippe," Sloane called out. "I fulfilled my part of the bargain. It's time for you to fulfill yours. Let her go."

Philippe laughed. "Oh, Ace . . . *mon ami* . . . did you really think I would be so foolish?"

Sloane took a draw on his cigarette, then said, as he exhaled, "Not really. But if there was any chance, I had to take it."

Tommy interrupted. "How do we know it's the right film?"

Philippe lost his smug smile. He surveyed the reels of celluloid stacked in the dust. "Check it," he barked. "I am warning you, old comrade, if this is a trick, I will show you that there are much worse things a woman can endure than death."

Cautiously, Tommy approached the film. The eyes that had glared condemnation before now avoided Sloane's gaze. He picked up a reel and crouched down on his haunches, unspooling the first frames.

As he did, Sloane said softly, "You were right, Tommy. I killed Marie."

Tommy ignored this, but Sloane saw him flinch. As he

unfurled several more feet of film and held it to the morning light, Sloane continued in an unhurried tone. "You have every right to hate me. Every right in the world."

Tommy put down the reel, picked up another, and repeated the process of examining the footage. But a vein in his jaw throbbed.

"I defiled the love you felt for her because I couldn't understand it. I was a twisted son of a bitch. I was scarred, and I saw a scarred world all around me. But now that I know what it is to love someone more than I love myself, I know how you felt about her. And I understand what I did to you."

"Just shut up," Tommy spat out. With an angry jerk he snatched up a third reel.

Sloane gentled his tone. "I'm just telling you how sorry I am. Sorry I trusted Philippe. Sorry I brought you to this. Sorry I wasn't a better friend to you when you needed one."

Tommy was staring at a frame of film, but it was clear now that he wasn't seeing it.

"The truth is, Tommy, while they were calling me a hero, you were a better man than I. Because you knew how to do something I didn't. You knew how to love."

Tommy stood on trembling legs.

"Forgive me, Tommy. Please."

Abruptly, Tommy turned his back, as if he couldn't take any more.

Philippe, dragging Liana by the arm, joined them and asked, "Well? Is it the correct film?"

Grimly, Tommy nodded.

Philippe arched a cocky brow. "So . . . now . . . the moment we have all been waiting for."

Resigned, Sloane shrugged, "Then I guess there's nothing more to be said."

He put the cigarette to his lips, took a deep drag, and

blew out the smoke like a man having a last pleasure before his execution.

Then, with a last glance at it, he flicked the cigarette. It landed on one of the stacks of film. In the blink of an eye, the highly combustible nitrate stock exploded into flames.

Within seconds, the entire collection was reduced to charred reels and smoldering ashes.

A curtain of numb stillness descended upon the courtyard. No one moved. The flames died down and the ashes began to scatter on the breeze like confetti after a parade.

It hit Philippe then that his meticulously calculated scheme had just gone up in smoke. His hand fell dully to his side. As it did, Liana saw her opportunity and reached for his arm. Snapped back to his senses, he tried to pull away, but, with both hands, she yanked his wrist to her mouth and savagely bit down.

He yelped and the pistol clattered to the courtyard stones. Philippe scrambled to retrieve it, but Liana, tugging on his wrist, threw herself in front of him to block his path and swiftly kicked the gun toward Ace.

But before it reached its destination, Tommy bent and retrieved it. In a fury, Philippe hauled back and smacked Liana across the face, sending her tumbling to the ground. Ace rushed to her side. Pushing back her hair, he stroked her smarting cheek. Her head was spinning but she put a brave face on it and told him, "I'm all right." He helped her to her feet as she leaned on him for support. They righted themselves to find Tommy, like a sleepwalker, holding the gun on them.

"Kill them," Philippe hissed. "Both of them."

"Think, Tommy," Sloane coaxed. "It's not too late to get yourself out of this mess. Get rid of Philippe and this whole conspiracy collapses. None of his henchmen is crazy enough to murder the High Commissioner and his staff."

Philippe's mustache bobbed furiously. "Don't listen to him. Pull the trigger, damn you."

"You've had your helping of revenge," Sloane continued, "and it doesn't taste very good, does it?"

Philippe charged for Tommy. "If you're not going to do it, give the gun to me."

Still in a daze, Tommy swung the gun toward him, stopping him short.

Ace pressed his advantage. "Don't listen to Philippe. Listen to the good inside you. This is your chance to be the hero you always wanted to be. Your grandfather must have faced a moment much like this at Shiloh."

He took a step forward but Tommy checked him by swinging the gun on him.

"He's trying to direct you," Philippe wheezed, "like a stupid actor in one of his scenes."

Tommy was staring at him wildly. Unsure what to do, he lowered the gun.

Sloane pressed on in a coaxing tone. "We're in the air, Tommy. You and me, as always. The Red Baron's squadron is coming in fast. Only this time, *you're* at the controls, not me."

Seething, Philippe screamed, "You bumbling American *peasant*! Shoot the bastard. *Now!*"

Tommy was shaking so badly, he could barely hold the gun. Like a cat treed by a pair of hounds, his gaze darted back and forth between his two tormentors. He took a breath. Then he raised the pistol, closed his eyes, and pulled the trigger.

Epilogue

April 17, 1921

Los Angeles

Searchlights fanned the night sky over downtown Los Angeles. A string of limousines—Isotta-Fraschinis, Pierce-Arrows, Bugattis—pulled up before Sid Grauman's Million Dollar Theater on Broadway, discharging a glittering array of stars. Douglas Fairbanks, Mary Pickford, William S. Hart, Lillian Gish, Norma Talmadge, and Richard Barthelmess all waved to the admiring crowds who'd waited outside for most of the day to catch a brief glimpse of their favorites. Even Gloria Swanson was in attendance, dressed to the nines, every inch the reigning glamour queen of Hollywood. Her makeup bore the unmistakable mark that would soon be known as the "Nelson Reilly Touch." Above her, the marquee announced to the world:

Premiere Tonight!
Tehani of the South Seas

Finally the last limousine in the cortege pulled to a stop. A uniformed usher opened the door with a dramatic flourish. A handsome man stepped out, resplendent in tailored tuxedo, his sun-kissed hair brushed dashingly off his face, his commanding blue eyes radiating an easy confidence. He reached inside, then handed out the woman they'd all come to see. Her trend-setting bobbed haircut and dazzling white sequined dress—showing a daring amount of silk-stockinged leg—elicited a gasp from the crowd. These two, they knew, were the star of the picture and her celebrated director. The crowd hadn't seen the picture yet, but the Hollywood press was ablaze with stories about the landmark South Seas adventure. Everyone who'd had an advance peek acclaimed it and noted its perfect timing. *The Four Horsemen of the Apocalypse* had become Metro's biggest hit ever, sparking a national craze for the tango and ushering in a vogue for romantic epics. Valentino's smoldering sexuality had created a thirst for a new kind of star: exotic, sensual, empowered. Already, Liana was being hailed as the "female Valentino," and pictures of her—both as Tehani and as herself—graced the covers of every magazine on the stands.

As the crowd let out a cheer, Liana waved to them and smiled. Then Sloane led her up the red carpet through the forecourt where Tahitian dancers, brought over for this event, had been entertaining the crowd through the afternoon and early evening. They passed into the grand foyer and luxurious lobby, where a platoon of uniformed ushers snapped to attention.

There, a small group of friends had gathered to greet them: the cast and crew, who hadn't seen each other since leaving Tahiti and were treating this gala night as a reunion; various old Hollywood friends of Liana's, including her cohorts from the Swanson masquerade;

and the three most important friends of all. When everyone else had exchanged giddy greetings and good luck wishes and drifted off to find seats, these three remained behind.

Nelson, the nearest of them, rounded on Liana with cocked head and eagle eye, double-checking his handiwork for any telltale flaws. "I've outdone myself," he pronounced at last.

"Better than Swanson?" she teased.

He took on the aspect of a thief about to crack a safe, and, lowering his voice, confessed, "I told Swanson I had to go to my grandmother's funeral this afternoon so I had to make her up early in the day. She's probably spent the afternoon with her face in the Frigidaire." They put their heads together and giggled at the absurdity of the image. "But really, sweet, you look divine. My inspired trim of your butchered hair is getting all the stares. It's so modern, so chic! By tomorrow all the dollar-a-day shop girls will be clamoring for the Nelson bob."

"Do I ever get to take the credit for anything where you're concerned?"

"Naturally, darling. For having magnificent taste in friends!"

Reverend Dale took Ace and Liana's hands in his own and squeezed them warmly, but with a barely perceptible moisture in his palm.

"Not nervous?" Sloane asked him.

"You'd think I'd be accustomed to public speaking, but yes, a bit."

"There's nothing to be nervous about. Just think of the audience as being the biggest conglomeration of hypocrites and sinners you're ever likely to find in one place."

Dale chuckled, but as they were about to move on, he

detained Sloane. "Your father would be proud of you," he told him. "And so would Tehani."

Liana saw the emotion that threatened to choke Ace. Lowering his lashes, he gave a silent nod and squeezed the Reverend's hand.

And finally Tommy . . . standing back, appearing awkward in his tuxedo . . . watching them as if uncertain of his standing. Cleared of criminal charges by the High Commissioner himself, he'd reluctantly returned to Los Angeles with Liana and Sloane. The two men had talked over their differences on the voyage home, with Sloane trying to persuade Tommy that they both had things to be sorry for, so they might as well call it a draw. Outwardly Tommy had agreed, but it was clear from the emotional distance he'd kept that he still harbored feelings of guilt and shame. Liana worried about him, but Sloane assured her that he would come around. Now, standing before him, Ace said, "I have something for you."

Tommy took an involuntary step back, as if the hand Sloane was reaching into his pocket might come out bearing a snake. Instead, he handed forth a flat leather case. Guarded, Tommy flicked the clasp with his thumb and opened the top. Inside was a bronze cross overlaid with crossed swords and the head of the French Republic, suspended by a red and green striped ribbon: the Croix de Guerre.

Tommy lifted dead eyes. "I told you I don't want your—"

"It's not mine. It's yours. It just arrived." He took the accompanying certificate from his pocket and read, " 'For extraordinary valor on the Western Front photographing enemy movements at enormous personal risk, and for foiling a conspiracy in Polynesia that might have brought discredit to the honor of France: Thomas Crenshaw.' "

Tommy held the coveted medal uncertainly. "It's . . . mine?"

"You earned it," Sloane told him sincerely. "Congratulations, Tommy. I'm happy for you."

Tommy's lips quivered. "Ace . . ." he began.

But Sloane put his arm about his shoulders and cut off his apology. "Let's go see our picture, shall we?"

Together, they went inside to find their seats.

The auditorium beyond was filled with a who's who of Hollywood. But all eyes were focused on the newcomers as they made their entrance and glided down the long aisle to the roped-off seats in the row of Paramount brass. Hobart, sitting among them, gave a flamboyant salute. Greenburg, once the film's fiercest enemy, was beaming at them, pumping Sloane's hand as if he were a long-lost son. Adolph Zukor himself had come in from New York for this auspicious occasion. He, too, shook Sloane's hand, slapping him companionably on the back. As Sloane had predicted, all had been forgiven when they'd viewed the final cut and smelled a gigantic hit.

Their final worry—the flurry of publicity six months before about Liana's scandalous family past—had not only been put to rest but converted into an asset when Robert Sherwood, the foremost critic of the day, published a story last week gushing over his advance peek at the film. In the course of the piece, he pointed out that being the daughter of a duchess who married an earl made Liana a countess in her own right. Overnight, she became an object of fascination not just to the moviegoing public but to Hollywood proper, a town impressed by only one thing other than itself: royalty.

As the lights dimmed and a spotlight swept toward the screen, the master showman, Sid Grauman himself, stepped onstage and raised his hands to quell the groundswell of applause. "Ladies and gentlemen, I'd like to welcome you all tonight to this occasion, which is a special evening for our industry, and for me personally. The first million-dollar picture for my Million Dollar Theater."

There was an appreciative chuckle before he continued. "I've seen the photoplay you're about to witness, and let me tell you, it's a wowzer! As you know, the world premiere of this spectacular motion picture is a charitable benefit. The astronomical price you paid for entry tonight"—another chuckle—"will go to help the islanders of the South Pacific. But let someone who knows what he's talking about explain. I give you the director of *Tehani of the South Seas,* Mr. Spencer Sloane."

Liana squeezed Sloane's hand briefly before he bounded upstage to thunderous applause, followed by a hush of anticipation. He took the spotlight and said, "On behalf of the entire cast and crew of *Tehani,* I want to thank you all for your generosity in coming here tonight. I went to Tahiti to make a picture about the corruption of paradise. But I found an even greater corruption than I'd expected. The colonial government was brutally exploiting the people of Tahiti, stealing the black pearls that are their only hope of economic sustenance in the modern world. Because of our film, that government has been replaced and a more enlightened regime is sincerely trying to reverse the damage. Your contributions tonight will go toward helping that effort and creating a cultured pearl industry run by the Tahitians themselves. One lone missionary has spent the last few years fighting this injustice and helping to return their birthright to the people of the South Seas. So if I may, I'd like to present to you the real hero of this film, Reverend Jeremiah Dale."

Dale walked uneasily toward the center of the stage. He seemed temporarily dazed by the bright lights and wave of applause. When it died down, he began to speak hesitantly.

"This is a new experience for me. I'm not accustomed to such a large congregation."

The laughter and applause that followed his words built his confidence, and he continued. "Mr. Sloane has called me the hero of this picture you're about to see. But with all due respect, I must decline the honor. It is Mr. Sloane who has brought our plight to the attention of the world. With his film, he has proved that motion pictures can be more than just entertainment. That they can lift the spirits and enrich the soul. That they can show us hitherto unknown worlds and ideas in a personal way that touches our hearts and becomes a part of our lives forever. It is *he* who has returned the precious black pearls of Tahiti to their rightful owners. And he who has immortalized their story in the magic of moving pictures."

As he walked off the stage, the lights dimmed further and the house orchestra—augmented tonight with traditional Tahitian instruments—began to play the overture. The house went dark. As the haunting melody reached its end, the Paramount logo appeared and the movie began. Over the next two hours, no one moved. No one seemed to breathe. The audience was transported by the visual grandeur. Through it all, Liana held Ace's hand in the dark, as mesmerized by the saga as everyone around her.

When the last image faded from the screen, there was a dead silence. Then the sound of a single pair of clapping hands. Then another and another until everyone was applauding. As one, they surged to their feet and cheered, "Bravo! Bravo!"

As the house lights came on, the audience flowed toward Ace and Liana, everyone eager to be the first to congratulate the director and his Tehani. Hobart, with uncharacteristic humility, grabbed Sloane's arm and said, "It was an honor to work with you." Gloria Swanson elbowed her way to the forefront and took Liana's hand. "My dear, you were splendid. I couldn't have done it better myself. And I *love* your hair!" Doug Fairbanks, with Mary Pickford at his side, told them, "This is going to be a big success, but the real test will be how you follow it up. I've got some ideas I want to discuss with you. Why don't you drop by Pickfair on Saturday and we can talk about it?"

Amidst the barrage of praise and invitations, Liana realized that the elite of Hollywood were peering wistfully at her the way she used to look at *them.* Despite the reaction to Sherwood's column, it was a startling revelation. In this one evening, she'd became a star. Just a few short months ago, she would have relished this as life's supreme gift. But tonight, watching Sloane as he graciously acknowledged the acclaim, she knew that the real gift she'd received was standing right beside her. And she couldn't wait to get him alone.

Eventually the audience began to head for the limousines waiting to take them to a lavish post-premiere party at the Coconut Grove, which had opened that week and was the new Hollywood "in" spot. As they passed, Liana caught their comments.

"Wasn't she something? And those love scenes . . . did they sizzle! Did you ever think you'd see anything like that in a moving picture?"

"Did you hear she's a *countess*?"

"My dear, those nude scenes . . . they were so tasteful, so artistic, so beautiful . . ."

"So romantic!"

"She was fabulous. But how is she ever going to find a role to follow *this*?"

"Don't you just love that short haircut of hers? It's so smart. I'm going to get mine cut just like it!"

She was reeling by the time they'd escaped from the stuffy lobby into the night air and made a dash for their own limousine. They fell back into the plush seat and Sloane rapped on the glass partition that separated them from the driver, motioning him to go ahead.

Once they were underway, he smiled at her. "The world is at your feet, Liana. How does it feel?"

"My feet are tired. I'm glad to get off them for a while." So saying, she reached down and removed her heels. "I think Tehani had the right idea. Bare feet beats shoes any day."

He laughed. "I guess I don't have to worry about this going to your head." He took one of her feet into his lap and began to massage it. Moaning her pleasure, she lay back in the velvet folds of the seat.

"Go to my head? When everyone's already saying I'll never find anything half as significant to follow it up. For all I know, I'll be a one-hit wonder. Maybe we *should* go to Pickfair Saturday and see what Doug Fairbanks has to offer."

"I don't need Fairbanks's ideas, thank you all the same."

"My, aren't we touchy!"

"Actually, I have an idea for something that may be *very* significant to you."

She sat up. "Tell me!"

His smile was mysterious. "Not yet."

She leaned closer, taking her foot from his lap and grabbing his face with her hands. Raining it with kisses, she pleaded, "Don't tease me. Tell me before we get to the party. We only have a few blocks to go."

"We're not going to the party. At least not immediately."

She saw now that the driver was heading in the opposite direction. "Where are we going?"

"Nowhere. Anywhere."

She arched a delicate brow. "Are you falling back into your role of enigmatic director so soon?"

"I wanted some time alone with you first to give you your present."

She brightened. "A present? For me? Why, Ace, you shouldn't have."

"Can't a director give his star a little something to show his appreciation? Of course, if you don't want it . . ."

"Where is it?" she cried. Playfully, she began to pat him down, searching for it. "Is it here? No, not here. There? No, that's your lighter. Is it bigger than a bread box?"

"I'm not telling."

"Well, where *is* it?" Then, smiling slowly, she added, "I know. Is it here?" She put her hand on his loins. He swelled beneath her hand. "Oh, it *is* bigger than a breadbox!" Giggling, she reached to unfasten his trousers. "Thank you, darling. It's just what I wanted."

But he stopped her hand with his. "*That's* for later. I have a different present for you now."

"Oh, you've spoiled it," she pouted. "It *can't* be better than this."

"Do you want it or don't you?" he asked.

"Yes, darling, but do hurry, so we can get back to *this*."

She reached for him again, but he pushed her hand away and bent to retrieve something from under the seat. He handed it to her. An unassuming wooden box with the words "Roi-Tan" embossed on it.

"How lovely," she deadpanned. "You're giving me a box of cigars."

"Open it."

"I suppose cigars are just the thing for a celebration," she continued lightly. "I'll smoke them at the party. That should cause even more of a commotion than my haircut."

But then she lifted the lid and the smile died on her face. She went completely still. For inside the box, nestled in blue velvet, was a three-row necklace of perfectly matched black pearls.

Then she understood what he'd done. Knowing how much her mother's necklace had meant to her, he'd sought to replace it with one of her own. She should have felt overjoyed by the thoughtfulness of his gesture. But the sight of the pearls, so reminiscent of her mother's lost treasure, saddened her. Memories flashed through her mind. Her mother placing the pearls on Liana's neck as a child, telling her that one day they'd belong to her. The many times she'd secretly taken them from her mother's jewelry box, thinking of the day when she'd be old enough to wear them herself. The humiliation of their being sold to pay off debts. It was sweet of Ace to try and replace them. But it wasn't the same. It could *never* be the same.

She sat staring at them, trembling, knowing she should thank him but unable to muster the excitement and appreciation such an offering called for.

As if reading her thoughts, he said gently, "Look closer." He reached over and flicked on the small light at the side of his seat.

She couldn't bring herself to move, knowing her rejection of his gift showed.

He reached inside the box and held the pearls up so she could see the clasp. Large, made of platinum, extravagantly engraved with a stylized *W* amidst elaborate scrollwork.

In a stunned tone, she muttered, "These are the Wentworth pearls." When he said nothing, she added, "My mother's pearls."

He nodded.

Entranced, she held the cherished necklace to her cheek. With the pearls against her skin, she could sense her mother's presence, see her gracious smile. Smell her perfume. Feel her arms about her, bringing comfort and love.

She realized belatedly that her tears were spilling on the pearls. He handed her a handkerchief and she used it to wipe them lovingly. "How did you . . . how could you *possibly* . . ."

He shrugged, uncomfortable in the face of her profound emotion. "I tracked them down through the agent for the estate sale."

"But, Ace . . . these pearls are priceless. They must have cost you . . . *everything* you made on the picture . . ."

He took them from her and, turning her gently, fastened them about her throat. "We'll make other pictures," he said.

She felt the pearls on her neck with her hand, thinking of how she'd dreamed about this moment—when she'd first wear them as an adult—so repeatedly as a child. She'd thought she'd lost that dream. Now, miraculously, it had come true.

Because of him.

Moving like one still dazed, she turned back to him. "Ace . . ." Her tears made it difficult to speak. She tried again. "You couldn't have given me anything . . . that would mean so much to me. Anything in the . . ."

She couldn't continue. He reached for her and pulled her to him, holding her as she wept into his chest.

When she finally quieted and began to sniff, he took the handkerchief to dry her eyes.

"There's no way to thank you."

"You don't have to thank me. I did it because I hoped it would please you."

"*Please* me? That's the understatement of the year. But . . ." She paused, flustered. "I'm afraid I didn't know about opening night etiquette. I didn't get anything for you."

"Well . . . there *is* something you can give me."

"What? Anything!"

"You can star in my next picture."

She laughed as he dabbed at the tears that had streaked Nelson's makeup. "It must be a real doozy if you'll go to such lengths to soften me up."

"Who knows? You might even *like* this idea."

She touched her pearls again. "After this, you can film the phone book if you want and I'll be happy to star in it."

"It's not the phone book. But it *is* a book."

"What sort of book?"

"Well . . . it's historical."

"What is it? *The Countess of Monte Cristo*? *The Princess and the Pauper*? No . . . I have it. With your penchant for pirates, it must be *The Lusty Buccaneer*."

He gave her a piercing look before asking, "How's this for a title? *The Lady and the Highwayman*?"

Once again, she felt as if he'd knocked the wind out of her. "You're joking."

"No joke."

"You're actually suggesting . . . that we film my parents' story . . ."

"A story that needs to be told. But the right way. Not as a bedroom joke, but as the story of two incredibly passionate people who lived an epic love story and chose to die together. A dangerous man who steals from the aristocracy to help a cause. A lonely, tortured man who's given up on any hope of love or tenderness. Until this amazing woman comes into his life. A duchess who defies her own class to boldly ride by his side. A sexual woman who teaches him to love. We'll make your parents seem so appealing, so heroic, so . . . *enviable* that the world will fall in love with them. And their mystique will add to your legend. When we get through with this picture, people won't condemn you for being their daughter, they'll consider it the most fascinating thing about you."

"And I play my mother?"

"I certainly don't see you playing your father."

"Be serious."

"I'm perfectly serious. Think of it. It's irresistible. The public will eat it up."

After a thoughtful pause, she asked, "Why are you doing this?"

"Because I've come to admire your parents. Their wisdom brought us together and got us through our ordeal. I want the world to see them as you do. As *we* do."

"And . . . ?" She knew there was more.

"And . . ." He stroked her cheek, caressing the face he'd fallen in love with all those years before. A lifetime ago. The face that had made him want to live again. "And because I love you," he told her simply. "You did something for me that I never thought anyone could. You took the wound inside of me and healed it. If I can, I'd like to do the same for you. And the only way to do that is by showing your parents to the world as the glamorous rebels they were, not disgraced criminals."

It was so perfect, Liana was amazed she hadn't thought of it before. Her mind began to bubble over with possibilities. "I remember every story they ever told me. We'll have so many great scenes. Them dressing up as an old couple and holding up the train. The duel with the Prince of Wales. Oh, and robbing the theater. I can see it all now. What if we went to England and filmed it where it actually happened? And . . . I know! What about Doug Fairbanks as the highwayman?"

Laughing, he put up a hand to stop her. "We can iron out the details later. Besides which, I'm the director, remember?"

"But you'll need me as consultant. Don't forget, I'm the one who knows the real story."

"It's a novelty to propose an idea that you like," he said mildly.

"I suppose you brought the contracts with you," she mocked.

The corner of his mouth quirked. "As it happens . . ."

"And how long is *this* contract for?"

"For life."

She was so exhilarated—and so grateful—that her body couldn't contain it any longer. She had to express it. Brushing aside the cigar box, she put her hand on him once again. This time, when she moved to open his trousers, he didn't stop her. By the time she'd brought him out into her palm, he was hard. She leaned over and joyously took him into her mouth, channeling all of her devotion and gratitude into the act. She felt him swell even larger against her tongue, felt his hands at the back of her head as he brought her closer still and groaned his pleasure. She sucked him slowly, worshipfully, thanking him for all he'd given her, for taking her secret demons and transforming them into a glorious heritage. As she increased the pressure, he began to pump appreciatively into her mouth.

She drew away. "Aren't you worried that the driver might see us in the mirror?"

"Not especially." He pushed her head back into his lap.

She ran her tongue up the length of him and teased, "So I take this to mean that you're no longer threatened by a sexual woman?"

"Like any convert, I've got to make up for lost time."

Her gaze roamed his handsome face, ruggedly masculine but washed clean of the pain, the wariness, the suspicion that had held him aloof. Healed by her love. And saw in it the complete acceptance she'd always longed for; a celebration of who she really was, not what he wanted her to be. "I absolutely adore you," she told him. Then added, breathily, "Kiss me."

He fixed her with a mock frown. "You're *always* asking me to kiss you."

She favored him with an exaggeratedly timorous smile as she cooed, "Can I help it if I love the way you kiss?"

As she moved closer, he raised a hand and held her back. "You're insatiable," he scolded. But his eyes burned like blue flame.

As she sought his mouth with hers, she murmured, "Lucky for you . . ."

Author's Note

For those readers who might be interested in the story of Liana's parents, the lady and the highwayman, they were the subjects of my first book for Bantam called *The Last Highwayman*. Unfortunately, it's currently out of print, but perhaps can be found in used book stores or through used-book sellers on Amazon.com. I'd love for you to read it since, as my first published book, it holds a special place in my heart.

My thanks to all who helped me in the writing of this book: my agent, Meg Ruley, for her unfailing support and friendship; my editor, Abby Zidle, for her astute editing and for being such a pleasure to work with; Nita Taublib for her kindness, her patience, and her understanding; my much loved daughter Janie and Shaelah Lewis for their tireless help on our research trip to Tahiti. And finally, the one whose spirit permeates each and every book—who gave me courage when I needed it, hope when I'd lost it, and an answer whenever I asked. I'm nothing without you. I never forget it.

About the Author

KATHERINE O'NEAL is the author of six previous books set in various exotic corners of the old British Empire. She is married to William Arnold, noted film critic and author. They have a daughter, Janie, who shares their passion for travel and literature. In addition to the Bantam books, Katherine is a contributor to the recent anthology *Taken By Surprise* along with Susan Johnson and Thea Divine.

E-mail Katherine at KatherineONeal@aol.com.